THE DINOSAUR FEATHER

THE DINOSAUR FEATHER

S.J. Gazan

Translated from the Danish
by Charlotte Barslund

Quercus

New York • London

© 2008 by S.J. Gazan
Translation © 2011 by Charlotte Barslund
Originally published in Denmark by Gyldendals Bogklubber in 2008
First published in the United States by Quercus in 2013

Any member of educational institutions wishing to photocopy part or all of the work for classroom use or anthology should send inquiries to Permissions c/o Quercus Publishing Inc., 31 West 57th Street, 6th Floor, New York, NY 10019, or to permissions@quercus.com.

ISBN 978-1-62365-066-7

Library of Congress Control Number: 2013937744

Distributed in the United States and Canada by
Random House Publisher Services
c/o Random House, 1745 Broadway
New York, NY 10019

Manufactured in the United States

2 4 6 8 10 9 7 5 3

www.quercus.com

Contents

Chapter 1

Anna Bella Nor was dreaming she had unearthed *Archaeopteryx*, the earliest and most primitive bird known. The excavation was in its sixth week, a fine layer of soil had long since embedded itself into everyone's faces and the mood had hit rock bottom. Friedemann von Molsen, the leader of the excavation, was the only one still in high spirits. Every morning when Anna staggered out of her tent, sleepy and shivering in the cold, von Molsen would be sitting by the fire, drinking coffee; the congealed oatmeal in the pot proving he had cooked and eaten his breakfast long ago. Anna was fed up with oatmeal, fed up with dirt, fed up with kneeling on the ground that only revealed bones that were, of course, interesting in their own right, but were too young to be the reason she studied biology, and most definitely not the reason she was spending six weeks of her precious summer vacation living in such miserable conditions. The year was 1877 and, at this point in her dream, Anna got the distinct feeling something didn't add up. She was wearing her quilted army jacket and thick furry boots with rubber soles, but Friedemann von Molsen didn't seem the least bit surprised, even though he had a pipe in his mouth and was wearing a three-piece corduroy suit with a pocketwatch and a wool cap that rested on his ears.

They were in Solnhofen, north of Munich, and in addition to Anna and von Molsen, the group consisted of two local porters, two other postgraduate students, and von Molsen's brandy-colored retriever bitch, whose name also happened to be Anna Bella; a truly irritating detail in the dream. While they plodded across the same ridge as yesterday, von Molsen told anecdotes. His stories weren't particularly amusing and, by now, Anna had heard them so many times that she no longer derived any pleasure from having been dropped into a time in history in which any natural scientist would give their right arm to experience. Whenever von Molsen was about to speak, he would snatch his pipe from his mouth and point it in the direction of England. It was Darwin who had upset his sense of order.

In the 1870s Darwin's theory of evolution was starting to gain a foothold, but the mechanism that caused species to evolve was a matter of huge controversy, and though it fascinated von Molsen, he categorically dismissed Darwin's theory that evolution was driven by natural selection. When his feelings ran high, von Molsen would call Darwin a "stickleback." Anna failed to see how a stickleback could be the worst term of abuse von Molsen could imagine.

At the start of the expedition Anna had challenged von Molsen's argument, and this was how his interest in her had originated. Von Molsen was a man who encouraged curiosity toward the phenomena of natural science, and it was perfectly reasonable, he declared, to play devil's advocate in order to provoke a stimulating debate. This, on the proviso that one didn't seriously believe that in a few decades the stickleback's hypothesis would be accepted as common sense; that all living organisms, mice and men, birds and beetles, had evolved from the same starting point and that differences in their individual morphology, physiology, and behavior were entirely the result of adaptation and competition. "What would be the consequence of that?" von Molsen had demanded and pointed abruptly at Anna with his pipe, but before she had time to reply, he answered his own question.

"The conclusion," he declared, cheerfully, "would be that the genome wasn't a constant. It could be changed and no one would be able to predict what would cause it to change. As if everything, life and nature, was entirely random and unplanned. The whole business is insane!"

During an already notorious lecture at Oxford University, Darwin had recently argued that the vast gaps in fossil evidence for birds existed solely because such fossils had yet to be discovered. Once they were found, and this was purely a matter of time, the evolutionary game of patience would come out and it would be obvious to everyone, as it already was to Darwin and his supporters, that the driving force behind evolution was the process of natural selection. The man must be mad, von Molsen had exclaimed, and looked sharply at Anna.

The conversation had occurred on the fifth day of the expedition by which time Anna had already gained a reputation for being something of a chess wizard. They played on a small board with horn pieces, which von Molsen had conjured up from the left-hand pocket of his jacket, opposite the one in which he kept his pipe, and he balanced the board on his right thigh. Anna had slipped up when, in an attempt to support Darwin's views, she had mentioned a fossil that wouldn't be discovered for another seventy-four years, and had, in order to cover up her gaffe, dug herself into an even bigger hole by citing the feathered dinosaur from China, which two Chinese paleontologists would find and describe 124 years into the future. At this point, von Molsen had become so outraged that he accidentally knocked his own queen off the board. Anna felt like banging her head against one of the tent poles. "We're talking serious science here, not tomfoolery and nonsense," von Molsen had sneered as he picked up his queen. Anna gave up. After all, it was just a dream.

From that day onward Anna's mood had gone steadily downhill and this morning when von Molsen, in an exuberant state of mind, started gesticulating toward England with his pipe, Anna decided that, as far as she was concerned, the excavation was over. She would return to Munich, eat a decent meal, then take the train back to Berlin and from there travel home to Copenhagen. She rubbed her eyes and tried to wake up, but the wind swept heedlessly across the Bavarian plain and von Molsen had turned ninety degrees north and reinserted his pipe. In the distance Anna saw a hare rise onto its hind legs to sniff the air before it disappeared into the scrub. She sighed.

During the day, when Anna was awake, the year was 2007, and she was enrolled in the master of science program at the College of Natural Science at the University of Copenhagen, more specifically at the department of Cell Biology and Comparative Zoology at the Institute of Biology, where she had spent the past year writing her dissertation on a scientific controversy which had been running for more than 150 years. Were birds present-day dinosaurs or did they originate from an even earlier primitive reptile? She had just handed in her dissertation and her dissertation defense was in two weeks.

Scientific controversies were par for the course. People had argued whether the Earth was flat or round, whether man was related to the apes, the status of the Milky Way compared to the rest of the universe, with a fervor that ceased the moment sufficient evidence became available. The earth *is* round, man *is* a primate, and the Milky Way *does* mainly consist of red stars. However, the controversy surrounding the origins of birds appeared to be different. It rumbled on, even though, scientifically speaking, there was nothing left to discuss.

Von Molsen relit his pipe and the sweet tobacco aroma tickled Anna's nostrils. Someone started to make coffee. She could see and hear Daniel, one of the other students, clatter with a saucepan while he said something to von Molsen and hitched up his trousers, which tended to fall down. Daniel had been fairly chubby five weeks ago when the excavation began, but since then he had lived on the same food as everyone else: beans, oatmeal, cabbage, and coffee. Anna suspected that Daniel secretly questioned von Molsen's dismissal of natural selection. The day she had debated it with von Molsen and had completely shot herself in the foot by referring to the two as yet undiscovered fossils, she had exchanged glances with Daniel, who was standing a little further away pretending to secure a couple of guy ropes, and she thought she had detected something in his eyes. Something that told her he had genuine doubts as to whether Darwin's theory of natural selection was really as far-fetched as the older established scientists of the day were claiming.

Anna understood entirely why the new concept of evolution seemed unimaginable. For centuries the broad consensus had been that God had personally created every animal and plant and that the mouse and the cat, the beech and the maple were no more related than the desert and the firmament or the sun and the dew on the grass. Everything was God's work and one creature couldn't simply evolve into another, nor could animals and plants become extinct unless it was God's wish to remove the species in question from production. As far as birds were concerned, it therefore didn't follow that the sparrow was related to the starling, the flamingo, the shearwater, or any other bird, or that birds as a group were related to each other or to dinosaurs or reptiles or any other animal. They had been put on Earth, aerodynamic and fully developed, by God. *Voilà*.

The theory of evolution broke completely with the doctrine that the Earth and all its organisms had been created by one divine being, and this was a huge challenge: how could people suddenly accept that evolution happened by itself, without God's influence, just like that?

The dream continued. The sun was now high above Solnhofen. After a quick consultation about today's tasks and a cup of coffee as black as tar, they all got to work. Anna's area was a gentle slope behind the rest of the team, and she had only to raise her head to see where the others were and what they were doing. The lithographic limestone slab spread out beneath her like a huge blackboard. She scraped, eased away a couple of layers, brushed sand and soil aside, coaxed the earth; she took off her jacket and pushed up her sleeves. An isolated gust of wind from the south forced her to close her eyes to avoid the dust. When she opened them again and looked down, she saw the fossil. The wind had removed nearly all the excess material, and though another two layers needed to be removed before the creature would lie fully revealed, there was no mistaking it. Beneath her, bathed in the light from a yellow sun, lay *Archaeopteryx Lithographica*, one of the world's most precious fossils. It was slightly smaller than a present-day hen and had one wing beautifully unfurled. In this respect the dream was a bit of a cheat, she thought, because she instantly knew what she had discovered. She recognized the small bird from hundreds of photos; only two weeks ago, in the vertebrate collection at the Natural History Museum, she had been studying the impression—which the Germans had reluctantly allowed a Danish paleontologist to make—of the Berlin Specimen, as *Archaeopteryx Lithographica* was known. She recognized the flight feathers, which lay like perfectly unfurled lamella against the dark background, she saw the relatively large tail feather, the wondrously faultless location of the rear and front limbs and the arched position of its flawlessly formed skull, which made this specimen superior to anything else discovered so far. In 1861, the newly discovered London Specimen had been sold to the British Natural History Museum for £700. Now Anna had uncovered one of the ten most beautiful and significant fossils in the world: the Berlin Specimen.

Her instinctive reaction was to punch the air and cry out in triumph to von Molsen, who was standing some distance away in deep thought, holding his pipe, but what she needed now was a plan. Anna had to beckon von Molsen in a manner that made it clear she had stumbled across something extraordinary, while simultaneously sounding sufficiently vague in her conclusion so von Molsen wouldn't get the impression that she already knew what she had found. That would surely make him suspicious.

Von Molsen turned around instantly when she called him and came toward her with reverence. When he reached her, he knelt down by the excavation and stared for a long time at the fossilized animal that was emerging. Carefully, he worked on the last two layers of the limestone sediment, whereupon, with great awe, he traced the perfect body of the small bird with his finger. Anna knew that the bird was 150 million years old.

"Well done, my girl," he said. When he turned to look at her, she noticed that one of his eyes was almost purple. Her find had shaken him to his core.

"Mom?"

Von Molsen laid his pipe on the ground, took out his magnifying glass and, right at this point when Anna absolutely didn't want the dream to end, it started to dissolve.

"Mom, I want to get into your bed," a little voice pleaded. Anna clenched her fists and woke up in Copenhagen.

The light in her bedroom was dim. Lily was standing next to the bed, in her onesie, with a soaked diaper, which Anna Bella grabbed hold of as she swung the child into her bed. Lily snuggled up to her. It wasn't even six o'clock yet. Pale, white dawn light was starting to creep in, but it would be another half hour, at least, before any objects would be visible. Her sheets were freshly washed and felt crisp.

A figure was standing between the window and the door to the living room. It was Friedemann von Molsen. She couldn't see his face, but she recognized the broad-brimmed felt hat he wore against the merciless sun. Anna's heart pounded inside her ribcage. She wanted him to disappear. Von Molsen watched her silently, just as lifelike as he had been in her dream.

"If I wait long enough," she told herself, "the light will make him go away."

She knew she must be imagining this. She had to be. And yet she saw him just as clearly in the gray dawn as she saw the tall dresser next to the door, the green vase on top of it, and the silhouette from the lilies she had bought yesterday and put in the vase.

Later, when she looked back at this morning, she knew exactly what von Molsen was.

He was an omen.

CHAPTER 2

Monday morning, October 8. The Institute of Biology was an H-shaped building squeezed in between the Natural History Museum and the August Krogh Institute in the University Park in the Østerbro area of Copenhagen. The main building was a narrow rectangle of four floors, which bordered Jagtvejen on one side and a cobbled square on the other.

Anna Bella parked her bicycle outside the entrance to Building 12, which housed the department of Cell Biology and Comparative Zoology on its second floor. It had been a terrible morning. When she tried to drop off Lily at nursery, Lily had sobbed and refused to let go of her in the coat room. Through the window in the door Anna could see the other toddlers, see them fetch their cushions and get ready for morning assembly. Lily was inconsolable. She clung to her mother, smearing snot and tears into Anna's jacket.

Eventually, one of the nursery teachers came to Anna's rescue. Lily's sobbing grew louder. Desperation gushed from the pores of Anna's skin. She looked at the nursery teacher with pleading eyes and the nursery teacher lifted Lily up, so they could pull the snowsuit off her.

Anna suffered from a permanently guilty conscience. Cecilie, Anna's mother, looked after Lily almost all the time. Cecilie had volunteered her help six months earlier when Anna's studies had become increasingly demanding.

"If you're to have any hope of finishing your dissertation within the allotted time, you can't possibly leave the university at four o'clock every day to pick up Lily from nursery," she had argued.

And that had been that. Lily loved her granny, Anna told herself, so why not? It was the obvious solution.

For several months she had worked virtually around the clock, and although she had finally submitted her dissertation, she still had to prepare for her forthcoming thesis defense. No matter how much Anna missed her daughter and knew very well that the temporary arrangement had gotten out of hand, there simply was no room for Lily in the equation. And, as she kept telling herself: Lily liked being with Granny.

"Stop it, Lily," she snapped. "I have to go now. Granny will pick you up today. You're sleeping at Granny's tonight. Now let go of me!" She had to tear herself loose.

"You go," the nursery teacher said, "I'll deal with her."

When Anna had finished locking up her bicycle, she caught sight of Professor Moritzen in her office on the ground floor. Anna tried to catch her eye, but the professor was hunched over her desk and didn't look up.

Hanne Moritzen was a parasitologist in her late forties, and four years earlier she had taught Anna in a summer course at the university's field center in Brorfelde. One night, when neither had been able to sleep, they had run into each other in the large institutional kitchen that belonged to the Earth Sciences department. Hanne had made chamomile tea, and they started talking. At first the topic was biology, but Anna soon realized that Hanne, in contrast to other professors she had met, wasn't particularly interested in talking shop. Instead they discussed favorite books and films, and Anna found herself genuinely warming to Hanne. When dawn broke, they agreed it was pointless to go back to bed, and when the bleary-eyed kitchen staff arrived, they had just started a game of cards.

Later they had bumped into each other in the faculty lounge, said hello, exchanged pleasantries, and then had lunch together several times. Anna admired Professor Moritzen's serenity and sense of purpose. It was now a long time since their last lunch. Once she had defended her dissertation, she would make it up to all the people she had neglected: her daughter, Hanne Moritzen, herself.

Finally, Hanne looked up from behind the window, smiled, and waved to Anna. Anna waved back and walked through the revolving doors to Building 12.

The department of Cell Biology and Comparative Zoology consisted of offices and laboratories arranged on either side of a long, windowless corridor. The first office belonged to Professor Lars Helland, Anna's internal supervisor. He was a tall thin man without a single wrinkle. This was remarkable. Biologists, as a rule, made a point of never protecting their skin when doing fieldwork. The only clues that revealed he was in his late fifties were white flecks in his soft beard, a slowly spreading bald patch, and a photograph on his desk of a smiling woman and a teenage girl with braces on her teeth.

Anna was convinced that Professor Helland loathed her; she certainly loathed him. During the nine months he had been supervising her dissertation, he had barely taken the time to offer her any guidance. He was permanently crotchety and uninterested, and when she asked a specific question, he would go off on an irrelevant tangent and couldn't be stopped. It had angered Anna from the start and she had seriously considered making a formal complaint. Now she had resigned herself to the situation, and she tried, as much as possible, to avoid him. She had even left her dissertation in his cubbyhole last Friday, rather than hand it to him in person. When she checked the cubby for the fourth time, her dissertation was gone.

The door to Professor Helland's office was ajar. Anna tiptoed past it. Through the gap she could see part of Helland's recliner, the last centimeters of two gray trouser legs, feet in socks and one shoe lying carelessly discarded with the sole facing up. Typical. When Helland was in his office, he spent most of his time lying in his recliner, reading, surrounded by a Coliseum-like structure of books and journals piled up in disarray around him. Even on the very rare occasions they had met, Helland had been reclining as if he were a nobleman receiving an audience.

Helland wasn't alone. Anna could hear an agitated voice and she instinctively slowed down. Could it be Johannes? She tried to make out what they were talking about, but failed. She would have to find out later, she thought, and accelerated down the corridor.

Anna and Johannes shared a study. Johannes had finished his graduate degree, but he had been allowed to stay on because he was cowriting a paper with Professor Helland, who had been his supervisor as well. Anna could vividly recall her first day in the department last January when Helland had shown her into the study where Johannes was already working. Anna recognized him instantly from her undergraduate days and had spontaneously thought "Oh, shit." Later she wondered at her reaction because, until then, they had never actually spoken.

Johannes looked weird, and he was weird. He had red hair and looked at her as though he were leering at her with droopy eyes behind his round, unfashionable glasses. For the first three weeks, she deeply resented having to share and office with him. His desk looked like a battlefield, there were half-empty mugs of tea everywhere, he never aired the room, never tidied up, every day he forgot to switch his cell phone to silent and though he apologized, it was still infuriating. However, he seemed delighted to have acquired someone to share the tiny study with and talked nonstop about himself, his research, and global politics.

During those first few weeks Anna deliberately kept him at a distance. She went to the cafeteria on her own, even though it would have been normal to ask if he wanted to join her, she gave curt replies to his questions to discourage him from striking up a conversation, and she declined his friendly suggestion that they take turns to bring cakes. Yet Johannes persisted. It was as if he simply failed to register her aloofness. He chatted and told stories, he laughed out loud at his own jokes, he brought in interesting articles she might want to read, he always made tea for both of them and added milk and honey to her cup, just the way she liked it. And, at some point, Anna started to thaw. Johannes was warm and funny, and he made her laugh like she hadn't laughed in . . . well, years. Johannes was extraordinarily gifted, and she had allowed herself to be put off by his peculiar appearance. Nor were his eyes droopy, as she had first thought, they were open and attentive, as though he were making an effort, as though what she said really mattered.

"You're wearing makeup!" she exclaimed one spring morning, not long after they had become friends.

Johannes was already behind his desk when Anna arrived. He was wearing leather trousers and a Hawaiian shirt, his hair was smoothed back with wax and his long white fingers were splayed across the keyboard. His glasses magnified his brown eyes by 50 percent, so when he looked at her, there was no way she could miss it.

"I'm a goth," he said with a mysterious smile.

"You're a what?" Anna dumped her bag on her chair and gave him a baffled look.

"And things got a bit wild last Friday. I was in drag," he continued, surprisingly. "I thought I had got all that stuff off." He waved her closer. "Come on over, I've got something for you to look at."

He showed her some pictures on the web while he talked. The club he had been to was called the Red Mask and events were held the first Friday of every month. The club's name was inspired by the Edgar Allan Poe short story *The Masque Mask of the Red Death*, and it was a meeting place for goths from all over Scandinavia. Goths were a subculture, Johannes explained when he saw the blank expression on Anna's face and pointed to a photograph. Anna failed to recognize the slightly androgynous-looking woman with red hair, black lipstick, and dramatic eyes, wearing a tight black corset, a string vest, leather trousers, and studs. The caption below the photo read *Orlando*. Anna frowned.

"It's me," he said, impatiently.

"You're kidding!" Anna exclaimed, thinking she really was an idiot. It was obvious: Johannes was gay!

"What does 'Orlando' mean?" she asked.

Johannes looked exasperated.

"Orlando is a reference to the eponymous hero of the novel by Virginia Woolf, obviously. Orlando starts off as a man and is later transformed into a woman. Like me, at nightfall." He laughed. Anna gawked and said: "Okay."

"But, no, I'm not gay," he added, as though he had read her mind.

"So what are you then?" Anna asked, before she could stop herself.

"I'm into women." He winked at her. "And, in addition, I'm a goth. From time to time I go to goth parties in drag; women's clothing, that is."

"So do you all have sex with each other or what?" Anna blurted out.

Johannes raised his eyebrows. "Sounds like someone's interested in going?"

"Shut up." Anna threw an eraser at him, but she couldn't help smiling. "That's not why I'm asking. I was just curious. You look like a . . ." she nodded in the direction of the screen. Johannes followed her gaze.

"Yes, I'm well and truly dolled up," he said, pleased with himself. He drummed his fingers on the table and looked at Anna as though he was debating with himself whether or not he could be bothered to explain this to her.

"There's no sex at the Red Mask," he said eventually. "But quite a few people belong to the goth scene as well as the fetish scene. Me, for instance." He gave her a probing look. "That club is called Inkognito, and events take place twice a month." He scratched one eyebrow. "And yes, there we have sex. There are darkrooms, and people arrive dressed in latex and leather. Here you can be hung from the wall and given a damned good thrashing if that's your thing."

Anna held up her hand. "Yes, thank you, Johannes. That will do."

"And prudes are very much in demand on the fetish scene. Very." Johannes flung out his arms by way of invitation. Anna threw a notebook at him; Johannes parried by rolling his chair backward. He roared with laughter. Anna could restrain herself no longer and joined in. With Johannes, everything seemed so easy.

The only time the harmony between them soured was when the subject turned to Professor Helland. Shortly after they had become friends, Anna asked Johannes what was bothering Helland. In her opinion, he was always in a hurry; he was grumpy and vague. To her great surprise, Johannes seemed genuinely baffled. What did she mean? Helland had been a brilliant supervisor for him, he protested, beyond reproach.

"Don't you find him distracted and apathetic?" she asked.

Johannes didn't think so at all.

One day they almost had a fight about Helland. Anna happened to mention that she often fantasized about playing practical jokes on the supervisor; hiding his favorite reference book, for example, or removing a small, but vital part of his dissecting microscope, which was worth millions of kroner—just a tiny bolt so the lens wouldn't focus or the eye pieces couldn't be adjusted to fit the distance between Helland's eyes. Or how about grafting mold onto his wallpaper? Or releasing a couple of mice in his office? Something that would wind him up without resulting in serious repercussions for her? They were enjoying a tea break and had discussed a film they had seen, they had been laughing, but Johannes paled when she shared her fantasy.

"That's not funny," he said. "Why do you say stuff like that? That's really not funny."

"Hey, relax," Anna said, instantly embarrassed at suddenly finding herself isolated with an evidently highly inappropriate idea.

"You can't go around playing tricks on people," Johannes had muttered.

"It was just a joke," Anna said.

"It didn't sound like it," Johannes said.

"Hang on, what are we really talking about?" Anna asked, defensively, and turned on her chair to face Johannes who was bent over his keyboard. "Are you saying you think I would actually hurt Professor Helland?"

"No, of course not." But Johannes sounded unconvinced.

"It's beyond me why you always have to defend him," she continued, outraged.

"And it's beyond me why you always have to attack him." Johannes gave her a look of disbelief. "Honestly, Anna, just give the man a chance."

"He's not committed," she said and could hear how ridiculous that sounded.

"And so he deserves mold on his wallpaper that will give him a headache, itchy eyes, and a runny nose?"

"It was a joke!"

Johannes studied her closely.

"Tell me, why do you have to be so harsh sometimes? Your tone . . . it can be really cutting. And Helland isn't so bad. In many ways, he's cool."

Anna turned to her screen and hammered away at the keyboard. She was close to tears. Johannes reheated the kettle and made more tea.

"Here, gorgeous," he said, affectionately, placing a cup on her desk. He nudged her softly.

"It was just a joke, all right?" she mumbled.

"But it *wasn't* funny," he replied and went back to his desk.

From that day on Johannes and Anna avoided discussing their mutual supervisor, even though Anna was finding Professor Helland's behavior increasingly bizarre. One evening, after taking Lily to Cecilie's, she cycled to the Institute to work. It was dusk and the parking lot behind the building was filled with dancing blue shadows. There was the leafy scent that carried the end to an unusually chilly summer. Pigeons were pecking at the ground by the bicycle stand. They scattered when her bicycle keeled over. Johannes had gone home hours ago, which was a shame.

Professor Helland materialized out of nowhere in the twilight. He stood with his back to her, completely rigid, right where the birds had just been congregating and he looked like a wax figure. He seemed unaware of the birds and didn't turn around. Anna felt unnerved and carefully walked toward him. The light was fading, and she moved in a soft curve, hoping he would, at least, say "hi." But still he didn't turn. He remained with his back to her, apparently doing nothing. Anna looked for his car, but she couldn't see it. She looked for his bicycle, but couldn't see that either. Nor did he have car keys in his hand, or a bag slung over his shoulder, and he wasn't wearing a jacket. She was just inside his field of vision now, so she cleared her throat. Helland turned his head and stared blankly at her; he opened his mouth to say something, but only a bubbling sound and some white froth emerged from the corner of his mouth.

"Are you all right?" Anna called out; she was frightened now.

"Gho whay," he mumbled and lashed out at the air. He gave her a furious stare, but the blow had missed if, indeed, it had been Helland's intention to push her away.

"Gho whay," he repeated, a little louder. Some froth dripped from his mouth and disappeared into the darkness.

"You want me to go away?" Anna asked.

Helland nodded. "Yes, go away," he said, very clearly this time.

Anna had left him there. Her heart had pounded all the way up to the second floor where she let herself into the photocopier room, which faced the parking lot. She stood in the dark window, watching Professor Helland. He stayed there for a while. Then he shuddered deeply, jerked his head, and shook first one, then his other leg and disappeared around the corner to the main parking lot.

She decided to tell Johannes about the incident the next day, and, to begin with, he looked annoyed with her for breaking their tacit agreement not to discuss Helland. But then, to Anna's huge surprise, he admitted that he, too, had noticed that Helland wasn't firing on all cylinders. Johannes and Helland were working on a paper based on Johannes's dissertation and, to be honest, Helland hadn't displayed his usual professional acuity.

All of a sudden Anna said: "And what's that thing he's got in his eye?"

Johannes looked blank.

"He's got something in his eye," Anna said, pointing to the corner of her own right eye. "A small hard pouch of some kind. Do you think he's ill?"

Johannes shrugged. Anna had been unable to figure out if Helland really did have something wrong with his eye, because the only times she ever caught a glimpse of him were when he hurried down the corridor, inevitably leaving mayhem in his wake, roaring "morning!" at the open door to their office before disappearing into the elevator.

Johannes bent over his keyboard again, and Anna decided to drop the subject.

Anna had moved to Copenhagen in 1999 when she was accepted into the biology program at the university. Jens, her father, was already living there, and he had helped her find the apartment in Florsgade. Jens and Cecilie had divorced when Anna was eight. Anna had stayed on the island of Fyn with her mother, in the village of Brænderup, just outside Odense, the largest city on the island. The village consisted of around fifty houses; the community was close-knit, and it was a lovely place to grow up. For years Anna was uncertain as to whether or not her parents had permanently split because Jens, like some hopeful suitor, never stopped visiting them. Anna knew it had been a source of friction to the girlfriends Jens dated after Cecilie; not that Jens and Anna spent much time discussing their feelings, but he had once remarked that it happened to be the case. His girlfriends resented that he would rather spend Christmas with Cecilie (and Anna), would rather go on vacation with Cecilie (and Anna), and never forgot Cecilie's birthday (but managed, on two occasions, to forget Anna's). Anna knew her father loved her, but he worshipped Cecilie. Anyone could see that.

Anna had once told her best friend Karen that she thought parents liked each other better than they liked their children. They had both been ten years old at the time. They were building a secret hideaway, and Anna had asked Karen why grownups seemed to like each other more, and why children seemed to come second, and Karen had said that was just not true. Karen's mom said she loved Karen more than anyone on the planet. That grownups could choose whether or not they wanted to be together, but that you loved children all the time, for as long as you lived, and that you never regretted having them. Karen and Anna had almost ended up having a row. In the middle of it all, Jens called them into the kitchen for toast and chocolate milkshakes. Jens and Cecilie must have been divorced at that point but, nevertheless, Jens was there, in the kitchen, reading the newspaper by the window. And making toast.

The girls came in and Karen said to Jens: "You don't really like Cecilie more than Anna, do you?" He lowered the newspaper, appearing shocked. Anna was small with dark hair; Karen's hair was blond and curly.

"Why on earth do you want to know that?" he had replied, and Anna had blushed. She hadn't wanted Jens to know about this, not at all, she hadn't wanted Karen to ask him. Anna glared defiantly at the tablecloth. She couldn't remember what happened next, only that she refused to play with Karen for the rest of that day and that she took back the special stamp she had given her, even though Karen said she couldn't do that. However, that evening Jens told her something. When Anna had been born, Cecilie had been very ill, back problems of some sort. She was in great pain and had been in and out of hospital, Jens explained, and even though Anna only weighed six pounds, Cecilie hadn't been allowed to lift her. That had made her feel really sad. Jens tucked Anna into bed and kissed her forehead.

"And that's why I take good care of Cecilie," he said. "Special care."

Anna nodded. Anna, too, always tried really hard to please Cecilie.

"But I love you more than anyone, Anna," he said, and suddenly looked very serious. "Parents just do. Otherwise something's wrong."

The next day Anna gave the stamp back to Karen. Along with a small rubber animal that could walk down the window all by itself.

When Anna told Jens in the spring of 2004 that she was pregnant by Thomas and they had decided to keep the baby, Jens's response was, "Why?"

They were in a café in Odense and had just bought a luxurious dressing gown as a birthday present for Cecilie. They were having coffee before going to Brænderup where Cecilie was cooking dinner.

Anna gave her father a furious look.

"Do you want me to start with the birds and the bees, or how much do you know already?"

"I didn't think you and Thomas were getting along very well."

"It's better now."

"How long have you two known each other?"

"Almost five months."

"How old are you?"

"Have you forgotten how old I am?"

"Twenty-five?"

"Twenty-six."

"And how many years of your degree do you have left?"

"Three years."

"Why do you want to keep the baby?" he asked for the second time. "The last time I saw you, you wanted to break up with Thomas because he . . . how did you put it? . . . only cared about himself. You weren't sure you could cope with that. And he was working all the time. Have you forgotten that?"

"You don't like him."

"I don't know him very well."

"But what you do know, you don't like."

Jens sighed. "I do like him, Anna. He's all right."

A pause followed. Anna gritted her teeth. Her legs were itching, and she had to make a real effort not to scream out loud. Suddenly Jens hugged her.

"Congratulations," he mumbled into her hair. "Congratulations, sweetheart. I'm sorry."

Afterward they had made a beeline for a baby supply store and bought a dark blue stroller for Jens's grandchild. A dark blue parasol was included, and Anna twirled it while Jens paid. The stroller was a display model and slightly faded on one side, but there was a waiting list to get a brand new one. And Jens didn't want to wait, no sir. He said "my grandchild" ten times at least, while they were in the store. The cashier glanced furtively at Anna's stomach, which was as flat as a pancake. Anna giggled.

When they came back to Cecilie, the aroma of roast lamb filled the whole house. Cecilie was standing on the kitchen table hanging a paper chain along the window. Jens rolled the stroller into the kitchen.

"What's that?" Cecilie said.

"What do you think it is?"

"A stroller."

"Bingo!"

"I'm menopausal," Cecilie said, and spat out the pins she had been holding in the corner of her mouth.

Anna started to laugh, and Jens did a round with the pram in the kitchen as he called out to Cecilie:

"Get down, Granny, roll your walker to the fridge and give me your best bottle of champagne. From now on I want to be known as 'honored Granddad.'"

It wasn't until then that it hit her. Cecilie dove off like a rock star and hugged Anna. Half an hour later, when they were sitting at the kitchen table and the champagne bottle was empty—Anna hadn't had any, and Jens and Cecilie were in high spirits—Cecilie suddenly said:

"Who's the father?"

Anna felt movement under the table and knew Jens had tried to kick Cecilie. Anna looked from one to the other.

"You'll be the death of me, the pair of you," she sighed and went up to her old room to watch TV.

The next morning when Anna got up, Jens and Cecilie were looking up something on the Internet.

"I'm moving to Copenhagen," Cecilie announced. Jens carried on searching while Cecilie got up to toast some bread for Anna.

"You just sit down," she said and put butter, milk, and cheese on the table, as well as her homemade jam and a cucumber. She made a fresh pot of tea and poured Anna a cup. When she had set down the teapot on the table, she looked at Anna and said, "I'm sorry I asked you who the father was. Of course it's Thomas. I was just under the impression that things between you two weren't good. That it was only a question of time before . . ."

"Well, you were wrong," Anna interrupted her.

Cecilie smiled a fleeting smile.

"I like him very much," she said, with emphasis.

The truth was that things between Anna and Thomas were a total nightmare. They had known each other only five months, and they didn't live together. Obviously, they would live together now that they were having a baby.

It had started with a chance meeting in a bar in Vesterbro. He was way out of her league, she thought, when she spotted him by the window to the courtyard where he stood with his arms folded, feet at ten to two, with a very straight back and a cigarette in a clenched fist. His T-shirt was rather tight, but it was probably hard to resist the temptation to dress like that when you had a great body, which he did.

Smug, Anna had thought. Thomas was a doctor at Hvidovre Hospital, he was currently training in his specialty, and he was in his mid-thirties. His hair was short, almost white; his skin was fine and freckled, and his eyes were very intense. He left at ten to two; just like his feet, Anna thought, as she watched him exit the bar.

He called her two days later. She had told him her name, and he had found her on the Internet. Dinner? Okay. From then on, they were dating.

It had gone wrong almost immediately. Anna still couldn't understand exactly how it had happened, but the fact was that she had never been so miserable in all her life, and how this was linked directly to her being madly in love got lost in the drama. Or it did at the time. Thomas loved her, he told her so. But she didn't believe it. You're a bit paranoid, he laughed. Anna, however, loved him to distraction. The more he kept her at arm's length, the more she loved him. She didn't have a clue what was going on. She didn't know if they were a couple, if he loved her (he said he did), or if he didn't (he behaved that way). He would arrive several hours late, or fail to show up altogether without a phone call of explanation. She didn't know if they had a future together; she didn't know where he was, why he said the things he said, why sometimes she was allowed to go out with him and his friends and other times not: "Why would you want to do that, sweetheart?" She could offer no reply. She just wanted to go.

Thomas told her to calm down. "Don't ruin it, it's fine as it is," he would say. She tried, but it didn't work. Thomas had only met Anna's parents a few times, and none of the occasions had been a success. Anna had never met Thomas's parents. In the spring Thomas wanted a two-week break; "I love you Anna, never doubt that, I just can't have this pressure all the time," he had said and looked irritably at her. In fact, he had been so exhausted after an all-night argument, which Anna had started, that he nearly gave a patient the wrong medication. During their two weeks apart, Anna did a pregnancy test.

"Looks like we're having a baby," he said and smiled when they met up again. Anna stared at him.

"Are you pleased?"

"I would have chosen a different time," he said.

They moved in together shortly before Lily was born. That was nearly three years ago.

The Natural History Museum was an upward extension of the Institute of Biology, and it towered like a decorated ferry over the surrounding buildings. The top two floors of the museum were open to the public. The rest of the building consisted of laboratories and offices symmetrically arranged around a fireproof core where collections of insects, mollusks and vertebrates had been gathered, identified and preserved by Danish scientists for hundreds of years. The Vertebrate Collection on the third floor housed a vast amount of vertebrates; downstairs were two invertebrate departments with mollusks, and furthest down was the whale basement, which included the mounted skeleton of an adult baleen whale.

Anna's external supervisor was Dr. Tybjerg. He was a vertebrate morphologist who specialized in the evolution of cynodont birds. He was Professor Helland's polar opposite. He had brown, thinning hair, dark eyes, a small nimble body, and he wore pebble glasses at work that made Anna smile because he looked like a parody of himself. Dr. Tybjerg was shy and very earnest. He never canceled their meetings, and he always arrived well prepared, bringing with him any books he had mentioned at their previous meeting or a photocopy of an article he had promised her. His speech was staccato. He added impressive amounts of sugar to his strong black tea. To begin with he had found it hard to look her in the eye and had clammed up like an oyster on the few occasions Anna had asked him personal questions.

Dr. Tybjerg was the first person to take Anna to the Vertebrate Collection.

"You can't learn about bones from books," he said, as they walked down the corridor to the collection. "And you must never," he added, giving Anna a stern look, "draw any conclusions about bones from drawings or photographs—never!"

Dr. Tybjerg unlocked the door and disappeared down aisles of cupboards. Anna stopped, overwhelmed by the unfamiliar smell of preserved animals, before venturing further inside. It was neither dark nor light. It was like a drug-addict-proof bathroom: you could see enough to find the toilet paper, but not a vein in your arm.

The Vertebrate Collection consisted of a large room divided by display cases with glass doors behind which stuffed animals were exhibited and cabinets with drawers containing boxes and cases in varying sizes, in which the boiled and cleaned bones were stored. Dr. Tybjerg marched down the aisles with familiar ease and stopped halfway.

"This is where the birds are kept," he said, cheerfully.

The air-conditioning was making a strange noise, and there was an awful smell. Anna peered into the cabinets with their rows of birds, neatly lined up. Ostriches, a dodo skull, and tiny sparrows of every kind. Dr. Tybjerg moved down an aisle to the left and disappeared around the corner.

"This is a sacred place," he said from somewhere in the twilight, and Anna could hear him rattling doors. She walked close to one of the display cabinets, pressed her nose against the glass, and tried to make out in the gloom what kind of bird was on the other side. It was large and brown, with a plump tail feather. Its wings had been spread out, as if the bird had been about to take off or land when it died, and Anna spotted a stuffed mouse that had been placed in its beak for illustration. Its wing span was six feet, at least, and the bird made all the others in the cabinet look like a flock of frightened chickens.

"A golden eagle," Dr. Tybjerg said. Anna nearly jumped out of her skin. He had gone around the cupboards and come up behind her without her noticing. He held two long wooden boxes under his arm. She reached out her hand to support herself against a cabinet.

"Don't touch the glass in the door," he warned. "It's genuine crystal. You'll break it."

"Does it have to be so dark in here?" Anna asked.

"Come on," he said, ignoring her question. Anna followed him. Back in the corridor she realized her legs were shaking.

"Now, let's take a look at this," Dr. Tybjerg said, as he settled down at a table by a window. "This is a *Rhea Americana*." Carefully, he lifted a bird skull out of the box.

"It's a secondarily flightless bird and so has a skeleton that is quite like that of predatory dinosaurs, in that it has an unkeeled sternum. This makes it a good skeleton to practice on," he explained, "because when it comes to flying birds, everything is welded together. The bones of secondarily flightless birds, however, are somewhat reminiscent of those of primitive birds. Now, let's go through it together."

Anna made herself comfortable and watched Dr. Tybjerg take out the bones from the box and spread them out on the table. A build-your-own-bird kit. He started pairing them up and Anna watched, fascinated. She had no idea where anything went, but she liked the gentle movements of his hands.

They remained at the window for nearly two hours. Dr. Tybjerg asked Anna to reconstruct the skeleton after having demonstrated it to her a couple of times. She had to be familiar with the many reductions and adaptations of the bird skeleton in order to appreciate the dispute that would be the subject of her dissertation, Dr. Tybjerg stressed. A group of expert ornithologists led by the well-known scientist, Clive Freeman—had Anna heard of him?—still refused to accept that birds were present-day dinosaurs. Anna nodded. Clive Freeman was professor of paleoornithology at the department of Bird Evolution, Paleobiology, and Systematics at the University of British Columbia, and he had published several major and respected works on birds.

"He is a very good ornithologist," Dr. Tybjerg emphasized. "He really knows his stuff. And if you're to have the slightest hope of demolishing his argument, you need to be conversant with those areas of avian anatomy and physiology to which Freeman constantly refers, and on which he bases his totally absurd claim that birds aren't dinosaurs."

Dr. Tybjerg stared into the distance. Professor Freeman and his team had no scientific grounds on which to base their argument, he went on, as fossils and recognized systems of taxonomy confirmed the close relationship between birds and dinosaurs.

"And yet they persist." Dr. Tybjerg fixed Anna's gaze, and his eyes narrowed. "Why?"

Anna sat with the coracoids and tried to figure out which one would fit into the sternum.

Dr. Tybjerg seemed to approve of her choice by passing her a scapula. As he gave her the bone, he looked at her urgently and prompted, "Two hundred and eighty-six apomorphies."

"Sorry?"

"They dismiss two hundred and eight-six apomorphies."

Anna gulped. Now what was an apomorphy again? Tybjerg twirled a small, sharp bone between his fingers.

"You need to review all of their arguments and all of ours," he said. "Pair them up and go through them. Once and for all. Together we will wipe the floor with him." Coming from Tybjerg, this expression sounded odd. Anna looked out at the University Park.

"We'll publish a small book," he added. "A manifesto of some kind. The ultimate proof." He stared triumphantly toward the ceiling.

Anna had gotten up to leave when Dr. Tybjerg suddenly said, "By the way . . ." and tossed a key across the table. It seemed as if it had slipped out of his sleeve. Anna caught it and, without looking at her, Dr. Tybjerg said:

"I did *not* just give you a master key."

Anna quickly pocketed the key and said: "No, you certainly didn't."

Dr. Tybjerg had entrusted her with a key that was normally forbidden to students. Now every door was open to her.

Anna's curiosity was rekindled as she left the museum. She asked Johannes about Tybjerg.

"A lot of people don't like him," was his immediate reaction.

"Why?" Anna was genuinely surprised. Johannes suddenly looked as if he was having second thoughts.

"I don't want to be seen as a tattler," he said, eventually.

"For God's sake, Johannes, give me a break," Anna exclaimed.

He thought it over. "Okay," he said. "But I'll make it brief. Word has it Tybjerg is an insanely gifted scientist. He was hired by the museum to keep track of their collections when he was still a schoolboy. He's supposed to have a photographic memory, but he's socially inept and really quite unpopular. For years Tybjerg and Helland have been some sort of team . . ." He wrinkled his nose. "When he was younger, he taught undergraduates. In fact, he used to teach me. But there were complaints."

"Why?"

"He can't teach," Johannes declared.

"That's weird," she said. "I've just spent all afternoon with him, and I thought he explained things really well."

"Not to a classroom full of students. He gets nervous and he drones on as if he were reading aloud from some long, convoluted text he knows by heart. I think he's a bit nuts, I mean, seriously. They only keep him on because he knows everything there is to know about the Vertebrate Collection. More than anyone in the whole world. It's like hiring someone with autism to look after a vast record collection. He knows where everything is and what it's called. But they would never offer him tenure. To be employed by the University of Copenhagen, you have to be able to teach." He paused before he added: "Dr. Tybjerg is weirder than most."

Anna rested her head on her keyboard.

"Lucky me, or what?"

"What do you mean?"

"One of my supervisors is useless and the other one is a weirdo."

"Don't start all that again," Johannes said. "We've already been there. Helland's all right."

"I'm just saying."

"Yes, and I would rather you didn't."

To begin with, every word and every scientific argument in the controversy about the origin of birds was watertight and unassailable. Anna accepted that, as her starting point, she probably had to take Helland's and Tybjerg's positions at face value in order to even begin to understand the vast network of scientific implications; later she could form her own opinion. However, she honestly couldn't see why Helland and Tybjerg were right and Freeman, according to them, was wrong.

"Birds are present-day dinosaurs," she wrote on a sheet of paper, followed by: "Birds are direct descendants of dinosaurs." Then she drew two heads, which bore some resemblance to Tybjerg and Helland, on the paper and pinned it up on the wall. She took another sheet, drew another head—supposed to be Freeman's—and wrote on it: "Birds are not present-day dinosaurs," followed by: "Modern birds and extinct dinosaurs are sister groups and solely related to each other via their common ancestor . . ." Who was that again? She looked it up and added "Archosaur" to the paper and stuck it on the wall.

"'An archosaur is a diapsid reptile,'" she mimicked her textbook, and shut her eyes irritably. Now what does *diapsid* mean? She looked it up. It meant that the skull had two holes in each temporal fenestra. As opposed to synapsids and anapsids which had. . . . She chewed her lip. What exactly was a *temporal fenestra*? She looked it up. The opening at the rear of the skull for the extension and the attachment of the jaw muscles; a distinction was made between the infratemporal and the supratemporal fenestra, and what were they again? Anna looked them up.

The days passed in a blur, and she could feel her frustration escalate. She was writing a dissertation, not some trivial essay. The whole point was that she would contribute something new, not merely summarize a well-known controversy by repeating existing material. She tried to explain to Cecilie that it had taken her three days to read four pages, and Cecilie stared at her as though she had fallen from the sky. But it was true. Every word was alien, and every time she looked up one word, more terms followed and eventually she had looked up so many terms in so many books and followed so many references that she could no longer remember what she had initially struggled with. There was never a one-word explanation; every term described nature's most intricate processes, whose terminology she had learned as an undergraduate, but she could barely remember it these days, so she was forced to look that up as well. After one month, her frustration had evolved into actual fear. Was she plain stupid? The bottom line was she grasped so little of the controversy—which clearly enraged both Tybjerg and Helland—that it was embarrassing.

In a fit of despair she started reading Freeman's book *The Birds* from start to finish. Dr. Tybjerg had mentioned it several times and dryly remarked that when Anna was capable of pulling it apart, she

would be ready to defend her dissertation. Anna had had the book
lying on her desk for weeks. Every day when she left, she put it in
her bag, intending to read it, and every night she managed seven
lines before falling asleep. Time to bite the bullet now. Suddenly
spurred on by the promise that everything would fall into place
once she had read it, she immersed herself in the book.

Freeman's book was a masterpiece. It was filled with wonderful color photographs and illustrations, and throughout the text he
argued seriously and soberly. He backed up his views with well-
argued scientific conclusions, made references to existing literature,
and allowed for doubt to remain where certain points had yet to
be decided. Had it not been for Helland, and especially Tybjerg's
ardent assertion that Freeman was wrong, Anna would have bought
Freeman's sister-group theory on the spot. Freeman was without a
doubt someone who knew what he was talking about, and this was
the man she was supposed to "wipe the floor" with? When she had
finished reading *The Birds* she had eighty-two pages of handwritten
notes and hadn't grown even a bit wiser; rather, she had become
truly terrified of the task that lay ahead of her. With *The Birds* in her
arms and her heart pounding, she decided to come clean with Dr.
Tybjerg.

Dr. Tybjerg was waiting for her in the cafeteria at the Natural
History Museum, and Anna didn't even have time to sit down in the
chair opposite him before her misgivings poured out of her.

"Dr. Tybjerg, I fail to see why Professor Freeman's scientific position is wrong . . . I think his argument sounds convincing."

Dr. Tybjerg pursed his lips.

"Well, then you haven't read enough," he said with zen-like calm.

"It's taken me three weeks to read *The Birds*," Anna groaned.

"Why on earth did you read all of it? You can flip through it.
That's more than enough for anyone." Dr. Tybjerg took the book
from her.

"This book is a flash in the pan, nothing more." He quickly
thumbed the pages. Then he smiled. "But I do understand why it can
seem a little overwhelming. Freeman appears convincing because

he has convinced himself. Such people are always the worst." Dr. Tybjerg paused and then looked as if he had come up with a plan.

"Drop the book," he ordered her. "Instead, read at least fifteen papers written by people who argue that birds are present-day dinosaurs, and fifteen papers by people who disagree. This will make everything clear to you. And stay away from books for the time being. Many of them are good and you can return to them later, but this one," Dr. Tybjerg slammed *The Birds* on the table, "is nothing but whorey propaganda."

Anna exhaled through her nostrils.

"And one final thing," he added, giving her a short, sharp look. "You need to assume I'm right. You'll be convinced in time, but until that happens you need to accept my position. Otherwise you'll quite simply lose your way."

Dr. Tybjerg's face told her the meeting was over. Anna nodded.

Anna spent the next three days searching the database for published papers at the University Library for Natural Science and Health Studies in Nørre Allé. She kept reminding herself Tybjerg was right.

The first day was an exercise in futility. There were tons of papers for and against, but she didn't come across anything that convinced her that Helland and Tybjerg's argument was more valid than Freeman's. It wasn't until day two that things improved. She had compiled over forty papers at that point, she had photocopied them and spread them out on the table in front of her, and she was just about to give into frustration again when a tiny flicker of light appeared in the darkness.

If Tybjerg was right, *if* it really were the case that the kinship of birds to dinosaurs was as well supported as Tybjerg and Helland and . . . she did a quick count . . . around twenty-five other vertebratists from all over the world agreed it was, then it had to follow that their scientific position was the stronger, at least for now, as Dr. Tybjerg maintained. If that were true, well, then it was indeed remarkable that reputable journals such as *Nature, Science,* and, in particular, *Science Today,* which owed their existence to their scientific credibility, continued to assign column inches to it. Anna still was not convinced that this was the case, but that seemed secondary now. The situation would have been different if a sliver of doubt remained. *If* birds might have been dinosaurs, *if* fossilized evidence had yet to be discovered, which Anna could see had been the case in the 1970s and 1980s, *if* the feathered *Sinosauropteryx* hadn't been found in 2000 or the feathered *Tyrannosaurus* in 2005. But there was plenty of fossil evidence. The feathered dinosaur was a reality, and it was clear in every single paper that argued in favor of the close kinship between birds and dinosaurs that the authors were convinced birds were dinosaurs. *Utterly* convinced.

Anna stared into space.

Dr. Tybjerg had told her that the editorial committee of a scientific journal typically consisted of five people with a science background, which, broadly speaking, meant that fifteen people from the three leading journals, *Nature, Science,* and *Science Today,* were in supreme command of which scientific topics would reach the public. Fifteen people. That's not many, Anna thought, and in order to avoid giving preferential treatment to certain subjects or areas of research, those fifteen people had to consider very carefully if what they published did, in fact, reflect the actual work being carried out across the world. And this was where things didn't add up. Even though experts agreed that birds were present-day dinosaurs, Anna found in every other journal, at least, new contributions to the debate. She could feel the excitement pump through her body. Quick as lightning she sorted the papers into two piles, then she highlighted the names of the authors in yellow, and when that was done, she leaned back and smiled. There were twenty-four full-length papers and minor contributions in the pile that supported the kinship of birds to dinosaurs; there were twenty-three contributions in the pile that didn't believe that birds were present-day dinosaurs. Together, Dr. Tybjerg and Professor Helland accounted for five of the articles in the one pile; the remaining nineteen had been written by sixteen other vertebratists from universities all over the world. It was a rather convincing spread.

Then she went through the pile with twenty-three papers. These were written by three different authors. Clive Freeman, Michael Kramer, and Xian Chien Lu. Clive Freeman and Michael Kramer were responsible for nineteen out of the twenty-three articles. Anna got up and found a computer with Internet access. First she looked up Xian Chien Lu and discovered that the Chinese paleontologist had died the previous year. That left only Clive Freeman and Michael Kramer. It took Anna eight clicks to learn that Michael Kramer had completed his graduate degree at the department of Bird Evolution, Paleobiology, and Systematics at the University of British Columbia in March 1993, been awarded a PhD grant in 1993 by the same department, and had written his thesis there from 1997–2000, after which he had been employed as a junior professor in June 2000. Anna's eyes scanned his résumé and soon found what she was looking for: his MSc and his PhD supervisor was Professor Clive Freeman, his internal PhD examiner was Professor Clive Freeman, and the Senior Professor at the department of Bird Evolution, Paleobiology, and Systematics was Clive Freeman. For the first time since Anna had started her graduate work, she felt she had made a breakthrough.

Anna had just taken off her jacket, shaken thoughts of Lily's upsetting meltdown at the nursery school from her mind, and switched on her computer when she pricked up her ears. She knew every sound in the department. The groaning extraction system, the shrill smoke alarms, the Monday, Tuesday, and Thursday noises of students conducting experiments, the sound of Helland's busy footsteps, of Johannes's snail's pace shuffle, of Svend Jørgensen and Elisabeth Ewald, the other two professors in the department, who wore soft rubber soles and clicking heels, respectively. However, the sound Anna was now hearing didn't fit in. Someone was running, then they stopped, and she heard Johannes call out for Professor Ewald in a half-strangled voice followed by the sound of running feet again, and then Professor Ewald's voice and then Professor Jørgensen's. Frowning, Anna rolled back her chair and stuck her head out into the corridor. Johannes was standing in front of Professor Jørgensen's lab, his arms flailing.

"He's just lying there . . . I think he's dead. He looks dreadful. They're coming, emergency service said, they're coming right away; they said I wasn't to leave him, but I can't look at him. His tongue . . . it's his tongue." Anna stepped into the corridor and joined the trio, who started moving away from her before she reached them. They were running now. Anna started running too, and ten seconds later they stopped in front of Helland's open door.

For a moment they all froze. Professor Helland was lying in his recliner. He was still wearing the gray trousers that Anna had seen only minutes earlier through the gap in the door when she arrived. He slumped slightly, his arms hung rigid to either side, and his eyes were wide open. In his lap, as though he had been reading it, lay Anna's dissertation. There was blood on it. Then she noticed his tongue.

It was lying on his chest. One end of it looked like an ordinary rough, flesh-colored tongue, the other was a severed, bloody limb, elongated and shredded like prepared tenderloin. Johannes was standing behind them, whimpering, and Anna, Professor Ewald, and Professor Jørgensen reacted simultaneously by retreating to the corridor.

"Jesus Christ!"

They had arranged to meet to discuss their paper, Johannes stammered, his hands and eyes fluttering. "I was on time," he said. Helland had failed to answer the door, so he had pushed it open, and there was Helland, rattling, his tongue had fallen out of his mouth, that was how it had looked, as though it had let go of Helland's mouth at that very moment and dropped down onto his chest. Johannes had grabbed him, only the whites of Helland's eyes were showing; Johannes had panicked, run to the back office and called 911.

Professor Jørgensen went to the men's room across from Helland's office and threw up.

"We have to go back inside," Anna said. "What if he's still alive? What's if he's not dead yet? We have to help him."

"I'll go," Professor Ewald declared.

"We mustn't touch anything," Johannes called out. "They told me not to."

"Calm down, Johannes," Anna said. She felt dizzy. Professor Jørgensen emerged from the men's room white as a sheet. Then they heard the sound of the approaching emergency vehicles.

"Bloody hell," Professor Jørgensen said, rubbing one eye with the palm of his hand.

The emergency vehicles were close now, and soon they heard people thunder up the stairs. Two uniformed police officers and an ambulance doctor arrived; the doctor disappeared immediately into Helland's office and thirty seconds later another pair police officers arrived. One of the officers entered Helland's office and the other three started asking questions. Professor Jørgensen and Professor Ewald talked over each other and Anna fixed her eyes on a button on the floor. The two professors disappeared down the corridor with one of the officers, and Anna stared at the button until a warm spot on her head told her Johannes was looking at her.

"Right, we had better have a chat," a police officer said to Anna and Johannes. They spoke for five minutes. Johannes repeated what he had already said, and Anna explained who she was and said she had seen Helland's trousers through the gap in the door as she passed on her way to her office, that she had heard agitated voices coming from inside, and yes, it might just have been one agitated voice, and no, she hadn't heard exactly what had been said. Johannes kept staring at her. Anna tentatively held out her hand to see if it was trembling. It was.

The doctor emerged in the doorway and quietly briefed the two police officers, who nodded. One officer took Anna and Johannes a little farther down the corridor, where he told them to sit down.

"Please wait here. We'll be a few minutes," he said and returned to Professor Helland's door. Anna watched as the two officers cordoned off the entrance to Helland's office and a section of the corridor with red-and-white police tape.

More police officers arrived, uniform and plain clothes. Two of the plain-clothes officers put on thin, white boiler suits and face masks and disappeared into Helland's office. A tall man came over to Anna and Johannes and introduced himself as Superintendent Søren Marhauge. He had brown eyes, freckles, and short hair, and he looked kindly into Anna's eyes.

At Anna's suggestion they went to the small library, which lay between Professor Jørgensen's and Helland's laboratories. Søren Marhauge had a soft voice with a strange, slow drawl, as though he struggled to articulate his thoughts. Anna grew impatient. She thought he asked her the same question over and over, and by the time there was a knock on the door twenty minutes later, she had nicknamed him the World's Most Irritating Detective. An officer poked his head around the door, whispered a message, and the meeting was over. The World's Most Irritating Detective disappeared down the corridor and Anna returned to her study. The corridor was teeming with police. She groaned to herself. In two weeks exactly she would defend her dissertation which, at this very moment, lay in Professor Helland's office, soaked in blood.

CHAPTER 3

It was early Monday morning, October 8. Søren Marhauge was driving to Copenhagen, his car right behind a red Honda. He was Denmark's youngest police superintendent, based at Copenhagen's Police Department A, Station 3 in Bellahøj. It was well known that Søren had risen quickly through the ranks because he could "knit backward" as he called it. He possessed an extraordinary eye for the true nature of things, and many of the most spectacular conclusions reached in Department A had been achieved by Søren. At the age of thirty he had been promoted to superintendent. That was seven years ago.

Søren was in a hurry, so he overtook the Honda. He was late because he had stopped in Vangede to have breakfast with Vibe. Vibe and Søren had dated for seventeen years, but three years ago they'd split up. They had lived together in Nørrebro in Copenhagen, but Søren now lived in a house in Humlebæk, north of the city. Vibe had since married and lived with her husband in a house by Nymosen in the suburb of Vangede.

When they were still a couple, Vibe and Søren had done everything together. Picked strawberries, taken the train together all through Europe, traveled to India, shared student housing, and opened a totally unnecessary joint bank account. They had even worn matching rings. In those seventeen years it had never once crossed Søren's mind that Vibe might not be the right girl for him. Vibe was his girl. The end. They had met at a high school dance, their teenage romance continued into adulthood, and no one ever questioned it, least of all Søren.

Then one morning Vibe woke up wanting to have a baby. Having children wasn't something they had ever really discussed, and when Vibe first brought it up Søren didn't take much notice. But the genie was out of the bottle. Vibe's biological clock had started ticking and soon the putative child became a sore point. Søren didn't want children. He explained why: he had no parental urges at all. He thought that in itself was a good enough reason. Vibe began screaming at him. Vibe, who had been good-natured and sweet all through their time together, refused to accept his ridiculous position: there are two of us in this relationship, she argued. Søren tried to explain again. Needless to say, he only made matters worse. He went for a walk to think it through. He felt no desire to be a father, but *why?* For the first time since meeting Vibe, he wondered whether it was because he didn't love her enough. That evening—without screaming—she made the very same point: if she wanted a child so badly and he wouldn't give it to her, then it was because he didn't love her. I do love you, Søren protested, desperately. But you don't love me *enough*, Vibe had replied. She had her back to him and was taking off her earrings while Søren thought about what she had said. Slowly, she turned around. Your hesitation says it all, she declared, I think we should split up. Her eyes were challenging him.

Obviously they weren't going to split up. Vibe was his best friend, his closest and most trusted ally. She knew Elvira and Knud, she knew why he had grown up with his grandparents; she was family and he loved her. Søren hugged her tightly that night and they agreed to give it some time or, more accurately, they agreed that if Søren didn't change his mind very soon, he would have to go.

*   *   *

Søren was born in Viborg in Jutland. For the first five years of his life he lived with his parents. His maternal grandparents, Knud and Elvira, lived nearby in his mother's childhood home which lay outside a small village, on a hill, with a garden that sloped steeply down behind the house. The lawn was impossible to mow, and the long tangled grass offered numerous places to hide. Søren had hardly any memories of his earliest childhood, but he remembered Knud and Elvira's red house vividly, probably because it was there that Knud had told him his parents had been killed in a car crash. Knud and Elvira had been looking after him that weekend; Søren's parents had borrowed their car and driven off on an adventure. He remembered being told at the far end of the garden one summer's evening with Spif, the dog, standing next to him, barking. The next childhood memory he could clearly recall was their move to Copenhagen, to the house in Snerlevej. Knud and Elvira were teachers and both got jobs at the nearby public school, which Søren also attended. Søren lived in Snerlevej for the rest of his childhood. Far, far away from the red house.

Søren and Vibe had been together for almost six months when Vibe figured out that a generation was missing between Søren and the couple she—up until that moment—had assumed to be his parents. It hit to her one summer's day when Søren was in the kitchen making iced tea. Elvira had already gone outside; they could hear her spreading a cloth over the garden table and insects buzzing in the uncut grass. While Søren mixed the tea in a pitcher, Vibe studied the wedding photograph of Søren's parents that was standing on the sideboard in the dining room. Suddenly a dark cloud of wonder spread across her face, and she scrutinized the photograph as if seeing it properly for the very first time. She looked as if she wanted to say something, but then thought better of it.

Later, they were lying on Søren's bed listening to records.

"Who were the people in the photograph?" Vibe asked, at last. Søren turned over and folded his hands behind his head.

"My parents," he said. Vibe was silent for a moment, then she jerked upright.

"But they can't be," she burst out.

"Why not?" Søren looked at her.

"Well, because you can't change your eye color, and in that picture, Knud has brown eyes and . . ." she frowned. "And now they're blue. Your parents have blue eyes." She looked at Søren. "And yours are brown," she whispered.

Søren rolled over, rested his elbows on the mattress, and cradled his chin in his hands. It would only take a minute to fetch the dusty box from the attic and show it to Vibe. After all, it was no secret that Elvira and Knud were his grandparents, though they never talked about it. It was just the way it was.

"Knud and Elvira are my grandparents," he said. "My parents died when I was five years old. In a car crash. The photograph on the sideboard is of them. My parents on their wedding day. Their names were Peter and Kristine."

Vibe lay very still.

It was Jacob Madsen's father, Herman, who inspired Søren to become a policeman. Jacob also lived in Snerlevej, and he and Søren were friends. Herman Madsen was a sergeant in the CID, and Søren looked up to him. Jacob had an older sister and a mother who worked part time in a library. His family was different than Søren's. Jacob's parents weren't hippies. Not that Elvira and Knud were—not proper hippies anyway—but their left-wing politics regularly created mayhem in the living room, where meetings were held and banners painted. They frequently protested against nuclear power, and though Søren was proud of his grandparents, he always enjoyed walking down the road and into the haven of peace that was Jacob's house. Jacob's father would come home from work and make himself comfortable in his winged armchair with the newspaper, Jacob would lie on his bed reading comics, and Jacob's mother would be in the kitchen making mashed potatoes or hamburgers. At Søren's they ate oddly concocted casseroles, salads topped with chopped up leftovers, and a lot of oatmeal.

When dinner was ready at Jacob's house, his mother would strike a small gong and everyone would gather. When Jacob's father joined them, the children would go very quiet. Sometimes, but not always, he would tell them the stories they were so desperate to hear. They knew from experience that if they pestered him before they had eaten, he would usually remain silent; however, if they were good and only said "pass the salt please," and let Jacob's father eat some of his dinner in peace, he would open up.

"Herman, not while we're at the table," Jacob's mother would sigh.

The children waited with bated breath until Herman started telling them about murdered women, kidnapped children, hidden bodies, and vindictive ex-husbands. The two boys, especially, were riveted once Herman got into his stride. At some point he started giving the boys murder mysteries to solve, and Søren got so excited about going to Jacob's house that Elvira, rather anxiously, asked if it really was all right with the Madsens that Søren ate with them three times a week. Oh, yes, Søren had replied. It became a kind of real-life game of Clue where Herman knew who the killer was, where the murder had been committed, what the motive was, and which murder weapon was used, but it was up to the boys to come up with a plausible scenario. Herman taught them how to think, and Søren displayed considerable aptitude. Though he was only twelve years old, he could spot connections and produce explanations that, at times, were really quite far-fetched, but that to both Søren's and Herman's surprise—and to Jacob's irritation—often turned out to be correct. Søren had no idea how he did it. It was as if he visualized a network of paths through which he could, quite literally, trace the solution to the mystery. He could keep track of everyone involved in the case, even though Herman would frequently throw in some red herrings to confuse the boys. In addition, Søren was a skilled bluffer with the ability to ask seemingly innocent questions, only to suddenly come up with the answer to the whole mystery.

When Jacob went off to boarding school, Søren felt awkward going to his house. Besides, he had started high school and met Vibe, and the riddle-solving faded into the background, except on Sundays when Herman washed the family's Peugeot on the drive-way. Søren would swing by for an update on the week's events at the police station, and Herman would always have a mystery for him to crack. It wasn't until Søren was an adult that he started questioning just how much of what Herman had told them had actually been true. After all, he must have had a duty of confidentiality.

At eighteen Søren left home and got his own place in Copenhagen. One day, a year later, when he returned home for a dinner with Elvira and Knud, a moving van was parked outside Jacob's house, but there was no one around apart from four moving men carrying boxes and furniture. The next time Søren visited his grandparents, two unknown children were playing on Jacob's old front lawn. Søren watched them and made up his mind to become a policeman.

Søren quickly became the family's official detective, charged with finding lost items such as reading glasses, user manuals, and tax returns. He asked a lot questions, and nine times out of ten he would locate the missing object. Knud's reading glasses lay on top of his shoes in the hall where he had bent down to scratch his ankle, the user manual for the coffee maker was in the trunk of the car, on top of a box of telephone books for recycling, and the tax return was found in the ashes in the fireplace because Elvira, in a moment's distraction, had scrunched it up and thrown it there.

"How do you do it?" Vibe asked one evening when Søren, after a most unusual interrogation, reached the conclusion that her calculator had accidentally ended up in the garbage can in between some old magazines. He even offered to go downstairs to check—there was a chance that the trash might not have been collected yet. Five minutes later, he presented Vibe with her calculator.

"I knit backward," Søren began. Vibe waited for him to continue.

"When you solve a mystery," Søren explained, "you should never accept the first and most obvious explanation that presents itself. If you do that, it's just guessing. You'll automatically assume that the man with blood on his hands is the murderer and the woman with the gambling debt is the grifter. Sometimes that's the way it is, but not always. When you knit backward, you don't guess."

Vibe nodded.

* * *

In December 2003 Vibe attended a course in Barcelona with her business partner, and Søren was home alone. While she was gone, he caught himself enjoying the solitude. Vibe had started to look at him with deeply wounded eyes, and Søren had felt guilty for weeks. The whole point was that he did *not* want to betray her. In her absence he went to work, organized old photographs, watched *The Usual Suspects*, which held no interest for Vibe, and read *Calvin and Hobbes* while sitting on the toilet. At the end of the week he played squash with his friend and colleague, Henrik.

At first glance, Henrik was the ultimate cliché. He pumped iron, had a crazy number of tattoos (including a prohibited one on his neck, which had nearly cost him entry to the police academy), and his hair was never more than a few millimeters long. A small, aggressive mustache grew on his upper lip; Søren thought it looked ridiculous. While still a recruit, Henrik had married Jeanette and they had two daughters in quick succession. The girls were older now, teenagers, and Henrik was forever moaning how there was no room for him in their apartment because of all their girly stuff, clothes, shoes, and handbags, and when they go to school, he ranted, they look like bloody hookers, the sort we keep arresting in Vesterbro, and Jeanette just tells me to shut up, it's the fashion, she says, what's that all about? And Jeanette had started going to yoga all the time and he wasn't getting any, what the hell was that all about, no, he missed the good old days, when he was single, blah-blah-blah. His bark was infinitely worse than his bite. Søren knew perfectly well that Henrik loved his wife and daughters and would do anything for them.

Søren hadn't mentioned to Henrik that he and Vibe were going through a rough patch and whenever Henrik tried to pry with his *what's up, you getting any these days?* he deflected him. His private life was nobody's business. Nor had he told Henrik he was home alone, but when they were cooling off in the locker room after their squash game, Søren blurted out that Vibe had gone to Barcelona. He could have kicked himself. Henrik lit up like a Christmas tree;

the two of them were going to hit the town. He called Jeanette from the locker room, and Søren could hear an argument erupt—something to do with their younger daughter—and quietly hoped this would lead to their night out being canceled. But Henrik stood his ground. Bitch, he said, as he hung up, she can go to her power yoga some other fucking time. Time for them to have some beers.

"I don't know," Søren said, pulling his sweater over his head. "I was just going to get a pizza and watch a DVD at home. I'm bushed."

"You're a boring old fart, that's what you are," Henrik scoffed.

Søren said nothing.

They found a small bar in Vesterbro and got drunk. Henrik grew increasingly raucous, and Søren was desperate to leave when Henrik struck up a conversation with two women at the table next to them. One was called Katrine, she was from Århus, but had lived in Copenhagen for a few years while she was training to be a teacher; her course would finish just after Christmas. She was very dark, like a gypsy, even though she spoke with a strong Jutland accent. What did Søren do for a living? They got talking and, at Henrik's suggestion, they pushed their tables together. Later they went on to a club that Søren had never been to before. He felt strangely animated, oblivious. It was wonderful. His old life seemed so far away.

At two o'clock in the morning he decided to call it a night and went to find a cab. Katrine wanted to share it. She lived on H. C. Ørstedsvej and could be dropped off on the way. Afterward, Søren could barely remember how they had started kissing. It was so random. When the cab stopped outside Katrine's block, she invited him in. He nodded and paid the cab fare.

Katrine lived in a two-bedroom attic apartment with coconut mats, plants, and lots of books. She went to brush her teeth and he could have left then, but he stayed, flipping through a book with photographs of churches. She even unloaded her washing machine and hung her clothes out to dry on a rack in the living room, as though she was deliberately giving him a chance to reconsider. He told her about Vibe. His girlfriend, who was in Barcelona on business. Katrine just smiled and said Barcelona was great. He stayed.

They made love, and it was wonderful. Different, because she wasn't Vibe. Søren had been unfaithful to Vibe a couple of times at the beginning of their relationship, but that was years ago. Katrine felt and tasted different.

He stayed the night. The next morning Katrine got up and made toast and coffee for them. It was nice. They didn't exchange telephone numbers, and Søren went home.

Later that afternoon Søren was racked with remorse, the strength of which he hadn't believed possible. He took a shower, but it was no good. Henrik telephoned and behaved intolerably. She was hot, wasn't she, eh? Had he done something about it? Of course he hadn't. Søren pretended to be offended and ended the conversation. Vibe would be back in three days, and during those three days Søren forced himself to think about having children. His guilt had nothing to do with Katrine; he had already forgotten all about her. He had slept with her because he was stressed about Vibe and the baby business. He had tried to relieve his frustration by doing something completely unacceptable and outrageous. He didn't want to be that guy. Suddenly it was clear to him: he either had to get Vibe pregnant or he had to let her go so she could have children with someone else.

When Vibe came home, she was happy and relaxed. Søren wondered if she, too, had been unfaithful. In the days that followed, they appeared to benefit from their break. Vibe's eyes no longer held that hurt expression, and she seemed so absorbed by work that she was far too tired to think about having a baby and their relationship. They spent a lovely Christmas with Knud and Elvira, they cuddled in front of the fireplace and exchanged presents; on New Year's Eve they hugged each other for a long time when the clock struck twelve. Neither of them spoke, but it felt like a commitment. Søren woke up on the first of January believing the crisis had passed.

Then one evening, completely out of the blue, Vibe said that they had to talk about it. Barcelona had been amazing, inspirational, and when she came back, her work had meant as much to her as in the old days when she had worked late practically every night. But since they had completed their latest project, her life had become humdrum.

"And I can still feel it," she said, quietly. "I want to have a baby. My body wants to have a baby. I can't help it."

Søren sat down in the sofa and put his arms around her.

"Perhaps it's time for us to go our separate ways," he said. The tears started rolling down Vibe's cheeks.

"So you still don't want to? Never, under any circumstances?" she asked.

"No."

Shortly afterward Vibe went to bed. She didn't kiss him good-night, she just closed the door to the bedroom. Søren stayed behind feeling like a total dick. He didn't want to have children. The feeling couldn't be mistaken, but neither could he fathom what lay behind it. Was it about Vibe? Did he want children with another woman, but not with her? No, he didn't. So what was it all about? He grabbed a beer from the fridge and turned the TV volume to mute. The world was a dangerous place, that was why. Children might die, children *did* die, he thought, angrily. It wasn't all romantic, as Vibe imagined. Children were born only to end up in the morgue; young girls, half-naked, bruised, battered, and dead. Teenage boys high on designer drugs, beaten to a pulp by each other, or smashed up in cars or motorbikes driven by their drunk friends. Søren had accompanied countless parents to the morgue. He didn't want children. When he had finished his beer, his sadness overwhelmed him. They would have to break up, so Vibe could have her child with another man.

They decided to tell Knud and Elvira together the following Friday. It was a Tuesday and Søren was dreading the moment because Vibe was like a daughter to the old couple. He was convinced they wouldn't accept the reason for the breakup as they had both hinted, repeatedly, that they would like some great-grandchildren soon. Vibe slept on the sofa the whole week, even though Søren offered her their bed. She didn't want it. She was fine sleeping in the living room, she said.

That Friday, Søren picked Vibe up from work. They drove to Snerlevej and parked in front of the house. Søren loved to go back to his old home. He loved opening the door with the key he had been given when he turned ten and started making his own way to and from school, he loved the smell in the hall, a mixture of what was cooking in the kitchen and damp coats, boots, shoes, and old wool. There was always a bottle of red wine waiting on the radiator when Vibe and Søren came to visit, always delicious food and warmth, and after dinner they would play Trivial Pursuit, the men against the women. But that evening when Søren unlocked the door, something was clearly very wrong. Vibe followed behind him. They had hugged each other briefly on the garden path, and Søren had asked if she was sure.

"I'm sure I want a child," she had replied, and looked away. They went inside the house. Søren called out. The hall was cold, there was no smell of food or wine, and the hall light, which was always on when his grandparents were expecting guests, was off. They hung up their coats and exchanged baffled looks before Søren opened the door to the living room. Knud and Elvira were huddled together. Elvira was crying. She was sitting on Knud's lap, her head resting on his shoulder. Knud had both his arms around her. They stayed like this, even though Vibe and Søren had now entered.

"What's happened?" Søren exclaimed. Elvira raised her head and looked at him, red-eyed.

"Come here, my love," she said, patting the sofa. Vibe and Søren stared at them, paralyzed.

"No," Søren said. "Can't you just tell me what it is?"

Elvira was ill. She had a tumor in her breast, and the cancer had spread to her lymph nodes. She had been told that very day. It was terminal.

That night they reminisced about Elvira's life. That was what she wanted. Past summers, the plums, Perle, the goat kid they had bottle-fed in the back garden, about the time Søren had found her wedding ring in a jar of strawberry jam. They laughed and drank wine and ate pizza, which Søren went out to get. They lit candles, and the evening concluded with Vibe and Elvira beating the men so emphatically in Trivial Pursuit that Vibe suggested that Søren and Knud should ask for their school tuition back. At no point did Søren and Vibe tell Knud and Elvira why they had come.

*   *   *

When Katrine telephoned, Søren had almost forgotten her existence. He was at work, it was summer and it was seven months since their one-night stand. The weather had been mild and pleasant, and Vibe and Søren spent all their spare time in the garden in Snerlevej. Elvira was dying. They had installed a hospital bed in the living room for her three weeks prior, and since then she had deteriorated quickly. Vibe and Søren had still not mentioned their split to Knud and Elvira. They couldn't bear to and had agreed to wait until after Elvira's death. She deserved to die as happy as possible. Vibe had moved out at the start of April, but when they visited Knud and Elvira, they would catch the same bus or share the car, and when they walked up the garden path, they would hold hands. They still saw each other, both at home in their old apartment and in Vibe's new one. It felt good, but strange, titillating almost, to make love to Vibe in her new bed, in a bedroom with apple green curtains and wallpaper with tiny flowers, it was almost as if they had only just met. They went to the movies like they used to, went running together every Sunday, and even flew to Paris for a long weekend. A strange calm existed between them; limbo. A few times Vibe had cautiously asked him if his mind was made up, and he had kissed her forehead and said that she deserved better.

"And so does your child," he had added.

When he realized that it was *that* Katrine who was calling, his palms grew sweaty. His first thought was genital warts, his second, HIV. Tracking him down had been no easy task, she said with a nervous laugh, because she only knew that his name was Søren and that he worked at Bellahøj police station. She had been put through to several different people, and she was relieved she had finally found the right person. She laughed nervously again, and then she said gravely, "But Bo and I agree that I should."

Søren was baffled, who was Bo? Bo was her boyfriend, she explained, and she had met him shortly after the night Søren had spent with her. They had just moved in together.

"And Bo will be the baby's father," she then said.

Everything stopped.

Søren didn't understand a word.

It was surreal.

They spoke for a little while. Afterward he called Vibe and told her that he was working late and please would she go to Elvira and Knud's on her own and he would join them later? Is everything all right? she wanted to know. No, yes, he stuttered. Something has come up at work, he lied.

He worked through the longest day of his life without any sense of what he was actually doing. At five o'clock he drove to H. C. Ørstedsvej and rang the bell. The nameplate below the bell was new; in addition to Katrine's name it said *Bo Beck Vestergaard*. Upstairs, in Katrine's apartment, the situation became even more bizarre. Katrine was seven months pregnant, her belly beautiful and round.

"We're really looking forward to the baby," Bo said, narrowing his eyes.

Bo was assembling a changing table in the corner of the room. He was clearly putting in a lot of effort. However, Søren was the biological father, Katrine said, there was no doubt about it. Katrine didn't meet Bo until after she had found out she was pregnant, and Bo had been relaxed about the whole thing—after all, they were all adults, and he was very much in love with Katrine. Initially, they had decided not to contact Søren, but as Katrine's pregnancy progressed, they had second thoughts. They didn't want to lie to the child, but this was precisely what they were setting themselves up for if they concealed the baby's real parentage at this early stage.

Søren didn't know what to think. His jaw had dropped and panic stuck to the inside of his throat like an obstinate fish bone. Bo continued explaining. Søren would be kept informed and the child would be told when it was old enough, but Bo and Katrine agreed it would be too confusing for the child if there were multiple fathers around during the early years. Søren understood, didn't he? He wouldn't have to pay child support either, unless he absolutely insisted. Bo had his own business selling musical instruments, and Katrine had gotten a job at a school in Valby; she was currently on maternity leave. They would manage. In fact, they were asking Søren to keep a low profile and not interfere too much. Not until the child itself wanted to meet its biological father. It was clear, as far as Bo was concerned, the need would never arise. Søren nodded, asked a timid question and nodded again. He declared that he would need time to process it all. Bo looked pleased and saw him out.

Søren stumbled out into H. C. Ørstedsvej, clammy with sweat, his mouth dry. In a kiosk he downed two soft drinks straight from the refrigerated case while the shopkeeper eyed him suspiciously. What the hell was he going to say to Vibe? Vibe, who had blind faith in him, who still called him "the straightest guy in the world" to her friends, even though they had broken up, even though he hadn't been pre-pared to give her the child she so desperately wanted. He walked down to the lakes and began pacing up and down. He had to convince Bo and Katrine that it would be in everyone's best interest if Søren never became the baby's father. Not ever. Not on paper, not in real life. It would hurt Vibe deeply if the truth came out. Besides, he didn't want to be a father, for Christ's sake. Not to Vibe's child, not to Katrine's, and certainly not to Bo Beck Vestergaard's. It was completely out of the question. He had donated some sperm, that was all. It should never have happened. Katrine was supposed to have had her period, and afterward she was supposed to meet Bo, and they should have had a baby of their own. Why the hell hadn't he used a condom? He stopped at Saint Jørgen's Lake and kicked a low wall hard with his black leather shoe. When he had calmed down, he went to see Knud and Elvira.

"It's good that you're here now," Vibe said quietly, as he entered the living room. At first he couldn't see Elvira and, for a brief sec-ond, he imagined that she had got out of bed, fit and healthy, and gone out into the garden to pick elderflowers, but then he spotted her. She was lying in a fold of the comforter—at least that was how it looked. Søren held her tiny frail hand and sobbed his heart out. Three hours later Elvira sighed softly, and then she was gone.

In the weeks that followed Søren tried to brush aside all thoughts of the baby. There was much to do. A complicated case at work, orga-nizing Elvira's funeral, and then there was Knud, who was falling apart with grief. When Bo called two and a half weeks later, he screamed furiously into the handset that they should leave him the fuck alone, he hadn't asked to have a baby, and if Katrine could have been bothered to call him when she found out she was pregnant, he would have told her to get rid of it. Later the same afternoon, Søren called Bo back to apologize. He explained his mother had died and he was under a lot of pressure. To begin with Bo was distant and implacable, but as the conversation progressed, he softened.

"Okay," he said. "Call us when you're a bit more on top of things. After all, there's no hurry. Like we said, we would prefer not to have you hanging around. I'm sorry, but I'm being honest here. We just don't want to lie to the child. She deserves to know the truth so she can have a secure childhood."

"It's a girl?" Søren marveled.

"Yes," Bo said. "And we're calling her Maja."

Søren managed to visit Katrine once before she had her baby, one afternoon when he spontaneously drove past H. C. Ørstedsvej, rang the doorbell, and found her home alone. They didn't speak much, but she looked undeniably gorgeous on the sofa, big, round, and enigmatic as though she was hatching a golden egg. Suddenly, he heard himself promise to keep his distance, as Bo and Katrine had requested, and that he would be there if the girl wanted to meet her father when she got older. *If.* They sealed the deal with a cup of coffee and, as there was nothing more to say, Søren left.

Maja was born on September 8, 2004. Bo called him after the birth. He was rather monosyllabic and merely informed him the child had been born and that mother and baby were doing well. Then he hung up. Three days later Søren went to Frederiksberg Hospital. He had been racked with doubt, but in the end he had been unable to stay away. He bought a teddy bear for the baby and a bottle of lemon-scented lotion for Katrine. The young clerk in the drugstore helped him choose it. In the hospital corridor he hesitated before he entered the ward. What if they had visitors, what if it was inappropriate? But, for God's sake, *they* had chosen to involve him, so they had only themselves to blame. And, anyway, he wasn't some asshole who just stayed away.

To his surprise, the ward was nearly empty. There were no visitors and three empty beds waited for newly delivered mothers and their babies. Only the bed by the window was occupied, by Katrine, who was sitting with a faraway expression on her face. She looked up and smiled, almost as if she didn't recognize him, then she lowered her eyes. Søren approached her gingerly and placed his presents on one of the empty beds. Then he saw Maja. She was absolutely tiny and swaddled in a white blanket. The bear he had bought for her was five times her size. Maja's hair was long and black and her face all scrunched up. She was the spitting image of him. Søren was speechless. He looked at Katrine, then he leaned forward and kissed her forehead.

Everything changed. Not because there was a child at Frederiksberg Hospital who happened to share his genes, not because of her remarkable likeness to him, not because he had fathered another human being, technically, at least. No, it was because his brain was swelling to twice its normal size. He started to laugh out loud. Elvira had died, Knud was in mourning, and his relationship with Vibe was characterized by grief and anger, and yet he raced down Jagtvejen in his car, roaring with laughter. He hadn't wanted a child. He *still* didn't want a child. He hadn't wanted to sit down to talk it over with Vibe or Katrine or any other woman. But now that she was here, he wanted Maja. With every fiber of his being. He would never let her out of his sight, he would protect her against all evil. The feeling was like an unbreakable chain anchored in his stomach. That night he made a plan. He would visit Bo and Katrine as soon as possible and make it clear to them that the deal was off.

It was a fortnight before Bo said it was okay for him to visit. When Søren arrived, he had rehearsed his speech so many times, he was no longer nervous.

"I've decided that I want to be her dad."

Bo and Katrine had offered him coffee. Bo's cup froze in mid-air. He gave Søren an outraged look.

"You've what? You've no right to do that."

He slammed the cup down on the table. The noise startled Maja.

"Bo," Katrine began, cautiously. "Let's just hear Søren out." She looked up at Søren and smiled an almost imperceptible smile. Bo got up and went to the window, his back shaking.

"I know I can't be with her every day," Søren continued. "Probably not even every week, but I want to be in her life and not just as a last resort you call when you've got no one else. I'm in this for good. Bo is your boyfriend," he said, looking at Katrine, "and I realize that he will probably be Maja's dad in her heart. The one she plays with when she comes home from nursery, the one who reads her bedtime stories, the one she'll hate when she becomes a teenager." Katrine smiled. "And also the one who, on some level, will mean the most to her." Bo's back started to calm down. "But I want to be involved, and if you won't let me . . ." he took a deep breath, "then I will go to court." A deadly silence descended on the room.

Bo stayed where he was with his back to them, but Katrine said, "Okay, Søren. It's okay."

Bo didn't turn around, not even when Søren left.

From then on, Søren visited them every week. Maja was becoming increasingly alert and Bo less frosty. Søren made an effort when he was there. He asked Bo questions and listened attentively when Bo told him about a particularly bad diapering incident, a sleepless night, or an expression that might have been a smile. What he really felt like doing was bundling Bo up and hurling him out the window.

One November afternoon he found Katrine and Maja home alone. Katrine was breastfeeding, so Søren put the kettle on. When Maja had been fed, Katrine made coffee while Søren changed Maja's diaper and put clean clothes on her. From the kitchen, Katrine called out with a question about Vibe. Until now they had avoided talking about personal issues completely, primarily because Bo was always hovering by the front door in the hope that Søren might be overcome by a sudden urge to leave. Not surprisingly, this rather put a damper on their intimacy. Søren's reply was evasive, but when she had sat down again and Maja was lying between them, the whole story spilled out of him. His relationship with Vibe, which had started when they were teenagers, had to end because Vibe so fervently wanted to have a baby, and he didn't; Elvira, who had died never knowing that Vibe and he were no longer a couple though they still saw each other, and now Knud, who tried to carry on the traditional family Sunday lunch ignorant of the fact that Vibe and Søren lived separate lives and pretended to be a couple purely to shield him from further pain. When Søren had finished, he picked up the little girl. They stood by the window and watched the cars. Maja opened and closed her mouth, and Søren told her that a blue Ford Fiesta had just run a red light. "He's lucky your daddy is busy holding you," he whispered, "or he would have given him a ticket." Katrine, still sitting on the sofa, asked if Vibe even knew about Maja. Søren didn't reply for a long time. Then he shook his head.

When he left Maja and Katrine an hour later, he had made up his mind. Katrine had given him a photograph of Maja, which he had put in his wallet, behind his driving license, and the time had come. Knud would learn that Vibe and Søren were no longer together, and Knud and Vibe would learn of Maja's existence. He dreaded Vibe's reaction, there was no denying that, but he suddenly yearned to tell the old man that he was a great-grandfather. He started by calling Vibe to check that she was free this Sunday—she was, she had no plans apart from their usual lunch at Snerlevej. Then he called Knud. No one answered the telephone. He called back later the same day, but still nothing. In the evening, he grew increasingly worried and drove to his childhood home. He had called Knud fifteen times at least, and there had been no reply.

Søren found Knud in the kitchen, sitting on a chair facing the garden. His hand, resting in his lap, held a framed photograph of Elvira. On the kitchen table were two bags of groceries. Knud appeared incapable of summoning the energy to put them away. Søren hugged him tenderly.

"Is it very bad today?" he asked, carefully taking the photograph from Knud. In the picture Elvira was old and wrinkled and yet irresistibly alive. Knud turned his head and stared blankly at Søren.

"I've got cancer," he said, smiling weakly. "That's how bad it is."

That Sunday, they had lunch in Snerlevej as usual. Vibe had offered to make lasagna and salad. It was bizarre. Knud had bowel cancer, which had spread to his liver. There was nothing the doctors could do.

"And here was I thinking cancer wasn't infectious," Knud remarked dryly. He seemed neither scared nor sad; on the contrary, he praised the food and had second helpings. Afterward he suggested they have a cigarette.

"But you don't smoke." Søren was taken aback.

"Oh, yes," he said. "I do now."

They lit cigarettes and flicked the ashes onto their plates. It had been ten years since Vibe and Søren had quit smoking, and the three of them coughed and spluttered like teenagers. They all started to laugh and that was when Vibe suddenly exclaimed:

"Wasn't there something you wanted to talk to us about, Søren?" She gave him a searching look. "It certainly sounded like it the other day."

Now Knud was looking at him, too.

"Nah," Søren said. "You must have misunderstood. Everything's fine."

On December 18, when Maja was just over three months old, Bo, Maja, and Katrine flew to Thailand for Christmas. Søren loathed the idea. Thailand was far away, they would be staying at some hotel on an island, and he was convinced that Maja would have forgotten all about him by the next time she saw him. Katrine was busy packing when he came to wish them Merry Christmas. Bo, fortunately, was out. He gave Maja the world's tiniest bracelet with a four-leaf clover pendant.

"She really is far too young for jewelry," Katrine smiled. Søren watched her while she folded Maja's tiny onesies and placed them in the suitcase.

"Why can't you stay here?" he blurted out. Katrine laughed. Then she asked him if he had told his family about Maja yet. Søren was just about to lie, but he hesitated a fraction of a second. Katrine shook her head.

"How long are you going to keep your daughter a secret?"

Søren went to the window with Maja in his arms. This time, it was a Nissan Altima that ran a red light.

"I'll tell my grandfather on Christmas," he said. "When I've got some time off and everything has calmed down a bit."

"I would like to meet him," Katrine said.

His eyes widened. "Are you serious?"

"Yes," Katrine replied. "I really would. If you ever have the guts to tell him." Katrine winked at Søren. "Perhaps we could have lunch together, when we're back, all of us."

"Including Bo?" Søren winked back at her.

"Yes, of course," Katrine smiled.

Søren nodded. Then he laid Maja on the fleece blanket on the floor. She waved her arms, kicked her legs, and stuck out her tongue. She was starting to lose her hair, and her deep blue eyes studied Søren with curiosity. For the next half hour they drank coffee and chatted before Søren left. He kissed Maja's soft forehead and squeezed her tiny foot, warm and wriggling, inside her footed pajamas.

After Christmas, Vibe and Søren spent four days in Sweden where Vibe had borrowed a cottage from her business partner. Søren intended to confess to Vibe while they were there, and when they returned to Copenhagen he would also tell Knud about Maja. The woods behind the cottage seemed endless, and the snow scattered like crystals from the trees when a squirrel leapt or the wind stirred. Søren chopped firewood and gazed at the forest, briefly tempted to swap his life for one that was simpler and more manageable.

They played board games, read books, talked about Elvira, about the first Christmas without her and about Knud, who was putting on a brave face and had insisted they go to Sweden. Søren had rung him twice, but had only gotten the answering machine and he was just starting to worry when he received a voice mail from Knud. Everything was fine. Vibe and Søren spoke conspicuously little about their relationship, as though they had agreed to a truce.

"We're like brother and sister," Vibe exclaimed one day and lowered the book she was reading. Søren was standing by the window, looking out at the wild garden; he was thinking about Maja, how he was going to break the news, how he would tell Vibe. Now was an obvious moment. Right now. But Vibe was cuddled up in a blanket, her cheeks flushed with the heat from the wood stove, a pot of tea on the table, and she looked so peaceful. For the first time in a long time.

They made love only once. New Year's Eve. After a lot of salmon and wine. It felt familiar and comforting. They left early in the morning on January 2. Søren had still not told her about Maja.

They had stopped at a service station to buy milk when Søren saw the newspaper headlines: **ASIAN TSUNAMI DEATH TOLL REACHES 200,000**.

"What's happened?" Vibe gasped. A strange noise escaped from Søren's throat. They bought milk and a copy of every newspaper.

"It's just so awful," Vibe said, over and over. She was leafing through the newspapers. "It's unbearable." With tears streaming down her cheeks, she told him about an Australian mother who had been with her two sons when the tsunami hit and how she hadn't been strong enough to hold on to them both. She had had to let go of her older son, who was seven. Now he was gone. Vibe dissolved completely. Søren didn't utter a sound.

"Do you want to come in?" she asked, when Søren had parked in front of her apartment block. Søren shook his head.

Maja, Bo, and Katrine weren't on the lists of missing persons. Søren checked the homepages of the Danish Foreign Office every thirty minutes every single day. They weren't there. Why hadn't they called? He would scream at Katrine when he saw her. Teach her never to be so selfish again. He wondered whom to call. He couldn't think of anyone. Officially, he had no relationship with the Beck Vestergaard family. He had donated some sperm, and there was no one he could call. Vibe rang him several times, but he could barely breathe and he couldn't talk to her.

Bo called on January 5 in the evening. Søren had tried to eat some take-out food, but he had lost his appetite. He was standing by the window; the telephone was on the window sill. He answered it after the first ring.

The weight dropped off Søren, and halfway through January he took a sick leave. Bo called every day, but Søren ignored the telephone. Once, Bo tricked him by calling from a different number. Bo screamed at him, and Søren hung up. After that, Søren stopped answering his telephone. Twice, someone banged on his front door in the night. Søren knew it was Bo. He didn't open the door, instead he lay very still under his comforter. Eventually Bo gave up.

Søren spent his days with Knud, stroking the old man's hair and watching him waste away.

"Shouldn't you be at work?" Knud asked. Søren shook his head.

The night before Knud died, he lay in the living room in Snerlevej, hooked up to a morphine drip, dosing himself nearly all the time Søren was there. It wasn't until nine in the evening that Knud suddenly woke up and reached out for Søren. Knud's blue eyes were alert, but he struggled to speak.

"Vibe," he said.

"Vibe isn't here today. Do you want me to call her?"

Vibe had gone out to dinner. They had agreed that she would leave her cell phone on silent so that Søren could call her if Knud deteriorated. Søren reached for his cell.

Knud made a grunting noise, which stopped Søren in his tracks.

"No, don't call," he hissed. His eyes rolled a couple of times, then his eyelids closed heavily and just as Søren decided to get up and make some coffee, Knud's voice could be heard again.

"You should love your woman," he wheezed, "like I love Ella." Knud was the only one who had ever called Elvira "Ella."

"I look forward to dying," he said, and now his voice sounded strangely clear, like the Knud Søren used to know.

"Because I'll see her again." He smiled faintly. Knud was an arch-atheist. A tear rolled down his cheek.

"And I so want to see her again."

Søren fought hard not to cry.

"And Vibe . . ."

"We've agreed that I'll call her," Søren said again.

"Shut up," Knud snarled, as though it was less painful to rebuke him with a quick crack of the whip than with a lengthy explanation. Søren glanced at the morphine drip.

"Vibe is like a daughter to Ella and me." His voice was calm now. "But if you love someone, you should be willing to die for them." He closed his eyes. Søren sat still like a statue. Knud opened his eyes again and said: "And you're not willing to die for Vibe. This much I know." Those were his last words.

Søren rested his head on his grandfather's emaciated thighs, covered by the blanket, and sobbed. He thought he would never be able to stop. He could feel Knud's hand move slightly, but Knud was now too weak to reach his head. Søren was Denmark's youngest police superintendent, he could identify a murderer from the mere twitching of a single, out-of-place eyebrow hair, he could knit backward, and everyone he had ever loved had died and left him behind.

Søren parked his car in the basement under Bellahøj police station. He walked up the stairs, filled the coffee machine in the kitchen, switched it on, and went to his office while the water dripped through the filter. It was all a long time ago now. Elvira, Maja, Knud. Three years. Søren contemplated the sky. It looked like it might snow, even though it was only October. He was rummaging around on his desk, looking for a report he had to finish writing, when Henrik burst in without bothering to knock first.

"Hi, Søren," Henrik said. "Fancy a lecture at the College of Natural Science?"

Søren looked perplexed, but he reached for his jacket and started putting it on.

"A very upset guy by the name of Johannes Trøjborg dialed 911 an hour ago saying his academic supervisor lay dying in his office. Sejr and Madsen followed the ambulance, and they have just called in to report that the deceased, as he is now, is a Lars Helland, age fifty-seven, a biologist and a professor at the University of Copenhagen. The preliminary findings from the paramedic who attended the scene suggest that Helland died of a heart attack." Søren started taking off his jacket. "But," Henrik raised his hand to preempt him and checked his notes, "Professor Helland's severed tongue was lying on his chest, and young Mr. Trøjborg has lost his shit. The deputy medical coroner and the boys from forensics are on their way. Are you coming?"

Søren rose and zipped his jacket. They went to the garage and drove at high speed to the university. Henrik told a completely unfunny joke, and Søren watched the sky, which looked as if it were about to burst.

CHAPTER 4

Clive Freeman lived in Canada and was professor of Palaeoorni-
thology at the department of Bird Evolution, Palaeobiology, and
Systematics at the University of British Columbia—where he had
worked for almost thirty years. He lived on Vancouver Island, not
far from campus, and he specialized in bird evolution.

It was generally accepted that birds descended from a primitive
reptile, the thecodont, and the most likely candidate for the role
of the ancestor of all birds was the archosaur *Longisquama*. Most
scientists—people whom Freeman respected—argued that modern
birds were living dinosaurs. Professor Freeman disagreed.

Clive had grown up in the far north of Canada, the only child
of the famous behavioral biologist David Freeman, one of Canada's
most important wolf experts in the latter half of the twentieth century. David taught his son all there was to know about the woods;
the life cycle of trees, the forest floor, and the flora and fauna. There
was never any doubt that Clive would grow up to be a biologist.

When Clive turned twelve, he made up his mind to specialize
in birds. Birds were the most advanced animals on the planet. The

primitive reptile they descended from was also believed to be the ancestor of turtles and crocodiles. A bird skeleton was streamlined, its bones were hollow and filled with air and provided the bird with superior movements, its plumage was perfect, and its egg-laying process was second to none. People never thought about that when sparrows pecked their lawns or pigeons soiled the windshields of their cars. This appealed to Clive. It was as if he alone had spotted the ruby in the dust.

Clive's father didn't care for birds.

"It's actually shocking how little you know about the local wolves, given that your father is a world-famous expert," the elder Freeman remarked one day. He had tested Clive on the subject of mammalian teeth over dinner, and Clive hadn't been very success-ful. He could remember molars and premolars. "And eye-teeth," he had added. Clive's father gave him a long, hard stare.

"Eye-teeth are premolars, you moron," he said after a lengthy pause, then he got up and went to his study. Clive had been on the verge of telling him something about bills. The structure of the bill was unique, evolved, and adapted to such an extent that Clive could barely believe it. Long, thin bills, short, stubby, curled bills. Herbi-vore, omnivore, or carnivore, there was a bill for every imaginable purpose. Clive's heart was set on birds, and he didn't mind that they weren't mammals.

Clive was offered a place to study biology at the University of British Columbia in Vancouver when he was twenty and knew all there was to know about birds. He ran to the mailbox the day the letter arrived and tore it open. When he learned that he had been accepted—something he had been expecting—he looked back at his childhood home. Somewhere inside it, his father was clinging des-perately to his books. Clive never wanted to end up like him. There was more to life than academia. The sun warmed Clive's forehead, and he closed his eyes. As a child, he had worshipped and feared his father—he still did, as a matter of fact. However, as Clive's knowl-edge of natural science had expanded, it had become impossible to believe *everything* his father told him. Besides, natural science was changing with new methods, modern behavioral research, and a world of technology that Clive believed to be the future, but that David Freeman had very little time for. In recent years their discussions had become so heated that Clive's mother would sometimes take her plate to the kitchen to eat in peace.

In a few weeks he would put his childhood behind him. Perhaps this would improve their relationship? Perhaps David would visit him in Vancouver, proud that his son was following in his footsteps?

That evening, he told his parents about the offer and informed them he would be leaving home soon.

"The gait of birds is clumsy and ridiculous," David Freeman observed, and carried on eating.

Clive's mother said: "Stop it, both of you."

Clive visualized himself leaving the table, casting a patronizing glance at his father's bald patch, and taking his plate to the kitchen before going to his room to read. But instead he turned to his father and remarked calmly that even if one accepted birds didn't walk with much elegance, it followed it was even more impressive that many of them still used their feet for walking, given their highly evolved ability to fly. After all, wolves could *only* walk. They didn't master an alternative form of movement.

David said he couldn't hear what Clive had said. Clive repeated his words, louder than strictly necessary.

David responded by firing off Latin terms for bones, but he messed up describing the wolf's leg, whose construction he regarded as superior to that of a bird's in every respect. Clive's mother passed the potatoes and poured water into glasses. She shot Clive a quick, pleading look.

Suddenly Clive pricked up his ears.

What was it David had just said?

"What did you just say?"

Clive's mother sat absolutely still and David's face froze halfway through his argument, his hand suspended in midair, his mouth half-open. They both knew it. In his outburst, David had referred to a small bone, which in more primitive mammals was located between the talus bone and the tibia, though any fool knew that the bone in question had been reduced through evolution. David Freeman had made a mistake, Clive had heard it, and David knew that he had.

Nothing happened for several seconds. The air stood still and Clive's heart raced. Then David pushed back his chair and walked out.

For two days Clive was ecstatic. David had finally been put in his place. He came downstairs for meals and would join in the conversation, though he was somewhat subdued. Even Clive's mother livened up and said, "Don't you think so, darling?" several times.

"Yes, yes," David muttered.

Clive was the center of attention as he talked about the reading list he had been sent and the forthcoming term. His mother listened and David stayed silent. This had never happened before. Clive suddenly thought his father looked old, eaten up by the antagonism he had harbored over the years and, seized by a rare moment of tenderness, Clive called David "Dad," which he never normally did.

Two days later, Clive decided to suggest to David a final walk through the woods before his departure. It was Clive's fondest childhood memory, and he wanted to take a dew-fresh one with him to Vancouver. He was leaning against the kitchen table, drinking a glass of milk, while he summoned the courage to go to David's study, when something in the garden caught his eye. Their lawn was a curved piece of land, scattered with Arctic plants; Clive's bird table was at the far end, and behind it four large rocks broke the surface of the earth. Then the woods began.

There were dead birds all over the lawn. Three, seven, twenty, his eyes flickered as he started counting. He slammed down his glass and ran outside. There were dead birds everywhere. Limp balls of feather lay on the ground, on the naked area under the bird table, even on the board itself where Clive usually scattered seeds. Horrified, he inspected the feeding table. It was bare with the exception of a few husks whirling around in the wind. He checked the ground where the spike of the table had been pushed in, and that was where he saw the red pellets. There weren't many left, but enough for him to know what they were: rat poison.

Clive went straight to his room and packed his bags. He didn't want to spend another second in his father's house.

In Vancouver, Clive rented a room from an elderly lady who lived in a villa. Her front garden was a mess, and Clive volunteered to tidy it up.

Jack lived next door. He was five years old when Clive moved in and had lost his father a few months previously. He was a beautiful boy with watchful eyes and one day, when Clive was gardening, he came over and started digging his toe into the ground. Clive asked him if he wanted to help.

Jack and Clive dug a hole for a rose bush the old lady had asked for and, together, they studied everything they unearthed: beetles, worms, pupae ready to burst, skeletons, and a recently deceased mole whose coat still was soft and black. Jack wanted to know all there was to know about nature.

College began the following week, and Clive soon became very busy. There were compulsory lectures on campus, and he had essays to read and write. Clive told Jack he had to entertain himself during the week. He wouldn't have time for him until nine o'clock Saturday morning. Jack would show up at nine on the dot in the front garden under Clive's window with his bucket, his dull pocket knife, and his butterfly net. To begin with, they stayed in the garden, but when they had examined every square inch of it, Clive took Jack into the woods, taking water bottles and packed lunches, reference books, and collection boxes for their findings.

Clive taught Jack to dissect an animal on a flat rock. A mouse, a rabbit, a pigeon. Clive bought scalpels from the supplies store on campus and made a big deal out of telling Jack how sharp they were. The boy gazed at him, wide-eyed. The first animal they opened up had died from natural causes only a few hours earlier. It was very fresh and didn't smell at all. Clive guided the scalpel in Jack's hand and when the animal was laid out and its abdomen revealed, he asked Jack if he wanted to dissect the spleen.

"The spleen is bluish and shaped like a plum, that's all I'm going to tell you."

Jack picked up the scalpel, lingered a little, and then he took a deep breath. Soon the boy—pale but smiling—held the shiny organ in the palm of his hand. He had specks of dried blood on his cheek and his hair was tousled, and when Clive praised him, his face lit up.

This became their game. Clive would tell him which organ to remove and Jack would do it. When Jack turned ten, he was a skilled surgeon, not just in terms of dexterity but also speed. Rarely more than fifteen minutes would pass from the time they found, or killed, an animal before Jack would have dissected it. Clive ruffled the boy's hair.

Clive watched Jack's mother from his window. She had four children, of whom Jack was the youngest. She worked at the checkout in the local supermarket, but she never seemed to recognize Clive when he did his shopping. She had bags under her eyes, she smoked too much, and yet there was something attractive about her. She had slim tanned arms and a narrow back. Not that Clive had any desire to take on another man's children. Thanks, but no thanks. Jack, of course, wouldn't be a problem. He was a good boy, Clive's boy, but Clive found the other children irritating. The oldest one was a young man of sixteen—seventeen years, an apprentice mechanic somewhere. Clive would see him come home in the evening, hear him argue loudly with his mother, and watch him tinker with a car in the front yard, chucking beer bottles on the grass as soon as he had emptied them. One evening, he came home late and Clive heard a violent argument erupt inside the house. "Whore," the young man shouted. Jack's mother howled and something got broken. After that night Clive rarely saw him, and Jack told him his big brother had moved out. The middle children were fourteen-year-old twins. The girl was pretty, but had already acquired the same slutty look as her mother. From his window, Clive would watch her smoke furtively, put on makeup, and change into high-heeled boots behind the hedge when she went out in the evening. She would end up like her mother, anyone could see that. Have too many kids she couldn't support when her boyfriends walked out on her. Her twin brother was no better. He looked like a mini version of his older brother, and when he was home alone he would sit in a deckchair in the garden and masturbate under a blanket. Clive could see from far away what he was doing; he could see what kind of magazines were lying on the grass next to the deckchair. Clive's throat tightened at the thought of what Jack had to look forward to.

Clive started buying Jack presents. New scalpel blades and a pair of binoculars with Jack's name engraved on them. He gave him reference and activity books, he let Jack have his scientific journals when he had finished with them. When they were out in the woods, Clive looked after Jack. He would help Jack across the stream, he would lend him his hat if the sun was blazing and Jack had forgotten his own; he only gave the boy challenges he could meet, and he listened to his answers. The boy deserved to be looked after properly when he was with Clive. Once in a while, he would clutch Jack's chin and turn his face to his to emphasize something it was important for Jack to understand, or grab his arm if Jack was fidgeting and losing concentration. Obviously Clive never hit him, but it was essential Jack stay focused or he would never find the strength to break free from his background.

"Would you like to dissect a larger animal?" Clive asked. Jack was now so skilled at dissection that hares and hedgehogs no longer represented much of a challenge. It was early one Sunday morning and the mist lay thick under the rising sun. Clive carried a spade, and he had a flask of hot chocolate and some sandwiches in his backpack. Jack nodded unconvincingly. They began by building a trap in a clearing. Clive concentrated on the construction of the trap, and how they would lift up the animal once it had fallen in. Suddenly he became aware that Jack had stopped. He was standing a little distance away, and he didn't look happy.

Clive went over to him and knelt down on the path, making their eyes level.

"What's the matter?" he asked, softly.

"I don't like always having to kill the animals," the boy said. Clive embraced him.

"But nature's like that," Clive said into Jack's hair. He smelled innocently of forest and sweaty child.

"Then why don't you do it?" Jack said, wriggling free. Clive let go of him.

"We'll do something else," he said.

"Okay," Jack said, relieved.

They walked further into the woods.

"I wish you were my dad," Jack said out of the blue.

Clive smiled.

"Well, we can always pretend," he said, lightly.

The weekends passed and weeks became years. When Jack turned thirteen, Clive's present to him was a tree house in the woods. Clive had built it in secret and, on Jack's birthday, he suggested they celebrate the day by camping in the woods. Jack was up for it. They packed provisions, a camping stove, sleeping bags, comics, and torches and off they went. Jack looked puzzled when Clive suddenly stopped and dumped his backpack on the ground beneath a huge tree. Then Clive pointed out the cleverly concealed pegs he had hammered into the tree trunk to serve as steps. Jack obediently climbed up and disappeared inside the foliage. A cry of joy soon followed and Clive smiled as he climbed up. When he reached him, Jack was sitting on the narrow walkway in front of the entrance to the tree house, dangling his legs over the edge.

Clive had put up two shelves inside for their luggage and, at the end of the walkway, he had constructed a screened enclosure, so it was possible to pee over the edge in private. Inside the hut Clive had put up pictures of Jack and Clive. A friendship spanning eight years, where a child had become a boy and a boy had become a man. You could see it in their faces. The softness had left Clive's, who was now twenty-eight years old, but it was more noticeable in Jack's. His gaze was intelligent, his face slimmer, and his hair longer. The little boy was fading away.

That evening, they fried sausages in a pan Clive conjured up from his backpack and, for dessert they shared a bar of chocolate, which turned out to be cooking chocolate, but it tasted good all the same. They huddled together to keep warm and heard the owls hoot and the wapiti deer roar.

Early the next morning, while the moon still hung suspended in the sky, a nightingale sang very close to them. Jack was asleep and Clive looked at the boy's lips, which were sharply outlined in the moonlight. He wanted to reach out and touch Jack. At that moment, Jack turned over in his sleep and was now facing Clive. Clive could smell his breath; it was strong and alien, and he was hit by an unfamiliar surge of arousal. Not like the feeling he got when he thought about Jack's mother or the girls from college, but something infinitely deeper, as if unbridled lust had risen in him like an atoll from the sea. Clive struggled to breathe calmly and inched himself closer toward Jack's warm, sleeping body.

Jack jerked upright and moved away.

"What is it?" he murmured. "What's wrong?"

The light inside the tree house was still gray. Clive said nothing and pretended to be asleep. He was wide awake, but it wasn't until it was daylight, at least an hour later, that he stretched out and said he hadn't slept this well in a long time. Jack was already sitting on the walkway surveying the forest. They made oatmeal on the stove before they packed up and walked home. They said good-bye to each other by the garden gate outside Clive's house, and Clive could feel his legs shake. Jack moved in to hug Clive, like they always did, a brief meeting of their chests and a friendly pat on each other's back meant *thanks for today and see you later*. Clive shot out his hand to stop him. A surprised Jack shook it.

"You're a man now," Clive said. "Thirteen years old."

Jack beamed with delight, and his surprise evaporated. Clive picked up his backpack and walked down the path.

"See you," he called out over his shoulder.

Clive couldn't sleep that night. Breathless, he lay in his bed, his body throbbing.

*   *   *

Three months later, Jack's mother got a job in another city and they moved. Clive stood behind the window, watching the moving van being loaded. He heard the doorbell ring, he heard his landlady call out for him, and he watched a disappointed Jack walk back to the waiting van. When the van had disappeared around the corner, Clive uttered a deep cry of despair. Then he thought: it's better this way. Jack had changed recently, the little boy had gone completely. Clive missed him and had no idea what to do with the new Jack. Since the birthday camp out in the forest, Jack had canceled their Saturday arrangement twice, and the previous Saturday he had failed to show. He hadn't appeared until later that morning, his hair crumpled with sleep and a pimple on his cheek. Clive was sitting on the steps, carving a stick.

"Sorry, overslept," Jack mumbled. He was wearing Bermuda shorts and no shirt and stretched languidly. Clive muttered something and carried on carving. He felt as if Jack had died. The boy Clive had protected and looked after was gone, and a young man had taken his place. Jack glanced at him from under his curly bangs, and his downy upper lip pointed at Clive.

It's better this way, Clive told himself again long after the moving van had left. The way he felt about the new Jack was forbidden.

The next time Clive saw Jack, he could hardly believe his own eyes. It was 1993. Clive had married Kay, they had two children, and he had been appointed the youngest ever professor of the department of Bird Evolution, Paleobiology, and Systematics. Clive recognized Jack immediately. He was standing to the left of the entrance, glancing at his watch, a worn briefcase by his feet. He was tall with very dark hair, and he had the face of a grown man, but Clive recognized the sharp line of his upper lip. His eyes were still guarded, and the movement with which he swept aside his hair was the same it had always been. Clive felt flushed all over as he held out his hand to Jack. At first, Jack failed to recognize him, but then his eyes penetrated the soft beard Clive had grown and his face lit up.

"Clive, right?" he exclaimed, smiling. Jack was taller than Clive and, for a few seconds, they simply looked at each other.

"What are you doing here?" Clive said, at last.

"It's my first day," Jack said, smiling shyly. It was frightening how much he resembled his younger self. Clive couldn't help feeling proud. This was his reward.

"You taught me everything about nature," Jack said. "Everything I know. I'll never forget that."

"Don't mention it," Clive said. "You'll find a way to pay me back one day," he added, laughing.

Jack completed his biology degree and went on to do a PhD. He focused on the communication of natural science from the Renaissance up to the present day. Clive reviewed Jack's PhD and felt edgy about it. He had hoped Jack would specialize in ornithology, and he didn't regard the history of science as a proper subject. However, Jack was determined, and, shortly after his PhD had been accepted, he launched a new Canadian journal, *Scientific Today*, which quickly became the best-selling natural science journal in North America and soon also in Europe.

Eight years had passed since Clive and Jack had bumped into each other at the university, and they still met for lunch at regular intervals. They talked about science, they discussed recent university initiatives, they assessed scientific conferences, but they skillfully avoided ever mentioning their private lives, as though by tacit agreement. Sometimes they happened to stay in the same hotel during an out-of-town conference and, after the conference, they might dine together alone or with other colleagues. But it was never like the old days. It didn't even come close. Clive wondered why he didn't simply invite Jack and his wife, Molly, to his home for dinner. Kay would love it. She often remarked that they never entertained. But something inside him fought it. What would happen if the easy mood of a social setting loosened Jack's tongue? Might he tell Kay that Clive had played with him every weekend for years, even though he had been fifteen years older than Jack? That Clive hadn't had a single friend his own age? That Clive had taught Jack to kill and dissect animals but had never killed or dissected a single one himself? And what precisely did Jack remember about the night in the tree house? Clive shuddered. He had suffered beyond measure when Jack left, but it was all in the past now, and there it would stay.

In 2001 Clive published his life's work, *The Birds*. The day the book came out, he spent a long time sniffing it. He had worked on it for four years, and every single one of his arguments was solid. Soon his opponents—Darren in New York, Chang and Laam in China, Gordon at the University of Sydney, and Clark and his team in South Africa—would be convinced that birds were a sister group to dinosaurs and not their descendants. Most of all, he was anticipating the reaction of Lars Helland in Denmark. The Danish vertebrate morphologist was the opponent who tormented Clive more than anyone else. Helland never attended any of the ornithology symposia held around the world, so Clive had never met him in person, but Helland's papers were always meticulous and vicious. Every time Clive had published something on the evolution of birds, Helland could be relied on to provide an instant refutation, stating the exact opposite, as though he had nothing better to do than annoy Clive. However, Clive was convinced *The Birds* would silence Helland. Clive knew the Dane nearly always relied on the evolution of the *manus*, the bird's hand, to illustrate the relationship between birds and dinosaurs, and neither Helland nor Clive's other opponents had given much thought to the evolution of the feather. Consequently, Clive had decided the feather would be his trump card. He had studied the evolution of the feather for years. From now on, no one would be able to argue that feathers on present-day birds had anything to do with the feather-like structures found on dinosaurs.

When the book was published, it went straight to the bestseller lists in Canada and the United States. Every dinosaur-mad amateur biologist on the planet bought a copy. However, Clive's fellow scientists ignored it. It received only a few peer reviews in the more serious journals, and, on each occasion, in a rather dismissive tone, as though it was a curiosity to fill column inches rather than an important scientific work. Only *Scientific Today* allocated it a half-decent amount of space, but even so Clive was dissatisfied. He tried to call Jack to find out why his book had received such minimal coverage and been bounced to page 22, but Jack was unavailable.

Clive volunteered to speak at every upcoming symposium and carefully rewrote every chapter of *The Birds* as individual papers that he submitted simultaneously to scientific journals all over the world. He thought about his father. Had his father still been alive, he would have been proud. The reactions came just under a month later. Clive was prepared. He had already drafted his counter arguments because he knew exactly where his opponents would attack: the crescent-shaped *carpus*, the reduction of fingers, the ascending process of the *talus* bone, and the alleged feathers.

Clive devoured the new journals, convinced that his opponents would go straight for the anatomical discussion. However, apart from two responses written by minor scientists, none of his opponents criticized Clive's anatomical arguments; instead they focused solely on poor editorial control whose *lethargy had allowed Clive Freeman's original contribution to be published, thus causing a deeply regrettable undermining of the general credibility of the journals. The nature of the relationship between birds and dinosaurs isn't a subject worthy of a serious medium, because there is nothing to discuss. Birds are present-day dinosaurs. The end.*

In thirty-seven different publications.

Clive was consumed by a boiling rage. They were accusing him of incompetence. They were accusing him, Clive Freeman, a world-famous paleobiologist and a professor at the University of British Columbia, of scientific incompetence.

The most arrogant response came, not surprisingly, from Lars Helland who, on this occasion, listed an unknown, Erik Tybjerg, as his coauthor. This undoubtedly meant that Helland had told one of his PhD students to write his contribution. But the worst was yet to come.

The ultimate insult was that Helland's reaction appeared in *Scientific Today*.

Clive called Jack immediately to request a meeting.

*   *   *

When Clive saw Jack three days later, he was suffering from an upset stomach. They had arranged to meet at a bar across the street from the office of *Scientific Today*, and Jack was already there when Clive arrived. He was wearing dark trousers and a thin T-shirt, and a newspaper rested on his casually arranged legs. Clive's stomach lurched when Jack looked up, and he stared at Jack's lips. Clive slammed the journal on the table.

"What the hell is this?" he demanded.

"Clive, there are five other people on the editorial committee besides me," Jack said quietly.

Clive turned on his heel and left.

In the autumn of 2001 Clive was a guest speaker in Chicago. Normally, he kept strictly to material from *The Birds*, but the American audience was remarkably receptive, and Clive expanded on his feather argument. Asymmetrical feathers were linked to flight in present-day birds, and dinosaurs hadn't had feathers—obviously—first, because they didn't fly, second, because they were cold-blooded animals, and third: "Can you imagine *Jurassic Park*—with chickens?"

His joke brought the house down. Clive concluded with a challenge: "Show me a feathered dinosaur, and I will personally beg forgiveness from every advocate of the dinosaur theory!" He flapped his arms like a bird trying to take off. The laughter refused to die down.

That night, Clive drank too much white wine before he staggered back to his hotel room. The next morning, he woke up with a dreadful taste in his mouth and grabbed a soda from the minibar. While he was drinking it, he switched on the television and found CNN. For a fraction of a second, he thought he must be the victim of a cruel hoax. To the right of the anchor was a huge photograph, which, to Clive, looked like a dinosaur with clearly visible feathers.

At that moment, the anchor cut to a CNN reporter who announced, with cracked lips as though he had trekked all the way to Asia, that he was in the Liaoning Province in northeastern China.

"This is a sensation," the reporter panted. "Early this morning farm workers discovered what might be the world's first feathered dinosaur. Tonight, the first experts have already reached the area, and a few minutes ago they confirmed that the newly discovered fossil is not a prehistoric bird but a predatory dinosaur belonging to the Theropod family. The animal is believed to have lived between 121 and 135 million years ago, and the exciting feature is that it has fossilized but extremely well-preserved feathers running down in a ridge from its head and along its back. The tantalizing questions here in northeastern China are these: were dinosaurs able to fly and were they warm-blooded, or are these feathers astonishing proof that feathers weren't only used for flying but also for insulation? We'll know more once the experts have had a chance to examine this thrilling discovery in detail. Back to the studio."

Clive stared at the screen for nearly twenty minutes. Then he crushed his soda can.

Kay greeted him with a nervous smile when he came back to Vancouver. The telephone had rung constantly all morning and please would he call . . . and she reeled off the names of everyone from his colleagues at the department to national television stations. Jack hadn't called.

Clive made himself a sandwich, gave Kay's cheek a reassuring pat, and went to his study. Calmly, he ate his sandwich. The discovery in China was obviously a prehistoric bird, not a dinosaur. Dinosaurs didn't have feathers. He downloaded forty-eight e-mails and skimmed through them. With irritation, he opened one from Lars Helland. Typical. The Danish scientist just had to put his oar in, in his usual affable manner, of course, so that it might be mistaken for good-natured banter. Clive deleted the e-mail.

When he had finished on the computer, he leaned back and tried not to think about Jack. Why hadn't he called? Clive still hadn't met Molly, Jack's wife. They had just had their second daughter, and Clive hadn't even seen the first one yet. Once upon a time, Clive had been the sole recipient of Jack's rare, blinding smiles, the one who triggered his exclamations of surprise, the one who prompted him to press the tip of his tongue against the corner of his mouth in concentration when learning new facts. Now it was likely to be Molly and the two little girls. Clive was well aware that the distance was partly his own making. Jack had briefly met Clive's sons, Tom and Franz, one day when the boys had picked him up from the university parking lot, and had, on one occasion, met Kay at a conference dinner that Jack had attended alone. However, distance was one thing, deliberate avoidance was something else. Jack was conspicuously polite and friendly, and always had time for a professional discussion, but Clive found his private reticence unbearable. They didn't have to get together with their wives and children, the very thought caused Clive to break into a sweat, but Clive and Jack had a connection and it was as if Jack refused to acknowledge it, even when they were alone. It was absurd. Clive knew Jack better than anyone. He had Jack in his blood, in the tips of his fingers, which still remembered the feeling of ruffling Jack's dark hair.

Jack would know perfectly well that the discovery of an allegedly feathered dinosaur meant late nights for Clive, who would need weeks to defend his position and refute the implications that the media and every other idiot would draw from the discovery. Jack not letting Clive into his life might be a coincidence, it might even be Clive's own fault. But Jack not calling him, that was deliberate.

Clive called a meeting with his department that Monday, and later the same day they issued a press release announcing that UBC's department of Bird Evolution, Paleobiology, and Systematics was obviously excited at the discovery of a feathered dinosaur, but that they had nothing further to say until they had been allowed to examine the specimen themselves. Afterward Clive completed an application to view the animal, knowing full well that it would be a great deal of time before permission was granted. Jack still hadn't called.

The following January, the two Chinese paleontologists, Chang and Laam, finally described and named the animal and announced that it wasn't a dinosaur. Clive was triumphant. They named it

Sinosauropteryx, concluded it was an ancient bird, and consequently no one was surprised that it had feathers.

However, Clive's joy was short-lived. Fossils started pouring out of China's soil, literally, and in every subsequent case, Chang and Laam had no doubts: these weren't ancient birds, they were dinosaurs. And they were all feathered.

Clive sent a reminder regarding his application, and when it was finally approved he flew to China immediately. It took him two weeks to examine *Sinosauropteryx,* and he also had a closer look at *Caudipteryx* and *Protarchaeopteryx.* Delighted, he called Jack and told him to hold the front page. Clive's enthusiasm was infectious. "This is a rotten line," Jack laughed, "call me when you get back."

Clive spent another two days in China before flying home. He was overjoyed. *Beipiaosaurus, Sinornithosaurus, Microraptor, Caudipteryx,* and *Protarchaeopteryx* were obviously all ancient birds but *not* dinosaurs. Furthermore, the Chinese had turned out to be very welcoming, not at all reticent as he had been told, and the food was superb. One afternoon he strolled through a garden of cherry trees, whose white petals fluttered poetically onto passersby and wished Jack could have been there with him. If only they could have some time together. Jack was a science writer, one of the very best, but, of course, there was a price to pay. Jack shared Clive's scientific views, Clive knew that, but Jack self-evidently couldn't appreciate the discussion about the origin of birds fully, when he also had to consider so many other topics. If only they could have some time together, then Clive could explain the details to him. This would boost Clive's position enormously. *Scientific Today* was selling better than ever, everyone in the science community read it and wanted to publish in it. Jack and he would once more be an unbeatable duo.

Across from the cherry-tree garden was a market, where Clive bought two bronze beetles in a glass dome for his sons and a large piece of silk for Kay. When he got back, he would ask Jack if they could go away together. Just for a couple of days. Just the two of them.

*   *   *

When he got back to Canada, Clive went to see Jack. He had written most of his paper on the plane, and when he landed in Vancouver the major themes of his arguments were outlined. Triumphantly, he slammed it down in front of Jack.

"Did you have a good trip?" Jack asked, smiling.

"Yes," Clive said.

"Coffee?"

Clive declined. Jack went to get some for himself, and when he returned he closed the door behind him and called his secretary to say he didn't want to be disturbed for the next fifteen minutes. Fifteen minutes, Clive thought. Jack let himself fall into the chair behind his desk and looked at Clive.

"I can't print your paper," he said.

"What?"

"I've got doubts," Jack replied.

"About what?"

"About the origin of birds." He held up his hand to forestall Clive's reaction, but Clive was speechless.

"For years your position was reasonable. We were missing many decisive fossils, phylogenetic methods were still unreliable, and there were problems explaining the reduction of bird fingers. . . . During all that time I understood perfectly well why you didn't buy the dinosaur theory. But now? New evidence is discovered every week, Clive. And everything points to birds being present-day dinosaurs, don't you see? More than 250 apomorphies link birds and dinosaurs. Two hundred and fifty apomorphies! Including feathers. Feathers! Not to mention that more than 95 percent of the world's scientists today agree that cladistics is the accepted phylogenetic method. Everyone's using cladistics, except you. You have an impressive résumé, Clive. No one would think less of you if you changed your position—on the contrary. That's the very core of science. That a hypothesis stands until it's replaced by a better-supported one. Remember Walker? He dismissed his own theory when it no longer held up. He won a lot of admiration for that."

Clive stared at Jack and, in that moment, he hated him. He remembered once when Jack was little and had cut his finger on a knife and Clive had stuck his finger in his mouth. Suddenly, he could taste the blood again.

"I want my story on the front page," he whispered.

"We already have a lead story."

"I've been an ornithologist for thirty years," Clive said. "And now you're telling me that some fashionable paleontology theory is going to end my career?" Clive shot up from his chair, reached over the desk and grabbed Jack's jaw.

"Look at me," he hissed. "I was like a father to you. I got you out of that shit hole you came from. Everything you've got," he gestured toward the enormous desk and the stacks of journals, "you owe to me."

Clive let go of Jack's face and pointed at his paper lying on the desk. Then he left.

The next issue of *Scientific Today* was published in mid-August. On the cover was a photo of *Caudipteryx*, its left wing partly unfolded and beneath it the headline: THE EMPEROR'S NEW CLOTHES: THE CRETACEOUS TURKEY.

Clive was satisfied.

In the autumn of 2005, Clive was invited to take the hot seat at a major ornithology conference in Toronto, where he would participate in a live TV debate with a young Danish paleontologist, Dr. Erik Tybjerg, who appeared to have been promoted from being Lars Helland's PhD student to his errand boy. Clive had met the young scientist several times because Helland made a point of staying away from conferences, and he found Tybjerg intensely annoying. He was an upstart who thought he knew it all, and Clive would regard it as a considerable pleasure to bring him down on national television.

Clive made a last-minute decision to fly to Toronto via his hometown. Since the death of his father, he tended to visit his mother every other year. She was an old lady now, practically blind and living in a nursing home. Clive looked forward to seeing her lined face and feeling her hand in his. He left three days before the conference

and stayed at a hotel near the nursing home. When he wasn't spending time with his mother, pushing her around in her wheelchair,
he slept like a log in his room, ate well in the restaurant, and even
managed four walks around the local area before traveling onward
on the fourth day.

He landed in Toronto, rested and exhilarated. He was met at the
airport and driven straight to the conference center where he left
his luggage with a cloakroom attendant, collected his entry pass,
and strolled around the many interesting booths.

Half an hour later he took a seat in a comfortable red armchair on
the stage. Opposite was an identical but vacant armchair. The stage
was bathed in light and Clive found it hard to see properly, but he
was aware of a large audience taking their seats in the auditorium.
A well-dressed young woman came out to greet him, introduced
herself as the assistant to the producer, and asked if Clive was ready
to be hooked up to his microphone. Of course, Clive answered and
complimented her on her appearance. He noticed the young woman's perfume, and she stood very close to him while she attached the
clip of the micro port to his lapel.

"It's amazing, isn't it," she burst out. "Of course, I'm no expert.
But it came as a huge surprise to me!" She smiled at Clive, straightened his jacket, conjured up a powder compact from her pocket,
and began dabbing powder on Clive's nose.

"I'm sorry, I don't follow?" Clive croaked. The cable for the
microphone was choking him, and he tried to give it more slack.

"Allow me." the young woman said. "Turn around." Clive turned,
and she carefully lifted up his jacket. Clive felt the cable loosen and
became more comfortable.

"What did you mean just now?" Clive prompted her. His cell
phone had been switched off, and he hadn't looked at a newspaper
while visiting his mother. He suddenly got the feeling that the Presi-
dent might have been assassinated and that he was the last to know.

"It's really amaz—" the woman began, then she stopped to listen to something coming through her headset, excused herself, and
hurried off.

Dr. Tybjerg entered, grinning like an idiot in the sharp light, and pushed up his unfashionable glasses.

"Professor Freeman," he said, offering him a sweaty hand. Clive shook it. Tybjerg might be a walking encyclopedia, his knowledge was truly impressive, but he was devoid of charm.

"As a scientist you would have to rejoice, no matter what your views are, wouldn't you say so?" Dr. Tybjerg stuttered. "You must admit that it's hard to believe?"

"What are you talking about?" Clive said as calmly as he could manage, but he felt his voice tremble.

Dr. Tybjerg gave him a puzzled look.

At that moment the host appeared and explained the format of the debate to the audience. Professor Clive Freeman and Dr. Erik Tybjerg were introduced to each other by their full titles, to the audience and the viewers, after which the host handed floor to the two duelists. Clive made a friendly gesture to Tybjerg, who opened the debate.

"As you all know, the day before yesterday it was announced that the remains of a feathered Tyrannosaurus had been found in Mako-shika State Park in the state of Montana, close to Hell Creek where the world's first *Tyrannosaurus Rex* fossil was found in 1902."

Clive stared at Tybjerg. His jaw dropped.

The duel lasted thirty minutes, and throughout the whole ordeal Tybjerg was visibly nervous but quick-thinking. He listened attentively, he never interrupted Clive and every time he demolished one of Clive's arguments, he was thorough, meticulous, almost. When Clive declared that he wanted to examine the animal before form-ing an opinion, Tybjerg gave Clive a looked of genuine surprise and wonder, and said:

"How long are you going to use that argument? Until a feathered *Apatosaurus* turns up on your doorstep?" It was an obvious joke, but no laughed.

When the spotlights faded, the audience started to disperse and Clive studied his hands. He didn't dare look at Dr. Tybjerg, who hadn't moved since the stage lights dimmed. Afterward he had no idea what provoked him. A faint cough? The quiet superiority? Whatever it was, he glanced up and the second he met Tybjerg's eyes, he slapped him with the back of his hand. Dr. Tybjerg sprang up, horrified, touching his eyebrow, which had split open. Clive looked at his hand, at his wedding ring. It was stained with blood. When he looked up again, Tybjerg had left.

Then he heard footsteps.

"What happened?" the confused young assistant shouted.

"Uh," Clive began. He dusted off his clothes. The assistant looked at him and then in the direction in which Tybjerg had disappeared.

"Uh," Clive repeated and dusted his clothes again.

Back in Vancouver, Clive felt strangely accepting of the news. He refused to talk to the press, didn't reply to e-mails and telephone calls, and he informed the faculty press office that he had no plans to counter-attack.

"I have resigned myself to the folly of this world," he told the press officer. Then he called a meeting with his department where they agreed to keep a low profile while redistributing their work-load. The next allocation of research funding would take place in three years, and no one needed reminding that if they were unable to convince the world that birds were *not* descended from dino-saurs, they would never get another grant.

They decided to start three major excavations and an expensive developmental study to observe the cartilage condensation in bird embryos. Clive's junior researcher, Michael Kramer, would be head-ing the project.

Once that was in place, Clive headed home.

As Clive cycled through the forest, the sun shining through the trees, he thought about Jack. They hardly ever spoke these days. When Clive submitted a paper, Jack rarely acknowledged receipt, and when Clive rang with changes, Jack's secretary would deal with them. Clive had even called Jack at home and left a message, but Jack never called back.

Whenever Clive opened *Scientific Today* looking for his contributions, his joy at seeing them was diminished. Clive appreciated the expensive layout, the graphs, and the illustrations, but he felt no real pleasure. Jack and Clive had met in their passion for nature. Now he was alone.

Clive thought about the situation for a week, then he called Jack and invited him and Molly over for dinner. He practically pleaded with Jack to come.

"Jack," he said. "Let's put the past behind us. Let's do the right thing, let's not mix science and friendship." Jack replied with silence.

"I can't stand not seeing you," Clive suddenly burst out, and held his breath.

Finally Jack said: "All right, we'll be there."

Kay was delighted that the famous Jack Jarvis and his wife were coming to dinner.

"What an illustrious guest," she said, thrilled. "What will we serve them?"

Clive took the cookbook from his wife's hand and led her into the living room where he told her the whole story. Or, almost the whole story. Kay was fascinated.

"He must have been like a son to you. Why didn't you ever tell me? Fancy them moving away like that," she added. "That poor boy must have felt like he was losing his father all over again."

Clive nodded.

That Saturday Jack and Molly arrived right on time. Molly was radiant and very beautiful. She shook Clive's hand energetically and said what a pleasure it was to meet such a legendary scientist. Her husband had talked so much about him over the years, she said, but she had no idea that they had known each other since childhood.

"I was sorry to hear about the recent trouble," she carried on, cheerfully, "but Jack says that's how it is with natural science. All storms blow themselves out eventually."

Clive smiled and took their coats. What a chatterbox she was. He wasn't entirely sure what he had imagined but definitely not this.

"Odd," Kay said when the evening was over and Molly and Jack had left. "Molly is as outgoing and sparkling as Jack is closed."

Clive nodded. Jack had seemed a little sullen, but then again with the women chirping away, it had been hard to get a word in.

At the start of July 2007, Clive developed an earache and decided to leave work early. He had been troubled by a cold since Kay and he had spent two weeks in their vacation home, and it was getting worse, not better.

The study of cartilage formation in embryonic chickens was looking very promising. Clive didn't want to get his hopes up, but he had butterflies in his stomach as he followed its progress. He thought about Tybjerg and Helland. Helland still published, but it was nothing compared to Tybjerg, who was rapidly firing off papers. Even now, while Clive was awaiting the outcome of the condensation experiment and thus not publishing much himself, Tybjerg wrote one article after another, and in every single one of them he distanced himself from Clive's views.

Neither Tybjerg nor Helland had commented on the incident in Toronto. Clive was amazed that Helland had managed to restrain himself. Helland still e-mailed Clive every now and then with references to papers he thought Clive ought to read, or attaching silly natural history cartoons. But he never once mentioned Tybjerg. The outcome of the cartilage condensation experiment filled Clive with rapture. Neither Helland nor Tybjerg had any idea of what was about to hit them.

By now he had cycled through the forest. He looked forward to reading the latest issues of *Science, Nature,* and *Scientific Today* in his bag. When he got home, he made himself comfortable on the sofa and started with *Nature.*

And there it was. "Helland, et al." jumped out at him as early as page five, a lengthy and infinitely trivial description of the discovery of a dinosaur tooth on the Danish island of Bornholm in the Baltic Sea. Obviously, his esteemed colleagues couldn't help but remark how this find yet again proved the direct ancestry of modern birds to dinosaurs. Clive let the journal fall from the sofa.

Then he opened up *Science*. He had to flip as far as page seventeen before "Helland, et al." leapt from the page. What the hell? Again, the article's point of departure was some—in Clive's opinion—utterly insignificant excavations on Bornholm, and the article was riddled with guesswork and conjectures, bordering on fluff. Clive scanned a few more pages before letting the journal slide to the floor.

Finally, he started on *Scientific Today*.

Jack's beaming face greeted him from the editorial on page three, and Clive smiled back at him. They had seen each other only last Saturday, and the vibe between them had been really good, as it had been over the last six months. Kay and Molly had become fast friends, and Jack had been less defensive and recalled many of the things they had done together when Jack was a boy. Last Saturday he had mentioned the tree house. It must have been a big job to build, he remarked, and both women had turned to look at Clive. Clive's heart started pounding, but Jack was relaxed and smiling and seemed to have no hidden agenda. Yes, Clive had replied, it had taken some time. How annoying that we had to move so soon afterward, Jack continued. They were having dinner in Clive and Kay's freshly painted dining room when, out of the blue, Jack mentioned that his older brother had just been released from prison. "Is that right?" Clive said, relieved to let the tree house slip back into the past where it belonged.

"I never told anyone," Jack admitted. "It's not exactly something I'm proud of. But anyway, he's out now. Fifteen years inside."

Molly and Jack had visited him the previous day. Jack never explained what his brother had done, and Clive didn't want to pry. Fifteen years spoke volumes. Jack simply said that it had been good to see him. He'd got a job sorting bottles at a recycling plant, and he was pleased about that. Jack suddenly looked directly at Clive and said "thank you." The words hung awkwardly in the air, and Clive had no idea what to say. Molly's eyes welled up, and Kay got up to serve dessert.

Clive stretched out on the sofa, flipped past the photo of Jack and further into the journal. On page five, he nearly choked on his tea.

The paper took up six pages and at the top "Helland, et al." stood out. This was no minor puff piece run during a scientific dry spell. Clive sat up. The subject of the article was the femur of the Berlin Specimen, *Archaeopteryx*, which Helland and Tybjerg had visited Berlin to remeasure. The last approved measurement, undertaken in 1999 by the ornithologist Professor Clive Freeman, was not only highly inaccurate, it had also led to a series of unfortunate conclusions which—according to Helland, et al.—had distorted important arguments relating to the origin of birds to a very considerable extent. The question now was whether this data distortion was the result of that margin of error that should always be factored into science, or whether the measurements in question were the expression of deliberate manipulation. A brief summary of the incident at the 2005 bird conference in Toronto followed with a reproduction of the press release from Clive's department, which placed in this context sounded like a total surrender.

Clive was so outraged that he knocked over the teapot when he got up. This paper ridiculed him, and Jack had approved it. His thoughts whirred around inside his head so fast that he could barely keep his balance. He held the copy of *Scientific Today* away from his body, like a burning oven glove he wanted to chuck outside as quickly as possible. When he opened the front door to get rid of it, Kay was in the process of bringing in the groceries from the car. He tossed the journal aside, but it landed on his foot. He picked it up again and it stuck to his fingers. Kay came to his rescue and grabbed him by the elbows.

"Clive darling, what's happened?"

"Jack," Clive snarled. He shook his hand to free himself from the journal and a page with a colorful DNA double helix came loose and spiraled down to the ground. Finally Clive broke free of the journal and stomped past Kay, around the house, and into the back garden where he stayed for an hour.

He didn't come back inside until Kay opened the living room window and told him dinner was ready. At 9:30 p.m. he called Jack and suggested a meeting. No, no particular reason, nothing that couldn't wait. A game of chess, perhaps. And, by the way, there was something Clive wanted to discuss with him.

Jack came the next day, and while Kay and he made small talk, Clive said nothing. They retired to Clive's study for a game of chess. It was a mild summer evening, the window to the garden was open, and Clive could hear birdsong in the distance. He could also hear Kay loading the dishwasher in the kitchen. Jack, who pretended that nothing had happened, pondered his next move for a long time. Clive forced himself to remember that Googling "Clive Freeman" attracted 41,700 hits in 0.11 seconds. When on earth was Jack going to make his next move? Clive got up and mixed them both a drink.

"Why?" he hissed from the drinks cabinet. Jack gave him a baffled look. "Why do you want to destroy the credibility of the world's finest and most respected natural science journal?" Clive slammed down his drink so hard on the desk that it sloshed over.

Jack's reaction shocked Clive. Clive had imagined immediate contrition. Downcast eyes, a boy confessing to a man of superior intellect. The only thing he hadn't imagined was Jack's calm reply: "That's precisely what I'm trying to prevent."

"Then why have you allowed that article in *Scientific Today*? I demand to know why!"

Jack looked at Clive for a long time before he said: "Because it's my journal, Clive, and I decide which articles are published." Clive detected a faint tremor in Jack's voice.

"It's unscientific," Clive shouted, and stamped his foot. "And you know it! You know that their arguments aren't properly supported. What about the reduction of the fingers, what about the ascending process of the *talus*, eh?" Clive swirled the alcohol around in his glass and continued his rant.

"What about the crescent-shaped *carpus*, you moron, the orientation of the pubic bone, and the colossal ifs and buts, which you know ad nauseam, and which allow you—in contrast to those idiots from *Science* and *Nature*—to weed out these crazy articles about kinship? When did you turn into someone who shapes his scientific views to fit a trend? Have you lost your mind?"

Jack gave Clive a neutral look.

"I don't believe in you anymore," Jack said eventually. "True, the other side still have certain problems explaining the reduction of the hand, but we're talking about two hundred and eighty-six apomorphies, Clive, two hundred and eighty-six! A feathered Tyrannosaurus. What do you want? God to pop down from heaven and explain how it's all connected before you're satisfied? I've supported you professionally for years. I've done much for you. Much more than I should. Because you're . . . my friend. But it has to stop now. A feathered Tyrannosaurus, Clive. *Scientific Today* is a scientific journal."

"How do you know it's a Tyrannosaurus?" Clive sneered. "How do you know it's feathered? You want to put feathers on an animal that couldn't fly? You know as well as I do that the development of feathers is primarily and inextricably linked with the evolution of flight and didn't serve as insulation until later. And you also know Tyrannosaurus didn't fly. You haven't seen the creature. I haven't seen it, either. The structures may look like feathers, but they're likely to be the residual of a dorsal skin fold; they're *not* precursors of genuine feathers. That should be self-evident! You're publishing conjecture, it's unscientific! Have you forgotten you should never, ever, base your conclusions on what others have seen?"

"No, I haven't," Jack replied, "and when it's your turn to describe the animal, *Scientific Today* will be delighted to publish a properly researched article that may conclude that the discovery in Montana *isn't* a Tyrannosaurus, and that the skin structure *isn't* feathers. But not until your description is available and has been accepted. It's never been the intention of science to claim to have found the absolute truth, Clive, but to put forward the most likely hypotheses, and my job," Jack pointed to himself, "is to publish those papers that reflect the more probable ones, and right now, they aren't coming from you."

"Get out," Clive said icily. He pointed to the door. Jack got up.

"You shouldn't mix science and friendship," Jack said calmly.

"Get out," Clive repeated.

Jack left. Shortly afterward, Clive heard the engine of Jack's car start.

Kay came into his study.

"Why did Jack leave? What happened?" Her eyes were bulging. Clive said nothing. He was shaking all over. Jack was a traitor.

"Did you two fight?" she asked. "Clive, what did you say to him?"

Kay's mouth moved. Say something for God's sake, her lips mouthed, but there was no sound. Kay put her open, baffled face up to his; like a poker, she stoked the embers and the fire flared up. He struck her. The angle was unfortunate and the impact of his wedding ring made her cheek swell up. Horrified, she touched her face and stared at him. Then she left.

Clive stayed in his study and tried to calm himself down. He reread some of his old articles, and a few hours later he felt better. He went through the house to find Kay. It was dark and quiet. The dishwasher was beeping, and the door to the garden was ajar but Kay wasn't in the kitchen or in the garden. He went upstairs to the master bedroom. The door was locked. Outside the bedroom door, to the right, lay a comforter and his pillow. Clive knocked on the door, but there was no reply. He started hammering on it.

"Open the door," he commanded.

There was no sound from inside. Clive went downstairs and watched television. Close to midnight, he fell asleep on the sofa.

CHAPTER 5

She was unmoved by Professor Helland's death. Monday evening, as Anna climbed the stairs to her apartment, she was ashamed of her reaction. The apartment was empty and cold, so she turned up the heat and closed the door to Lily's room. She hated Lily not being there, and without a child in the bed the small colorful comforter seemed creepy. She slumped on the sofa, where she stayed for a long time staring into space. At two o'clock she went to bed, but though she was exhausted she couldn't fall asleep. She tried thinking about Helland's wife, who had lost her husband, their daughter, who had lost her father, and about the times Helland had been kind to her. But it was no use. Her heart remained untouched.

Helland had let her down, indirectly belittling her academic work through his lack of engagement and had, in every respect, been a useless supervisor. For nearly a year he had let her flounder. She didn't care that he was dead, and she almost didn't care how he had died, either. She tossed and turned, kicking off her blankets. Finally, she got up to go to the bathroom.

* * *

After the short preliminary interview, they had been driven to Bel-lahøj police station in separate cars. Anna with Professor Ewald, Johannes with Professor Jørgensen. Professor Ewald dissolved into tears, her hands were shaking and she kept blowing her nose and fidgeting with a soggy tissue.

Somewhere along the way, Anna snapped: "What are you crying for? You couldn't stand Helland."

Professor Ewald looked mortified.

"We worked together for twenty-five years. Lars Helland was a good colleague," she wailed.

Anna glared at the window, knowing full well that the two offi-cers in the front were watching everything that was going on in the back. Every word, every breath, every revelation. She was also well aware that she wasn't coming across as terribly sympathetic.

At the station they were interviewed again by the World's Most Irritating Detective. He appeared to have eaten beets for lunch; Anna noticed a purple stain at the corner of his mouth when it was her turn. She was asked the same questions as before, and she gave the same answers. At one point when she irritably repeated herself and made it clear that she had already answered this question, Søren Marhauge raised his eyebrow a fraction and said: "Please under-stand that we need to do our job properly. An apparently fit and healthy man has been found dead in his office with his tongue sliced off. Imagine he was your husband or your father. I'm sure you would want us to be extra thorough, wouldn't you?" His voice was mild but firm, and he held her gaze a little too long. Anna looked away. When she had read through and signed her statement, she was free to go.

It was three o'clock that afternoon when she caught the bus back to the university. She was thinking about Dr. Tybjerg. She was due to meet him in an hour. Did he already know what had happened? Anna had no idea how quickly the news would reach the Natural History Museum, but the parking lot had been teeming with police cars, so it was likely to be soon. Then it struck her that she might be the one who told him. Dr. Tybjerg was bound to be deep inside the collection and wouldn't have spoken to anyone. A strange sense of dread filled her. She turned her head and looked out the window. The sky was still heavy and gray. Then another thought occurred to her: what if her dissertation defense was canceled? She couldn't bear to wait any longer. The whole situation was already a nightmare, but if her defense was postponed for weeks, until after Christmas even, she would get seriously depressed and Lily would definitely start calling Cecilie "mom." Last Friday, Anna had handed in four copies of her dissertation; one for Helland, which was now lying, blood-smeared, in a sealed evidence bag somewhere at the police station, one for Dr. Tybjerg, one for the unknown external examiner from the University of Århus, and one for the University Library for future students to use. Surely the library's copy could be given to Helland's replacement? Her defense was in two weeks, so someone already familiar with the subject should be able to gain sufficient understanding of the argument to be able to examine her. How about Johan Fjeldberg? Professor Fjeldberg was a highly respected ornithologist at the Natural History Museum, and she knew that he had worked with Dr. Tybjerg before. When she met with Dr. Tybjerg, she would make him promise that her dissertation defense would go ahead.

There were fewer unfamiliar cars in front of Building 12 now. The door to Professor Helland's office had been sealed. Professor Ewald and Professor Jørgensen had yet to return, and the whole department felt strangely deserted. Anna shuddered and quickened her pace. She stopped just as she reached the door to her study. It was ajar, and she could hear there was someone inside. A cough was followed by the sound of an office chair rolling across the floor. Anna's heart started to pound. She was convinced she had locked the door when they left. She heard another small cough, then two footsteps, before the door was opened fully.

"Shit, you scared me!" Anna practically shouted. "How did you get back here so fast?"

Johannes held his head in his hands.

"Christ," he said, heaving a sigh of relief. "I didn't even hear you. My interview didn't take long, so I waited for you, but when you didn't show, I left."

Anna gave him a quick hug and sat down in her chair. An echoing silence ensued, then she said, "What the hell's going on? Was Helland murdered?"

Johannes looked upset.

"I don't know what to think," he said, rubbing his eyes. "It's unreal. Besides, I only got two hours' sleep last night, which makes it difficult to think clearly. How about you?"

"I don't care," she said.

Johannes was shocked.

"I don't believe you."

"But that's how I feel," she mumbled. She turned halfway in her chair and gave Johannes a lost look. "I feel completely indifferent about his death." She turned her attention to her screen and started checking her e-mails. Johannes carried on looking at her as though he wanted to say something. An e-mail had arrived from Cecilie, attaching a new photo of Lily. Had Cecilie already picked her up from nursery school? The message had been sent at 2 p.m., which could only mean Cecilie had collected Lily after lunch, even though Anna had asked her several times not to pick up Lily until after three so she wouldn't miss out on the nap. Anna stared at the photo. Lily was wearing a new dress, and her hair looked somewhat different. Had Cecilie given her a haircut? Anna tried to figure out if the photo was misleading her or whether Cecilie really had snipped off Lily's baby curls. Johannes was still looking at her.

"Why didn't you get any sleep last night?" she asked, without taking her eyes off the screen. Lily's eyes shone as if she couldn't be happier anywhere but where she was right now. In Granny's bed with all the picture books Granny had borrowed for her from the library.

Johannes was exhausted; he buried his face in his hands again. The movement made Anna turn around.

"It's a long story. I met someone at the Red Mask a few weeks ago," he said, "and we hit it off. No, not in that way or, at least, not as far as I was concerned. And now I'm dealing with a stalker. I haven't experienced anything like this, ever. E-mails, phone calls in the middle of the night . . ." He smiled, embarrassed. "Anna," he added, interrupting himself. He swallowed. "I feel really bad . . ."

"But if you're not attracted to the person, then that's it. You'll just have to be honest and—"

"No," Johannes stopped her. "I feel really bad because I . . ." he looked anguished. "I accidentally told the detective that . . . I don't know why, but I accidentally told him—"

At that moment Anna's cell phone rang. She rummaged through her bag, but by the time she found it, it had gone to voice mail. It was Tybjerg's number, but he left no message. Anna briefly wondered whether he was calling because he had just heard the news. She tossed her cell on the desk and turned her attention back to Johannes.

"I'm sorry, what did you say?"

Johannes looked remorseful.

"I told the detective what you said last spring," he said, at last. Anna was puzzled.

"What did I say last spring?"

"That you wanted to play pranks on Helland. I told the police that you didn't like Helland all that much," Johannes sighed.

Anna stared at him.

"But why?" she said.

Johannes shrugged.

"Because I'm an idiot. I'm sorry. I know you're not involved." Johannes looked shattered.

"I really—" Anna began. Then her cell rang for the second time. "Damn it," she fumed and checked the display. It was Dr. Tybjerg again.

"Dr. Tybjerg?" she answered.

"Anna," Tybjerg whispered. "Have you heard what's happened?"

Anna gulped.

"Yes," she replied.

"I have to cancel our meeting today. I can't . . ." The signal was bad. "You'll have to come some other time. Next week."

"Next week?" Anna pushed her chair away from the desk. "You're not serious? We have to meet, Dr. Tybjerg. I have my dissertation defense, and I want . . ." She took a deep breath and braced herself. "I *have* to have that defense, please," she insisted. "It's terrible what's happened. But my defense has to go ahead, do you understand?"

"I can't," he said, and hung up.

Anna turned to Johannes. Her eyes filled with tears.

"Don't worry," she said in a thick voice. "You're not the only who's let me down."

"Anna . . ." Johannes pleaded. "I'm so sorry. I don't know why I said it. And that's what I told the detective, Marhauge. I told him that you definitely had nothing to do with Helland's death. I was beside myself."

Anna got up.

"Where are you going?" Johannes whispered, as she headed for the door.

"To the museum to find Dr. Tybjerg."

"Does it have to be right now? Can't you stay for a while? I have to go soon, and I don't want to leave . . . until we've made up."

"That's not my problem," Anna said, icily.

She heard Johannes heave a sigh as she walked down the corridor to the museum.

Dr. Tybjerg could invariably be found in one of three locations: his basement office, the cafeteria, or at the desk below the window by the door to the Vertebrate Collection, measuring bones. She tried the collection first. No sign of Tybjerg. Then she tried the cafeteria. Still no Tybjerg. Some young scientists had gathered around a table. Anna could smell pipe tobacco. That left only his office.

Anna had been puzzled by Tybjerg's office ever since she first saw it. Dr. Tybjerg was one of the world's leading dinosaur experts, but his office was small and damp as though the faculty were trying to keep him out of sight. Two walls in the tiny room were filled with books from floor to ceiling, Tybjerg's desk stood against the third wall, and at the fourth, below the basement windows, was a low display cabinet with dinosaur models and Tybjerg's own publications. The door to his office was locked, and Anna peered through the window but it was empty and the light was off. She called him on her cell phone. No answer. Finally, she found some scrap paper in a trash can and wrote him a note: *We need to talk. Please call me to arrange a new meeting.* She stuck the note to the door.

At that moment the light in the corridor timed out and she realized just how dark it was. Outside, someone walked past the low basement windows, and she saw a pair of legs wearing red boots, heels slamming against the cobblestones. Her heart raced as she stumbled along the corridor. She found the switch near the door to the stairwell and turned on the light. It was empty and quiet.

Anna and Karen had been friends since they were children. They were in the same class at school and were always together in the village of Brænderup, where they grew up. One day, while roaming around Fødring Forest, they met Troels. A hurricane had raged recently and there were fallen trees everywhere, their roots ripped out of the earth like rotten teeth. The girls had been told not to play in the forest under any circumstances.

They were jumping on the slimy leaves and daring each other to leap into the craters because they had heard stories that the wind might cause the trees to swing back up and crush you. Karen was the braver; she stood right under the roots of a dying tree and clumps of earth sprinkled onto her shoulders as she reached out her hands toward the sky in triumph. They had strayed further and further into the forest, until they remembered a giant ladybug made from the stump of a tree that had been felled. They wondered what might have happened to it during the storm and decided to investigate; after all, they weren't far away. What if the ladybird had been uprooted and was lying with her legs in the air?

They discovered Troels sitting on the ground, leaning against the ladybird. They didn't notice him at first. They were busy chatting and patting the ladybird. It wasn't until Anna climbed up on its wooden wings and had made herself comfortable that she spotted a tuft of hair sticking up on the other side. It belonged to a boy with freckles and a sad look on his face.

Anna said "hi" and tossed him a pine cone, which he caught. The next hour they were absorbed in their play. The darkness came suddenly, as if big buckets of ink had been poured between the trees. Troels grew anxious and said: "Shouldn't we be going home now?" The girls nodded. Oh yes, they ought to. The three of them skipped through the forest and, as they reached the edge, the beam from a torch picked them out and they met Troels's father for the first time.

Cecilie's reaction would have been: "Where on earth have you been, you horrible little brats," then she would have hugged them and pretended to be mad.

Troels's father said nothing. He slowly pointed the torch from one face to the next.

"Sorry, Dad," Troels whispered.

"See you later," Anna said, taking Karen's hand. If they cut across the field, they could be home in twenty minutes.

"Oh, no," Troels's father said. "You're coming with me. You'll walk to the parking lot, where my car is, like good girls, and I'll give you a ride home. Is that clear?"

Anna had been told her whole life never to go with strangers. Never ever. The three children plodded down a gravel path in total silence, past dimly lit houses, in the opposite direction to where Anna lived.

When they reached the parking lot, she tried again: "We'll be fine from here. Thanks for walking us . . ."

Troels's father stopped and made a half turn. Anna couldn't see his face very well.

"Get in," he ordered them and opened the door to the back seat. Anna was about to protest, when she saw the look in Troels's eyes. Just get in, they pleaded. The car smelled new, of chemicals, as though every fiber had been cleaned. She helped Karen put on her seatbelt. The car glided through the darkness, away from the forest and out onto the main road. Troels sat, small and dark, on the passenger seat next to his father.

*   *   *

Cecilie opened the door, a towel wrapped around her head. She was in the process of dyeing her hair; Anna could see tinfoil sticking out over her ears. Cecilie was wearing a faded robe. Music was coming from inside the house, and it smelled of mud.

"Hi, kids," she said cheerfully. Then she noticed Troels's father behind them. A deep furrow appeared on her brow.

"What's happened?" Cecilie's eyes widened. Had the man hit them in his car? Were they all right?

"Good evening, ma'am," Troels's father said. "In the future, I suggest you keep a closer eye on your children. I found them in the forest, playing under fallen trees." He paused, then he clapped his massive palms together. "It's a dangerous place to be."

"Get inside, girls," Cecilie said to Karen and Anna. Something Anna didn't recognize flashed in her mother's eyes.

"Thanks for your help," she said in a monotone voice, and closed the door.

When the car had disappeared, Cecilie started pacing up and down in the kitchen, and she didn't stop until Jens came home.

"What are you accusing him of?" Anna heard Jens say in a low voice. "Giving the girls a ride home and staring at your robe?"

After the summer break, Troels started in Anna and Karen's class. It was five months since their meeting in the forest, but they hadn't forgotten him. Their teacher introduced him, and Troels's face lit up a little when he saw them. He had grown taller, but his expression was the same, and his eyes were still very dark.

During recess Karen asked him anxiously, "Did your dad get really angry last time?"

And Troels smiled broadly and said, "Oh, no, not at all."

That afternoon Anna and Karen walked home together from school. The golden wheat swayed in the fields. At some point they stopped and decided Troels would be their friend.

A week passed. They spent every recess with him, walked home from school together, and one day, when they were about to say good-bye, Anna asked if Troels wanted to come to her house. He looked at his watch and smiled. Yes, please, he would like that very much. They played in the garden and when it started to rain, they went inside and made themselves sandwiches. The girls swapped stickers, and Troels handled the pictures very carefully and examined them closely. He, too, liked the ones with glitter babies and puppies the best.

Cecilie came home and Troels got up politely to shake her hand. The telephone rang at that moment, so Anna wasn't sure if Cecilie had remembered who Troels was. When Troels went to the bathroom and Cecilie had sat down with a cup of tea, Anna whispered that he was the boy they had met in the forest last March. Cecilie paled.

"You can visit us anytime you like," she said, when Troels came back. "Anytime you like."

"Thank you very much," Troels replied.

Cecilie bought a scrapbook and ten sheets of stickers for Troels. Anna felt so jealous she wanted to cry. Troels unwrapped his gift as though he had been entrusted with a blanket full of precious eggs. His face lit up, then he looked miserably at Cecilie.

"I can't accept this," he said and carefully pushed the present away. Anna picked up the scrapbook and admired the pictures. Big cherubs on clouds, glitter babies, animals, and baskets of flowers. If Troels didn't want them, she certainly did.

"Of course you can," Cecilie said warmly. "Now you can swap, can't you? They're a present."

"No," Troels said, still wretched. "I really can't. I'm not allowed to accept presents."

Cecilie narrowed her eyes and studied him.

"Hmm," she said. "Well, you can't take them home, obviously. They need to stay here."

Anna stared at her mother.

"They'll still be my stickers, you understand, but I'm not very good at swapping, so I would like you to do it for me. Extend my collection. Do you think you can do that?"

Troels nodded and opened the scrapbook with awe. With the same deference, he removed the wrapper and gazed at the stickers. Later that afternoon, when it was time for him to go home, he placed the scrapbook on the bookcase in the living room, where it remained until his next visit. The scrapbook lived there for years.

It was not until four months later that Anna and Karen visited Troels. It was at the start of December, and after school they caught the bus to his house, a huge, newly built bungalow a few miles outside the village. They sat on the floor in Troels's room making Christmas decorations out of paper and were listening to music when Troels's father came home from work. They heard him speak on the telephone in the hall in a loud voice, then he swore at something before he suddenly popped his head around the door.

"Hello, girls," he said, showing no signs of recognizing them. Shortly afterward he came back and put a bowl of chips and three sodas on the floor.

"Troels's mom wants to know if you would like to stay for dinner?"

Karen and Anna exchanged looks.

"Yes, please," Anna said quickly.

Chips and sodas! For dinner they had pork tenderloin in a cream sauce and for dessert they had chocolate ice cream. Troels's mother was a petite, elegant lady who worked as a real estate agent in Odense. Troels's sister was fifteen years old and really pretty. She had very long hair, she wore lip gloss, and she said, "Pass the potatoes, please," in a terribly grown-up way. Anna felt a pang of infatuation and glanced at Troels. He smiled at something his father had said, replied and laughed heartily when his father expanded on and repeated the punchline. Anna took it all in.

Troels's father started telling vacation stories. On vacation in Sweden, Troels had fallen off a jetty when trying to measure the depth of the water with a stick, which was far too thin and had snapped under his weight. Troels had wailed like a banshee, he was so scared, but the water was less than three feet deep and rather muddy. The girls imagined Troels screaming and dirty, and they laughed. His father hosed him down in the garden behind the cabin. On the same vacation, Troels's father recalled, they had visited a traveling fair where one of the stalls had a board with a man on it, and if you could hit a red disc with a ball, he would plunge into a tub of water. Troels's father had persuaded the stallholder to replace the man on the board with Troels, who had been moaning all afternoon that he was too hot. Troels got dunked repeatedly and had duly cooled down. Anna and Karen laughed again.

"And then there was the time when Troels wouldn't stop wetting his bed," Troels's father began. "Do you remember, girls?" he said to Troels's mother and sister who had started clearing the table.

"Not that story, please," Troels's mother called out from the kitchen where she was scraping leftovers into the trash. "The girls won't want to hear that."

Troels's father leaned toward Anna and Karen.

"Troels wet his bed until he was six," he announced.

Anna looked uncomfortably at Karen who seemed to be mesmerized by Troels's father.

"We were at our wits' end, weren't we, Troels?" his mother said, still at the kitchen table. "All of us, you included, isn't that right, darling?"

Anna looked at Troels, and something inside her turned to ice. Troels made no reply, silent, as his half-eaten chocolate ice cream cone slowly melted in his hand.

His mother carried on while she dried a baking dish, "We tried everything. We tried bribing him with candy and toys, we gave him more allowance, we even made him wear his soaked pajamas all day, but it was no good. He just continued wetting his bed."

Karen was still smiling, so Anna kicked her under the table.

"And do you want to know how it stopped?" Troels's father asked, blithely.

"Ouch," Karen exclaimed and sent Anna a furious look. Anna glared back at her. Finally, Karen noticed Troels.

"Tell the girls how you stopped wetting the bed, Troels," his father ordered him. Troels whispered something.

"I can't hear you," his father said. "Speak up."

"When I pooped my pants on my first day of school," Troels said in a flat voice.

The girls looked at each other.

"And you can't poop your pants at school, can you?" his father went on. "The other children will laugh at you. So you have to stop, don't you? If you ever want to have any friends, that is." His father gave Troels a friendly slap on the back and roared with laughter.

"Stop it!" Anna burst out. "Stop it!"

But his father had already got up to leave, the dishwasher had been loaded, his sister had disappeared, and his mother was folding clothes in the laundry room; they could see her through the open door.

"That was a lovely meal, thank you," Anna muttered. "I have to be home by seven."

When Anna and Karen had put on their shoes and coats and shouted "bye-e!" from the utility room, Troels was still sitting at the table with the melting ice cream cone in his hand.

"Bye, see you tomorrow," he said and gave them a pale smile.

Cecilie called Troels's parents one day to tell them she could use some help around the garden and offered Troels fifteen kroner an hour to do the work. While Cecilie spoke to Troels's father, Anna was in the kitchen, listening to her mother's high-pitched chirping. Cecilie slammed down the telephone at the end of the conversation and when she joined Anna in the kitchen, she smiled stiffly and smoothed her dress.

"Done," she said. "Five hours a week. Thank God." She flopped down on the kitchen bench next to Anna.

"Phew," she exhaled and smoothed her dress again.

One evening, when Anna was twelve years old, she overheard her parents talking about Troels. It was the late 1980s, and by now Jens had officially moved to Copenhagen but he visited them constantly. They had just said goodnight to her, but before she fell asleep Anna remembered she had forgotten to give her mother a letter from school and got out of bed.

Halfway down the stairs, she heard Jens ask: "What makes you think he hits him? You have to be able to prove it, Cecilie. It's a serious charge."

A pause followed. Then Anna heard Cecilie cry.

"I want to help, but I can't!" she sobbed. "That beautiful, fragile boy. Look at him! He's suffering, and there's absolutely nothing I can do about it."

Jens said something that Anna couldn't hear, and Cecilie replied: "I know, Jens." She sounded irritated now. "I'm aware of that. You've told me a thousand times. I just can't bear it that he has to live like that."

Cecilie blew her nose. Anna was getting cold on the stairs and hoped that one of her parents would notice her. That they would carry her to the living room and let her fall asleep under a blanket while their voices grew muffled, just like when she was little. Silent tears rolled down her cheeks. Right now she hated Troels. Her parents seemed to prefer him to her. She felt alone in the world. They started discussing Jens's job. Eventually Anna went back to bed.

One summer day Troels dropped by unexpectedly. He seemed happy. His parents had gone to Ebeltoft to pick up a new car and wouldn't be back until the evening. Cecilie and Jens were entertaining old college friends, and the lawn was teeming with children. The sun was shining, there was iced tea and sandwiches, and swallows were dive-bombing the garden. Troels watched the chaos, rather intimidated; he hadn't been expecting this. Two boys, Troels's age, were playing football, but Troels didn't want to join in. He sipped tea and Cecilie introduced him to everyone.

"This is Troels. He's goes to school with Anna."

"He's gorgeous," Anna heard Cecilie's friends whisper.

Jens decided they should all play baseball. Everyone leapt from their chairs; four large stones were found, along with a bat and a yellow tennis ball, and two teams picked. The mood in the backyard was light-hearted and boisterous. Anna and Karen rolled their eyes at the silly grown-ups. They were both wearing makeup, but none of the adults had said anything. It was Troels's turn to bat. He said,

"I don't want to"—not very loudly, but loud enough for Anna to hear it, and she was some distance away. Troels sent her an apologetic smile.

Jens's old friend, Mogens, who was bowling, encouraged Troels.

"You can do it," he said warmly. He positioned himself behind Troels and guided his arms in a horizontal arc through the air.

"Keep the bat high," he instructed him. "Don't let it drop." He tapped Troels's drooping elbow. "And watch the ball."

Troels's arm was still limp.

"Come on! Concentrate. It's not that hard!" Mogens called out. Anna instinctively glanced at her mother. Cecilie wanted to say something. She raised her hands as if to object. Next to Troels, Mogens was a gentle giant.

"What do you think this is, eh?" Mogens roared with laughter and grabbed Troels's white, freckled arm and dangled it. "Flab?" he chuckled. Troels looked vacantly at Mogens, who was ducking and diving like a boxer, throwing mock punches at Troels.

"Come on, son, show us what you're made of!"

Troels raised the bat and hit Mogens over the head. *Clonk.* Mogens clutched his head. Everyone went very quiet.

"What did you do that for?" Mogens gasped.

Troels ran off, and Cecilie chased after him. They had been gone for nearly an hour when Anna decided to look for them. She found them in the back seat of the car. Troels looked red-eyed and lay with his head in Cecilie's lap. She stroked his hair. He didn't want to go back to the party, even though Cecilie assured him that it would be all right. That Jens would definitely have explained to Mogens why Troels had hit him. This puzzled Anna. Troels refused point-blank. He wanted to go home. Cecilie hugged him, and she and Anna watched Troels ride his bike unsteadily down the road before his speed increased and he was gone.

In the garden, the mayhem had come to a halt and people were sitting around again. Mogens was pressing an icepack against his head. He still looked stunned. An eerie silence reigned.

"Are you all right?" Cecilie asked.

"Yes," Mogens replied. "I'm so sorry."

"Yes, you humiliated him," Cecilie replied.

"Hey, listen," Jens objected. "That's not fair."

"No, I mean it. Not deliberately," she said, addressing Jens. "I know that. And 99 percent of boys would have reacted differently. But not him."

"No, it was a real pity," Mogens said, miserably, and touched his sore head again.

When Troels turned seventeen, he had his tongue and his nose pierced and he started wearing tight trousers and Doc Martens. The skinny boy was gone. Troels was now almost six feet tall, he had large, supple hands and broad shoulders. He had come close to being expelled from high school, but Cecilie intervened and pleaded his case. He didn't visit them as often as he used to, so Anna and Karen no longer knew as much about what he did or who he was with, but he told them that he sometimes took the train to Århus or Copenhagen to go to a gay club. The girls thought it sounded very exciting.

One day, Troels stopped by to ask Anna if she wanted to go for a bike ride. After riding for a while, he grew hot, pulled his jumper over his head, and bared a torso mottled with bruises.

"What on earth's happened to you?" Anna was shocked.

"I went home to see my dad and to wash my clothes," Troels said, giving her a cheerful look.

"He hit you?" Anna whispered.

"Yes, but I hit him back."

Anna stepped hard on the pedals to keep up.

"And do you know something?" Troels gave Anna a complicit look. "It's a real pain that I look like this." He rose up on his pedals with studied indifference.

"Why?" Anna panted.

"I've been spotted by a modeling agency in Odense."

"You're kidding!"

"No, it's true. They want to make a portfolio about me. They said they could get me a lot of work."

They spent the rest of the afternoon discussing Troels's future modeling career. Paris, New York, and Milan all beckoned. Anna promised she would definitely visit him. They ended up on a fallow field where they lay among meadow flowers, gazing at the sky and fantasizing about champagne fountains and silver confetti descending from the ceiling. Or rather, Anna did. Troels sat next to her. His back hurt too much for him to lie down.

In 1997, the year Anna, Troels, and Karen graduated from high school, it seemed the summer would never end. It was so hot their clothes stuck to their bodies, and the nights, too, were warm, azure, and endless. The three friends were euphoric; the world was theirs and they felt that if they exhaled simultaneously the heavens would expand forever. They went to parties in houses owned by people they didn't know and drank themselves senseless. Houses empty of their friends' parents who were away on vacation, where neglected houseplants were shoved aside so the windows facing the fields could be flung wide open, where they could crash and sleep under the sky, if they felt like it, or accidentally start a small fire, as happened early one morning in late July. The teenagers watched in contrite silence as the fire engines pulled up, and then stared at their feet while a fireman held up a cigarette butt to their faces and lectured them. Of course, it wasn't the actual butt that had started the fire, merely one of the many strewn across the garden. The next day, the party carried on as if nothing had happened, houseplants pushed aside and windows thrown open.

Later, when Anna looked back on that summer, she wondered if things might not have ended so badly between them if it had rained. They rarely slept, and when they weren't partying they hung out in Karen's small apartment in Odense, eyeing each other like wild animals.

It all happened one night when Karen had scored some cocaine, and they snorted it all at once. Anna went to the bathroom, and when she returned, Karen and Troels had gotten the bright idea that now was a great time to try group sex. Well, why not, Anna thought.

Her mouth felt dry like sandpaper, and she went to the kitchen to get a drink of water. When she returned, Karen and Troels were dancing around, naked from the waist up.

"I thought you were gay," Anna exclaimed. Troels and Karen collapsed in heaps of laughter.

"And we thought you were open-minded," Karen called out. They gestured for Anna to join them.

They climbed into Karen's bed, and Anna and Troels started kissing while Karen pulled off his trousers. Troels started laughing into Anna's mouth, because Karen was fumbling, and temporarily let go of Anna to come to Karen's aid. Troels and Karen began kissing, and Karen managed to pull Troels's pants down. His dick was pierced. Anna stared at Karen's hand enclosing it. Troels closed his eyes, and Anna could hear him gasping with pleasure while he continued kissing Karen. Anna rolled aside. At some point, Karen opened her eyes, looked at Anna and held out her hand to her, but before Anna had time to take it, Troels lifted Karen up and turned her over, so she lay on her back, her curls spilling over the pillow. His dick pointed momentarily at Karen and then it disappeared inside her. They both shut their eyes. Anna sat up. Everything went black. She kicked at their joined bodies and hit Troels right on the hip, sending him rolling with a howl. His mouth opened, his erection subsided, and Karen looked from one to the other, confused. Anna flew at Troels, and let her clenched fists rain down on his face, his chest, and his stomach, as he lay halfway across the bed. Troels's face went white and his eyes burned.

"Stop it, Anna," he hissed. But she didn't stop. Karen tried to grab Anna, and Troels, who had passively let the blows fall, got up to gather his clothes. Anna pushed Karen aside and slumped on the bed. Troels had put on his jeans and he pulled his T-shirt over his head as he left through the front door. He didn't close it behind him. His footsteps echoed down the stairs, then he was gone.

Karen sent Anna an outraged look and said: "What you just did, Anna Bella, was fucking unnecessary."

That was ten years ago.

CHAPTER 6

As Søren began to think about leaving the office on Monday October 8, he was firmly of the opinion that Professor Helland's death would be classed as one of Mother Nature's enigmatic early recalls, and decided to wrap up the case as quickly as possible. Lars Helland had dropped dead—that was all there was to it. Hearts stopped beating in Denmark every day; even in people who, like Professor Helland, biked fifteen miles to and from work, and never smoked or drank. Admittedly, the severed tongue was a bit out of the ordinary, even to Søren, but it was a relatively common occurrence for people to sustain serious injuries in the process of dying. Søren had seen broken necks, smashed teeth and skulls, burns, shattered bones, and skewered torsos inflicted by everything from barbecues and radiator valves to lawnmowers and cast iron fences. Helland must have suffered convulsions of some sort and had bitten off his own tongue before he died.

Convinced the case would soon be closed, Søren had started his preliminary interviews at the university. The first person on his list was the rather strange-looking and practically transparent biologist, Johannes Trøjborg, who had reported the death. He had been in the department because he was co-writing a paper with Professor Helland. He was hoping to get his PhD application approved, despite the PhD and Human Resources Committee having already turned his application down—twice. Søren had met many oddballs in his time, people whose head and body decorations were so extreme that you could barely make out the naked person underneath them. Johannes, however, was one of the most peculiar creatures Søren had ever seen. His transparency reminded Søren of those little white creatures you find under paving stones. Johannes's hands were long, slender and silken, his skin stretched tight and pale across his face and he stooped. Only his red hair and intelligent eyes contradicted Søren's impression of being in the presence of something stale and musty.

Johannes appeared to have nothing but positive things to say about Helland, and only when Søren held a gun to his head—metaphorically speaking, of course—did he reluctantly agree that Helland's behavior had recently been unfocused and distracted. But then again, he quickly added, Anna wasn't the easiest person in the world to get along with, either. Søren failed to see the relevance, and Johannes spluttered as he explained that Anna and he had differed wildly in their opinions on Helland's qualities, both as a human being and as a supervisor, a topic they had discussed several times over the summer. Johannes paused, then he blurted out that Anna had, in fact, been toying with the idea of playing pranks on Helland. Pranks? Søren gave Johannes a baffled look. What did he mean? Johannes blinked as though he had said too much. Nothing, it was just. . . . He looked away. Anna was angry with Helland, he admitted at last. She felt he had let her down. She had a young child to look after, so she was already under pressure, and she had grown disproportionately mad at Helland in a way that Johannes didn't like. They had argued about it. Søren listened.

All of a sudden, Johannes asked Søren if he was aware that someone had made threats against Helland. He mentioned it casually, his tone bordering on flippancy, but then rushed to make it clear

Helland himself had laughed and declared the threats to be pranks. Johannes didn't know the nature of them, he only knew Helland's interpretation, which was that someone at the university bore a grudge and had decided to send him some nasty e-mails. Søren wanted to know if Johannes suspected the sender might be Anna Bella Nor. Johannes dismissed it instantly. Of course not! It would never cross Anna's mind. Professor Helland was a member of several committees and his administrative influence was considerable; he knew that he was an obvious target for people's dissatisfaction. He was on the PhD and Human Resources Committee—to name but one—Johannes explained, and was thus in a position to decide the future academic careers of several biologists.

Søren nodded slowly, thanked him and had just closed the door behind him when he remembered something. Johannes looked up, surprised, when the door opened again and Søren popped his head around it.

"Does that mean," Søren said kindly, "Professor Helland was involved in rejecting both your PhD applications?"

"Yes," Johannes said, calmly. "It does."

Søren left, a touch perplexed. Johannes was clearly upset about Helland's death and hunted high and low for a logical explanation; he had accidentally implicated his colleague, Anna Bella Nor, but then had gone on to defend her, as though it was Søren and not Johannes himself who had made the insinuation. Just as well this was a straightforward case, Søren thought, it saved him from having to dig more deeply to find out what Johannes Trøjborg had actually meant.

Anna Bella Nor's turn was next. They met in the small library, and she sat with her back to him, but turned around warily when he approached. She had short, brown hair, an oval face, and a slender, yet strong body, he thought. There was something sullen about her movements, as though she minded being here very much. Her eyebrows and lashes were dense and black. Her eyes were indescribable; at first sight they seemed muddy, but when she said something with emphasis, they shone golden. To his surprise, the pace of the interview was sluggish—it was clearly a matter of great inconvenience to Anna Bella Nor that Professor Helland had died. She came across as angry and fraught, and at one point she said outright: "My dissertation defense is in two weeks. This really is very bad timing, to put it mildly."

Søren asked about her relationship with Helland and learned that Helland was slightly better than useless, and Anna had even considered making a formal complaint about him to the Faculty Council. He also learned that Helland had upset everyone, including Johannes, though Johannes wouldn't admit it.

"Johannes is a friend," she interjected, and narrowed her eyes, "but he's horrible at reading people. He's just too nice, and he has convinced himself it's his mission on earth to excuse every single reprehensible act. Johannes can always find a reason, and do you know something?" Anna gave Søren a hard stare. "Sometimes even the best explanation isn't a justification. Professor Helland didn't care about me at all, and that's a fact."

She went on to tell him that Professor Ewald and Professor Jørgensen hadn't been huge fans of Professor Helland either, and, as far as Anna could see, with good reason. Helland had managed to get himself a seat on every single academic and administrative committee there was, and was consequently responsible for myriad things that affected the daily running of the department. Anna refused to specify what they were: "Trust me, they'll bore you to death, seriously."

What Anna was at pains to point out was that Helland had twice removed the electric kettle, which she and Johannes had bought and kept in their study, and taken it to his office without asking. At this point, Søren's fingers had begun to itch with irritation, and he told Anna to leave out irrelevant information, whereupon Anna looked straight at him and said: "You want to know about Helland's relationship with his colleagues at the institute? How better to describe the climate that surrounded him than by explaining what a petty, self-important, emotionally stunted fascist he really was?"

Søren was genuinely impressed at how swiftly Anna could weld so many words into such a hard-hitting sentence.

The next thing he wanted to know was if Helland had seemed all right lately.

Anna replied: "I tended to avoid him, but he was always quite odd. The strangest thing recently was his eye. Whatever it was, it was bad."

She had first seen it in the early summer and thought little of it, but recently she had noticed that the growth had. . .

"*Bigger* isn't the right word," she said. "But it grew more visible, as though it was changing character and hardening." She fell abruptly silent.

Søren thanked her and asked her to remain at the department from where she would be driven to the police station. Anna demanded to know why and looked most unhappy when Søren explained it was procedure. When he left and closed the door between them, he could feel himself sweating.

The two professors were next on his list. They were speaking quietly in Professor Ewald's office and exuded an atmosphere of profound trust. When Søren knocked, they both rose and asked him to take a seat in a stylish, but rather uncomfortable chair with a metal back and a thin seat pad. Professor Jørgensen was the doyen of the department and had, Søren quickly realized, partly retired, but was still working on a range of research projects.

At first glance, Professor Ewald came across as the most normal of the four biologists. She was petite, but she had the edge over the rest of them—expensive, well-fitting clothes, a good haircut, modern glasses, and discreet makeup. At second glance, however, he realized that she was fundamentally a worrier. While they spoke, Søren unobtrusively checked out her airy office where every surface was covered with biological specimens. Her subject was invertebrates, she told Søren, and when he looked baffled, she said: "Animals with no spine," and gestured in a way Søren took to indicate that the numerous animals decorating her shelves and window sills were all such unfortunate creatures.

The professors were terribly upset. Professor Ewald admitted openly that she was plagued by horrible guilt, and Professor Jørgensen nodded in agreement: they had both loathed Helland. Unequivocally. Helland and Ewald had worked in the department for over twenty-five years, Jørgensen even longer, and when they looked back at their careers, the only obstacle had been Helland. He had poisoned the working environment and prevented joint and targeted research by constantly looking out for number one. Further, he was a member of several administrative committees and Professor Ewald and Professor Jørgensen strongly agreed this was the equivalent of giving a baby a razor. Helland had no administrative skills whatsoever, and yet he got himself elected chair of several university bodies, with chaotic consequences for the department every single time. Once, for example, Helland forgot the submission date for joint grant applications, despite the fact he had been reminded of the approaching deadline on an almost daily basis in the preceding six months. The department had been forced to survive a whole term on the remains of the previous year's grants, students had to pay for photocopied handouts, the annual field trip was canceled, and they had been forced to use faulty microscopes.

Two years ago, Helland had been elected head of the department, which meant he was given overall responsibility for the two units that made up the department of Cell Biology and Comparative Zoology, and in those two years he had practically brought the department to its knees. Helland's incredibly poor performance and his cavalier treatment of students as well as budgets had sparked a lot of friction, not only among Jørgensen, Ewald, and Helland, but also between Helland and several of the cell biologists who worked on the floor above. The corridors had frequently echoed with arguments, and Professor Ewald said she had come close to resigning on numerous occasions. Unfortunately, having tenure as a scientist at the college of Natural Science was a dream job and she knew she would never get another post like it. Then there was the responsibility toward the students. Morphology was a popular subject, and she felt duty-bound to educate new morphologists—a task that fell almost exclusively to her because Helland quite simply didn't appear to share her sense of duty, even though teaching was a compulsory part of their employment contract with the university.

Søren failed to understand the latter; as far as he had been informed, the department had only two postgraduates, Anna Bella Nor and Johannes Trøjborg, and surely Helland was supervising both of them?

"Yes . . ." Professor Ewald hesitated. "But they are his only post-graduate students in the last *ten* years. During the same period, Professor Jørgensen and I have supervised at least forty postgradu-ates, of which the vast majority finished their PhDs long ago and are now in full-time employment. Those students are our *only* hope, and even though it's undeniably tough to teach undergraduates, supervise postgraduates, and deliver new groundbreaking research that maintains our international reputation as a nation of scientists, you have to take your job seriously, not only as an employee of the college of Natural Science, but also as a human being." Professor Ewald's eyes were fiery.

"The truth is, we were both surprised. At Johannes and Anna. Pleasantly surprised, I hasten to add." She stopped and looked at Professor Jørgensen.

"But . . ." Søren prompted.

"Neither of them needed a laboratory to do their work," Profes-sor Jørgensen answered for her. "Johannes wrote a theoretical dis-sertation, and Anna has done the same."

"What does that mean?"

"They didn't spend time with Helland in the laboratory; he didn't have a student trailing after him for years, which meant he didn't need to do any research because there was no one to keep an eye on him. Johannes and Anna based their dissertations on existing literature, and though that's almost certainly twice as hard as writing a practical dissertation, it undoubtedly represented a minuscule effort, if any, on Helland's part. Of course it troubled us. It was the principle of it."

A pause followed. Then Professor Ewald said, "Still, it's dreadful what's happened. You wouldn't want that for your worst enemy." She looked as if she was about to say something else, but stopped and exhaled lightly.

"Was that what he was?" Søren probed. "Your worst enemy?"

"No," Professor Ewald replied firmly. "He was frequently a pain in the ass, he really was. But after twenty-five years, you learn to live with it."

Søren cocked his head. At the same time, the light outside changed and the office grew darker, almost black. Professor Ewald leaned forward and switched on a lamp on a low trolley. The base of the lamp was a brass octopus twisting its tentacles up a gnarled stick as though it was trying either to climb out of the sea or pull the white silk shade into the sea with it. Søren wondered if the creature were an invertebrate, too. When Professor Ewald had settled back into her chair, Søren continued.

"Speaking of pain . . . have you any idea what the problem with Helland's eye might have been?" he asked innocently, and looked from one to the other. The professors seemed genuinely baffled.

"There was something wrong with his eye?" Professor Jørgensen frowned.

"Johannes and Anna both mentioned a growth of some sort in Helland's right eye, they said it had become more noticeable in recent months. Did you see anything?"

The professors considered this. Then Professor Ewald began, tentatively: "This may sound odd . . ." she sighed, "but I never actually looked at him. Not closely. We would say hello in passing, but since Helland, in his year as head had practically handed over the head of department job to Professor Ravn upstairs, I hadn't needed to discuss administrative issues with him. That was last spring, wasn't it?" She looked to Professor Jørgensen for confirmation. He nodded.

"The atmosphere here was affecting me badly, you see." She was looking at Søren now. "However, about six months ago I came to a decision. I finally stopped believing things would ever change. I decided to regard Helland as a necessary evil, like a motorway at the end of a garden you have spent precious years cultivating. I didn't want to leave. I'm fond of the students and I love my research. And last year I realized I had only two choices: I could resign or I could learn to put up with Helland. Since then I haven't had much contact with him. We used e-mail to exchange internal messages, but apart from that I avoided him. So, no, I hadn't noticed that something might be wrong with his eye."

Søren saw she was resting her hands calmly in her lap and looking straight at him.

"Me neither," Professor Jørgensen added.

"And what about his health in general? Anything stand out?"

Again both professors looked puzzled. Then Professor Jørgensen remarked, "Something must have been wrong for his heart to stop beating without any warning. He suffered death throes, I imagine? Since he bit off his own tongue?"

"The autopsy will establish that," Søren said in a neutral voice.

"Perhaps he was an undiagnosed epileptic?" Professor Jørgensen suggested.

"So you never noticed anything?" Søren cut him short.

"No," they replied in unison. Søren got ready to leave, but sensed hesitation hanging in the air. He looked closely at Professor Ewald.

"Did you want to add something?"

Professor Ewald frowned.

"This is going to sound silly . . ." she looked away. "No, it's too absurd."

"Tell me anyway," Søren prompted her.

"As I was saying, we e-mailed occasionally about practical matters. For instance, we shared the SEM computer at the end of the corridor and a couple of times Helland didn't show up when he had booked a session, so I e-mailed him to ask if I could use his slot."

"You chose to e-mail him even though his office is about a hundred feet down the corridor?" Søren asked.

"Yes," Professor Ewald said, curtly.

"All right, go on," Søren said.

"And if I have to come up with something that might seem a little out of the ordinary, then this is it"—she laughed a hollow laugh—"his spelling was deteriorating."

Søren and Professor Jørgensen were speechless.

"His spelling?" Professor Jørgensen said.

"Yes," Professor Ewald replied. "His last two or three e-mails were so appalling I could barely read them. As though he had bashed them out in seconds and simply couldn't be bothered to spell-check them before hitting 'send.' I took it as further evidence of how little respect he had for me. But, now that you mention it, it does seem a bit strange."

They both nodded and Søren made a mental note.

Still convinced that Helland had died from natural causes, Søren arranged for the four biologists to be driven to the police station where he formally interviewed them and their statements were written down and signed. Anna still looked disgruntled.

As he and Henrik drove down Frederikssundvej, Søren quickly reviewed the case, purely to assure himself that he hadn't missed anything. Professor Helland clearly couldn't compete with Santa Claus in the popularity stakes, that much was obvious, but Søren had yet to stumble on anything that might hint at uncontrollable rage, and without that it was quite simply impossible to rip someone's tongue out. He smiled to himself. Anna Bella was the only one who appeared remotely combative, but the idea that she would mutilate her supervisor was far-fetched.

"What's so funny?" Henrik wanted to know.

"Nothing," Søren said and looked out of the window.

At half past four in the afternoon, Søren sat in his office wondering if he could write his report now, even though he was still awaiting the result of the autopsy. It would probably arrive tomorrow, but he was pretty sure he knew what it would say: Lars Helland had died from heart failure. Once he put that in his report, the case would be closed. The only thing stopping him was that he had yet to talk to Professor Helland's allegedly close colleague, Dr. Tybjerg. After interviewing Anna and her colleagues, he had gone to the Natural History Museum to find him. The place had been like an enchanted forest. Søren had started by asking for Dr. Tybjerg at the reception and had been directed through a door and into a complicated maze of deserted corridors, where he instantly got himself lost. It wasn't until he had been into four empty offices and knocked on six locked doors, which no one answered, that he met a living human being. It was an old man sitting behind a desk, writing. A huge poster depicting thousands of colorful butterflies of all sizes hung on the wall behind him. The old man directed Søren further down a corridor and up to the third floor where Dr. Tybjerg was supposed to be sitting by the windows overlooking the park.

Five minutes later, Søren was lost again and when he, finally and with the help of a young woman, found the desk where Dr. Tybjerg was supposed to be when he worked with bones, all he could see was an angle-poise lamp, which was switched on, a pencil, and a chair. He hung around for a while, but after ten minutes he grew impatient and decided he had had enough. He found something that appeared to be a cafeteria and informed the catering assistant, who was wringing out a cloth, that he was a police superintendent and insisted on speaking to Dr. Tybjerg this instant. The woman glanced around, said, "He's not here," and resumed cleaning.

Someone at a table in the cafeteria, however, told Søren Dr. Tybjerg's office could be found in the basement, in the right-hand wing; that is, down the stairs in the central wing, then right through two swing doors, and then down to the basement. Halfway down one of the basement corridors, the one facing the University Park, was an office and through that office was another office and that belonged to Dr. Tybjerg. Søren stomped back to reception where he asked, in his most polite tone of voice, the student staffing the counter to get hold of Dr. Tybjerg. The student rang various numbers. Søren drummed his fingers on the counter.

"He's not in his office, in the collection, the cafeteria, or the library," she said. "All I can do is e-mail him."

Søren left his name and number with a message for Dr. Tybjerg to contact him. Then he drove to Bellahøj police station and worked in his office. He had just made up his mind to go home when his telephone rang.

"Søren Marhauge."

"It's me." It was Søren's secretary, Linda.

"Hello, me," Søren said.

"The Deputy Medical Examiner just called."

Bøje Knudsen, the Deputy Medical Examiner, worked in the basement of Rigshospitalet, Copenhagen's central hospital. Søren had never been able to decide whether or not he liked him. Bøje had a twinkle in his eye, and though Søren appreciated that a certain amount of professional detachment was required, Bøje still came across as strangely aloof. One day Bøje had read his mind and remarked, "Søren, my dear friend, if I broke down and cried every time I felt like it, the hospital would be flooded. But, trust me, my soul is grieving." Søren had warmed a little to Bøje, but he had yet to be convinced. Søren himself was more thick-skinned now than he had been at the start of his career, that went without saying, but he told himself this made him neutral and composed rather than cold.

"Why didn't you put him through?" Søren asked.

"He wouldn't hear of it. He told me to give you his regards and to tell you that if he were you, he would hurry over to the hospital."

Just before five o'clock Søren drove to the hospital and parked under two poplars stripped bare by the advancing autumn. The blacktop was slippery with fallen leaves, and the wind seemed to blow simultaneously from all four corners. He felt a profound sense of unease. He announced his arrival at reception and took the elevator down two floors to the Institute of Forensic Medicine. It was the second time in one day he had walked through a desolate grid of interconnecting passages and corridors, but this time he didn't get lost. He greeted a few familiar faces in passing before he heard music from the radio and Bøje's humming. He knocked on the open door and entered. Bøje was behind his desk. It looked like he was expecting him.

"There you are," he said, as Søren entered.

Søren took a seat and Bøje glanced at him. Then he looked down at a sheet with indecipherable hieroglyphs and up at Søren again. He rolled his lips and tapped the table once with his finger.

"Today I performed an autopsy on one Lars Helland," he began.

"And?" Søren wished he could extract the information from Bøje now and absorb it later at his own pace.

"He died from heart failure," Bøje went on, and nodded. Søren nodded back. It was what he had expected.

"And his tongue?"

"He bit it off himself. His heart failed after a series of violent epileptic seizures and because no one was there to put a splint in his mouth, his tongue bore the brunt of the fits."

"Right, okay, I might as well get going then," Søren said, getting up and letting him know through his facial expression he was annoyed at having been summoned to the hospital.

"In theory, yes," Bøje shrugged. "Unless I can interest you in a charming detail which, in all likelihood, induced the seizures?"

Søren sat down again. Bøje peered at Søren over the rim of his reading glasses.

"It was an agonizing death, Søren," he then said. "It's not uncommon for the tongue or the lips to be bitten through in places, but I have never come across a case where the tongue was severed."

"I think your memory is faulty. There was the Lejre case and that one from Amager," Søren objected.

"Yes, but in those two cases—actually I know of three, but never mind," Bøje glanced at Søren. "In each severed-tongue case, other instruments were involved. It requires huge force to bite off a tongue. It isn't something you just decide to do," he said emphatically, and then his expression softened.

"And as it doesn't look like anyone was directly involved in Helland's death, it's my theory he experienced extreme convulsions which led, among other things, to the severing of his tongue and heart failure shortly afterward. There is no doubt that Lars Helland died a brutal and painful death." Bøje was looking urgently at Søren now.

"But, Søren Marhauge, my friend," he said, amicably. "That's nothing compared to the hellish agony he must have suffered while he was alive." A sincere and almost naked horror briefly revealed itself in Bøje's eyes, before he managed to herd his feelings back into their box.

"What do you mean?" Søren asked.

"He's riddled with bugs," Bøje said.

"Bugs?"

"Parasites of some sort, but I'm a forensic examiner, not a parasitologist, and I'm ashamed to say I've been unable to identify the little devils. All I can tell you is they are everywhere in his tissue. The strongest concentration is found in his muscles and central nervous system. It's unbelievable. For example, his brain is filled with encysted organic . . . growths. Do you understand what I'm saying? A parasite of some kind. I've sent samples to the chief medical officer at the Serum Institute, obviously. We'll know what we're dealing with tomorrow."

Søren was speechless.

"Yes, that's exactly how I felt when I realized what the poor man had been through. I can't imagine how he was able to function on a daily basis."

"Where do they come from?" Søren asked eventually.

"I don't know."

"But is this normal?" Søren wanted to know. He had never heard about parasites in human tissue before. A tapeworm, yes, threadworm, giardiasis, bilharziasis even, he had heard of, and he knew the latter was widespread in the Third World, but they were unwanted guests in the stomach, the intestines and, possibly, in the blood, but not in actual human tissue. It was the most disgusting thing he had ever heard.

"I don't know," Bøje repeated. "Like I said, I'm no parasitologist."

"How many of them would you estimate he had in him?" Søren asked.

Bøje picked up his sheet.

"Around 2,600 in total, spread across nerve, muscle, and connective tissue . . . a relatively high concentration in his brain . . ." Søren held up his hand.

". . . and one in his eye," Bøje said. "It was visible."

Søren shook his head in disbelief. "Listen," he said. "Are you say-ing Professor Helland didn't die from natural causes?"

"Again I'm tempted to take a pass on guessing," Bøje said gravely. "On the one hand, his death is exceedingly natural. His system col-lapsed, and it was exclusively down to his superb physical condition and strong constitution that it didn't happen much sooner. And like I said: I don't know enough about parasites to be specific, but if I can speak off the record, my immediate and most pressing concern is obviously: how did the little devils get into him?" Bøje narrowed one eye.

"A disturbing thought," he went on. "On the other hand, Helland was a biologist, and who knew what he was up to? Perhaps it was a work-related injury? Perhaps he knocked over a dish in his lab?"

"The man was an ornithologist," Søren objected.

"The source of the infection could be birds. It's pure guesswork for my part, and I don't enjoy that, but we have a distinguished expert, Dr. Bjerregaard, on parasitology at the Serum Institute and I've already spoken to her. She promised me she would embed the samples in paraffin, slice them before going home today and exam-ine them first thing tomorrow morning. At twelve noon we'll have the answer. And then there is Professor Moritzen at the College of Natural Science. She's one of the world's leading parasitologists and worked for years in South America and Indonesia, which have huge parasite problems. She's definitely the right person to talk to. She can explain to you how all these little critters ended up inside Lars Helland." Bøje paused, then he held up his index finger.

"Meanwhile, I have some more fascinating information to share with you. Lars Helland had a fair number of recent fractures that were left to heal by themselves; not a pretty sight in some places. He had broken three fingers on his left hand, two on his right and two toes on his right foot within the last six months. Further, he had scar-ring on his scalp from violent seizures and two minor hematoma in his brain, neither of them in a dangerous location, but they're there."

Bøje had been hunched over his papers, now he looked up at Søren. "I can also tell you he has had brain surgery, eight to ten years ago? Not that it matters and, apart from the two hematoma, there is no sign of brain disease. I just thought I would mention it. Now, about the fractures. I called a colleague of mine in the ER and asked him to check their records. He owed me a favor and, yes, I do know it's illegal." Bøje raised his hand to preempt Søren's objection. "Helland never visited the ER in the last year. Not once. Obviously, he might have seen his own doctor, you'll have to check that, but he definitely never went to the ER here, even though several of his injuries would require immediate medical assistance. The damage resembles those of victims of domestic violence, women who are too scared to see a doctor because they know it would mean a week in jail for the husband. If Helland's body hadn't been crawling with parasites, I would have suggested he might have been abused. Now, of course, my guess is the fractures are connected to the parasites. Why he was never patched up is a different story altogether . . ." Bøje gave Søren a knowing look as if to say that was Søren's department.

"Could his injuries alone have killed him?"

"No," Bøje said. "Lars Helland died from 2,600 uninvited organic growths in his tissue. I'm 100-percent sure."

Søren's knees wobbled as he stood up.

After his visit to the hospital, Søren drove home as though the devil was on his back. The sky had been gray and heavy all day, but while Søren had been in the basement with Bøje, patches of blue had broken through and the temperature had dropped. Søren rolled down the window and felt the sharp air against his face.

What the hell just happened?

He pulled behind a truck and reduced his speed.

Easy now.

Once he got home, he cooked dinner and sat down to eat. Suddenly, he felt crawling and prickling underneath his clothes. His groin itched, and after he wolfed down his food he took a shower. His cheek tingled, and so he shaved. Finally, he tried to check himself for head lice and spent ages staring at his big toenail. Did he have a fungal infection? How had those ghastly creepy-crawlies entered that poor man? He couldn't come up with a single explanation. Had Helland eaten one of them? How had it multiplied? Had it reproduced once it was inside him? Was it airborne? Or in the drinking water? He paced up and down the living room. Then he fetched a beer and told himself to give it a rest.

Early the following morning, Søren drove to Copenhagen, bursting with pent-up energy. From the car he called Helland's widow, Birgit. He got the answering machine. He asked her to call him as soon as possible. Then he called his secretary and asked her to find the number for Professor Moritzen, a parasitologist at the University of Copenhagen. He liked making Linda laugh, but this morning he failed. She called him back three minutes later. He had to move to the slow lane to write down the number and hoped none of his more officious colleagues were around. He called Professor Moritzen and pulled back into the fast lane.

"Hello?" Hanne Moritzen answered at the first ring. She sounded sleepy and distant. When he introduced himself, she went very quiet for a moment.

"Is Asger all right?" she whispered, almost inaudibly. Søren had done this a million times before, so he quickly reassured her.

"I'm not calling about your family."

He heard her breathe a sigh of relief and gave her two seconds to process the false alarm before saying, "I would very much welcome your help regarding some parasites we've found in connection with a death. Yesterday, Bøje Knudsen, the Deputy Medical Examiner, told me no one knows more about parasites than you."

Professor Moritzen was clearly relieved.

"Is it urgent? I drove up to my cottage late last night, and I wasn't planning on returning to Copenhagen until Wednesday."

Søren thought about it, and they agreed he would call her back when he knew more about just how urgent it was. Professor Moritzen wanted to know what questions he might have and Søren concluded the conversation by saying: "I'm afraid I can't disclose that at this stage, but I'll obviously explain the circumstances to you, if it turns out we need your expertise. For now, I would like to thank you for your time."

Søren was about to hang up when Professor Moritzen said, "Does this have anything to do with the death of Lars Helland?"

"You knew Lars Helland?" Søren said before he could stop himself.

"Yes, we both worked at the institute, but in different departments. I've just heard what's happened. I'm very sorry." She sounded genuinely upset. They ended the conversation.

Søren parked in the basement under Bellahøj police station and was slow-clapped by his colleagues when he arrived for the morning briefing, five minutes late. He summarized Bøje's unofficial conclusion and saw how nausea colored every face. Søren's colleague reported on his visit to Helland's widow and daughter the day before. This had, not surprisingly, been depressing. The daughter, Nanna, had been on her own, and the officer had stayed with her while Mrs. Helland rushed home. The girl had cried her heart out, and her mother sat on the sofa hugging her for a long time before the officer had been able to ask them questions. A family friend was called to comfort the daughter. Mrs. Helland insisted her husband was in great shape. He was a cycle-racing enthusiast, a hobby he had enjoyed for years, and he also played squash and was a runner, but then Mrs. Helland remembered Helland's father had died from a heart attack at an early age, and soon convinced herself that a similar fate had now robbed her of her husband. At this point, everyone looked at Søren, as though a collective decision had been made that he would be the one to go back to the villa in Herlev and break the news to the widow about Helland's uninvited guests.

No one touched the pastries, quivering with yellow custard, on the table.

At noon, Søren and Henrik arrived at the Serum Institute. It was yet another trip through a bewildering maze of clinical corridors, and Søren gave up trying to find his bearings. The woman escorting them swept through the building with familiar ease, pressed buttons, turned corners, opened doors, and led them, at last, to a light and pleasant laboratory. A woman rose from one of the microscopes, smiled, and introduced herself as Dr. Bjerregaard. She offered them a seat in a low office at the center of the room.

"I've looked at the samples," she said, once they had sat down. "And there's no doubt the parasite is an advanced cystic stage of the pork tapeworm, *Taenia solium*. It takes between seven to nine weeks for a viable cysticercus to grow and, in my opinion, the patient was infected three to four months ago, at the most." She looked briefly at the two police officers.

"*Taenia solium* is a member of the phylum *Platyhelminthes*, or as they're more commonly known, flatworms. In its adult stage, *Taenia solium* is a parasite in humans where it feeds on intestinal fluid. Inside the intestines, it deposits proglottids, as they are called, which leave their host through feces. Each proglottid contains approximately forty thousand fertilized eggs. From human feces, the eggs access the secondary host, also known as an intermediate host, which, in the case of *Taenia solium*, are pigs. Pigs acting as intermediate hosts, by the way, are the primary reason why *Taenia solium* cysticercosis is mainly found in countries where animals and humans are in close contact, for example, in households in developing countries where people defecate in areas accessible to pigs. We know of hardly any cases in the West, where animals and humans live separately, nor in Muslim or Jewish areas, where pork isn't consumed."

Again she looked briefly from Søren to Henrik, and didn't appear to have much faith in their ability to keep up with her. She seemed to be contemplating something; then she rose and produced a whiteboard, which descended silently from the ceiling. She grabbed a felt-tip pen and accompanied her explanation with simple drawings.

"Inside the pig, the egg hatches and the bloodstream transports the larva until it attaches itself to muscle tissue, nervous tissue, or subcutaneous connective tissue, where it develops into a cysticercus, a dormant cyst, whose further development isn't triggered until the pig is eaten—by humans, for example." Her hands flew across the board. "Inside the human stomach, the cysticercus wakes up from hibernation, attaches itself to the intestines where it grows into a tapeworm, thus completing its life cycle."

Søren felt nauseated. He stared at his notepad, where he had scribbled down a few words. He was about to say something, but Dr. Bjerregaard beat him to it. She put the cap back on her pen.

"A tapeworm is harmless and won't necessarily cause its host to fall ill," she said. "As a result, you can host even very long tapeworms for a long period of time without knowing that you're infected. In the vast majority of cases, the tapeworm is discovered by chance, during an operation or an autopsy. They normally grow six to eight feet long, and when a tapeworm is discovered, the host is given medication that kills the tapeworm and it's expelled from the host with feces. Unpleasant, certainly, but as I said, quite harmless."

Søren was close to retching. At the same time his brain was troubled by a discrepancy.

"I'm not sure I quite understand," he stuttered. "Professor Helland didn't have a tapeworm, but carried . . ." Søren checked his notes, "cysticercus." Dr. Bjerregaard waited patiently.

"That's correct. However, I haven't finished my explanation," she said calmly. "The life cycle of parasites is a complex area, even for a great many biologists, and in order for you, as lay people, to understand what I'm telling you, I need to give you some basic information." She suddenly looked at the two men as though she was enjoying herself tremendously.

"Yes, of course. Sorry," Søren said. Henrik looked sick.

Søren expected Dr. Bjerregaard to launch into the second half of her disgusting lecture, but she merely said, "The logical conclusion is . . . ?" She looked sternly at the two men.

"That Helland ate shit," Henrik blurted out. "Gross."

Søren glared at Henrik.

"It means," he said, addressing Dr. Bjerregaard, "that Helland somehow ingested a tapeworm egg." On realizing the implications, he fell silent.

"Or, to be precise, 2,600 eggs," Dr. Bjerregaard interjected. "If that's the number of cysticerci Bøje found in the tissue of the diseased, then it would equal 2,600 eggs."

Søren managed to suppress his revulsion to such an extent that he could follow her logic. "But he didn't ingest a whole . . ." he checked his notes again, "proglottid?"

"That would be impossible to know."

Søren detected a microscopic smile at the corner of her mouth.

"If the proglottid carried more than forty thousand eggs, you would have expected many more than 2,600 cysticerci. However, there might be several factors why only 2,600 managed to develop." She shrugged. "The point is Lars Helland acted as the intermediate host, and that happens very rarely in these latitudes. During my thirty years here, I've only come across three cases of human intermediate host infection, and they were all discovered in people who had recently returned from countries with a high prevalence of *Taenia solium*, such as Latin America, non-Islamic Asia, and Africa. Do you know if Helland spent time in a high-risk country?"

"We'll be checking that. The parasite theory is still very new to us," he said, by way of apology, and continued, "How can you tell how long the cysticerci have been in Helland's tissue?"

"The host body forms calcium capsules around the cysticercus, to protect itself from the foreign object, and in the capsule, the cysticercus awaits its next developmental stage. You can determine the exact age of the cysticercus by measuring the thickness of the calcium shell. This would normally take place in pigs, which will be eaten sooner or later, and this places an upper limit on how calcified the capsule becomes. However, humans are unlikely to be eaten, aren't they? The growth of the cysticercus is generally very slow, and as Helland's cysticerci were fairly large, I would estimate that they'd developed over a long period of time. The capsules were thick and the cysticerci would undoubtedly have demanded more and more room. To begin with, they would have caused Professor Helland only mild irritation, but in time they would have become a pathological condition, and I can't imagine how he coped with it. Cysticerci have a preference for the central nervous system, and from records—from Mexico, for example, where the occurrence of humans infected with cysticerci is high—82 percent of cysticerci had attached themselves to nerve tissue. Otherwise they prefer muscular and subcutaneous tissue, in that order."

"What about symptoms?" Søren asked. Bjerregaard pursed her lips.

"The symptoms of an infected patient depend on several factors. Generally, you'll expect to find a positive correlation between the number of cysticerci and the extent of the symptoms. However, it depends on where the cysticerci are located. Forty thousand cysticerci located exclusively in muscle tissue can, in theory, cause less damage to their host than five unfortunately located cysticerci in nerve tissue. Muscular tissue tolerates the uninvited guests surprisingly well, and their presence may not cause muscular pain until the very late stages. However, if they are located in the central nervous system, it's a completely different matter. As the cysticercus grows, it takes up more room and diverts blood supply from the surrounding tissue, and the tissue in the central nervous system is of far more critical importance for functionality than muscular tissue, for example. If the central nervous system is attacked, the patient will experience severe seizures of an epileptic nature, the same as have been observed in brain tumor patients. In addition, the patient will experience sudden blackouts, and very likely suffer from severe motor problems and spasms. Bøje Knudsen informed me the deceased had a fairly high concentration of cysticerci in his brain tissue, and he showed signs of multiple fractures and falls. That makes perfect sense."

She allowed the conclusion to hang in the air before she continued. "If the cysticerci are discovered in time, the patient will be given medication and/or surgery, depending on the number of cysticerci, their location, and how advanced their development is. In the case of the deceased, the cysticerci weren't discovered which, in itself, is incredible. To me, it's a physiological mystery how the deceased managed to go to work on the day he died."

A moment of silence followed, then Dr. Bjerregaard said, "Anything else I can do for you gentlemen today?"

Søren was taken aback. He wasn't used to being shown the door before he had announced he had no further questions. Dr. Bjerregaard glanced at her watch and pursed her lips again.

"Can you explain how Helland was infected?" Søren said, refusing to be brushed off.

"No," Dr. Bjerregaard replied. "I certainly can't."

She sounded almost hurt, and Søren realized what a stupid question it had been. It was the equivalent of asking the mechanic what caused a car crash.

"But, like I said," she carried on, giving Søren a final look, "either he ingested feces, or something which had been in contact with infected feces—and all things considered, that's highly unlikely. Or he worked with live tapeworms and was accidentally infected, which doesn't really add up, either. There are parasites that infect their host through the skin, the blood-sucking Japanese mountain leech, for example, which causes bilharziasis, but *Taenia solium* has to be ingested via the digestive tract to complete its life cycle, so even if we assume the deceased had a work-related accident, I still can't see how he could have been infected. You would expect a biologist who happens to drop a test tube to take precautions immediately, and you would most certainly not expect him to go to lunch without washing his hands after an accident involving *Taenia solium*. My guess is Professor Helland must have spent time in a high-risk area within the last six months, and that was where he was infected. It's still hard to imagine how, but as I said, it does happen."

Søren looked at Dr. Bjerregaard for a long time, before he said, "And if it's none of the above?"

Bjerregaard stood up.

"The deceased lived in excruciating pain and died as a result of this infection. The idea that he was infected accidentally is unpleasant enough in itself. The suggestion that someone infected him deliberately, well, that's not a thought I would like to pursue. Besides, to my ears it sounds highly implausible. It requires biological competence to extract a proglottid from infected feces, and it would be difficult for a layperson to clean that kind of organic material without destroying it. And even if you were successful, the rest of the plan seems rather far-fetched. It's regrettable and horrifying that the deceased died under such dramatic circumstances, but I find it hard to see how a crime could have been committed. Very hard." Bjerregaard's face made it clear their meeting was over.

"How do you store your material?" Søren persisted. Dr. Bjerregaard flashed an irritated look at Søren before she relented.

"It's impossible to gain access to material here at the Serum Institute, if that's what you're insinuating. That's self-evident. We store far more dangerous material than tapeworms. HIV, hepatitis C, Ebola, avian flu. And it's obviously impossible," she shot Søren a sharp look, "to force entry and steal such material. And if anyone were to succeed, only an expert would know how to treat the material to keep it alive. If someone broke into our basement and nicked a test tube, the contents would die and, consequently, cease to be infectious before the thief was halfway down the street."

"Are you the only facility that stores live organic material?" Søren wanted to know.

"We store the majority. But, as you may know, there's the parasitologist, Hanne Moritzen, at the University of Copenhagen. And Professor Moritzen has a substantial supply, otherwise she wouldn't be able to do her work. But she's Denmark's biggest expert, and I can promise you she treats her material with the utmost care. She'll be awarded a Nobel Prize for her brilliant work in the Third World one day. She would never take safety lightly. Never."

This declaration concluded the meeting, and Søren and Henrik left the Serum Institute in silence. When they were back in the car, Henrik was about to say something, but Søren stopped him.

"No," he said. "Just no."

They drove through the city without speaking. Søren leaned back in his seat and looked out of the window, where trees and houses rushed past. He felt he was on very thin ice.

* * *

Back at the station, Søren went to his office and drank three cups of tea. Professor Helland had died from 2,600 parasites in his nerve and muscular tissue, and he had sustained multiple fractures and other injuries. What the hell did it all mean? Before he had time to think it through, he called Mrs. Helland to ask if she was at home. Ten minutes later he was on his way to Herlev. If Professor Helland had been murdered, and this was now a possibility, Søren could no longer ignore the fact that there was a 98 percent probability the killer would be found among family or close friends. Birgit Helland had just gone straight to the top of his list of suspects.

Mrs. Helland offered him a seat in a large, airy room and called down her daughter from the first floor. Both women were red-eyed. Without revealing any details, Søren explained that Helland appeared to have suffered from a tropical infection, and the police were looking for a possible link between the infection and his death. Mrs. Helland's reaction was a cross between denial and shock. A tropical infection? That's impossible, she said, over and over. Her husband had never visited the tropics. He had a fear of flying. It had been a source of endless frustration, as the vast majority of bird symposia and conferences were held abroad, and every time he had had to send his young colleague, Erik Tybjerg. He only traveled to places he could reach by train or by car. Nanna sat beside her mother, crying. Mrs. Helland obviously wanted to know more about the tropical infection, but Søren said that at this stage in the investigation, he was unable to provide her with further details. Investigation? Mrs. Helland's jaw dropped, and Søren explained that while a heart attack was regarded as "natural causes," they had now learned something that meant yesterday's conclusion no longer applied. Helland's death was now being treated as "suspicious," and this forced him to withhold certain information due to the ongoing investigation.

Mrs. Helland was outraged. "Are you suspecting me? Because if you are, just go on and say so."

"I'll do everything I can to find out how and why your husband died," he said, avoiding her question. "Until then I'm asking you to trust me. Will you do that, please?"

She looked skeptical, but Nanna nodded. Eventually Birgit Helland agreed.

Nanna left to go to the lavatory, and Søren started asking about Professor Helland's health.

"Lars was in great shape," his widow protested.

"So, in your view, he was well?"

"Of course, I've just said so. Nearly nine years ago Lars had surgery for a brain tumor. It was discovered early, the tumor was removed, and there's been nothing since. He went for regular check-ups. He was in great shape," she repeated.

"So no signs of illness?"

"No!"

Søren thanked her, got up and left, unable to decide whether Mrs. Helland simply knew nothing about parasites or fractures, or whether she was devious enough to hide it.

When Søren got back to the police station, he called the Natural History Museum and asked to be put through to Erik Tybjerg. The telephone rang for a long time before the switchboard operator informed him Dr. Tybjerg wasn't in his office, but she would send him an e-mail asking him to call back. Søren sighed.

There was a knock on the door and Sten appeared. Sten was the crime squad's computer analyst, and since yesterday he had been busy examining Helland's computer. Søren had barely given the computer a second thought; he had been convinced he wouldn't have to devote much time to this case. Overcome by sudden guilt, he asked Sten for his verdict.

"Professor Helland's e-mail account was opened in February 2001," Sten began. "Approximately 1,500 e-mails are stored on the server, and I've been through them all." He looked drained.

"The vast majority are work-related, apart from those he sent to his wife, Birgit Helland, who works at the Humanities College of the University of Copenhagen, and to his daughter, Nanna. The only interesting thing I discovered was that for the last four years Lars Helland exchanged twenty-two e-mails with a professor of ornithology at the University of British Columbia—a guy named Clive Freeman. Mean anything to you?"

Søren shook his head.

"They disagree about something," Sten went on, "and they refer repeatedly to each other's papers in various scientific journals, such as *Scientific Today*, which I've heard of, but also a range of other journals that I haven't. To begin with, their correspondence is relatively balanced, but it changes in early summer. The tone of their e-mails shows they're trying to maintain the illusion that they're fine, honorable scientists engaged in a duel, but it becomes obvious on numerous occasions that Freeman is increasingly cornered and Helland is enjoying it big time. Twice, Freeman actually threatens Helland." Sten handed Søren a printout with highlighted sentences.

"At the end of June, there is unexplained silence. Nothing in their correspondence up until then indicates why, and even though I did some searching on the Internet, I haven't been able to find a plausible cause for their sudden ceasefire. However, shortly afterward, on the ninth of July, to be exact, Helland starts receiving anonymous e-mails." Sten pulled out a new file and extracted a small pile of printouts. "And now the tone is brutal and blunt. Someone is threatening Helland."

"Did Clive Freeman send them?" Søren asked.

Sten shook his head. "I'm fairly sure he didn't. The tone is completely different. The person making the threats has only one aim: to scare Helland. The threats consist of one sentence only."

Søren waited.

"'You will suffer for what you have done.'"

Søren frowned. "Did Helland reply to them?"

Sten nodded. "And he seems to find the threats highly amusing. Perhaps he thinks they're coming from Professor Freeman and are merely empty threats, or maybe . . . well, he just doesn't take them seriously."

"Sender unknown, you said?"

Sten nodded again. "A Hotmail address. Whoever created it registered themselves as 'Justicia Sweet.' Neat, eh? The person who threatened Helland could be anyone."

Søren buried his face in his hands and groaned.

"Anything else?" he asked.

"There is. I don't know how important this is, but Helland seems to have unfinished business with another colleague." Sten narrowed his eyes. "In the ten days leading up to his death, there was a fierce exchange of opinions between the deceased and Johannes Trøjborg." He paused to let the sentence take effect.

"However, in contrast to the exchange between Helland and Freeman, it was easy to figure out what the problem is. They appear to be cowriting a scientific paper and Johannes Trøjborg expresses dissatisfaction with Helland's lack of effort. Johannes wants Helland to pull out, so Johannes becomes the sole author of the paper, and Helland is refusing."

Søren nodded, and Sten carried on.

"There's more. I only started noticing it in the e-mails Helland sent over the last five to six weeks. He became very careless. His e-mails are littered with typos, and those sent in the last three to four weeks are practically illegible. Have a look at this." Sten handed Søren a printout which read:

I ca'nt elph yu bcase we d'nt argee. Soory, se yo tmorrrow at mu office a 10 a..m as arrrnged. L.

"You wouldn't call that standard spelling, would you?" Søren remarked, and then he realized the obvious.

"Sten," he exclaimed and looked utterly revolted. "Helland's brain was teeming with parasites. No wonder he couldn't type."

When Sten had left, Søren called Professor Moritzen again to insist on a meeting. She was still in her cottage, she protested. Søren checked his watch, asked her for the address, and told her he would be there as quickly as the highway traffic would allow him. Reluctantly, she agreed.

Then he called Johannes Trøjborg. Søren's intuition told him that the account given by the transparent Johannes was genuine. Still, he wanted Johannes to explain why he hadn't mentioned his disagreement with Helland. The telephone rang repeatedly, but no one answered.

*　*　*

Søren found Professor Moritzen's cottage, with great difficulty, in a resort at Hald Beach. It was a small, well-maintained cottage on a huge plot, like a building block on a football field. The cottage consisted of a single airy and sparsely furnished room, with a few Japanese-inspired objects placed directly on the floor. Hanne Moritzen served an almost white but surprisingly strong tea in Japanese cups and offered Søren something he thought was chocolate, but it turned out to be a foul-tasting Japanese concoction. She laughed when she saw the look on his face.

She's not a happy woman, Søren thought instinctively, and felt sad. Anna Bella Nor wasn't exactly a picture of happiness, either, but she had her rage, and rage, at least, sparked life. Hanne Moritzen had given up, and her defeat had left permanent traces in her dull silver eyes. However, she was articulate, precise, and far more accommodating than Søren had expected after their telephone conversation. She was wearing soft clothes, and her hair was loosely gathered in a ponytail.

Søren tried to explain the situation as best he could. He passed on Dr. Bjerregaard's best wishes, though she hadn't asked him to. Hanne Moritzen went pale when Søren summarized the autopsy and mentioned the 2,600 cysticerci, and he noticed how her eyes flickered and her hands trembled slightly before she regained her composure. Søren asked to use the bathroom and when he came back, she had calmed down and gave, without prompting, her opinion on the matter. She was adamant Professor Helland couldn't have been infected at work accidentally.

"He was a vertebrate morphologist," she said, as if that explained everything, and then she added: "He hasn't been in contact with parasites in the course of his work since the obligatory introduction to parasitology at the start of his degree in the 1970s. It's a highly specialized field, and Lars Helland went completely in the opposite direction. Parasitology and vertebrate morphology are about as far removed from each other as psychiatry and orthopedic surgery."

In the next half hour Professor Moritzen confirmed all of Dr. Bjerregaard's hypotheses.

"The last registered case of cysticercosis in Denmark was in 1997," she informed him. "The patient, a twenty-eight-year-old male, presented with violent skin symptoms after a lengthy stay in Mexico. We soon located nine cysticerci in his subcutaneous tissue and all were surgically removed. And do you know how he was infected? He got caught up between two gangs of boys hurling mud at each other, and the mud hit his mouth. It sounds very unlikely, but it was the only explanation we could come up with. There are plenty of other parasites that are easy for people from Western Europe to pick up, parasites that infect you directly through your skin, through food and drinking water, from unhygienic toilets or sexual transmission. But an actual cysticercus infection is rare, if hygiene levels are generally high. If we're talking about the tapeworm itself, well, of course, that's another matter. Raw or undercooked meat is a constant source of infection, and the human penchant for raw meat is, for some inexplicable reason, considerable."

"So, in your opinion, a natural infection is unlikely?"

"No," Professor Moritzen said. "A natural infection is the *only* explanation that is even vaguely possible, but it still remains highly improbable. I just don't buy that Helland had an accident in his lab."

"Why not?"

"Because he had no contact with parasites," she said, emphatically. "There is no living material in his department."

"Might he have become infected during a visit to the department of parasitology?"

"In theory, yes, but it's unlikely."

"Why?"

Professor Moritzen looked directly at Søren.

"Because I'm the head of that department, and I know who comes and goes, what leaves the department, who with, and why. It's a legal requirement."

"Dr. Bjerregaard estimated that Helland became infected three to four months ago," Søren stated, and looked back at her.

"That, too, sounds highly improbable," she said, locking eyes with him.

"Why?"

"Because it seems very unlikely that anyone could live in that state for several months. Have you ever pricked yourself on a cactus?" she asked. Søren shook his head.

"Its spikes are thin and transparent but scalpel-sharp and they dig deep into the palm of your hand. After just a few hours, they cause irritation and in only a few days each cut turns into an infected abscess. Imagine the same thing occurring in vital tissue. It's unrealistic, don't you see?"

Søren nodded.

"But maybe Helland's an exception?" she suggested. At first, Søren thought she must be joking, but her silver eyes looked gravely at him.

"Perhaps the locations of the cysticerci were such that he could still function? We know from brain tumors that it's a question of where the pressure is. Some people collapse when the tumor's the size of a raisin, others are fine until it's the size of an egg." She shrugged.

"This has really shocked you," Søren said, scrutinizing her. "You're trying to hide it, but I can sense it."

"Death *is* shocking," Hanne Moritzen replied in a neutral voice. "And I, more than anyone, can appreciate the hell he must have been living in, if Dr. Bjerregaard's time line is right. Of course I'm shocked at such an unpleasant death, and of course I want to know how it could have happened. I'm also sorry for his daughter. It's hard to live without your father." She flashed Søren a look of defiance.

"So you didn't know Lars Helland personally?"

"No," she replied. "He taught 'Form and Function' in the second term when I was a student. He was a good teacher. When I started working in the same building as him, we would run into each other from time to time and we would say hello. That's all."

"Are you married? Do you have children?" Søren asked.

"Excuse me, how is that relevant?"

He just stared at her and repeated his question.

"No, I've never been married, and I have no children," she then said. "Getting to this level in my profession requires many sacrifices."

Søren nodded. "Do you know if Professor Helland had any enemies?"

Hanne Moritzen laughed a hollow laugh, but didn't look even vaguely amused.

"Of course he had enemies. Professor Helland was a brilliantly gifted man who was never afraid to take center stage. If the rumors are to be believed, he drove his closest colleagues to the brink of madness. That's a recipe for making enemies, some might say. People who court controversy are often hated. Like I said, I barely knew him, but I instinctively liked him. He had drive, and he entered the arena of academic debate with all guns blazing—it made him a real asset to the faculty. For example, for years he has been at the forefront of a completely ridiculous and—allegedly—scientific row about the origin of birds. It provided the faculty with loads of press coverage even though, in my opinion, it's a total waste of column inches."

"Why?"

"Because birds are dinosaurs. The end. Kids can read that on the back of cereal boxes. When Anna told me it was the subject of her dissertation and she would be spending a year or more explaining Helland and Tybjerg's storm in a teacup, I was outraged. That dissertation will do nothing for her career, and I tried telling her that. It's much ado about nothing, if you ask me. That Canadian, whom Tybjerg and Helland are squandering their grants doing battle with, is a fool, and—"

"Are you saying that Clive Freeman—"

"Oh, yes, that's his name," Professor Moritzen interrupted him.

"Do you think he might have infected Helland with parasites as an act of revenge?"

Hanne Moritzen laughed out loud.

"No, I promise you I don't think that for a second! I can't imagine why anyone would go around infecting other people with parasites . . ." She hesitated. "That would be completely insane."

"I understand that you know Anna Bella Nor. Do you know anyone else from Helland's department?" Søren asked.

"Yes, I know them all, of course. Though I don't know the man Anna shares a study with very well. I've said hello to him a couple of times, when I popped in to see Anna."

"But you and Anna Bella Nor are friends?"

"In a way, yes. . . . She attended one of my summer courses, and we got along really well."

Søren saw a hint of warmth touch Professor Moritzen's eyes.

"I always wanted to have a daughter," she said and almost looked shy. "Anna reminds me a little of myself when I was younger." She smiled a wry smile before she continued. "I also know Professor Ewald and Professor Jørgensen from the faculty. The three of us have been working there a lifetime."

She got up and lit the fire in the fireplace. Søren had run out of questions. He got up to leave and she saw him out. It had started to snow. Large fluffy snowflakes descended in columns toward the ground, which was already white.

"Snow at this time of the year," Professor Moritzen commented, and shivered.

"Yes, it's a very odd autumn," Søren said, and shook her hand.

"I'll be driving back to Copenhagen early tomorrow morning," she said. "If there is anything else, I'll be in my office."

Søren nodded.

As he drove toward Copenhagen, he suddenly missed Vibe. Uncomplicated, gentle Vibe, who always held her blond head high and looked on the bright side of life. The department of Natural Science could do with a few people like her.

Chapter 7

Tuesday night Anna lay awake and it wasn't until four o'clock the following morning that she fell in to a deep, dreamless sleep. She woke up at 8:30 a.m. and called Cecilie. Everything was fine. Lily was happy and hadn't missed her mom at all. Anna took a bath and ate a bowl of muesli.

"She hasn't missed you at all," she sneered as she put on her army jacket and boots. She would pick up Lily at 4:10 p.m., and she would be with her daughter tonight. At last.

It was past ten when Anna entered the department of Cell Biology and Comparative Zoology. In the corridor she met Professor Ewald, who was carrying four thermoses. They had last seen each other at the police station where Professor Ewald had been in tears, and yesterday neither Professor Ewald nor Professor Jørgensen had come to work.

"Ah, there you are," she said, looking straight at Anna. "Could you give me a hand, please?"

"What are you doing?" Anna asked, baffled.

"Making coffee. We're holding a memorial gathering for Lars in the senior common room in half an hour. Just the department and people who knew him through work."

Anna blinked and took the thermos Professor Ewald handed her.

"Don't you normally hold memorial services after the funeral?"

"Yes," Professor Ewald said. "But Professor Ravn wants it done this way. Helland has only been dead for two days, but rumors are already spreading like wildfire all over the university. Ravn intends to use the service to try to quash them. Lars will be buried on Saturday, and you're welcome to attend, if you feel like it." Professor Ewald's gaze lingered briefly on Anna.

"So what are the rumors saying?" Anna followed Professor Ewald into the kitchenette, where the older woman slammed the thermoses on the kitchen table and spoke in a shrill voice.

"Rumor has it that Professor Helland was murdered and the police think the killer is someone who knew him very well and might even have worked with him. And do you know something else?" she snorted. "I find those rumors odious. *If* he was murdered, well, then it's either me, Professor Jørgensen, Johannes, or you who are the prime suspects. And that doesn't bear thinking about."

"Or any one of the five hundred employees at the faculty who wanted Helland dead. Metaphorically speaking, of course," Anna added quickly.

Professor Ewald started to cry.

"I can't get the image of him out of my head," she sobbed and hid her head in her hands. "By God, I hated that man, but he didn't deserve that."

Something occurred to Anna.

"Professor Ewald?" she said.

Professor Ewald had sat down on a chair and was cleaning her glasses.

"Do you think Dr. Tybjerg will succeed Professor Helland?"

Professor Ewald momentarily looked lost.

"Tybjerg from the Natural History Museum?"

"Yes, Helland's colleague. My external supervisor."

"No, I can't imagine that," she said without hesitation.

Anna wrinkled her nose.

"Why not?"

"I don't know why Lars thought it was his job to push Erik Tybjerg like that. Dr. Tybjerg is extremely talented, there's no doubt about it, but if you ask me, he's completely unsuited to the University of Copenhagen and acts primarily as Helland's errand boy. For years it has been a mystery why Helland drags Tybjerg with him everywhere, even sending Tybjerg in his place. This will stop now, obviously. A Chair is the public face of a department and Tybjerg's clearly unsuitable. He was once allowed to teach 'Form and Function' for one term here because Helland assured us that he could. It was a complete disaster; the students complained about him. He spoke far too quickly, as if he was chanting, and when the students couldn't understand what he said, he lost his temper and walked out."

"But he's my supervisor," Anna said miserably. "My only supervisor."

"Honestly, Anna." Professor Ewald put on her glasses and said gently, "At the time you began your dissertation, some of us did wonder why you had been lumbered with those two. However, it seems to have worked out all right, so—"

"But I still think Dr. Tybjerg's a good supervisor," Anna protested. "A thousand times better than Professor Helland—no, a million times better."

Professor Ewald gave her a neutral look.

"Is that right?" she said eventually. "But you must agree that he's a bit peculiar? And the University of Copenhagen is a respected state institution, not a madhouse."

Professor Ewald got up and poured coffee into the thermoses.

Nearly thirty people gathered in the senior common room. Dr. Tybjerg was standing at the far end, his hands folded, and he was staring at the floor. Anna was relieved to see him and tried to catch his eye, but he didn't look up. Johannes rushed in at the last minute and squeezed in behind Anna, just as the door was closed. She turned to look at him. He smelled of fresh air and frost, and his wild, messed-up ginger hair gave him a haggard appearance. They had both spent the previous day working in the study and something of a toxic atmosphere had reigned. Johannes had made several attempts to strike up a conversation, but Anna had cut him dead. She had things to do. Twice, he had asked if she was still mad at him for what he had said to the police. She had denied it. He had begun making yet another apology, and she had held up her hand to stop him. "What's done is done," she said, "forget it." The truth was, she was hurt. Johannes was the last person she had imagined would let her down. When he flashed her a tentative smile in the senior common room, she intended to smile back, but instead she turned around to look at Professor Ravn.

The Head of Department started by lamenting the death and sending his condolences to Professor Helland's widow, Birgit, and their daughter, Nanna. It was a terrible loss to the department. Helland had worked there full-time since 1979 and published countless papers; a huge loss to the department, he said again, a loyal colleague. Anna was only half-listening as she stared at Dr. Tybjerg, trying to make him look up, but to no avail. Professor Ewald sobbed noisily. Helland's funeral would take place at Herlev Church this Saturday at 1 p.m. and the department would send flowers.

What was wrong with Tybjerg? Anna couldn't catch his eye, and he was standing absolutely still. Then Professor Ravn cleared his throat and said he would like to take this opportunity to ask for everyone's help with ending the rumor that Professor Helland had been murdered. He had been in close contact with the police, as he put it, and according to the information he had been given, there was every reason to think that Professor Helland had died of a heart attack. He fell silent and an eerie unease spread. The gathering started to dissolve and, out of the corner of her eye, Anna spotted Tybjerg heading straight for the exit. She went after him, but didn't catch up with him until far down the corridor leading to the museum.

"Dr. Tybjerg!" Anna called out. "Hey, Dr. Tybjerg. Wait. Have you got a minute?"

Tybjerg turned around, looked at her, but carried on walking. Finally Anna caught up to him.

"Hey," she exclaimed, irritated. "You got a train to catch or what?"

Tybjerg gave her a fraught look.

"No," he snapped.

"I've e-mailed you, called you, and dropped by your office. Where have you been hiding?" They reached the door to the stairwell; Dr. Tybjerg went up the stairs two at a time with Anna at his heels.

"If we presume a normal room temperature, rigor mortis will set in three to four hours after clinical death has occurred. After twelve hours it will, in most cases, be complete. The biochemical explanation of rigor mortis is simple ATP hydrolysis in the muscle tissue. This is not good, Anna," he said. "It's not good at all."

"No," Anna said, trying to fathom what Dr. Tybjerg was referring to. Helland's death? The rumors that he might have been killed? That Tybjerg would have to complete any outstanding research on his own? That Anna's viva might have to be canceled? What?

Dr. Tybjerg stopped abruptly and Anna nearly crashed into him.

"I can't talk to you right now. Not here. Come to the museum later. I'll be in the collection." Tybjerg looked urgently at her. "Don't tell anyone you're going to see me. Just let yourself in. I'll meet you there. Okay?"

"Tonight?" Anna frowned.

Dr. Tybjerg nodded, and then he disappeared.

Anna stood there for a moment. She could feel her heart pounding. Then she clenched her fist and closed her eyes. She had Lily tonight; she couldn't meet Dr. Tybjerg in the Vertebrate Collection. Shit! She considered chasing after him, but dropped the idea. Johannes was waiting for her outside the senior common room.

"You coming?" he called out.

She joined him, bristling with frustration. Her dissertation defense was in twelve days. Twelve days!

"Do you have to shuffle your feet like that, Johannes?" she snarled.

Johannes gave her a puzzled look, his face gray from lack of sleep; Anna felt ashamed at her behavior and was about to ask him how he was, but she couldn't find the right words.

"You're still mad at me," Johannes said, when he had closed the door to their study behind him. Anna sat down and switched on her computer.

"I know you're still mad at me. Can we talk about it, please?" he said gently.

Anna leapt up like a jack-in-the-box and shoved her chair at him. This made Johannes roll backward, frightened. Why couldn't he just leave her alone? Why couldn't he just shut up? Why was he even at the college? He had finished his thesis a hundred years ago, why couldn't he be somewhere else writing his grant application, somewhere he didn't disturb her all the time? She was fed up with being interrupted. She was fed up that no one took her work seriously. Not Helland, not Tybjerg, and now, it would appear, not Johannes either. Anna wasn't thinking straight, she just exploded. Johannes blinked, then he took his jacket and his bag and walked out.

Anna sat down, flabbergasted. On impulse, she ran out into the corridor and yelled: "What kind of a friend are you, anyway?" She stamped her foot and Johannes stopped. He turned around and walked back to her, until only their breaths separated them.

He said, "Anna, I'm your friend, and you would know that if you just took a moment to think about it. I've apologized for what I said to the police. I shouldn't have done it, but I was upset. Nothing gives you the right to be so hard on me, to give me the silent treatment for days. Everyone's under a lot of pressure right now. Not just you. I'm your friend," he repeated, "but right now I'm drowning in my own problems and I don't have the energy to be your punching bag. Helland has died, and yes, that's terribly inconvenient for Anna Bella and her dissertation, but the man's dead! Don't you get it?" Johannes wagged a finger at her. "His daughter has lost her father, Birgit has lost her husband, I've lost my . . . friend. Do you think you could snap out of your self-pity for just one second and realize not everything in the world revolves around you? I don't have time for your whining right now. Helland's dead, and I've enough of my own shit to deal with. I can't sleep, and I can't take any more." He spun around and walked down the corridor. Suddenly, he turned, looked at her sweetly and sneered, "And anyway, you don't need others to take your work seriously, Anna. You're quite capable of doing that yourself."

When Johannes had gone, Anna closed the door to their study. The tears started rolling down her cheeks. It happened again and again. She was treated unfairly and when she retaliated, her reaction obliterated everything and the injustice *she* had suffered faded into the background. Just like with Troels and Karen. Suddenly, it was all her fault they were no longer friends. As if Troels was completely blameless! It was also her fault Lily's father no longer lived with them.

"No guy will put up with the way you behave," Thomas had said, conveniently ignoring the reasons for her behavior. And countless times Jens had said, "Don't be so hard on your mom, Anna Bella!"

As if Cecilie had never been hard on her!

And now Johannes. It was *he* who had blurted something utterly ludicrous to the police, but suddenly *she* was the one being unreasonable!

It took her a long time to calm down. She blew her nose and made herself a cup of tea. Once her anger subsided, she felt ashamed. Johannes was her friend, she knew that. He was right. He had helped her so much in the past year.

At the start of June, she had hit her second dissertation crisis and come close to throwing in the towel. She had read everything about the controversy surrounding the origin of birds and familiarized herself, in detail, with the scientific implications of feathers. She had long been convinced that Helland and Tybjerg's position was scientifically the stronger, and that it was nonsense for Freeman to carry on fighting to convince the world of the opposite. All experts agreed that birds were present-day dinosaurs, and that predatory dinosaurs, theropods as they were called, had undergone an evolutionary reduction when they started hunting their prey by leaping between knolls and tree stumps before moving on to trees. Once up there, they developed first a primitive gliding flight between treetops and, later, actual flight. All the evidence pointed to dinosaurs having feathers, even before flying became a part of their behavior.

What prompted the crisis was that Anna had no idea what to do with her newfound knowledge. Countless scientists before her had attacked Freeman's position. World-famous vertebrate scientists everywhere, ornithologists, laden with PhDs and chairmanships, had taken Freeman's arguments apart in papers, at symposia, and in books. But Freeman had remained immune to these experts. How could she, Anna Bella Nor, ever come up with a contribution that might add or change anything? Surely that was impossible? All she could do was repeat what had already been said and write a historical dissertation that reviewed the controversy from Solnhofen up until the present day. It would be nothing but a synopsis, and no student could be awarded even a pass for work that was ultimately a summary. She had to add something new.

Johannes had come to her rescue.

He had said: "Have you examined Freeman's underlying premises properly?" and she had nearly throttled him. Johannes was forever boring her with science theory and had written a highly intellectual theoretical science dissertation about Cambrian arthropods and been awarded a first. However, her dissertation was about bones and feathers, she had no use for his philosophical musings, she thought, and she had told him so. She had brushed him aside and carried on wallowing in her crisis. Finally, Johannes lost patience with her and gave her an ultimatum.

"Tomorrow morning, 10 a.m., in the lecture hall. If you don't show, you're on your own forever. I mean it."

That evening she reluctantly conceded that it would be in her best interest to show up.

When Johannes had failed to arrive by 10:10 a.m., she had been on the verge of leaving. She had just gotten up and reached for her bag when he stormed in, gasping for breath.

"Great," he panted, "you're here."

"It sounded like an order yesterday, not an offer."

Johannes pulled off his jacket and faced her.

"Anna," he said calmly, "it *is* an offer. You want out?"

Anna didn't dare nod even though everything inside her urged her to.

They went up to the board.

"Take a seat," Johannes said, pointing to the tall desk. She climbed up and looked at the empty board.

"Right, Anna Banana . . ." he said and quickly massaged his forehead. "When you say the word 'science,' most people imagine a strict, objective discipline that is impersonal, general, and true. We like and accept that literature, architecture, and politics are subjective, but most of us would bridle at this being applicable to, say, chemistry or biology." Johannes cleared his throat. "The strictly objective view of science is represented, among others, by the philosopher Karl Popper, who lived from . . . ah, that escapes my mind. . . Popper was in search of an absolute set of rules for science, and he used the so-called hypothetical-deductive method, which says scientific theories must always be tested by conclusive experiments. Only when a theory could be falsified, could it be called scientific. Do you follow?" Johannes looked directly at Anna.

"Er, no," Anna said. "Popper thought a theory was false when it was scientific?"

"No, of course not, you dork. Popper thought it was only when a theory was *open* to testing and could, possibly, be disproved, that it could be deemed scientific.

"At the start of the 1960s," he continued, "a new school of thought in scientific theory was born that wanted subjectivity to be acknowledged and included in our understanding of science. One of the frontrunners was the physicist Thomas Kuhn, who pointed out the value of subjectivity in science. I just want to interpose," Johannes said tapping his upper lip lightly, "that of course there are many different ways to interpret Kuhn, so it's not *absolutely* certain I'm right." He gave her a teasing look before he continued.

"Kuhn was later supported by a woman I have the greatest respect for, the brilliant science theorist Lorraine J. Daston, who in an attempt to solidify the role of the subjective in science introduced a concept she named the Moral Economy of Science. So we're talking about a shift in perception, with on the one hand Popper's demand for an absolute set of rules for science and, on the other, a more relative attitude, as proposed by Kuhn and Daston." Johannes wrote Kuhn on the board following by a colon.

"Of course, none of them was a genius working in isolation who suddenly saw the light, that goes without saying," he added, "but to simplify matters I'll give you the shortened version, okay?"

Anna nodded.

"Kuhn demonstrated that a scientist's choices are influenced by the personality and biography of that scientist, and that ultimately subjectivity determines what the scientist chooses. Kuhn, you won't be surprised to hear, attracted huge criticism and was accused of having a completely irrational understanding of science, but he responded by pointing out that making room for disagreement doesn't equal throwing open the doors to a misleading and totally subjective understanding of science, as long as"—Johannes raised his index finger—"the scientists in question are 100-percent loyal to their own explanations and can argue convincingly in case of any breaches of that loyalty." Johannes planted a hand on the desk either side of Anna and stood very close to her.

"Have you examined whether Freeman is consistent within his own work? Is he loyal to his own choices, and when he changes his explanations, is his argument satisfactory?"

"I don't know," Anna said.

Johannes took a step back.

"Let's move on," he said, and spent the next fifteen minutes reviewing Lorraine J. Daston's concept of the Moral Economy of Science. Anna listened in awe and made notes as Johannes's talent for abstract thinking unfolded before her.

"I think that's enough for today." He smiled. "But first let's summarize." He looked gravely at her. "Over to you."

"What?"

Johannes nodded.

Anna took her notes and jumped down from the desk. Suddenly the situation reminded her of her forthcoming dissertation defense, and her heart started pounding as she wiped the board, picked up a piece of chalk, and carefully accounted for her understanding.

Johannes looked pleased when she had finished and said: "Find out if Clive Freeman adheres to universal and established premises for sober science. If he doesn't," he snapped his fingers, "then you've got him."

"And if he does?"

"Then you're screwed," Johannes laughed.

Anna was about to sulk, but then she felt it. There was something. Something almost terrifyingly intangible, but vital. Something she could work with.

Over the following weeks she studied Popper, Kuhn, and Daston in detail, and as the days passed, two points emerged: scientists who contradicted themselves couldn't claim their theories were scientific; and scientists must, at any given time, be able to substantiate effectively any theories they propose or reject.

She revisited the controversy with a fresh pair of eyes. She reviewed Freeman's arguments for the umpteenth time, and they were just as well oiled, indisputable, and professional as they always had been, but to Anna's huge astonishment Freeman's scientific premises didn't bear scrutiny. Spurred on by renewed enthusiasm, she attacked Freeman's book *The Birds* again, and the contradictions sprung from the pages like mushrooms after a rain shower. Triumphantly, she slammed the desk and when Johannes, who had just entered the study at that point, gave her a quizzical look, she got up and kissed him on the cheek. Johannes giggled.

"I don't know how to thank you," she said. A scent of something dark and perfumed surrounded him.

"Ah, well," he said, shyly, "you'll think of something."

Two students walked noisily down the corridor, past the study, and interrupted Anna's train of thought. She massaged her forehead and felt ashamed. Her way of thanking Johannes had been to scream at him, and he hadn't deserved it. She tried calling him on his cell, but he didn't answer. She left a message and asked him to call her back. The air in the study was oppressive and uncomfortable. She called Dr. Tybjerg to cancel their meeting that evening, but there was no reply. Then she did some preparation for her dissertation defense. Just after 2 p.m. she packed up and left, locking the study behind her. Johannes still hadn't returned her call. She was outside in the cold air when she heard someone tap on a window. She turned and saw Professor Moritzen.

"Can I come in?" she mouthed. Hanne nodded.

"Have a seat," she said, when Anna entered her tasteful office. Anna sat in a molded chair and, without asking, Hanne handed her a cup of tea.

"I'll get straight to the point," she said with a quick glance at Anna. "I've a favor to ask you. Can this remain just between the two of us?"

Anna nodded.

"I presume you've heard about Helland?"

"Yes, of course."

"Good." Hanne looked briefly relieved. "Yesterday I had a visit from a police officer, Søren Marhauge. I've seen him here a few times, so I assume you know who he is? Very tall guy with short hair and dark eyes?"

Anna nodded a second time.

"He wanted to know if it was at all possible that the material came from my department, and—"

"What material?"

"The proglottids, obviously."

"I don't follow."

"Ah, so you don't know that . . ." she said.

"Know what?"

Hanne sighed and told Anna what she knew. Anna was shocked.

"Who did it?" she whispered.

"I refuse to believe that anyone did," Hanne said dismissively. "The material was in my care, and everyone who needs to work with live material must be approved by me before the material is released, and afterward they must account for how it was used in detail. Everything happens under strict control, and the people who work in the laboratory are colleagues I trust." She took a sheet of paper and reeled off a list of names. "All of us have worked with parasites our entire professional lives and we're very careful. Besides, it requires imagination to even think of infecting someone with mature eggs. It would have been much easier to push Helland out in front of a car, or shoot him even," she remarked drily.

"Could someone have stolen the material?"

"No!" Hanne sounded momentarily offended, then she sighed again. "Of course it's possible—in theory. It's also theoretically possible to steal the crown jewels. But it's very unlikely. You need to know how to treat the material, or it will die. Live organisms are complicated." She paused.

"So what's your explanation?" Anna asked.

"I think he was infected on a trip abroad," she said. "I know the police claim that Helland has never been outside Europe, but he doesn't have to have been. *Taenia solium* is cosmopolitan, because it spreads via pigs, so even though the number of incidents is infinitesimal, it's still a possibility. My conclusion: he must have been infected elsewhere." The expression in Hanne's eyes suddenly changed.

"I don't know if you're aware, but there is no permanent Parasitology department at the Institute of Biology now, nor will there be any teaching next year. The course and the department will be closed due to cuts."

"I don't understand." Anna was genuinely puzzled. "You still work here."

"I do, but when I leave, it's all over." Her eyes shone. "We weren't awarded a single grant to fund graduate programs, PhDs, or postdoctoral studies this year, and that means when the money runs out, well, that's it." Hanne fished out a thin string of pearls from under her blouse and started fidgeting with it.

"The Faculty Council controls the distribution of faculty grants and, like in any other council, they agree to an overall plan. What

to invest in and why. It's important for Denmark to have a com-
petitive research profile that not only matches what happens elsewhere in Europe, but also in the rest of the world. That said, few
people believe the Faculty Council bases its decisions exclusively
on what's best for Denmark." Hanne gave Anna a hard stare. "Of
course, a certain amount of nepotism exists in the charmed circle
that is the Faculty Council. You scratch my back and I'll scratch
yours. A mechanism that has undoubtedly enjoyed great popularity
since the government slammed its coffers shut," she added tartly.
"I'm not saying it's an easy job, and that's why I've always avoided
administrative work myself. You won't believe how much money we
need to save right now. Council members are under pressure, and
they experience, first hand, how even their own areas of research
are being slimmed down. They try to compensate for that in the
notorious faculty meetings. They trade pots of money and grants
like kids trade stickers, and when they make an announcement,
everyone holds their breath and crosses their fingers." She held her
breath for a moment.

"I do actually believe they're trying their hardest—up to a point—
and some level of self-promotion is unavoidable. Let me give you
an example: take the Natural History Museum's beetle collection.
We have one of the most impressive collections in the world, and
it's left to rot. There's no one to look after it, and no research happens within that field. Beetles are low status, they're not 'sexy.' The
Faculty Council shut down the department of Coleoptera Systematics, which used to be in this building. From an outside perspective, it seemed a small sacrifice, the department had only two staff,
Professor Helge Mathiesen, who was about to retire anyway, and
a very young scientist, Asger . . ." Hanne shook her head, as if she
had forgotten his surname. "He went into a total tailspin. Before
the summer break, he had a promising academic career ahead of
him, after the summer break, his department had been closed. For
a scientist who has micro-specialized within a specific field . . ."
Again she shook her head. "He's finished. It's the end of his science
career. That's the way it is. Certain areas of research are high status

because they reflect what's happening globally, others have high status because they're areas of interest to members of the council, whose decisions have huge consequences for all of us, depending on whether or not we work in a field that happens to be flavor of the month. Up until this year, I had never been directly affected by the council's priorities and have always been given my fair share. However, this spring, it was finally our turn. My turn. The department will be closing." Her voice rang hollow.

"They dropped the bombshell on the first day after Easter break. We have three years to finish our work. Research, which has already cost the Danish tax payer millions of kroner, and projects that—were we allowed to complete them—could save the lives of hundreds of thousands of people in the Third World where parasites kill people every day. Three years. That may not sound unreasonable to you, but it's the equivalent of building the Great Wall of China in an afternoon. It's a preposterous timetable." Hanne gave Anna a dark look. "My research is my life, Anna," she said. "I'm forty-eight, and I have devoted my life to my academic career."

Slowly Anna began to grasp the implications.

"And now you're scared you'll be fired on the spot if the material found in Helland is traced back to your department?"

"Yes," Hanne said.

"What do you want from me?" Anna asked.

Hanne shook her head softly. "Sorry, I was ranting. Listen, I can't start asking questions around your department. Not now, after what's happened. At worst, it will look suspicious; at best, it would be inappropriate. But I need to know about the investigation and, more importantly, in which direction it's moving." She looked almost beseechingly at Anna. "Will you help me, please?"

Anna placed her hands on her knees. "I'm not sure I understand. What do you want me to do?" she said.

"Keep your ears open. What are Svend and Elisabeth saying? What about the police? I know your chances will be limited, but just try to pay attention, please? And if you hear any rumors suggesting the parasites came from my stock"—for a moment she looked anxious—"please contact me immediately. It's important, Anna. I only have three years; after that the completion of our research projects will depend on outside funding, and I can promise you that if we are labeled as careless with potentially fatal material, we can forget about outside funding. The Tuborg Foundation is currently our main sponsor, and they only touch projects that are squeaky clean. I need to know if the ax is about to fall." She let go of the string of pearls, and it fell against her skin. "I need to be prepared."

Anna nodded slowly, and Hanne crumpled into the elegant sofa. She ran her hand through her hair and closed her eyes.

"I'm absolutely exhausted," she sighed.

Anna started wrapping her scarf around her neck and pulled up the hood of her jacket. Hanne kept her eyes closed and rested the back of her head against the wall.

"I need to pick up my daughter," Anna said.

Lily was kneeling on the ground, mesmerized by a polystyrene box full of seedlings, when Anna arrived to collect her. Her daughter held a watering can in her hand and listened dutifully as the nursery school teacher gave her instructions on how to water the seedlings. Anna sat down and watched her little girl from a distance. They had seen so little of each other and, for a moment, Lily seemed almost a stranger to her. She was her child. *Hers.*

All of a sudden, the sun broke through the large windows of the nursery school, and Anna heard Lily say, "My granny grows sunflowers."

The nursery school teacher listened, replied, and pushed back the soil around the seedlings where Lily's watering had been excessive, despite the instructions. Just as Anna was about to call her, Lily turned around. She dropped everything and leapt like a kid goat to her mother.

Anna noticed the earrings immediately. Two silver studs with glass beads. They caught the light. How long was it since she had last seen Lily? Two days? She decided not to say anything. Lily was pulling and pushing her, showing her around, jumping on the spot, climbing on to her lap, trying to slip her hands into Anna's sleeves and up to her armpits. When one of the teachers came to give Anna some information and she hushed Lily to make herself heard, Lily had a tantrum. She threw herself on the floor, kicking, so one of her socks fell off. Anna tried to distract her by pointing to a drawing of a clown and getting Lily to tell her about it. Lily ignored her. Anna tried to bribe Lily with the offer of hot chocolate. It appeased Lily, but only for a moment, then the tantrum resumed. Anna was at her wits' end and had no idea how to make Lily stop.

So she ended up scolding her. She didn't shout, but her voice was loud enough for one of the assistants to come over and help Lily put her coat on. Lily stopped crying and gave her mother a miserable look. Hand in hand, they walked down the path, out through the gate, across the communal garden and home to their apartment block. Anna promised herself she would never yell at Lily again. Back in the apartment, they watched *Teletubbies*. Anna nodded off next to her daughter and when she woke up, Lily was gone. Anna found her in her bedroom, where she was doing pretend cooking with beads.

"I want to go to Granny's," she said, when Anna came in and said hi. Anna squatted and tried to embrace her daughter.

"No, darling," she said, anxiously. "You need to be with me. You need to be with Mommy."

"I love Granny." Lily looked away and carried on with her cooking. She seemed contented. She babbled as she poured beads from one container into another and spiced up her dish with some chestnuts and four small birthday cake candles. Anna went into the kitchen and tried very hard not to cry. She cooked dinner. Cheese-and-bacon omelet with a green salad. She cooked peas and carrots for Lily as well. They had a nice time at the table. At first, Lily refused to eat and looked away when Anna tried to feed her. Then Anna pretended the fork had come alive and every time Lily tried to bite into it, it would squeal and hide behind the milk; then it would peek out and get scared the moment it saw Lily and her many teeth. Lily laughed so hard that she cried. A moment of harmony had been created. And then the witching hour descended on them, Lily rubbed her eyes and everything went wrong. It took Anna forty-five minutes to put her to bed. They read books and Lily's eyelids were heavy and drooping, but still she refused to go to sleep when Anna put her in her bed and switched off the light.

"Nooooooo," she wailed and pulled herself up to stand. Eventually Anna was forced to pin Lily to the mattress, and after a bout of kicking and screaming she fell asleep at last.

Anna stood in the dark kitchen, leaning against the table. She could see the lights in the other apartments across the street, cozy homes filled with life and warmth by the looks of it.

The telephone rang. She went to answer it. It was Cecilie. She wanted to know if everything had gone all right, how Lily was, had she been in a good mood, and had she discovered that she had left her teddy behind?

"Why did you have her ears pierced?" Anna asked.

Silence the other end.

"You had her ears pierced without asking me first," Anna said, a little louder this time.

"Yes, sorry about that," Cecilie said sincerely. "I didn't think you would mind. I thought we had talked about it? I thought you had said you would be okay with it. That it looked nice on little girls."

"You could have asked me, Mom," Anna said.

"Yes, you're right. Sorry, darling. No, I mean it. I'm really sorry."

"Piercings are prone to infections, aren't they?" Anna asked.

"They were a little infected on the first day, but it passed quickly. I put some antiseptic on them."

"Goodnight, Mom," Anna said and hung up. It was 8:30 p.m. and her blood was boiling.

Fifteen minutes later, Anna knocked on the door of the apartment below hers. Her downstairs neighbors had a daughter the same age as Lily. Lene answered. No, it was no problem, she said. They didn't mind listening to the baby monitor. Anna explained she wanted to go for a run and added, casually, "I'll just stop by the university on my way back. I'm working from home tomorrow, and I forgot an important book. Is that okay? I'm taking my cell, so just call if there's anything." It was her only chance to meet with Dr. Tybjerg.

Anna ran faster than ever. It took her only twenty-five minutes to cover the Four Lakes. The sky over Copenhagen glowed orange, as if the universe itself were on fire. She ran up Tagensvej and accessed Building 12 by swiping her keycard through the magnetized lock. It was black and silent inside. She went to her study, turned on her computer, and wiped the sweat off her neck and stomach with a kitchen towel. She glanced at Johannes's dark computer. He hadn't called back, and when she checked her e-mails she saw he hadn't replied to that, either. A sense of unease started to fill her. What if he didn't want to be friends anymore? She had yelled at him, she had crossed a line. Troels and Thomas had both left her because she had crossed a line. But Johannes was different, she reminded herself. He wouldn't just drop her. He was bound to call her eventually.

She found a sweater in one of her drawers and put it on. Then she went down the corridor.

She regretted her decision as soon as she let herself into the museum. The likelihood of Dr. Tybjerg still being at work was less than zero. He must have given up waiting for her and gone home. The building felt deserted. She switched on the light and started walking. She had a constant feeling of doors opening behind her, of hearing footsteps; after all, it was a distinct possibility, she told herself. There might be students around, busy with exam preparations, dissertations, or essays.

She was relieved when she reached the Vertebrate Collection. He was there. Or rather: he had to be there. At the entrance to the collection, a solitary lamp was lit on his usual desk, there was a pencil, a pile of books, and, when she looked more closely, she saw the box with *Rhea Americana*. He would never have left it out if he had gone home. She pulled out a chair and sat down. It was very quiet; only a fan hummed in the distance.

After less than five minutes, she grew impatient. Perhaps he was somewhere inside the collection looking for more boxes and had been distracted by something? She put the lid on *Rhea Americana*, picked up the box, retrieved the master key from her running pants, and opened the double doors leading to the Vertebrate Collection. The sweet smell of preserved animals and boiled bones enveloped her immediately, and she breathed through her mouth. The doors closed behind her with a deep, soft sigh.

Only the nightlight was on, so Dr. Tybjerg couldn't possibly be inside. He would have needed more light to work. Anna was just about to leave when she heard a rustle. The sound was coming from the right-hand side of the room. The blood started racing through her veins.

She heard another noise. It was a sniffle, followed by the long, slow groan of rusty hinges, then feet, shuffling across the room. Anna kicked off her sneakers without making a sound. The labyrinthine rows of cabinets were to her left and, in only four steps, they would conceal her.

At that moment, someone switched on a study light in the far end of the room and a soft, honeyed glow spread to Anna. Then she heard Dr. Tybjerg.

"Ah, well," he sighed. He whistled briefly, there was the sound of another hinged lid squeaking. Anna coughed. Tybjerg instantly fell silent and turned off the light. She heard footsteps and again the creaking sound of a hinged lid. She frowned.

"Dr. Tybjerg," she called out, tentatively. "It's me, Anna Bella."

There was a five-second pause, then another creak, after which the lamp was turned on again. Anna walked toward the light, and Dr. Tybjerg walked toward the sound. They didn't follow the same path, so when Anna turned a corner and could see the desk with the lamp, Dr. Tybjerg wasn't there. Suddenly, he appeared right behind her. She spun around and took a step backward.

"Anna," he said, sounding fraught. "You came after all." He stepped past her. Anna tried to understand why on earth Tybjerg was here. There was no obvious sign of collection boxes, bones, a notepad, or a magnifying glass.

"What are you doing?" Anna said, gently putting down the box of *Rhea Americana* on one of the desks. Dr. Tybjerg stared at his hands.

"Researching," he said.

"In the dark?"

Dr. Tybjerg's face looked sly and the faint smell of stress from this morning was now mixed with an unmistakable note of stale sweat. He kept looking at his hands. Anna turned on the lamps on the adjacent desks.

"All right, Dr. Tybjerg," she demanded. "What's going on?"

Tybjerg didn't speak for a long time.

"Anna, I'm scared," he said at last, glancing up at her. His eyes were dark.

"What are you scared of?" Anna asked.

"Helland's dead," Tybjerg whispered.

"Yes, Helland had a heart attack. It happens and it's not infectious." Anna tried to gauge if he knew more. Tybjerg looked at her for a long time, as though he was trying to pull himself together.

"I heard about his tongue," he said finally, and pointed to his own. "The tongue is a mucus-covered muscle, found only in vertebrates. Its upper surface is covered with papillae, of which four different types exist. The filiform papillae, the foliate, the circumvallate, and the fungiform. . . ." He stared into space. "Why was his tongue severed? I don't understand. There's something fishy about this, there's more to it." He paused and looked straight at Anna.

"Mold is a furry layer found on items such as food, and it occurs when the relevant surface is infected with, for example, *Mucor*, *Rhizopus*, or *Absidia*, not that I'm a mold expert." Baffled, he shook his head and let himself flop onto a chair. Anna pulled up a chair for herself and sat down opposite him. She was on her guard.

"I'm not really sure where you're going with this. . ." she began.

"He's here," Dr. Tybjerg said.

"Who?"

"Freeman."

"What makes you think that?"

"You don't get it, do you?" Tybjerg shook his head in disbelief. "There's a bird symposium this weekend and Freeman is one of the speakers. He's giving a so-called 'cultural contribution,' it says on the Internet—that's their way of saying that, scientifically speaking, his contribution is hogwash. And yet, he'll be speaking. For an entire hour. On utterly ridiculous subjects, which he's spoken on twenty times before. It's just a cover, that's what it is."

"What for?"

"I don't know how he did it, Anna." Dr. Tybjerg suddenly looked very worried. "But Freeman must have found out about your dissertation. That we intend to annihilate him once and for all. Helland and I have spent the last ten years deconstructing Freeman's scientific credibility, and we're slowly getting there. He's cornered now and—"

"Clive Freeman is an old man," Anna protested.

"He attacked me," Tybjerg whispered. "Two years ago. In Toronto. He was wearing a ring and he hit me with it, on purpose." Tybjerg touched his eyebrow, where Anna remembered he had a thin, white scar. She was taken aback.

"Didn't you report him?" she asked, horrified.

"And he sent threatening e-mails to Helland," Tybjerg said. "Helland treated it as one big joke, 'ha-ha, hilarious, don't you think,' he would say to me. He just laughed it off, but I saw things differently. I'm the only one of us who has actually met Freeman. Helland always sent me. I've debated with him before, but the last time . . ." Tybjerg gulped. "His eyes."

"What about them?" Anna said.

"They were filled with hate."

Anna sighed.

"So you're saying Freeman is using the bird symposium as his excuse to go to Denmark and murder Lars Helland?"

"Yes."

"And that you'll be next?"

"Yes." Tybjerg swallowed a second time.

"I hope you realize just how insane that sounds."

Tybjerg's face shut down and Anna instantly regretted her words.

"And what about me?" Anna forced Dr. Tybjerg to look her in the eye.

"I don't know," he whispered. "He must have found out we're about to deal him the fatal blow. I don't know if he's made the link to you." Tybjerg gave Anna a wretched look. "But I think you need to be careful."

"You're wrong," Anna said, lightly.

"Possibly, but I'm not taking any chances."

"But you're wrong."

Tybjerg focused on the darkness. He was in a world of his own.

"Helland died because his body was riddled with parasites," Anna said and waited for his reaction. Tybjerg continued to stare into space until, slowly, he turned to her.

"I don't understand."

"His tissue was full of *Taenia solium* cysticerci. Thousands of them; several were found in his brain and that's why his heart failed. The police are currently trying to establish whether the infection was the result of a crime. But whether or not it was deliberate, it couldn't have been Freeman. The infection had reached an advanced stage. The cysticerci were three to four months old. Big ones." Anna straightened her back. "So unless you think Freeman came here in the summer to infect Helland, then it couldn't have been him."

Tybjerg looked confused.

"I know this from Professor Moritzen and Superintendent Søren Marhauge. By the way, Marhauge is looking for you," she added.

"Leave now," Tybjerg suddenly urged her.

"Dr. Tybjerg, my dissertation defense is in twelve days, even if we have to hold it down here! I *have* to do it. Did the office forward my dissertation to you? I handed in three copies last Friday. Have they given you one?"

Tybjerg nodded.

"Have you read it?"

"You need to go now," Tybjerg said.

"Yes, I do," Anna said, but she waited. "Perhaps we could leave together?" she suggested.

"No, I've a few things to do," he mumbled. "Just go without me."

Anna shrugged.

"Okay, bye," she said. She started walking down the aisle, turned around and said, "See you, Dr. Tybjerg."

Tybjerg didn't reply, but turned his back to her. Anna pretended to leave, but slipped back inside and closed the door. She stood very still. Her sneakers were still on the floor where she had left them. She could hear Tybjerg mutter to himself. Anna tiptoed back to the light. Rather than retrace her original route, she walked two aisles further along. Then she peeked around the corner. Tybjerg had opened one of the cabinets and was struggling to pull something out. It was a thin mattress, which he rolled out on the floor. Then he undressed, took out a sleeping bag, climbed into it, and made himself comfortable on the mattress. He started reading a journal and munching an apple. Anna watched him for a little while, then she slipped silently out of the collection and started her run home.

It was 10:15 p.m. when she came down Jagtvejen, and though her speed was good, she was cold in her running clothes. She would defend her dissertation in less than two weeks, she had yet to prepare the one-hour lecture that would precede it, and she still had plenty of revision to do if she was to have a hope of answering the questions that would follow. When she had met with Dr. Tybjerg, she had intended to tell the police where he was the next day. Smoke him out, force him to examine her. Now she was having second thoughts. Tybjerg was clearly terrified and beyond rational argument. What if he had a breakdown? She had already lost one supervisor, and the last thing she needed was for Tybjerg to be out of action. She sped up as if she could run off her frustration.

Anna let herself into the communal stairwell and heard a door open upstairs. The timed light went out and Anna felt a pang of guilt. A run shouldn't last nearly two hours, not even with the bogus excuse of picking up a book. She reached out to turn on the light, but it came on before she touched the switch. She leaned forward and looked up the stairwell. A cold, defensive shiver ran through her.

Lene's face appeared in the gap between the banisters, looking down.

"Any problems?" Anna said, shamefaced, taking several steps at a time. Her downstairs neighbor was holding the baby monitor in one hand and Anna's key in the other.

"Who was that?" Lene asked. The light went out and Anna turned it on again.

"Who?" Anna was confused.

"That guy."

Anna looked perplexed.

"Didn't you pass a guy on his way down? He's just left."

Anna squinted.

"I didn't see anyone. I've been out running." Anna was still confused.

"There was a guy here just now," Lene persisted. "The baby monitor bleeped, and I went upstairs to check that everything was okay. He was sitting on the stairs by your landing. He was waiting for you, he said, and that was fine by me. I said you would be back shortly. Lily was sleeping when I went inside, so I don't know what set off the monitor. I put her comforter back and was going to call you to find out when you were coming back because we wanted to go to bed. I'd left your front door open, but when I was about to leave, the guy had made himself comfortable on your sofa, and I wasn't happy about that. I tried calling you to find out if it was okay."

Anna fished out her cell from her running jacket. Three missed calls.

"I'm sorry," she said. "It was on silent."

"Because I couldn't get hold of you, I asked him to wait outside. I explained you had gone running and he would just have to wait on the landing. I've never seen him before; I couldn't just leave him in your apartment when you hadn't mentioned anything about visitors, could I?"

Anna shook her head.

"I wasn't expecting anyone," she managed to say. She felt cold all over.

"But you must have seen him," Lene insisted. "He only just left."

"I didn't see anyone," Anna said. "Could it have been Johannes, my colleague from the Institute of Biology? Did he have red hair?"

"He wore a cap. And a long coat," Lene said. "I think he removed his cap when he sat down in your living room, but I don't know if his hair was red. More brown, I think. I'm not sure."

"It doesn't make sense," Anna said. "I used my key to let myself in downstairs and then I walked up. No one came down. I swear."

Lene looked tired and ran her fingers through her hair.

"Weird," she mumbled. "He raced down the stairs only a minute ago. I'd closed my door, thinking how odd it was for someone to visit you this late. I wondered if I should fetch Otto, and then I heard him leave in a hurry. As if he had changed his mind and decided not to wait for you. I went back out on the landing, I saw his hand glide down the banister, the light went out, you switched it back on and we spotted each other in the gap." Lene pointed to the curved banisters. Anna felt another chill down her spine.

"You turned on the light, right? Because it wasn't me," she said.

"No," Lene said. "I didn't turn it on. You did."

Anna raced up the stairs to her own front door, holding out her key as a weapon. Her hands were shaking, and it took three attempts before she found the keyhole. The apartment was dark. Anna ran blindly into Lily's room. She could make out the comforter, Lily's toy dog, Bloppen, which had keeled over, and her daughter's favorite embroidered pillow; she could even make out the stickers Lily had stuck on her bedposts, but she couldn't see Lily. She heard Lene behind her, and the two baby monitors screeched when they got too close. Lene switched off the transmitter and Anna turned on the light.

Lily twitched, but soon resumed sucking her pacifier energetically and carried on sleeping, rosy-cheeked and safe. Anna slumped next to her daughter's bed and buried her head in her hands. She was shaking all over and struggling to breathe. What did she think she would find? An empty bed? A blue-eyed doll? A child's corpse?

She heard the hiss of a kettle boiling and of cups being filled. The cups were carried into the living room, away from Anna who was still sitting on the floor, panting. Of course Lily was safe and sound in her bed, where else would she be? Anna dug her fists into her eyes. She had to repeat this rational explanation, a thousand times if necessary, or she would go crazy.

Anna heard Lene open the doors of the wood stove, heard the scrunch of newspaper followed by the sound of logs and a match being struck. Shortly afterward, Lene appeared in the doorway.

"Why don't you come into the living room?" she said.

Anna got up. A cup of tea was waiting for her and a white ribbon of steam wound its way up to the rosette in the stucco ceiling. Anna couldn't look Lene in the eye. A man had been waiting for her. He could have been anyone, and that was seriously weird. Anna would surely find out who he was tomorrow, or in a few days. A suitor who had gotten cold feet, was Lene's suggestion. She, too, thought the whole incident had been bizarre.

But Anna had panicked, and Lene had witnessed it. The tears started rolling down her face. Lene stroked her hand.

"I'd like to go to bed now," Anna muttered.

"But are you all right?" Lene asked. "I'll stay if you want me to."

"No," Anna said. "It's okay. I'm just tired."

Once Anna was alone, she took off her damp running clothes and sat naked on a chair in front of the fire. She opened the doors and let the warmth soften her skin. She checked her cell. Only one of the missed calls was from Lene. The other two were from Søren Marhauge's cell. Johannes still hadn't returned her calls. She rested her head against the back of the chair and spent a long time studying a framed photograph on the wall above the wood stove. It was black and white, and it had been with her since her childhood. Cecilie and Jens, very young, both with long, unruly hair and unlined faces. Jens had his arm around Cecilie's shoulder; it looked as if he was nudging her gently toward the lens. Anna was peeking out between them; she was laughing and her eyes shone.

Anna had always loved that picture, but suddenly she couldn't understand why. Cecilie didn't look happy at all. Her mouth was smiling, but her eyes were dead. Jens's arm rested heavily on her shoulder. If he were to let go, she would fall out of the frame. Jens's gaze showed determination that this picture would happen. As though he knew the moment must be captured, so the image could accompany his daughter into adult life and remind her of her happy childhood. Anna's own grin was broad, her eyes sparkled with euphoric stars, and she was on top of the world. But the adults were suffering.

Around midnight she had spread her own and Lily's personal papers across the living room floor. Her own were reasonably well organized; she had Cecilie to thank for that. Anna looked briefly at her own birth certificate. When Lily was born, Thomas and she had disagreed vehemently about what her name would be and finally, two days before the mandatory six-month deadline was up, they had drawn lots. "Or we'll just have to name her after the queen," Anna had joked, but had secretly breathed a sigh of relief when the winning ticket said *Lily*. When Anna herself was born, the rules would appear to have been less strict. She had been named Anna Bella Nor on November 12, 1978, when she was almost eleven months old. She put the birth certificate aside and began looking through Lily's papers, which she had chucked into a large buff envelope. The colorful child-health record book from the health visitor, the very first photographs from the maternity ward, and the plastic ID bracelet from the hospital. Anna had intended to create a scrapbook for Lily, but nothing had come of it. She and Thomas had broken up between Lily's nine- and twelve-month checkups. Their health visitor had been shocked when she came to see Lily and found Anna falling apart. Anna had made tea while the health visitor rolled colored balls to Lily.

Suddenly, the health visitor had said, "And I thought you were such a lovely family."

Anna knew she meant no harm, but she exploded with anger and screamed at the woman.

"We still are. With or without Thomas."

The health visitor had apologized, Anna burst into tears, and Lily refused to play with the colored balls.

Feeling a little sad, Anna flicked through Lily's child-health record book, scared to stir up memories that might upset her. The teething, the endless nights when Anna paced up and down with her inconsolable baby so as not to disturb Thomas, on the brink of insanity from exhaustion, yet simultaneously more ecstatic than she thought possible. Lily had gained weight, the numbers recorded for posterity in the health visitor's neat handwriting. Anna ran her fingertips over all the new skills Lily had acquired.

Anna's own child-health record book from 1978 was orange, the paper slightly furry, and the tone more businesslike than in Lily's. Curious to know more, Anna leafed through it. She had started crawling when she was eight months old, and she took her first steps two days after her first birthday, she read. The health visitor recommended cod-liver oil and hard-boiled egg yolk, and had written down how positive it was that Anna ate meat and fruit. There had to be a second book, Anna thought, as she looked through it. Recordkeeping in the one she was looking at now had begun in September 1978, when Anna would have been around eight months old, and ended in January 1979. *Anna says "oops" and "no,"* it read. Anna smiled. The name of the health visitor, Ulla Bodelsen, was neatly printed on a dotted line.

She got up, went to her computer and searched the telephone directory for Ulla Bodelsen. She got two hits. An Ulla Karup Bodelsen who lived in Skagen, and an Ulla Bodelsen listed as living in Odense. She noted both numbers and sat for a while looking at the note before she put it aside. *Anna says "oops" and "no"* echoed inside her head. She stared at the photograph again. The mouths of Cecilie and Jens were smiling, but Anna's smile was the only genuine one. She was three years old in the picture and had no hidden agenda. Just like Lily.

It was almost one o'clock in the morning when Anna went to bed. For the first time in days, she slept a sound, untroubled sleep.

* * *

When she woke up Thursday morning, she was cold. She lit a fire, turned up the radiators, made oatmeal, and put far too much sugar on it.

"Yummy," Lily said, skillfully scalping the oatmeal with her spoon. "More sugar, please."

Anna sprinkled a little more into her bowl and rubbed her nose against the back of Lily's neck.

"I'll pick you up early today," she whispered.

"I want to go to Granny's," Lily declared. Anna sat down at the table and looked into Lily's eyes.

"No, Lily, you're not going to Granny's today."

"Granny makes pancakes," Lily argued.

"You can have pancakes here," Anna said. "With ice cream."

"Ice cream," Lily exclaimed, overjoyed, and looked in the direction of the freezer.

"Not now, Lily. This afternoon," Anna replied.

"No, ice cream now."

Anna sighed, found another bowl and scooped two hard balls out of a tub. Lily hoovered the contents of the bowl and wanted more. In the end, Anna had to carry her howling daughter into the hall and put her into her snowsuit. But suddenly, Lily threw her arms around Anna.

"You're my mom," she said.

Anna was touched. "And you're my cuddle bunny," she replied, softly.

"Bloppen is coming with me to school," Lily declared.

"Then go find him."

While Lily rummaged around her bedroom, Anna zipped up her jacket and thought about Johannes, who had still not called, and then about the man who had come to see her last night. It had to be Johannes, who else could it have been? The World's Most Irritating Detective would surely have shown his ID. Anna sent Johannes another text.

Johannes darling. Please call me. I'm really sorry about yesterday. I'm sorry that I shouted at you. By the way, did you stop by last night? Please call!

Anna remembered the note with the telephone numbers for the health visitor. It was still lying next to the computer and she stuffed it in her pocket.

"Come on, Lily." She called down the hallway to Lily's room.

Lily was dawdling. Anna waited on the landing and called out again.

"Lily, come on."

At that moment she heard a security chain rattle and a dark gap appeared behind her neighbor Maggie's door. Maggie peered out, and when Anna said "hi," her face lit up, she closed the door, removed the chain, and joined Anna on the landing.

"Look at the state of you," she exclaimed. "You have Olympic-size bags under your eyes. Have you had gentlemen callers?" Maggie wore a floor-length dressing gown and her hair stood out on all sides.

"Not exactly," Anna said, but couldn't help smiling.

Maggie pulled the dressing gown tighter and suddenly glanced anxiously down the stairwell.

"So who is he then? It did seem a little odd."

Anna froze.

"What do you mean?"

The old lady scrutinized Anna.

"The man who came back last night. It all seemed very strange to me. The other day I asked him if he wanted a drink. I didn't want him sitting out here getting cold, did I? But he declined and, after last night, I'm very glad that he did."

"What do you mean, the other day?" Anna asked, massaging a spot on her upper chest through her jacket.

"The other day. Yesterday? Or was it two days ago? What are you doing?" Maggie asked, indicating Anna's hand. Anna sighed.

"It's nothing. It's my heart. It's racing. What did he look like?"

"He had lovely eyes . . . and he was tall. He looked nice. Nice and a tad nervous. He wore a hat and a long black coat. His hair was auburn." Maggie touched her ear to show where his hair had stuck out.

"It must have been Johannes. What did he say?"

"I was coming back with my groceries, and you know how I leave the bags on the landing and carry them upstairs, one at a time. When I came up with the first bag, there he was. Very polite, asked if he could help me, and then he carried my groceries upstairs. He said he was one of your friends, so I invited him in, but as I said, he declined. He glanced at his watch as though he was in a hurry," Maggie explained. "And yesterday, when I saw him sitting there again, I thought it odd and I nearly called the police. And then, suddenly, he was gone. Like the last time. As though he had changed his mind. Strange, don't you think? Either you need to see someone or you don't. I rushed to my balcony to check if the light was on in your apartment, but it was dark as the grave," she said dramatically and narrowed her eyes.

"It must have been Johannes," Anna repeated, to herself mainly. "Think back. When was the first time he came here?"

"Three days ago," Maggie declared.

Lily came outside with Bloppen tucked under her arm.

"Can I have a Gummi Bear, please?" she asked. Maggie shuffled back inside her apartment, closely followed by Lily. Anna remained outside. It was going to be a long day.

Anna received a text just as they entered the nursery school. She reached into her pocket for her mobile, but the mayhem of children and parents in the coat room distracted her. Lily ran ahead into the classroom and tugged the skirt of one of her teachers.

"Look!" she called out. "Look! It's my mom. Look, she's right there!" Lily pointed and a teacher came out to share Lily's excitement.

"Look, my one is the lion," Lily said, sticking out her lower lip. Since when had her speech developed so quickly? Anna thought. "I've got the lion, Anton has the rhinoceros, and Fatima has a fried egg," Lily explained and pointed to some small wooden shapes stuck to the wall above the peg rail.

"Do you have long to go before you finish your dissertation?" the teacher asked.

"No," Anna said, looking up in surprise.

"She misses you," the teacher said softly.

"She has her granny," Anna defended herself.

"Sure," the teacher said. "But you're her mother, and she talks about you all the time." Then she turned on her heel and left.

"I'm four years old," Lily said.

"No, darling. In five weeks you'll be three years old." Anna held up five fingers. "And I'll pick you up at four o'clock," she went on and removed one finger.

Outside the school she fished out her cell and smiled when she saw the text from Johannes.

Apology accepted. We're still friends. I just need to be alone for a while. Hugs. P.S. I was at home all of last night and didn't visit you. Must have been one of your other admirers]

Anna breathed a sigh of relief. Johannes wasn't upset. But then, who could the visitor have been?

She was on her way into Building 12 when her cell rang. It was Cecilie.

"No, you don't need to pick her up," Anna said, before Cecilie had time to say anything.

"Ah, right, well, okay. Bye then, Anna," she said, sounding hurt. Then she continued, "But it wouldn't be a problem today. My meeting has been canceled, and I could pick her up as early as two o'clock. Saves her wasting her afternoon at the school."

Anna lost her temper and screamed. "You're not picking her up, do you hear me?! Christ Almighty, why can't you leave us alone? I'll call you tonight." She ended the call and stuffed her phone into her pocket.

The seal on Helland's door had been broken, and as Anna walked past she could see crime scene investigators inside the office. She slowed down. They were wearing thin white boiler suits and spoke quietly to each other. The floor in the corridor was covered with dirty footprints, and Anna had an irrepressible urge to eavesdrop.

Why had the police come back? When she entered her study, she saw that Johannes's computer was gone. An official-looking form had been left on top of one of his piles of paper, briefly stating it had been confiscated by the police. Anna took out her mobile.

The police have walked off with your computer, she texted.

No reply.

Cecilie, too, stayed silent.

At noon Anna went to the cafeteria and bought two sandwiches and two cartons of juice before she made her way to the museum. She let herself into the Vertebrate Collection with her master key. The ceiling light was on and she found Dr. Tybjerg at a desk, writing on a lined pad. Several reference books and boxes of bones were beside him. Tybjerg looked up, startled.

"Oh, it's you." He sounded relieved.

"You slept here last night, Dr. Tybjerg, I know you did," she said.

Tybjerg studied his hands and Anna noticed how his nostril had started to twitch. She placed a sandwich in front of him.

"Why don't you sleep at home?" she demanded, losing patience with his paranoia. Dr. Tybjerg looked worried.

"Anna," he begged. "Promise me you won't tell anyone. Please!"

"Tell anyone what?"

"For the past eight months I've been living in my office," he confessed. "To save money. Traveling to excavations. . . it all adds up. I lost my apartment. No one knows yet. The last few nights I've been sleeping in here. Is that for me?" He touched the sandwich hopefully.

"Yes," Anna replied, and handed him a carton of juice. She was shocked to see Dr. Tybjerg rip off the wrapping and wolf down the food.

"You're also hiding from Freeman, aren't you?" she said.

Tybjerg was eating and didn't reply. Anna snapped. She removed the lid from one of the boxes, took out a bone, and slammed it down in front of her supervisor.

"This," she hissed, "is the hand of a bird. It has a half-moon-shaped carpus, which overlaps the basis of the two first metacarpal bones in the wrist common to all maniraptora, that is all birds, both ancient and modern. It's a homologue feature, which underlines the close kinship of prehistoric birds to modern ones. Freeman disagrees. He thinks the dinosaur's carpus may have had a feature that, at first glance, could be mistaken for a semilunar, but that the two bones only bear a superficial likeness, and this apparent similarity has no impact on their relationship." Anna sent the bone skidding across the desk and stuck her hand into the box a second time.

"And this one—" she started.

"Stop," Dr. Tybjerg implored her.

"—is the pubic bone." Anna ignored him. "Those of us who know better, know that both theropods and *Archaeopteryx* and a couple of enantiornithine birds from the early Cretaceous had an enlarged distal on the pubic bone, i.e., another homologue feature. Of course, Freeman denies this. Further, there is the dispute about the position of the pubic bone. And the dispute about feathers, about phylogenetic methods, about the stratigraphic junction, about the ascending process of the talus bone, about everything." Anna looked at Dr. Tybjerg.

"That's why he's come to Denmark, Dr. Tybjerg. To win an argument he has no chance of ever winning; not to kill Helland, or you, or me, or my daughter."

"Stop it," Tybjerg howled. His knuckles were white. He rose. "It's pointless," he said, taking the rest of his sandwich and disappearing down the dark aisles. She could hear him shuffle around and didn't know what to do. She slapped her head with the palm of her hand.

Her cell rang on her way back to the department. It was Jens.

"Hi, Dad," she said.

"Anna, hi." He sounded breathless. "I'm on a job. In Odense, as it happens."

"Right," Anna said. She was walking down the glass corridor that connected the museum and the Institute of Biology.

"Listen, Anna," he said. "Your mom just called me. She sounded quite upset."

"Right," Anna said again.

"What's going on?" Jens asked. "I understand that you're under a lot of pressure, but be nice to your mom, please? She does so much for you, Anna sweetheart."

Anna glowed red-hot with rage. She was speechless.

"She says you screamed at her and hung up. What's that all about?"

Anna finally got her voice under control.

"Please can you explain to me when my mother became so fragile?" Anna sneered. "Since when is she made of glass? Can you tell me that? She's had special treatment all my life. My whole freaking life."

"Anna," Jens said after a pause. "Calm down."

"No, I won't!"

"You calm down right now!" Jens shouted.

"Do you know what you can do? You can call my mother and remind her that Lily is my child. And when she accepts that, then she can call me. For God's sake, Dad, Cecilie cut Lily's hair and had her ears pierced without asking me first!"

Jens was silent.

Then he said, "She's only trying to help."

"I don't need any help," she said. "From you or her."

At four o'clock that afternoon, she picked Lily up from nursery school.

CHAPTER 8

Clive woke up in his house on Vancouver Island, wondering why he had slept on the sofa. Then he remembered hitting Kay. He showered and shaved in the guest bedroom. He put eggs on to boil, fried bacon, and made toast and tea. He put plates and utensils on a tray and carried it out to the garden, and then he set the table. The sun was shining, the air was mild and hazy. Kay always put a tablecloth on first, but Clive couldn't find one. He found some napkins instead and put the plates on top of them. Then he went upstairs to get Kay.

The door to the master bedroom was open and Clive could hear the water running in the master bathroom. He looked into the bedroom and saw Kay's suitcase on the bed. At that moment, she appeared from the bathroom. She glanced briefly at Clive. They heard a key turn in the front door.

"Mom," Franz called out. "Where are you?"

Kay went downstairs. Clive heard her say something.

"No, just go sit in the car," Franz replied.

Franz climbed the stairs to the landing where Clive stood. Franz was tall and tanned, and he worked out. He walked past his father and picked up Kay's suitcase.

"You're an idiot, Dad," Franz said quietly, on his way back.

"And you're a mama's boy," Clive retorted.

Franz sighed and walked down the stairs with the suitcase. Clive couldn't understand how he had managed to produce such a useless and pathetic excuse for a man. All brawn and no brain. Shortly afterward, he heard Franz rev the engine and drive off.

Downstairs in the kitchen, the saucepan had boiled dry and the eggs were blackened.

The first three days he sequestered himself in the house. He unplugged the telephone, switched off his cell phone, and didn't check his e-mails. On the third day, the temptation to look became too great, but Kay hadn't called or e-mailed him. Nor was there anything from Jack.

The kitchen looked a mess. On his first day alone, Clive opened every cupboard and lined up cans and dry foods to take stock of the situation. He had seemed to be well provided for, he had thought at the time, but his supply was dwindling fast. He went down the road to shop and as he walked, he pinched his nostrils. He and Kay had never had a real falling out. During their marriage she had walked out—once—and had been gone for three hours after an argument, but she had never left the family home for three days. He didn't like it.

Inside the supermarket, Clive got a cart and stomped angrily up and down the aisles. He bought plenty of cakes, corn on the cob, packets of cold cuts, toilet paper, two bags of chips, and a case of beer. The supermarket was practically deserted; it was mid-morning and the obese woman at the checkout was in a chatty mood. When all his groceries had been scanned, she helped him pack and when he picked up the bags, she said, "So, welcome to Patbury Hill. Probably won't be the last time we'll be seeing each other. You'll always have to go shopping." She laughed and winked at Clive. Clive glared at her.

"I've lived here for more than twenty-five years," he snarled.

The woman looked at him and giggled.

"Is that right? I don't remember ever seeing you before," she replied.

Clive turned on his heel and left.

When he got back, he sat down in his armchair with a small selection of cakes. He looked at his lawn. When he sat very still, the house felt so quiet, it was almost as if he didn't exist.

Franz and Tom were both married and Clive didn't really know them anymore. They had become rather remote since having children of their own. Young children were such hard work. When his own boys had been small, Clive would often sleep at his office to avoid the sleepless nights. Now Franz managed a gym, and Tom had an executive position with Canada Post. How hard could that be? His sons would come over for dinner every now and then, and they saw each other at birthdays and holidays—obviously—but it had been years since he and the boys had done something together. What a pair of sissies! They were always hugging Kay and chatting with her in the kitchen, when they should be manning the barbecue with their father. Somehow Clive had always felt a closer bond to Jack.

Michael Kramer called to ask why Clive hadn't been at work. He tried to coax him by telling him they had plenty of promising research results to analyze; the project would finish in two weeks and then they could write their report. With a bit of luck, they could show up at the 27th International Bird Symposium in Copenhagen in October with a poster. They had roughly ten weeks to get it done.

"Sounds great," Clive said. "You work it. I'm taking some sick leave. I've got an ear infection."

"At your age?" Michael sounded surprised.

"Yes."

"Are you okay?" his protégé asked.

"Never felt better," Clive said and ended the call.

He sat holding the telephone for a while, then he called Kay. "'New evidence is pouring out of the ground, Clive,'" he mimicked, while the telephone rang in his son and daughter-in-law's house.

Never heard such rubbish. There was nothing "new" about these bones, his idiot opponents had merely invented more fanciful interpretations. Franz's wife answered. She sounded polite, but a little curt. Finally, Kay came to the telephone.

"Yes?" she said.

"How long are you planning on staying away? Come home, Kay. The place is a total mess."

"Is that your way of apologizing?"

"Yes," Clive said, laughing. "You know what I'm like. I'm a scientist. Come on home, honey."

"Clive," Kay said, "you don't hit someone you love. And you don't call three days later and pretend it's no big deal, like you just did." She hung up.

He called back immediately, but no one picked up the telephone.

During three more days and nights when Clive barely slept, he wrote a paper. His manifesto. When he had finished, he printed it out, placed the document on his desk, and took a nap. He dreamt about Jack, but the dream turned into a nightmare. Jack and Michael had both . . . they were . . . no, he couldn't stand the thought of it. Jack and Michael couldn't be compared, they weren't even in the same league, and the mere thought that they. . . . Clive woke and touched his head. The sun had moved above the house and had been shining directly at his face while he snoozed. His stomach rumbled, but he had no appetite. He had tried every premade meal sold at the supermarket, every frozen pizza and casserole, every can and carton, and he felt sick. Their freezer was filled with food, but all of it required cooking. The previous day Clive had defrosted a leg of lamb and put it in the oven. How hard could it be? He promptly forgot all about it and when he finally detected the smell of roasting meat and raced to the kitchen, the surface of the meat was hard and dry. He picked at it, but it didn't taste anything like it did when Kay cooked it. It tasted of burnt fabric.

He rose and fetched his manifesto. He wanted to have it published, not in a journal, but as a small book. On its cover would be a 3D depiction of *Archaeopteryx*—without this "new" femur that Helland and Tybjerg had conjured out of thin air, and which was now reproduced in every recent print of the bird. In Clive's edition, *Archaeopteryx* would look exactly as it did when it was found in Solnhofen in 1877. Obviously Clive had been meticulous when he measured it in 1999. It was the most beautiful little bird in the whole world.

Clive sat down in the conservatory to proofread his text. His plan was to have it ready by the time he flew to Denmark.

He was deep in thought when there was a knock on the door. Someone put a key in the lock and Franz appeared.

"Hi, Dad," he said, quickly.

Clive straightened up and reached out for the manuscript, which had slipped into his lap.

"Hello, Franz," he replied, pushing up his glasses. "Do you want some coffee?"

Franz hesitated, then he shook his head.

"No, I'm a bit busy," he said. "I've come to pick up some clothes and books for Mom." He went upstairs. Clive stayed where he was and pretended to read. When Franz came back down he was holding a bag in one hand and, draped over his other arm, a garment bag containing Kay's black dress with polished anthracite stones. Clive loved that dress. It hugged Kay's hips and on the rare occasions when she wore it, she let her hair down and it would curl around her shoulders. The last time they had had sex had been an evening she had worn it. That was a very long time ago.

"What are you doing with that dress?" he demanded, hoarsely.

"Mom asked me to get it," Franz replied.

"No," Clive said. "That dress stays here." He grabbed the garment bag.

"Don't be stupid," Franz said, firmly. "Mom needs it."

"Why?"

"Molly and Jack are taking her to the theater," Franz replied.

"No," Clive said, snatching the dress.

Franz got mad and yanked the dress back from Clive. He stopped in the doorway and looked at his father.

"I don't understand you anymore," he said. "Not that I ever really have. But now I don't understand you at all." And he was gone.

Clive spent the rest of the afternoon trying not to think about Kay going to the theater with Molly and Jack. It was impossible. Jack in black tie, clean-shaven, his hair freshly cut, a look of concentration in his guarded eyes, his mouth relaxed and soft for once. Next to him, Kay in that black dress, pale and beautiful, sitting in an upholstered seat surrounded by expectant theatergoers, Molly's hand resting on hers in sympathy.

The four of them had been to the opera that spring, and it had been a magical evening. During intermission they had drunk a little too much prosecco and after the intermission, Kay accidentally sat down first, so Clive ended up between her and Jack. Clive was so thrilled to be sitting between the two people who meant the most to him in all the world that he could barely concentrate on the second act. Kay had slipped her hand in his, and all down his right side he could feel a quivering heat from Jack when he shifted in his seat, when he laughed, when he leaned forward.

Jack and Kay going to the theater without him was an unforgivable act of betrayal.

This conclusion calmed him down. The human animal was fundamentally lonely, but in contrast to sentimental daydreamers, he had faced up to it. His priority now was the restoration of his professional reputation. Kay would come back sooner or later. Besides, she had no money.

Three weeks later, Clive was back at the department of Bird Evolution, Paleobiology, and Systematics. He cycled to the university and strode down the corridor. Michael emerged from his laboratory.

"Clive, my man," he said. "Good to have you back."

"Good morning," Clive said, marching past the younger man to his office. The air was dusty and stuffy, so he opened the windows. His secretary entered shortly afterward with a pile of letters. Rumors of his return spread quickly, and at lunchtime Clive accepted Michael's invitation to join him and the rest of the team in the cafeteria. They were all delighted to see him.

After lunch they started preparatory work on their poster. Clive and Michael reviewed the results from the cartilage condensation experiment, which looked very hopeful. Michael showed him microscope images of the various developmental stages. It was clear the primary cartilage formation in embryonic birds resulted in the carpal bone, the fourth metacarpal bone and the development of the fourth finger, which meant the bird hand couldn't have evolved from the dinosaur hand, *unless* it was an example of mutation in both the symmetry of the fingers *and* in the hand's existing central axis, and that was highly unlikely—obviously. Clive whistled softly. It was all very encouraging. The scent of cologne rose from the V-neck of Michael's T-shirt and tickled Clive's nose. If Michael hadn't had a wife and two children, it would have been tempting to assume . . . Clive edged away from Michael a little.

"I'm buying you all dinner at the steakhouse," he burst out. "Time to celebrate!" Besides Michael, he invited John, Angela, Piper, his secretary Ann, the two PhD students, and two new masters students. His loyal team.

None of them could make it. Michael had promised to *babysit*.

Clive spent the evening trawling through the program for the 27th Bird Symposium on the web. Tybjerg, that egomaniac, was giving no fewer than four lectures, which came as no surprise to Clive, but he was extremely surprised to discover that Helland's name didn't appear anywhere. Helland, who never attended symposia outside Europe, finally had the chance to put forward his nonsense ideas in his home country, so why not take it? Very odd. On checking his inbox, Clive realized that it had been a while since he had last heard from Helland. He started rereading their correspondence but soon stopped. He knew no one as snide and mean as Lars Helland, and it ruined his good mood.

It was mild outside and when Clive had opened the French doors, he called Michael to discuss the poster. Michael's daughter picked up the telephone.

"I'm sorry, Professor Freeman, I'm afraid my dad's not here," she said.

"So who's looking after you?" Clive asked.

The girl laughed.

"I'm fifteen and my sister is thirteen, so we can manage on our own."

Clive was affronted.

"So where's your father?" he asked.

"I think he had a meeting at the university," the girl replied.

Clive thanked her and hung up.

He stared into space for a moment. Then he returned to his computer and clicked on the homepage of the Natural History Museum in Copenhagen where he discovered, to his delight, that they were putting on an exhibition about feathers. His joy, however, was short-lived. The title of the exhibition was "From Dino to Duvet." Would it never end? He bet Tybjerg was the curator of that blasted exhibition. One day, probably when Clive was dead and buried, sadly, natural history museums the world over would hang their heads in shame at how wrong they had been.

Clive heard nothing from Jack, and Kay remained with Franz. Clive was annoyed she hadn't bothered coming home yet, but he wouldn't have time to do anything about it until after the symposium. His future career depended on the condensation experiment and the Copenhagen conference, and he needed space to think. At night he dreamt of Jack. Dark, freaky dreams, filled with sounds and Jack's face lighting up in flashes, so all Clive had time to see was Jack's snarling upper lip. He started taking half a sleeping pill and, to his relief, the nights became black and empty once more.

On October 9 Michael and Clive flew to Copenhagen. He usually loathed the journey across the Atlantic, but when Michael secured them an upgrade to business class, his irritation melted away. Clive had gone to the lavatory and when he returned, there was Michael, grinning from ear to ear, and waving the boarding passes at him. They sat in supreme comfort the whole flight, discussing the presentation, while attractive cabin crew served drinks and snacks. Clive noticed how attentive and deferential Michael was. After Michael had finished his PhD, he had gone through a phase of wanting to decide everything for himself. Clive had been most offended. When you navigated a scientific minefield, as Clive did, you needed loyal support and not childish attempts at independence. He noted with delight that Michael had been brought to heel. He made hardly any objections, and when he did, his observations were insightful and only contributed to honing Clive's argument. Somewhere across the Atlantic, Clive was overcome by an urge to confide in Michael.

"I've a feeling this will be my last time," he said.

"What do you mean?" Michael said, stretching out in his seat.

"I don't know. . ." Clive hesitated. What exactly was he trying to say?

"The presentation is good," Michael prompted him. "The experiment bears scrutiny."

"Yes, perhaps that's what it's about," Clive replied. He looked out of the window. To the west, the setting sun painted the clouds beneath them tomato red, to the east, the European night awaited them, black and alien.

"My life seems to have reached a turning point," he said. "I'm thinking of retiring, if the presentation is a success." He had no idea what had triggered this.

Michael looked as if he was about to say something and he shifted uneasily, but when Clive finally looked up, Michael was engrossed in a magazine.

The hotel in Copenhagen was called Ascot and was located in the side street of a large, ugly square. The rooms were tiny and claustrophobic, and the sheets felt greasy, as though the washing machine had a faulty rinse cycle. There was no minibar. Clive called reception to get the code for wireless access, and having uploaded his presentation and the latest corrections to his server back in Canada, he fell asleep.

Wednesday morning Michael and Clive had breakfast in a large hall, which was half-empty and freezing cold. They had just sat down to scrambled eggs and newspapers, when two tall men entered through the revolving doors at the far end of the room. Clive watched them while they looked around. They began strolling in the direction of Clive and Michael's table. Michael was eating and reading his newspaper and didn't look up until the men were right next to them.

"Professor Freeman?" one of them asked, politely.

Clive stared at him. If Kay had died, he would . . . he would. . . . He didn't know what he would do. He closed his eyes.

"Professor Clive Freeman?" the man repeated.

Michael nudged Clive, and Clive opened his eyes.

"Yes," he croaked.

"I'm Superintendent Søren Marhauge from the Copenhagen Police. Could we have a word with you?" His English was perfect and fluent.

"Is it about my wife?" Clive whispered. The man smiled.

"It's not about your wife or any of your family," he said calmly. "It's about Professor Helland."

Clive was in shock. When the interview had finished and he left the police station, a young police officer had to help him into a taxi, as though Clive were an old man. The police officer placed his hand between Clive's head and the car for protection, as Clive had seen the police do with criminals. They had all his e-mails. The tall superintendent with the dark eyes had spread them out on the table in front of him. He was about to argue this was illegal, but it occurred to him that it probably wasn't. Lars Helland was dead, and the police were investigating all options, as Marhauge diplomatically phrased it, but Clive knew perfectly well what it meant. It meant Helland had been murdered. Marhauge had looked at him for a long time, scrutinizing him, Clive thought.

"We know you're not responsible for Professor Helland's death. I've checked your travel records, and you haven't been to Europe since 2004, am I right?"

Clive nodded obediently.

"You're here for the Bird Symposium at the Bella Centre?"

Clive nodded again.

"You're giving a presentation there on Saturday?"

"Yes, Saturday evening."

"Where were you in June?" the superintendent wanted to know.

Clive thought back. June was *before* Jack had betrayed him, and Kay had moved out.

"Nowhere," he replied eventually. "Nowhere at all."

June had been windy, and all he wanted to do was work. Kay had ordered him to take a break and they had gone to their cabin, where they lasted two whole weeks together. Kay made salads and he barbecued. They had several visitors, all couples, where the wife was a friend of Kay's and the husband was utterly dull. Jack and Molly had been busy. Finally, he had resorted to clearing out the shed, and Kay had remarked that this was a strange way to spend a vacation. And that was when Clive had snapped.

"I don't want to be on vacation," he shouted. "My work is too important. Look what happened the last time. I close my eyes for two seconds, and someone finds a feathered dinosaur!"

Kay gave Clive permission to return to work.

"And what did you do in July?" the detective asked.

He had been alone in the house, living on canned food, sausages, and bread.

"I worked," he said. "Preparing the presentation I'm giving on Saturday, among other things."

The superintendent handed him a sheet of paper. Clive read: *You will pay for what you have done.*

"Did you write that?"

"Of course not," Clive replied, outraged. "I don't threaten people."

Finally, he was allowed to leave.

*   *   *

When Clive returned to his hotel, he collapsed on his bed and dreamt about his own funeral. Kay wore a black veil and was in deep distress; the boys, looking suitably cowed, flanked her. The sobbing widow was about to throw herself on his coffin . . . when the dream suddenly restarted. This time the church was empty. His coffin rested, white and lonely, in front of the altar; the priest rushed in and went through the motions. Clive tried to call out from his coffin, tell him to make more of an effort, but the priest didn't hear him. Then the door at the back of the church was opened, a solitary mourner entered and took a seat at the farthest pew. The priest beckoned him to the front—after all, there was plenty of room.

"The deceased had very few friends," the priest whispered. "Not even his widow is here. I'm delighted to see you."

The mourner approached. Suddenly Clive recognized Tybjerg. He sat in the first row, in Kay's place.

At first, Clive thought Tybjerg had started clapping, but then he realized someone was knocking on the door to his room. Dazed, he let Michael in. Together they went down to the hotel bar for a drink, where they discussed Helland's death at length before going to the Bella Centre. It was Wednesday evening and they had time for a quick look around the science fair.

Michael nudged him.

"Over here," he whispered. Clive followed his finger, which was pointing at an electronic screen listing the program for the symposium. Clive squinted.

"What?"

"Tybjerg's name has been removed. Look." He tapped the screen lightly. "It says 'Canceled. Please note replacement speaker' next to the four lectures Tybjerg was due to give."

Clive stared at the screen.

"He must be upset," he mused. "After all, Helland was his mentor. Imagine how you would feel, if I had been murdered."

Michael smiled. "Yes, can you imagine that!"

Thursday morning Clive ventured into the streets. A cold wind was blowing. He had consulted a map and located the university, where he had an appointment with Johan Fjeldberg. He had walked for thirty minutes when the College of Natural Science appeared to his left. The complex was unappealing: three tall 1960s blocks and several lower, yellow-brick buildings, each one more devoid of charm than the next. He walked through a park. At the museum reception he asked for Professor Fjeldberg, who appeared shortly afterward. Fjeldberg chattered away while he led Clive through a maze of restricted access doors and corridors. This business with Helland was dreadful. Such a good colleague. A brilliant man. Clive smiled and nodded. Fjeldberg said rumor had it Helland had been murdered. Fjeldberg simply refused to believe it.

"People are paranoid," he scoffed. "One rumor even claims he was killed by parasites."

Clive gave Fjeldberg a horrified look.

"Parasites?"

"Yes, his body supposedly was riddled with them," Fjeldberg snorted.

They had reached the elevator, and while they waited for it Fjeldberg looked at Clive.

"How well did you really know him?"

"Well," Clive began. The two men entered the elevator. "I knew him quite well. Professionally, we were polar opposites."

Fjeldberg nodded.

"But privately we were really quite good friends," he lied. "I'll be there on Saturday, at his funeral, I mean."

"I've never really understood people who can't make the distinction between work and friendship," Fjeldberg mused. "Can you? Helland excelled at keeping things separate. He picked fights with practically everyone, but he never allowed an argument to influence his personal opinion of them. In fact, there were times I thought he was fondest of those he had the biggest fights with. He loved confrontation. There'll be a huge turnout on Saturday, I imagine. He was a highly respected man. Even by his academic opponents."

Clive smiled, and he kept on smiling.

"Is Erik Tybjerg here?" Clive asked, feigning innocence. "I would like to express my condolences. He's an old friend. Tybjerg and I fight like cats and dogs, of course, but purely professionally. I think it would be appropriate for me to shake his hand."

Fjeldberg glanced at Clive as they stepped out of the elevator.

"Funny you should mention him," he began, tentatively. "Because Tybjerg appears to be missing."

"Missing?"

"Yes, several people are looking for him. Including the police." Professor Fjeldberg gave Clive a mystified look. "He doesn't respond to e-mails, he doesn't answer his telephone, and he's not in his office."

"Perhaps he needs some space," Clive suggested, compassionately. "After the sad news, I mean."

What on earth was going on? Surely there was a limit to how many of his arch enemies could die or vanish before he would receive a more heavy-handed treatment by the authorities.

"Yes, perhaps," Professor Fjeldberg replied. "Here we are."

Clive had heard accounts of the Vertebrate Collection at the Natural History Museum in Denmark and his expectations were high, but even so, a ripple of anticipation ran through him when Fjeldberg and he entered. The ceiling was high and the room was filled to bursting with fine, original wooden cabinets with glass doors. The porcelain handles on the cabinets and drawers bore Latin inscriptions explaining which animals were kept behind the glass. Beautiful, hand-painted posters hung in the few places where there were no cabinets. Everything was unbelievably old and tasteful. There were study areas where each desk was equipped with angle-poise lamps that were at least fifty years old. The desks were made of dark varnished wood, and each had an old, leather-upholstered armchair with wooden armrests.

"It was the moa skeleton you wanted to see, wasn't it?" Fjeldberg found a stepladder and started climbing it.

"Here we go," he said, opening one of the glass doors.

"Do you need a hand?" Clive asked. With his thin legs in khaki trousers, Fjeldberg looked old and very frail balancing on the ladder.

"You can take the old beggar, when I manage to get him out." Fjeldberg pulled out the drawer and stood on tiptoes.

"What on earth?" he exclaimed. "He's not here." Professor Fjeldberg felt inside the drawer. Then he climbed down.

"I don't believe it."

Clive stayed behind, somewhat baffled, while Fjeldberg marched back to the entrance. He switched on the ceiling lights and a rather merciless white glare revealed a layer of dust everywhere.

"He must be here somewhere," Clive heard Fjeldberg mutter to himself.

Clive tried to find him between the cabinets by following the sound of his footsteps, now here, now there, but as Fjeldberg appeared to be checking the room from end to end, he escaped from Clive, who eventually decided to stay put. The room was a little eerie, in a deserted, beautiful way. He shuddered. A *Pteropus Lylei* hung suspended above his head with its wings unfurled. It had tiny white teeth, and its eyes were hollow sockets.

"Found it!" Fjeldberg exclaimed triumphantly. Clive started walking and found the old man at a large desk.

"Someone has been studying it, but didn't check it out. And omitted to put it back. It happens. We have a number of students working with birds at the moment. Including one of Helland's, by the way. It could have been her. Her dissertation defense is coming up, so she has a good excuse, I suppose," he added and sighed.

"Oh, so what will she do now?" Clive asked. Professor Fjeldberg sighed again.

"I don't know much about it, she's registered with another department. But as far as I know she's only waiting to defend her dissertation, then she can graduate. I don't know who will examine her in Helland's place. We don't have that many paleoornithologists in Denmark . . . Perhaps you might extend your stay and examine her?"

Clive was well aware that Professor Fjeldberg was teasing him.

"I would have to fail her," he said, archly. "If she has written her dissertation in line with Helland and Tybjerg's scientific arguments, I don't think she has grasped even elementary evolution, and that surely is a fundamental requirement for a biologist."

Fjeldberg looked briefly at Clive and said, "Why don't we say I let you work here for a couple of hours until . . ." He glanced at his watch. "12:30 p.m.? Then I'll pick you up, and we can have a bite to eat. I've ordered in, sandwiches and so on."

Clive nodded.

The door closed behind Professor Fjeldberg and Clive was alone. He pulled out a chair, sat down, took out his magnifying glass, and started examining the skeleton. *Dinornis Maximus*. Fabulous. In relatively recent studies, scientists had successfully isolated DNA from bones of the long-extinct bird and proved the female had been 300 percent heavier and 150 percent taller than the male. Clive wasn't sure he believed it. He carefully held the talus bone in both hands. He found a pad and made some notes. Then he started looking for the rudimentary front limbs, which had to be in the box somewhere. An hour later, he was in an excellent mood. The synapomorphies between this secondarily flightless bird and, say, *Caudipteryx* and *Protarchaeopteryx*, which Tybjerg and Helland alleged were dinosaurs, were striking. More than ever, Clive was convinced that many of the animals, which Helland and Tybjerg claimed were dinosaurs, were in fact secondarily flightless birds from the Cretaceous and not dinosaurs at all. As far as he could determine, their skeletons were practically identical.

A noise made him turn around. The hairs on the back of his neck stood up. It sounded like a suppressed cough, and there was some barely audible scraping; he thought he could hear breathing. He rose and sniffed the air like a deer. The building sighed. Someone walked down the corridor outside. Clive relaxed his shoulders. He was in a public place, he reassured himself, yet he suddenly became very conscious of the far end of the Vertebrate Collection, which was lost in darkness.

He thought about how Helland had died. It was a revolting death. It was one thing to perish in an instant, another to die slowly as parasites in your tissue grew bigger. Worms, larvae, maggots. Clive shook his head to make the images go away. He hated the little monsters. They should be eliminated from the animal kingdom. He had once had a tick in his groin, which he hadn't discovered until it was the size of a pea and purple and bloated like a plum. Kay had removed it with tweezers.

The memory distracted him. The darkness seemed to grow more intense; suddenly he thought the bones stank of old membranes and sweet decomposition. He got up and put the bones he had managed to study back in their box. He opened a couple of cabinets and pulled out some drawers. They were neat and tidy. One drawer contained teeth, another feathers, sorted according to size and color. Some cabinets contained pelts, others held specimens floating in spirit in glass jars. For a long time he gazed at a dissected dromedary eye, which stared back at him. He breathed out. He couldn't shake off his unease. The darkness was mighty and menacing. He gave up and headed for the exit.

He found a seat in the corridor and stared out the window. It made no sense to start looking for Fjeldberg, he would only get himself lost. He decided to snooze. When Professor Fjeldberg arrived shortly afterward, he laughed and said the collection tended to have a soporific effect on everyone. Quiet as a womb and a few degrees too warm. They walked down the corridor, and Fjeldberg talked about the weather. After lunch, they discussed a possible joint project, and Clive almost forgot the spooky atmosphere in the collection, almost forgot Helland might have been murdered and Tybjerg was missing. Fjeldberg proposed an interesting project and when the two men parted, the seed to a future collaboration between the University of Copenhagen and UBC had been sown. Clive even dropped his planned rant about the feather exhibition.

"I'll see you on Saturday," Professor Fjeldberg said, and pressed Clive's hand warmly.

Later that evening, Clive and Michael had dinner at a fancy restaurant. Clive studied the menu with dismay and was about to object when Michael said, "The department is paying!"

"What do you mean?" Clive said, surprised.

"The board told me to treat you to a meal fit for a king. This restaurant has a Michelin star." Michael leaned across the table to whisper this information.

"Why?"

"Because their food is superb."

"No, I mean why have you been told to treat me to a meal fit for a king?"

"You deserve it," Michael laughed and raised his glass in a toast. There was a tiny, insincere glint in the corner of his eye. Clive was suddenly reminded of the evening when he had called Michael, and Michael, according to his daughter, had been at a meeting at the university, though he had told Clive he was babysitting. He confronted Michael with this. Michael smiled.

"I don't really remember. When did you say it was?"

Clive continued to stare at him.

"It was the day I returned from my sick leave. The day you gave me the result of the cartilage condensation experiment."

"Ah." Michael's face lit up. "That's right. We had a departmental meeting, and—"

"You held a departmental meeting without me?" Clive interrupted him and lowered his menu.

"Yes, because you didn't show up. We decided you probably weren't feeling well enough yet. We actually didn't start until seven thirty—in case you were late."

Clive said nothing. He had no recollection of there being a departmental meeting that night. He always attended such meetings. Irritated, he raised his menu.

"I don't know about you," he said. "But I'm having the lobster."

CHAPTER 9

Anna's cell rang while she was shopping in the Netto supermarket on Jagtvejen. She didn't recognize the number.

"Yes," she said, absentmindedly.

"Anna Bella," a hesitant voice began.

"Yes, that's me. Who is it?"

"Birgit Helland."

Anna froze.

"Is this a good time?" Mrs. Helland asked.

"Oh, yes," Anna lied, trying desperately to think of something appropriate to say when you unexpectedly find yourself talking to the widow of a man you couldn't stand.

"My condolences," she said, sounding like an idiot, and quickly added: "It must be very hard for you."

"Thank you," Mrs. Helland said quietly. "I have something for you," she continued. "From Lars. I thought perhaps you might like to visit to collect it. I would like to meet you. Lars often spoke about you." Birgit Helland's voice was subdued but determined, as though she had rehearsed her lines. Anna had no idea how to respond.

"For me? Er, yes, of course. Do you want me to come over now or later?"

"Now would be good. If you can. The funeral is on Saturday, and on Sunday Nanna and I will go away for a while. So, if you could manage today, that would be good. Otherwise it won't be for some weeks, and . . . well, I would like to meet you. I'm really sorry he can't be there for you. Really very sorry. He was so looking forward to your dissertation defense."

I bet he was looking forward to grilling me and failing me, Anna thought, but Mrs. Helland said: "He was so proud of you."

Anna thought she must have misheard.

"Pardon?" she said.

"When can you get here?" Mrs. Helland asked.

"I just need to take my groceries home and then I'll make my way to your house."

"I appreciate it," Mrs. Helland said. "See you very soon."

The Hellands's villa was in a suburb called Herlev, set back from the road and hidden behind a maze of scrub and bushes crippled by the frost. The gate was freshly painted. Anna heard birdsong in the front garden and spotted several feeding tables laden with seed balls and sheaves of wheat. She rang the doorbell. Birgit Helland was a tiny woman, just under five feet tall. Her eyes were red and her smile was pale.

"Hello, Anna," she said, holding out a hand that felt more like a small piece of animal hide than something human. The house was clean and tidy, airy, and light. In the living room were books from floor to ceiling on the windowless wall facing a colossal garden. Mrs. Helland invited Anna to sit down on one of two white, wool-upholstered sofas and disappeared into the kitchen. Shortly afterward she appeared with cups and a teapot, which she placed on the coffee table.

"I'm really very sorry," Anna said.

"I'm so glad you could come," Mrs. Helland said. "We're in a state, I'm afraid." Tears started rolling down her cheeks, and she did nothing to stop them.

"I'm so sorry," Anna said again.

"For the first two days the telephone wouldn't stop ringing. The Dean, the Head of the Institute. Former postgraduate students, colleagues from all over the world. They all wanted to offer their condolences. Most out of genuine compassion, but quite a few just called out of politeness. I can't imagine why anyone would offer their condolences if they didn't care about the person who died, can you?"

Anna shook her head.

"A lot of people didn't like Lars. I can see why. Lars wasn't an easy man." She smiled. "But then, who is?" She looked gravely at Anna. "The telephone has stopped ringing now," she added, glancing at the table where it stood.

"You didn't call," Mrs. Helland said. "Why not?"

Anna gulped.

"Lars was sure you didn't like him." She looked kindly at Anna. "Though he never cared very much whether or not people did. 'Never mind,' he would say. 'That's their problem. That will stir things up.' Lars loved stirring things up. It always bothered me, though. Because it was so unfair. He was a good man." Mrs. Helland smiled again. "A very unusual, but good man. He was a wonderful father to Nanna."

Anna was about to reassure Mrs. Helland that there was no need for her to justify her late husband's behavior, when Mrs. Helland said: "I don't know why I'm telling you all this." She smiled and looked down at her hands. "Either I hide myself away, never to be seen. Or I tell everyone about Lars. The supermarket cashier, the bus driver, the cold caller, everyone is forced to listen to my grief."

"I know how you feel," Anna said. Mrs. Helland poured more tea.

"He often mentioned you," she said. "I think he was fascinated by you. And Lars was usually only interested in birds." She smiled wryly. Anna reddened and wanted to protest, but Mrs. Helland carried on: "'She loathes me,' he would say about you. 'But she would rather die than admit it.' He respected you, Anna," she said.

Anna didn't know what to say. Everything she had ever said about Helland suddenly tasted bitter.

"I don't know what to say," she admitted.

Mrs. Helland continued looking at her.

"We had our differences," Anna said, tentatively.

"Well, of course you did. Lars had with most people. He was like that. He believed you had to court controversy to achieve anything at all."

A pause followed.

"Do they suspect you, too?" Mrs. Helland asked out of the blue.

"Do they suspect you?" Anna was shocked.

"They don't say so openly. The superintendent does. He wants to come across as a friendly teddy bear, so he ums and ahs. All he's prepared to say is that Lars appears to have suffered from a tropical infection and they're treating his death as *suspicious*. And then he assures me everything will be investigated very thoroughly. But he's hiding something because he suspects me, I'm sure of it." Mrs. Helland suddenly got up and sat next to Anna. She clasped Anna's hands and looked desperate.

"We're losing our minds," she wailed. "Neither of us can sleep. Until last Monday, Lars was a perfectly healthy man, and now he's dead. Why would anyone want to murder him? And what's this about a tropical infection? It's utterly ridiculous."

Everything inside Anna resisted. Mrs. Helland was sitting too close to her, and something in Anna's throat tightened.

"You're lying," she croaked.

Mrs. Helland stared at Anna. "What do you mean?"

"Your husband was ill," Anna said. "I saw him. He was seriously ill. Why do you say he was well when we both know that isn't true?"

Mrs. Helland pulled back.

"I don't understand . . ." Her lips quivered.

"What was wrong with his eye?" Anna continued.

"That small polyp?"

"Yes, what was it?"

"His father had one of those." Mrs. Helland faltered. "It was something inherited."

"No," Anna insisted. "It wasn't. And you know it."

Mrs. Helland looked stubbornly at Anna. "Lars wasn't ill. I don't understand why you keep saying he was. I loved him. He wasn't ill." Mrs. Helland started crying. "All I wanted to do was give you this," she said and picked up a small white box from a circular table next to the sofa. The tears were rolling down her cheeks.

"It's from Lars," she sobbed. "Your graduation present."

Reluctantly, Anna accepted the present.

"Open it," Mrs. Helland ordered her.

Anna took the lid off the box and removed the bright yellow cotton. Underneath it was a silver chain with a pendant. The pendant consisted of two charms, an egg and a feather. Anna swallowed and looked up at Mrs. Helland.

"It's beautiful," she gasped.

Mrs. Helland smiled, red-eyed. She was still sitting far too close, Anna could smell her tears, feel a vile heat from her body. Anna didn't want to stay there any longer. Not another second.

"I don't know why you're lying, but I know that you are. And, as long as you're lying, don't expect anything from me. Thanks for the tea."

She didn't realize how much she was shaking until she was outside in the street.

Anna caught the bus back to the university. She called Johannes, but it went straight to voicemail. When she reached the exit with Bellahøj police station and the bus turned into Frederikssundvej, she spotted Cecilie on the sidewalk. She was stooping and had covered her head with a scarf. When she looked up and saw the bus, she started to run. She didn't see Anna. Despite the weather, she was wearing boots with stiletto heels and a beige jacket with a fur collar, which was fashionable, but not very warm.

Why were they so different? Why did Anna have a mother who often looked at her as though she were from another planet? Cecilie was now parallel to the window where Anna was sitting, two-thirds back in the bus. Her foot slipped, but she recovered her balance. She pushed her way onto the crowded bus and stood where Anna could observe her, unnoticed. Cecilie looked rough. She always wore red lipstick, but today her lips were cracked and devoid of color, and she looked as if she had been crying. Over Anna? Over Lily? Yet she hadn't called. Jens had called. Seven times, since she had hung up on him. He was like the spy character from Stratego, willing to sound out the terrain, to die for the flag. Anna had ignored it and let the call go to voice mail.

Cecilie was clutching a strap. Anna was half-hidden by a night bus timetable, and if she moved her head she would be out of sight. She watched her mother and felt like crying. She missed her. When she had met Thomas, she had finally dared to separate from Cecilie. You can go now, Mom; you can get fat, bake cakes, but go, please. I have my own family now, I don't need you anymore. Not in that way. She wanted Thomas to provide everything that had previously been Cecilie's responsibility. Comfort, support, solidarity. For a short period, she convinced herself she had succeeded. Because she wanted it so desperately. Then her house of cards collapsed, and Anna fell flat on her face. And who picks you up when you're down? Your mother.

Cecilie turned her head, and Anna could study her profile. She's thinking about me, Anna thought. And yet she doesn't call me; still she chooses to wait until I come to her. It was the game they always played. They got off at the same stop along with fifteen other passengers. Anna was among the last to leave. Cecilie didn't look up but walked down Jagtvejen as quickly as her high-heeled boots would allow her. Anna stopped at the corner and looked at her mother as she disappeared.

At the university she met Professor Ewald in the corridor.

"Why don't I give you a lift on Saturday?" the professor offered. "To the funeral, I mean. I could pick you up at twelve fifteen?" She looked cautiously at Anna; they had barely spoken since their minor run-in the other day.

"Yes, please," Anna said. "I had actually decided not to go, but I've changed my mind."

"I'm so glad," Professor Ewald said, warmly.

"Any news?" Anna asked.

"No." Professor Ewald shrugged. "Only that dreadful rumor." Her eyes shone.

"What rumor?" Anna feigned ignorance.

"Rumor has it he was full of parasites, cysticerci from *Taenia solium*. That there were thousands of them in his tissue and that's what caused his death." Professor Ewald gave Anna a look of horror.

Anna gulped. Should she confirm it?

"Don't listen to rumors," she said and put her hand affectionately on Professor Ewald's shoulder. Professor Ewald nodded.

Anna continued down the corridor. She wanted a word with the World's Most Irritating Detective. Why on earth were those parasites a secret?

She was starving. She went through Johannes's drawers and found some crackers. They were stale and sweet, but she ate the whole packet. Then she drank a glass of water, switched on her computer, checked her e-mails, proofread the conclusion of her dissertation for the umpteenth time, chewed a nail, scratched her head, and when she had finally run out of displacement activities, she called Ulla Bodelsen in Odense.

The telephone was answered on the fifth ring, when Anna was about to give up.

"Yes?"

"My name is Anna," Anna said. Her heart was beating wildly.

"Hi." The voice sounded friendly.

"I know this might sound weird," she said quickly. "But I'm looking for a woman who used to be a health visitor in the Odense area about twenty-eight, twenty-nine years ago. I know that her name was Ulla Bodelsen, and . . . er . . . I found your number on the Internet."

The voice laughed. "Fancy that, I'm on the Internet. All that is completely beyond me. I'm retired now, but you're quite correct. I worked as a health visitor for Odense City Council for more than thirty-five years. How can I help you?"

It was a straightforward request, but Anna was nervous and thought her story sounded lame. A father and a daughter. Jens and

Anna Bella. The mother hospitalized with a bad back, father and baby alone. Could Ulla recall them?

"Ah. That's no easy task." She laughed again and it sounded as if she was weighing up her response. "But I ought to remember," she continued. "Fathers and babies, there haven't been many of them. It was mostly mothers. But then, back in the 1970s, there were quite a few. They had equality in those days," she quipped. "And Anna Bella, that's an unusual name. Were you named after anyone?"

"An apple, I think," Anna replied.

"Hmm, it doesn't ring any bells."

Anna's heart sank. "Ah, well," she sighed.

"Where did you live? Perhaps your address might trigger my memory."

"In the village of Brænderup, outside Odense. Hørmark svejen was the name of our street," Anna said.

A pause followed.

"Yes, that's right. I used to visit there all the time. All those communes. They kept having children." She laughed again. "But no, I'm sorry, I don't think I can help you."

"But it has to be you," Anna persisted. "We lived there, your name is in my health record book. It must have been you. I'm trying to find out something about that time, why my parents—"

Ulla Bodelsen interrupted her. "Now I remember him!" she exclaimed. "Your father. His name was Jens. He was a journalist, wasn't he?"

"Yes," Anna exclaimed. "That's him!"

"The poor man was under terrible pressure trying to work from home and look after a baby at the same time. It proved impossible, no surprise there, and as your mother was still in the hospital, he decided to quit his job. You wouldn't believe the state the house was in, and he was at the end of his rope from sleep deprivation and working too hard, so I supported his decision. We spoke regularly, until he called one day and said he didn't need my help anymore. I never found out why. I called him a couple of times, but he said everything was fine. I remember the child now. Gorgeous little thing, she was. She was dark and . . . you can't shut me up now," she laughed. "Old people are like that when you allow them to wallow in the past."

Anna was confused. "The child," she said. "That was me."

Ulla went quiet, then she said, "No, she couldn't have been you. The little girl was called Sara. I'm sure of it. My mother's name was Sara, and when I was young I knew that if I ever had a daughter of my own, I would call her Sara. So, of course, I noticed every little Sara, I met."

Anna was flabbergasted.

"So the name Anna Bella means absolutely nothing to you?"

"No." Ulla Bodelsen was adamant.

Anna felt like screaming. It couldn't be true. The man, Ulla remembered, was Jens, Anna was sure of it! Brænderup, the communes, Cecilie's absence, Jens who had to manage everything on his own, it *was* them! Her life. Her childhood. There was no Sara. Ulla Bodelsen had to be wrong.

"Please may I visit you?" Anna asked out of desperation.

"But, child," Ulla Bodelsen said, "even if I am your old health visitor, I won't be able to recognize you, it's been almost thirty years. You're a grown woman now, not a toddler."

"No," Anna said. "I know, but perhaps you'll recognize my daughter."

Another silence.

"Of course you can come," Ulla said then.

"As early as tomorrow?"

"Tomorrow is . . . Friday? Well, that'll be fine."

When Anna had ended the conversation, she was trembling.

Who the hell was Sara?

She wasted the next half hour on her computer. Googled something, tried to compose an invitation to her dissertation defense, but who was there to invite? She looked up Karen's address on the Internet. This was something she did regularly, and every time the address came up as somewhere in Odense. This time Anna's jaw dropped when the search results appeared. Karen had moved and was now living in northwest Copenhagen, not far from Anna and even closer to the university! It had to be her. Karen Maj Dyhr. There could only be one person with that name. She stared at the telephone number for a long time. She twirled on her chair, looking around the room. Johannes's computer was still missing, and the mess on his desk was unbelievable. She wondered why he hadn't replied to her text about his computer being confiscated. If anyone had removed hers without asking, she would have had a fit. She texted him again.

Haven't you hibernated for long enough now? No response. Damn! She called him. It went straight to voice mail. Thoroughly annoyed, she began going through his drawers. Chaos everywhere. Papers, notes, and books. She wasn't looking for anything in particular, nor did she find anything interesting. It was almost two o'clock. She switched off her computer and packed up her stuff. She wanted to speak to Johannes. He had said they were still friends, so he had to talk to her. They couldn't go on not speaking.

She was about to leave when she remembered the necklace. She took out the small white box. Fancy Professor Helland buying her a present. No man had ever given Anna jewelry. The pendant couldn't be mass-produced; after all, how many people would appreciate the significance of an egg and a feather? Helland must have had it made especially for her. She held up the chain and put it on. Then she left. As she passed Helland's office, she said out loud: "Sorry, but there's no way I'm thanking a door."

She caught the bus to Vesterbro and headed for the street where Johannes lived. As she crossed Istedgade, she was reminded of a winter's night, a long time ago, when Thomas and she had left a bar where they had spent three hours. It had snowed in the meantime, Copenhagen had been enchanting and they decided to walk all the way home. There was white virgin snow, the clouds had long since disappeared and they could see a million stars. In front of their block, Thomas had pressed Anna up against the wall.

"Let's not go inside," he whispered. "It's beautiful out here."

"Love me," Anna said suddenly. "Love me, no matter what happens."

"Anna," he said. "I love you no matter what. It's you and me forever. With kids and the whole kit and caboodle." He laughed. Anna had started to cry.

The next morning all the snow was gone. That was four years ago now.

Anna crossed Enghave Plads, where the winos still hung out even though the temperature had dropped to below zero. It had started snowing and she pulled up her hood. She had visited Johannes several times, and it had always been enjoyable. Johannes had treated her to a selection of unusual sandwiches of his own design and made tea in individual cups rather than in a pot. Every time he brought her a fresh cup, it would be accompanied by a crunchy biscuit on the saucer. On one occasion, he had starting quizzing her about her private life. Not just superficial information, such as *grew up in a village outside Odense, single parent*, but personal stuff.

Johannes had long since told Anna everything about himself that mattered. His father had died when he was very young, and he had acquired a stepfather, Jørgen, when his mother remarried. His stepfather owned a furniture emporium and hoped Johannes would take it over one day. It had been very hard for Johannes to fight this expectation. He hadn't really pulled his life together until he joined the goth scene, where he had met a uniquely accepting community. In a voice that came close to breaking, Johannes had told her about his younger sister. In return, Anna felt she ought to be honest about her own life.

At first, she tried to get away with the edited version, and initially Johannes bought it. But the next time they met he had said: "Anna, you really can trust me."

It had taken Anna two hours to tell him the story about Thomas. She had gotten pregnant and Thomas hadn't been pleased. Anna had raged and cried. She didn't want an abortion. Neither of them had worried about contraception for almost three months! When Thomas finally acquiesced, Anna convinced herself she had read too much into his initial reaction. A child was something abstract to a man, and he had simply been incapable of relating to it. They were going to live happily ever after.

Shortly after Lily was born, the rug was pulled from under Anna's feet. Lily woke up four to five times every night, and Anna could barely breathe when Thomas came home from work; it felt like she had a metal hoop clamped around her chest. She cried; she screamed. She hammered her fists against his chest, woke him up at night because she couldn't bear to be alone. Thomas withdrew from her. He worked late, went to bed early, ignored her when she spoke to him. And yet she didn't see the split coming.

With her voice subdued and her head lowered, she confessed the most shameful moment of her life to Johannes.

Lily was eleven months old and could say "Dad" and "Mom" and "hi" though she still didn't walk. One Saturday, when Anna and Lily came back from swim class, Thomas's stuff was gone. She had been out for four hours. The stereo and two framed posters were missing from the living room, the espresso maker had gone from the kitchen, and Thomas's office was empty. On the floor was a box containing the instructions for the dishwasher and the warranty for the blender. He called her later to say: "We're not together anymore." How stupid did he think she was?

The shock hit her that night and lasted three months. She couldn't sleep and kept shaking all over; she sweated and had palpitations. Lily cried and cried and wanted to get into Thomas's office. Anna tried to breastfeed her and kiss her clammy forehead, reassuring her everything would be all right, but Lily just screamed even louder. Seeing her eleven-month-old daughter grieve was the worst thing Anna had ever experienced, and she had no idea how to console her. The latch on Thomas's office was worn and the door kept opening of its own accord. Lily would crawl in and sit on the wooden floor, rocking back and forth, in an attempt to comfort herself. Finally, Anna nailed the door shut.

"Come on, darling, have some food," she whispered, but whenever Lily saw Anna's breasts, which she used to worship, she would howl. At last, Anna squeezed out a drop of milk and tasted it. It was bitter. After four days of hell, she called Jens, who called Cecilie, and an hour later, Cecilie moved in. Cecilie wanted to open the door to Thomas's office, but Anna threw a fit. Eventually Cecilie gave up, and the door remained closed.

"It must have been hard for you both," Johannes said, when she had finished.

"For me and Cecilie or for me and Lily?" Anna asked.

"No, for you and Thomas," he said.

"Don't you dare defend Thomas!" Anna sneered. "We can't be friends if you take his side!"

Johannes looked at her for a long time.

"No man wants to desert his woman and his child, Anna. No one in his right mind would do that. And, yes, it was hard for him. It was probably a thousand times harder for him than it will ever be for you. His pain will last his whole life. You'll find another man, Lily will have another father. But Thomas will never have another you. Never."

Anna started crying.

"Thomas said it was all my fault."

"Yes, of course he did. What else could he say? How else would he explain himself? I don't doubt for a second that you were hard work, Anna. You screamed and shouted, you hit him and you turned his life into a living hell. You've just told me. You give off twenty thousand volts. But nothing, nothing excuses cowardice. He could have done anything. Bound you, gagged you, had you committed or called the police, or fined you every time you freaked out, but he should have given you a chance. He should have given his family a chance. Leaving like that was cowardly. And you can't live with a coward. Period."

It was the *period* that had touched Anna the most. Johannes's assurance. What Thomas had done wasn't okay. Period. Later, they had talked about forgiveness, and Johannes had asked Anna if she intended to forgive her ex. Anna replied she didn't know if she could.

"But you have to," Johannes insisted. "Promise me you'll forgive him. For your sake and for Lily's." He looked at her earnestly, and she looked away. Johannes stood up and grabbed her firmly by the shoulders.

"Anna, I mean it. If you don't forgive him, you'll never move on. Promise me you will." Anna nodded, but Johannes didn't let go of her.

"I'll hold you to your promise," he said. "And don't take too long," he added. "Hey, look at me!" Anna looked into his eyes without blinking.

"Johannes. I'll forgive him. I promise you. Not today, please? But soon."

Anna turned into Kongshøjgade and stopped dead. Three police cars were parked in the street outside Johannes's apartment and a dozen people had gathered outside the stairwell, which was cordoned off with red-and-white police tape. Slowly, Anna walked closer, her heart pounding.

CHAPTER 10

Thursday morning Søren woke up far too early. He gave up trying to go back to sleep and got up. He lit a fire in the living room, heated frozen rolls in the oven, and forced himself to enjoy two minutes of home life wherein he wasn't thinking about the case. At 7:20 a.m. it began to get light. Søren put on thick socks as he contemplated how cold it was for October. Perhaps it was a sign of a hard winter to come?

Søren remembered the ice winter of 1987 when Denmark had been landlocked with Sweden for over two months. Søren had been seventeen years old and Knud had taken him ice-fishing. They had put snow tires on Knud's Citroën, set off in severe frost and brilliant sunshine, and driven across the ice to Sweden. A state of enjoyable mayhem had reigned on the ice with cars weaving gingerly in and out between each other, people on foot chatting as they pulled children on sleds, and skaters with scarves flapping in the wind. When they reached Sweden, they headed north. Knud had borrowed a friend's cabin on an island.

"How can we fish when the lake is frozen solid?" a baffled Søren had asked as they walked across the ice to the island. Knud winked conspiratorially at him.

They had lazed about all weekend. They played cards or Mastermind and ate chocolate in the cabin. They threw logs on the fire and went for a walk around the island. Knud had brought a dartboard and they played outside until the light faded, wearing gloves so they could hold bottles of beer without getting frostbite on their hands. Knud asked Søren what was on his mind these days. Søren's initial reaction was that it was a weird question, but then he got the urge to confide in his grandfather. Tell him the things he thought about, the people he thought about, who his real friends were and who weren't, why he had been bored on a school visit to the Royal Theatre for a stage version of *Hosekræmmeren*, though he loved the original short story, why he didn't have time for a girlfriend right now but there were some girls he liked; there was this girl in his class, her name was Vibe, she had completely green eyes.

It was evening now, there were millions of stars over Sweden, and they sat outside gazing at them, even though it was at least minus ten degrees. Knud made hot cocoa and warmed their sleeping bags by the fire and there they sat, like two fat caterpillars, in the darkness, in Sweden. Suddenly Søren turned to his grandfather and raised a subject they rarely discussed.

"There's a boy in my year called Gert. He lost his parents when he was ten years old. Car crash. He's gone completely off the rails. He cuts school, he drinks, and never does his homework. I think he might be expelled. They say he used to live with his aunt. I don't know him all that well. I think she got fed up with him. So he went into foster care. Two different homes. Finally, he was sent to boarding school. He's back with his aunt now, but only until he finishes school. *If* he finishes, that is."

Knud stared into the darkness. The constellations were clear and the darkness between them endless.

"But I'm not unhappy, Knud," Søren said. "I know Peter and Kristine are dead. I know they were my parents, and they loved me. But I'm not sad. Not about that." He fell silent.

They sat next to each other without speaking for almost five minutes. Then, in a thick voice, Knud said, "Sometimes, when I look at you, I miss them so much I think my heart will break."

Søren said nothing, but he took Knud's hand.

Søren decided to go to work early rather than try to relax at home. The rising sun made the sky glow flaming red. The heater was on. Søren switched on his radio but turned it off again. He needed silence to review the last few days. The College of Natural Science simultaneously fascinated him and drove him insane. Practically all its staff were friendly and helpful, and they had answered his questions willingly, yet he still felt as if he had made no progress. As if they weren't telling him everything.

The forensic evidence turned out to be equally inconclusive. There were prints everywhere in Helland's office. Anna Bella Nor's, Johannes Trøjborg's, Professor Ewald's, and Professor Jørgensen's along with a million others. It made no sense. Nothing significant had been found on Helland, only a micro-layer of soap with a hint of lavender, which merely confirmed Helland had showered before going to work on the day he died. There were no prints, no skin cells, no sweat, and no saliva that wasn't Helland's. Everything confirmed if Helland had been murdered, it had technically happened three to four months ago.

The previous day Søren had been informed that Professor Freeman had checked into Hotel Ascot. He was briefly cheered up by this; but a) Freeman was clearly here for the bird symposium, and b) Søren didn't for a moment believe that an ageing ornithologist from Canada had traveled to Denmark four months ago to infect Professor Helland with parasite eggs. Nevertheless, Søren and Henrik went to pick him up at his hotel, and while in the car, Søren wondered if his decision to interview Clive Freeman was an act of desperation rather than real investigation work. When you had nothing to go on, you clutched at straws. The interview did indeed prove to be a waste of time, and when he sent the professor home two hours later, the case had progressed no further. It remained bizarrely devoid of clues.

Søren spent the rest of the day at his desk growing increasingly frustrated. Finally, he decided to turn the spotlight back on Erik Tybjerg, and just after 4 p.m. he returned to the Natural History Museum. This time, his first port of call was the reception, but the receptionist was unable to help him.

"By the way, you're not the only person looking for him," the young woman behind the counter added. Søren was exasperated. What kind of workplace was this where you could just vanish without anyone taking the slightest notice? He asked to speak to the head of the institute. The young woman gave him a skeptical look but picked up the telephone and dialed a number. Ten minutes later a man appeared and introduced himself as Professor Fjeldberg. He was bony and gray, but his eyes sparkled.

"How can I help you?" he said, politely.

"I'm Superintendent Marhauge," Søren said, showing him his badge. "I would like to see Dr. Tybjerg's office. I've been looking for him for the last two days in connection with the death of Professor Helland. I would like to stress Dr. Tybjerg isn't a suspect, but I would very much like to talk to him to establish Professor Helland's movements up to his death." Søren sounded like he was reading from a script, and the older man looked at him for a long time.

"You know very well I can't let you into Dr. Tybjerg's office without a warrant."

Søren looked resigned. Professor Fjeldberg continued: "But I'll allow it this once. I, too, have been wondering where he is."

They followed a different path through the confusing building, and it wasn't until they reached the windowless corridor that Søren realized where they were: in the basement facing the University Park. They entered the laboratory in front of Tybjerg's office, and

Søren had a look around. The room looked unused. The trash cans were empty and the microscopes were shrouded.

"Here you are," Fjeldberg said when he had unlocked the door to Tybjerg's office. "How long will you need?"

"Twenty-five minutes," Søren said.

Fjeldberg lingered in the doorway. "Is it true about the parasites?" he asked, hesitantly.

Søren groaned inwardly. "What do you mean?" he said, feigning ignorance.

"Is it true that Helland died because he was riddled with parasites?"

Søren laughed briefly. "You know I can't discuss the case with you. But the parasite story is news to me."

"I knew it couldn't be true!" Fjeldberg exclaimed triumphantly, and marched down the corridor.

"Damn, damn, damn," Søren muttered to himself as Fjeldberg's footsteps faded away. The parasite rumor was spreading like wildfire. He entered Tybjerg's office. It was small and full to bursting without being messy. There were bookcases on two walls, a display cabinet against the third, and a desk against the fourth. No old mugs or glasses, no journals lying around. Tybjerg had around fifteen classical music CDs lined up next to his computer, but otherwise very few personal possessions were in evidence.

Søren studied the room for a long time. It looked like something out of an IKEA catalogue rather than the office of a real human being. He read the book spines and discovered that Dr. Tybjerg's own publications took up almost two shelves. They were mostly journals with Post-it notes attached to the pages where his articles appeared, but there were also a dozen books with his name on the title page. His most recent work was a reference book on birds that had been published earlier that year, Søren read on the title page. *An A to Z of Modern Dinosaurs*, it was called.

Hey, what was this? He pulled out a thick volume and discovered a beaker with a toothbrush and a disposable razor behind it. He removed more books and his eyes widened. Shaving cream, shampoo, a bottle of aftershave, a cheap plastic comb, stacks of clean underwear, socks rolled up in pairs, three pairs of jeans folded double. When he searched the other shelves, he found personal items behind every book. More clothes, more toiletries, four novels, a stamp collection, a blanket, a torch, an old-fashioned Walkman, and a bag of audio books, including *Lord of the Rings*.

When Søren had checked everything, he replaced the books and once again the office became bland and impersonal. Behind the door he discovered a fold-out bed, without its mattress. Weird. Søren looked inside the bin, but it was empty. Then he caught sight of a card sticking out between two books. He pulled it out. It was a colorful postcard from Malaysia, the handwriting was sloped and childish. *Malaysia is great, but the food very spicy. Will be home soon. Cheers, Asger.* A postcard from a friend. He glanced at his watch, then he scribbled down his telephone number on a piece of paper and put it on Dr. Tybjerg's keyboard. He left the office with one clear goal: to find Tybjerg. He heard Fjeldberg's footsteps in the corridor.

On their way back to civilization, Søren tried to quiz Professor Fjeldberg about Dr. Tybjerg, but it proved to be difficult.

"He's good," Fjeldberg kept stressing. "Very good. Plenty of publications, a visionary. But not terribly well liked."

"Why not?"

"He's rather eccentric," Fjeldberg said, bluntly. "But then again, who isn't around here?"

"Can you be more specific?" Søren pressed him. Fjeldberg thought about it.

"Erik Tybjerg has been associated with this museum since he was fourteen years old. I first heard about him through a friend who worked with his foster father, and I contacted him at the beginning of the 1980s. Tybjerg has a photographic memory and he knows everything there is to know about birds. I tasked him with reviewing the collection, and he organized and arranged the whole thing and has been maintaining it ever since. He knows every bone fragment and every feather in every drawer. He graduated as a biologist, but though he has been a fixture in this place for the last twenty-five years, I don't really know him. We've worked together on several occasions, most recently in connection with a feather exhibition currently on public display upstairs. You must have experienced this yourself: some people you just can't get close to. Dr. Tybjerg is one such person. He always talks about his subject in an odd, rather chanting manner, and he works nonstop. My wife will tell you I work far too much, you have to in this business. The competition is very stiff. But I'm a slacker compared to Dr. Tybjerg. He's always here. In the Vertebrate Collection, in the corridor outside the collection, in his basement office, or in the cafeteria. Always. Last year, I even ran into him on Christmas Eve." Fjeldberg looked at Søren and added. "I had left my wife's Christmas present behind in my office, and I stopped by around 3 p.m. to pick it up. All the lights were off, and I could have sworn I was alone. Suddenly I heard footsteps. I turned around, thinking it must be the security guard, but it was Tybjerg. He was carrying a bag of shopping and seemed to be in a good mood. We wished each other a Merry Christmas and as he was about to leave, I casually said, 'Aren't you going home for Christmas?' He muttered something, but when I asked him to repeat it, he gave a different answer. He said he was an atheist. Like I said, he didn't seem sad at all, or I would have invited him to spend Christmas with us—I mean, if he had no family to go to. But he seemed fine. Scientific work clearly is his whole life."

Søren looked at Fjeldberg. They were back at the main entrance, where he had been met less than an hour ago.

"There's something I don't understand," Søren said. "Dr. Tybjerg's relatively young, he's talented, he publishes prolifically, he's dedicated and hard working, but according to your administrator with whom I spoke yesterday, he has never been offered tenure. Why on earth not?"

Professor Fjeldberg sighed, and Søren's seismograph reacted.

"Personally, I'm not surprised—it's a rare thing. We have to be selective, and there are many high-quality candidates out there." Fjeldberg looked straight at Søren. "What does puzzle me is how Tybjerg manages to work here as though he had tenure. He must have found a way, I can see that, but where does he find the money to fund his research? Of course, he has worked with Helland on several of his projects, but that . . . that'll come to an end now. I imagine he will be forced to apply for jobs abroad, and I think that would be a good thing. This is a very small pond, if you catch my drift. Dr. Tybjerg is hugely overqualified, scientifically speaking, but his social skills are poor. The University of Copenhagen is completely the wrong place for someone like him. Too many sharp elbows, too much professional jealousy, and meager prospects for an oddball like Tybjerg who can't teach, nor should he; he should be allowed to get on with his specialized research. That would be the ideal solution: Enough money to invest in scientists with social and educational skills and also in experts who research exclusively within a narrow field. But we don't have the money, it's as simple as that. So we only hire people with sound subject knowledge and teaching qualifications, i.e., people who can get along with others and teach them something."

"And Dr. Tybjerg isn't one of those?"

"No," Fjeldberg asserted with a forceful smile. "He isn't."

"Do you know Anna Bella Nor from Helland's department?"

"Yes. Well, that's to say, I know she's his postgraduate student."

Søren nodded. "And Tybjerg's. According to Anna Bella, he's her external supervisor, so he must have some teaching skills?"

Fjeldberg looked genuinely surprised. "Tybjerg? That sounds like a rather suspect arrangement between Helland and Tybjerg. According to university rules you cannot supervise a postgraduate student unless you have tenure. But you know . . ." he suddenly looked reflective. "There has been a lot of belt-tightening here these last few years. The government has cut our grants to the point where it's beyond a joke. At times we are forced to bend the rules to keep the wheels turning. Don't quote me on that," he added quickly.

"Why not?"

"You don't know how things are done here," Fjeldberg sighed. "And I don't want to make waves. In three years I'll become an emeritus professor, and I've got my retirement all planned. A cottage, some grandchildren, a happy old age."

"Okay," Søren said. "Off the record. You have my word."

Fjeldberg looked relieved. "I think Helland helped Tybjerg on the quiet. He probably had his reasons, but that's none of my business. Personally, I would never have picked someone like Tybjerg for my successor; I would have chosen a candidate likely to have a future with the university. Dr. Tybjerg will never get tenure here," Fjeldberg said again, and then he laughed. "He might be an expert, but he's also a misfit and since our system barely tolerates experts, it certainly won't accommodate experts who are misfits. Impossible."

He looked at his watch. "I'm afraid I'll have to end our meeting. Is there anything else I can do for you?"

Søren shook his head.

"I'll call you if there is. Thanks for your help so far."

"Don't mention it." Professor Fjeldberg rose and unlocked the door to the museum with a key attached to a snap hook in his trousers. Søren remembered something.

"Excuse me, Professor Fjeldberg!"

The old man turned around.

"What did you think he said to you, back then?" Søren asked.

Fjeldberg looked momentarily thrown.

"Dr. Tybjerg," Søren explained. "What was it you thought you heard him say when you bumped into him that Christmas?"

Fjeldberg's face lit up. "Ah . . . well, I'm almost certain that he said, 'This is my home.'" Fjeldberg looked wistful and shrugged. Then he was gone.

When Søren parked his car under Bellahøj police station twenty minutes later than his usual arrival time, the sun had risen fully and the sky retained only a faint hint of pink. Linda was already there, and he could smell coffee.

"There are pastries, if you want some," she said, pointing to a plate on her desk.

"Any news regarding Johannes Trøjborg?" Søren asked, prodding one of the pastries.

"No," Linda replied. "I called him several times, yesterday and this morning." She showed him a list. "But it goes straight to voice mail."

Søren pursed his lips and said: "Please would you get Henrik for me? If he's not busy, we'll go to Johannes Trøjborg's home in half an hour. I've got to speak to him."

Linda nodded.

"And Dr. Tybjerg?" Søren asked, feeling weary now.

"No luck there either," Linda said. "Answering machine at the university, no reply to e-mails, and when I tried his cell I got a recorded message telling me the number was no longer in service."

"Oh," Søren said, raising his eyebrows. "Didn't it go to voice mail when you called it the other day?"

"Yes, it did," Linda confirmed, "and when I called the telephone company, they informed me that Dr. Tybjerg's cell had been disconnected because he hadn't paid his bills. They had sent three reminders."

Søren nodded and turned to enter his office.

"I nearly had an argument with them," Linda added. "Imagine, they cut off his cell because he owed them 209 kroner. Petty, don't you think?"

"Rules are rules," Søren said.

"Yes, but even so. Such a tiny amount. I think that's mean."

"Just as well you work for the police and not for the telephone company, then. Your generosity would soon bankrupt them." He had an idea and looked at Linda. "Tell me, did we ever check his address with the National Register of Persons?"

"You mean: did *I* ever check it?" She sent him a teasing look. "I did. It's twenty-six Mågevej, second floor apartment in northwest Copenhagen."

"Thank you," Søren said and went into his office. A moment later he stuck his head around the door.

"I think I'll take a rain check on the pastries," he said. He was starting to see parasites everywhere.

*   *   *

Less than thirty minutes later there was a knock on his door and Sten appeared.

"Am I interrupting you?"

"No, come in."

Sten closed the door behind him. "I've finally ploughed through Johannes Trøjborg's e-mails. There was a lot of them." Sten took a seat opposite Søren's desk.

"We already knew he was fighting with Helland from Helland's computer, but . . ." Sten flicked through a pile of papers. "Yeah, here it is. It would appear that Lars Helland wasn't the only person at the Department of Cell Biology and Comparative Zoology to receive mysterious e-mails."

Søren leaned forward, intrigued now.

"Someone calling himself *YourGuy* sent three e-mails to Johannes in the last four weeks." Sten read aloud from a sheet:

"I want to see you again. Don't you get it? Call me! And the next one: *I'm crazy about you. I'm beside myself with desire because of what you let me do to you. Call me!"* Søren and Sten exchanged knowing glances. Sten read on:

"Hi, Jo. I crossed a line the other day. Sorry. I lost the plot because you're so gorgeous. I've tried getting hold of you all week, but you won't come to the door or take my calls. I respect you don't want to, but can we talk, please?" Sten lowered the sheet.

Søren drummed his fingers on the table and looked out of the window.

"What can I say," he said eventually. "Some kind of gay fling?"

"Take a look at this," Sten said as if he hadn't heard Søren and handed him a printout of a photograph. It showed an androgynous person, which Søren took to be a man due to the flatness of the chest underneath the corset. The hair was scraped back in oily furrows, the clothes were tight-fitting black leather, and he wore fishnet stockings. The lips were painted scarlet and the lipstick was smeared on one side, as if the lips were bleeding or had just been kissed. The eye makeup was theatrical. Thick lines of kohl and a decorative spider's web spread its silvery threads toward the left temple.

"Who's that?" Søren asked.

"I'm convinced it's Johannes," Sten replied. And now Søren could see it too. In a flash, Johannes's features grew visible behind the make-up. Søren gasped.

"Well, I'll be damned!" he said.

"Johannes is a goth," Sten explained.

"A goth?" Søren frowned.

"It's a subculture. I read about it on the Internet. Men and women worshiping the darkness and dressing up as everything from Count Dracula to dominatrixes in leather corsets. They love black-and-white makeup, and they have tons of piercings. The photo is from the Red Mask, which appears to be the most active goth club in Copenhagen. The club is open the first Friday of every month, and as far as I can see, its fame extends beyond Denmark. Photos are always published on the club's website. The caption below the photo simply says '3rd September 2007.' That's why I thought it had to be him." Sten smiled wryly before he continued: "Elsewhere on the website he calls himself Orlando, but his alias doesn't appear to be an attempt to disguise his identity, more like a part of the game that goths appear to be playing. Seriously!" he added, when he saw the skeptical expression on Søren's face. "They act out Count Dracula parties. It seems rather appealing. A club that practices tolerance, acceptance, and community. The goth scene, as far as I've been able to establish, appears to be a reaction to 1980s punk. Punks must have a particular look and share the same views. The goths have no time for that. *No code, no core, no truth.* That's their slogan. The unique, personal expression is everything."

"Is it a gay club?" Søren asked.

"No. Like I said: no code, no rules," Sten said. "Gays are welcome as are straight people. Many people show up in normal clothes and never reveal which team they play for."

"No sex?" Søren asked.

"No, no sex. That's probably why nobody bothers to disguise their identity. Johannes isn't the only one whose name is published. All that's kept secret is where events take place. If you want to take part, you sign up to a text message list. You get a text informing you when the next event is taking place, a few hours before doors open. The venue changes every time. Probably to avoid interfering neo-Nazis and other troublemakers." Sten shrugged.

"I don't get the impression that anything shady happens there," he went on. "We're talking about a group of adults with a penchant for horror, thrills, and darkness; who like to dress up. However, there are many overlappers on the goth scene."

"Overlappers?"

"People who are part of the goth culture and also active on the fetish scene, and let me tell you something. The goth scene may be open, but the fetish scene is hermetically sealed, like a frightened oyster. That club is called Inkognito. The same people are behind the monthly club events, but strict rules govern fetish arrangements. There's a total ban on pictures. Fetishists are usually older than people from the goth scene and typically more established with families and senior executive jobs, so consequently they're more protective of their privacy. The fundamental difference between the goth and fetish scenes is obviously sex. Fetish events take place in dark rooms where people can enjoy themselves anonymously. The sexual activities are fairly hard-core. You can be spanked, have clamps attached to your nipples, be suspended from the wall by pulleys and weights, there's Japanese bondage and things I had—obviously—never heard of until I read about it on the net late last night." Sten grinned at Søren. "But anyway, everyone's anonymous, even when they're having sex. You find a partner and do your thing. Johannes received several e-mails announcing fetish events, so I believe there's a good chance he was active on both scenes. I imagine Orlando met YourGuy at an event in one of the two clubs and has now gone missing because he's hiding from YourGuy. He sounds creepy to me," Sten added, snapping his fingers against the printouts.

Søren pondered this. "And you don't think YourGuy is just suffering from a regular crush and his tone is a bit rough because people on that scene talk to each other like that?"

Sten nodded. "You may be right, but what really got me thinking is that YourGuy's address is anonymous, or fictitious. He lists it as 'Donald Duck, 2200 Ducktown.' You can do that with free e-mail accounts. You can create an anonymous address, just like the person who e-mailed threats to Helland, and you can call yourself anything, Donald Duck or Bill Clinton, and if you also use an Internet café, well, then you're completely untraceable. The account was created on the eighth of September this year, and only three e-mails were ever sent from it: on the twelfth and the sixteenth of September, and four days ago, on the seventh of October. Of course I've spoken to the owner of the Internet café, whose server I've traced the e-mails to, but he just laughed when he heard my request. The café has twenty computers spread across three small rooms and has approximately two hundred users per day. They've no idea who comes and goes, so anyone could have written those e-mails. All we can be sure about is that he definitely didn't want to be identified, but why be secretive if it's just a regular crush?"

Søren nodded slowly.

"Why do you think that Johannes is gay? You've suggested this a couple of times." Sten wanted to know.

"It hasn't been confirmed yet. I think he might be, but Anna Bella Nor says he isn't. Why?"

Sten looked pensive. "I googled Orlando. It's the name of the central character in a novel by Virginia Woolf, written in 1928. Orlando is a young man who lives for four hundred years and is transformed into a woman along the way . . ."

"And?" Søren looked at Sten.

"I don't think Johannes is gay at all," Sten replied. "Members post comments after parties on the homepage of the Red Mask. Johannes is clearly a big hit among the women, and he flirts so much the temperature rises in cyberspace. I think he's experimenting with his feminine sides, and we're sufficiently ignorant to confuse it with homosexuality."

There was a knock on the door. Sten rose and Henrik entered.

"I think we're done, anyway," Sten said and nodded to Henrik. He stopped on his way out.

"Good luck with your shiny new clue," he said, shaking his head as he left.

Søren banged his forehead against the desk.

"Er, what's going on?" Henrik asked him. He stood with his arms folded across his chest, looking like a tough guy.

"I've lost my touch," Søren groaned into his blotting pad.

They left the station and Søren drove down Frederikssundvej.

"Why didn't you take Borups Allé? I thought we were going to Vesterbro?"

"There's something we need to check out first," Søren replied. "Johannes Trøjborg isn't our only missing person. Dr. Tybjerg hasn't responded to telephone calls, to e-mails, or even the friendly note I left on his desk. He lives on Mågevej, so I thought we might drop in on the way." They drove on in silence.

Søren and Henrik had been buddies since the police academy. During the short drive from Bellahøj to Mågevej, it struck Søren that they might have drifted apart. Henrik usually sat in the passenger seat, ranting about his family. He would tell anecdotes about his motorbike and trips he had taken on it. Or he would moan about women or football, or how he was thinking of taking English lessons because his kids were so good at English now they took the piss out of his pronunciation. When Søren turned into Mågevej and found an empty parking space in front of number twenty-six, he was acutely aware of how long it was since Henrik's tirades had stopped.

Søren let the key dangle in the ignition. He had never told Henrik about Maja. What if Henrik wanted to know more? Søren couldn't bear to talk about it, so he hadn't said anything. He had not told a living soul. He was alone with his grief, and now it had become encapsulated like a glass splinter.

"Fuck, my head hurts," Henrik exclaimed. He flexed one foot impatiently.

"Did you go out last night?" Søren asked.

"Yes, I met someone . . ." he began, but then he stopped, as if he had already said too much. "We had a few beers, you know."

"What, you and Lau?" Søren asked. Lau Madsen was a mutual friend and colleague.

Henrik grinned sheepishly.

"No, it . . . oh, fuck it. I've screwed up. I'll tell you about it some other time."

Søren stayed put, his hands on the steering wheel.

"So how about it?" Henrik snapped. "I thought we were looking for that Tybjerg guy, or what?"

Søren wasn't listening. "I know why you've become so secretive," he said. "And I'm sorry."

"What are you talking about?" Henrik asked.

Søren's voice thickened and he stared at his hands. "I'm apologizing to you. I know you can't be friends with someone who never gives you anything back." He didn't know what else to say.

Henrik watched him. Søren could feel his eyes boring into him.

"Why don't we do this some other time?" Henrik said. "I've had enough. And that's putting it mildly. Let's go."

Henrik got out of the car and went to the front door to read the names of the residents. Søren observed him through the windscreen. An uncomfortable feeling of anxiety fluttered inside his chest.

"His name's not here," Henrik stated when Søren joined him. "There's no Erik Tybjerg on the list. Are you sure it's number twenty-six?"

Søren stood next to Henrik and they noticed it at the same time. Someone had stuck a white label on top of the original name for the second floor apartment. It read *K. Lindberg*. Søren peeled away a corner and, as expected, the name underneath read: *Tybjerg*.

Before Søren had time to think, Henrik had rung the doorbell. They both straightened up and waited for someone to answer.

"He's bound to be at work," Henrik said, checking his watch. At that moment, a man came walking down the street with two heavy shopping bags. Henrik and Søren were both thinking the same thing—that this must be the tenant—when the man stopped and faced them.

"You looking for me? Are you debt collectors?"

"Is your name Lindberg?"

"It is. Karsten Lindberg. Something wrong?"

"We're police officers," Henrik said, showing him his badge.

"What's happened?" the man asked. He put down his shopping and looked frightened.

"Nothing," Søren replied gently. "It's got nothing to do with you or any members of your family."

Karsten Lindberg let out a sigh of relief. "Right, so what can I do for you?"

"You live here?"

"Yes, second floor apartment to the right. I'm renting it until next summer."

"Dr. Tybjerg sublet it to you?"

"Yes," the man replied, surprised.

"Do you know where Dr. Tybjerg lives while you rent his apartment?"

"Yes, I think so," he said without delay. "More or less. Los Angeles. He's a paleontologist or something like that, his subject is birds. He's teaching at UCLA for two semesters."

Søren tried his utmost to hide his astonishment. "How did you make contact with Dr. Tybjerg?"

"He put up an ad at the H. C. Ørsted Institute. I'm a biochemist. I was looking for a place to stay, and I happened to see his ad on the bulletin board. What's this about?"

"We're looking for Dr. Tybjerg," Søren said. "Was it an unfurnished sublet?"

"No, it's partly furnished. He removed all his personal belongings, but most of his furniture is still there. Suits me fine. It's just a pit stop for me."

"Do you have his address in California?"

"No, I have his e-mail address, but it's a Danish university address. In fact, he was causing me a fair amount of hassle a few months ago. I started getting a lot of final demands addressed to him, and the electricity and the landline were cut off. I tried to get hold of Erik for two weeks, but no luck. In the end, I was really angry with him. At long last he got back to me. He said he had been away on a dig. The whole thing was stupid. We had agreed I would pay money into his account and he would pay the utilities, but once he had left, I didn't hear from him. I presumed he had dealt with it. I certainly didn't think he would just stop paying the bills. I got him to transfer the bills into my name, temporarily. It was much easier for both of us. He was free to look after his bones and excavations, and I could get the light back on in my fridge and my telephone working again. He asked me to put all the letters aside, and I have. To be honest, some of them look very serious, and I've e-mailed him about it but he hasn't responded. What more can I do? I'm his tenant, not his mother. He had another letter from a debt collector recently," he said and immediately looked shamefaced.

"I don't really feel comfortable telling you all this. It's his private business. But there you have it. Do you want his mail or not?"

"Yes, please," Søren said quickly. What Karsten Lindberg was offering was technically illegal, but it would save Søren a lot of paperwork.

Søren went upstairs with him to get the letters. He carried one of Lindberg's grocery bags.

"What a nice cop you are," Lindberg said and smiled.

Tybjerg's apartment was small and impersonal. Two rooms and a stall shower in the kitchen. The kitchen cabinets were worn, and the windows needed cleaning. Søren picked up fifteen letters from debt-collecting agencies and said good-bye. When he got back to the car, Henrik was reading a garden catalogue.

"I'm thinking I might get myself a tiller," he said. "What do you think? Are you still a real man if you don't have a tiller?"

"I don't know about you," Søren said. "But I'm doing fine without one."

"Your garden looks like shit," Henrik sparred. They drove for a while in silence, then he added. "There's no way Tybjerg is in LA."

"No," Søren said. "But that's what he told his tenant. I wonder why?"

They drove down Falkoner Allé in the direction of Vesterbro. Several times Søren prepared to say something, but Henrik leaned back against the headrest and looked as if he was snoozing. Søren drummed his fingers on the steering wheel and maneuvered the car effortlessly through the traffic. He felt totally isolated. They parked in Kongshøjgade and Henrik let Søren enter Johannes Trøjborg's stairwell first. The stairs were worn in the middle; it had to be at least thirty years since they were last renovated. On each landing lay scrunched-up juice cartons, sweet wrappers, cans, and in one place a rubber strap that had once been pulled tightly around an addict's arm. The light worked on the first floor, but from then up all the bulbs were out, and the two men could barely see where they were going. It stank of urine.

"Jesus Christ," Henrik commented softly.

"Yes, lovely place, isn't it."

At last they reached Johannes's front door. It was quiet. Suddenly Søren's stomach lurched. Henrik stuck out his hand to ring the bell, but Søren grabbed his arm.

"Look," he said, pointing. The door was closed, but not completely. A faint crack, almost invisible in the dark stairwell, had caught Søren's eye.

"I've a bad feeling about this," he said, taking a pencil from his breast pocket and pushing the door. It swung open. The silence was deadly.

"We're going in," Søren announced.

The apartment was, if possible, even darker than the stairwell. Søren and Henrik stopped inside a small hallway with a kitchen to the left and a living room to the right. They could see a window, closed curtains, a cast-iron sofa with deep cushions and fabric draped across it; in front of the window was a dining table with four chairs. Henrik went into the kitchen and turned on the light. The kitchen was cluttered and filthy. Empty soft drinks bottles, stale food in opened containers, and a greasy grill, which had been removed from the oven but had never made it to the sink. It stank, and Henrik opened the door under the sink, which brought an over-filled trash can into view. Søren took two pairs of rubber gloves and two pairs of shoe protectors from his inside pocket and handed one set to Henrik. He could see where this was going; he had been a police officer for far too long.

They checked the apartment carefully and discovered Johannes in the bedroom. It was a grotesque scene. In an abstract painting of blood, Johannes was lying in his bed, his comforter carefully tucked in, looking like he was asleep. The blood had come from a dark hole to the back of his head.

"Shit, Johannes," Søren exclaimed. The two men were silent for a moment. The bedroom smelled stuffy.

"The time is ten eighteen," Henrik said laconically, took his cell and called for backup. Soon they heard the sound of approaching sirens. Søren watched the body and, for once, he found it hard to suppress his feelings.

"Johannes is my best friend," Anna had said.

The rest of the morning was pure routine. Bøje, the Deputy Medical Examiner, and the team from Forensics arrived simultaneously. Bøje quickly established that Johannes had been dead somewhere between twelve and twenty-four hours, which instantly filled Søren with guilt because it meant Johannes had been alive while they were looking for him. Why the hell hadn't he just answered his cell! The bloody trail on the floor proved Johannes had been killed in the living room, and Bøje asked the crime scene technicians to look for the murder weapon, a hard, pointy object. It took the chief technician three minutes to locate it.

"Right there," he said, waving his colleagues closer. They focused on one of the four decorative orbs on the corners of the cast-iron sofa.

"Blood, brain tissue, and hair," the technician informed Søren, who was watching from the hallway to avoid trampling on potential evidence.

Bøje glanced at the finial from where he was in the bedroom doorway and announced, "Looks about right," before resuming his work.

Søren and Henrik left the apartment and watched from the landing while the technicians identified evidence on the floor, the walls, and on fabric. Flashlight exploded from their cameras, and Søren scratched his head. His job now was to canvas the immediate neighborhood with door-to-door interviews. The coroner's assistant arrived with a body bag and removed Johannes's body; Johannes's bed sheets and his mattress were sealed and taken away. Bøje said good-bye and disappeared down the stairs. Just after 3 p.m. everything had been measured, photographed, and all the evidence collected. They had to wait for the autopsy, and it would be hours before they got any information. Søren would be none the wiser until tomorrow. He instructed five teams of two officers each to ring doorbells. When the apartment had been sealed, he plodded down the stairs. It was snowing lightly, but even so, a crowd had gathered outside the house, staring nosily at the stairwell and the red-and-white police tape flapping in the wind. Another four officers arrived—Søren waved them over and briefed them in the shelter of the stairwell. When they had been given their orders, Henrik joined Søren. Søren was freezing and couldn't feel his wool socks, in fact, he couldn't even feel his feet.

"We had better tell his parents," Søren sighed.

"I've taken care of that," Henrik said, patting his shoulder. "I sent Mads and Özlem."

Søren was grateful, and he listened to Henrik while he tried to memorize the faces of the spectators. The group was starting to break up, he thought, people were getting cold. Two elderly ladies, with granny trolleys and berets, were shifting from foot to foot next to three young men in neon pink quilted jackets and backpacks and a young woman with a child in a stroller. A younger guy was talking into his mobile, his cheeks were flushed and, to the far left, were a couple of women in their forties with two teenage children.

At the far end of the group was Anna.

She had put up her hood and her body language told Søren she had just joined the onlookers and was trying to push her way to the front. Henrik was about to say something, but he made no sound, and he tried to catch Søren's eye. A frightened Anna looked at the building, the police cars, and the cordon and, for a fraction of a second, she looked straight at Søren. Then she turned around. Søren set off after her. Brusquely, he pushed Henrik aside, skidded across the pavement, got caught up in the tape, pushed the young guys out of the way, finally got free of the crowd, and ran out into the road. The street corner was 150 feet from the stairwell, and Anna had already turned it and was long gone. He was certain it had been her. Her eyes, her mouth, the hood covering her hair. He turned into Enghavevej. Traffic was heavy and slow, and he stopped. A bus started to pull out, the driver beeping his horn at the cars who refused to let him out. Søren ran to the bus and tried peering inside, but the windows were steamed up. He banged on the side while he ran alongside it. He punched the tires, which began rolling, hammered on the door, and finally made eye contact with the driver.

"Get lost," mouthed the driver. "Catch the next one."

Søren fumbled for his badge, but the traffic eased and the bus accelerated, leaving Søren behind, cold and troubled.

"What the hell do you think you're doing?" Henrik shouted, when Søren returned to Kongshøjgade. He sent Søren a furious look.

"I thought I saw someone," Søren said, avoiding Henrik's eyes.

"Who?"

"Doesn't matter. It wasn't . . . him."

Henrik narrowed his eyes. "Since when do you chase suspects on your own?"

"Since today," Søren said, wearily. "I'm sorry. I can't make head nor tail of this case."

Henrik was visibly annoyed.

"Søren," he said. "Every police officer has to accept that not every case will be closed. So far, you have solved every case you've ever been given. You may have to accept this could be your first unsolved case. It won't kill you, nor will you be demoted to pounding the pavement, will you? Besides, it's not over yet. We've only just started! You and I will wait like good little boys for Bøje's report and then we'll come up with a battle plan, okay? Let's call it a day. I'll wrap things up here and catch a ride back with Mads. You go home. I'll write the preliminary report."

Søren nodded and got into his car. He sat there for a while, trying to calm down.

Søren drove down Falkoner Allé toward Nørrebro with a renewed sense of purpose. After crossing Ågade, he turned right and parked behind Anna's block. He walked around to the front door and rang the bell. For a long time. No reply. He rang the next-door neighbor. Time passed, then he heard an elderly voice.

"Yes?"

"Mrs. Snedker?" Søren said, reading the name next to the bell. "I'm a police officer. Please will you let me in?"

He heard a noise and thought she was opening the door, but she appeared to have had second thoughts because she replied: "And why would I believe you?"

Søren was taken aback. "Er, no why would you?" he said. Now what? The intercom hissed again.

"If you're the chap who has been waiting for Anna," the old voice snapped, "then I suggest you run back home to your mommy. We're not interested in whatever garbage you're peddling, or whatever it is you want. Be off with you." She hung up and Søren was left standing there. He took a few steps back and looked up at the building. On the fourth floor, opposite where Anna's apartment had to be located, he saw an old lady in the window. She was watching him and when he looked back at her, she waved. He pressed the bell again.

"I've never seen you before," the old lady said when she answered. "And don't think I'm stupid enough to let in a stranger just because he claims to be a police officer."

"Mrs. Snedker," Søren said with all the authority he could muster, "I'm going to give you a telephone number and you'll call directory enquiries and find out whose it is. You'll be told that it's the duty officer at Bellahøj police station. Then you wait two minutes before you call the duty officer and ask him if he thinks it's a good idea to let in a man who calls himself Søren Marhauge who claims to be a policeman, and if he says yes, you let me in, all right? I'll call them right now and give them my location. Do you follow?"

"Do you think I was born yesterday?" she said cheekily. "I promise you, sir, that I wasn't. I was born long before you were even a twinkle in your mother's eye."

Søren smiled. "Right, we have a deal, then."

She hung up. Søren called the duty officer and four minutes later, he had a call back to say his identity had been confirmed. A Maggie Snedker, born February 26, 1919, had just called. She had been highly suspicious, but they had reached an agreement in the end. The duty officer sounded amused. The intercom crackled and Søren was buzzed into the stairwell.

Mrs. Snedker was waiting on the landing. Her arms were folded across her chest and she looked fierce, but Søren detected an element of teasing in the corner of her eyes.

"You're a long way up, Mrs. Snedker," he panted, holding out his badge.

"You're right. The air up here is too thin for weaklings like you." She scrutinized his badge. "What do you want?"

"I urgently need to get ahold of your neighbor, Anna Bella Nor, and she won't open her door or answer her telephone."

"Now why wouldn't Anna open her door to a nice cop such as yourself?" the old lady asked. She was elegantly dressed and had long red nails. He couldn't believe she was over eighty. Her hair was thick, curly, and very soft, and Søren wondered if it might be a wig. Elvira's hair had turned silky and fine when she reached her early sixties, and she had had it cut quite short.

"What's this about?" Mrs. Snedker asked. "That poor girl has suffered enough. First there's that cad who abandons her and the baby. I've no time for him. Lily hadn't even turned one. What a charlatan. Anna's a good girl, she really is. But she's unhappy. And when you're very sad, you put on a brave face. She doesn't fool me, though. So, what do you want?" The old lady's eyes were as piercing as a nail gun.

"I'm afraid I can't go into details, but it's nothing very serious," he assured her. "You wouldn't have a spare key?" he tried.

"Of course I have, but I'm certainly not giving it to you." Mrs. Snedker gave him a stern look; she measured him from head to foot, and he had a strong suspicion she was checking him out.

"Why don't you join me for a drop of something?" she offered, looking at her watch. "It's four o'clock and Anna is probably picking up her little munchkin from nursery school, such a cute girl. Can you believe it? Imagine deserting a little thing like that? Anna may not be the easiest woman in the world to live with, but then again, no one ever said living together was meant to be easy, eh? And what about the child? It's been nearly two years since she last saw her father." Mrs. Snedker leaned forward as she whispered the last sentence. Søren picked up the scent of a dusty, heavy perfume. Mrs. Snedker turned resolutely on her heel and disappeared inside her apartment.

"Er . . ." Søren began, but she ignored him. He followed her into a dark, rustic-style hallway and into her living room, the likes of which he had never seen. The floor was covered with thick-piled rugs, and there was no space left on the walls. Pictures in heavy gilded frames, plates and photographs, and on the end wall, broken only by the balcony door, there were books from floor to ceiling. A gramophone, which had to be at least fifty years old, sat in between the books. Mrs. Snedker was standing by a low drinks table, pouring a rust-colored liquid into two glasses.

"Ah, there you are." She sounded delighted.

"I don't drink while I'm on duty," Søren said, not very convincingly.

"Nonsense," she said.

Søren studied an old gun mounted on the wall. The metal was freshly polished and the woodwork was in good condition, but the weapon looked hundreds of years old.

"It used to belong to Count Griffenfeld," Mrs. Snedker explained. She had followed his eyes. "Stunning example, isn't it? Right, down the hatch." She handed him a glass, knocked back her drink and frowned when Søren swallowed only half of his. She went to the window and looked out.

"Oh, look, there they are," she said, triumphantly. Søren joined her. She was right. A figure, holding a small child by the hand, had just stepped out of a low, black wooden building Mrs. Snedker informed him was Lily's nursery school. Anna was dragging the child, who was wearing a snowsuit.

"Just time for a little more Dutch courage, my friend. Now what's that about?" She looked outraged at Søren's half-full glass. He put it down on the table.

"Listen," he said. "What did you mean when you said someone had been waiting for Anna?"

"Of course," Mrs. Snedker said. "I wouldn't want to force you." She emptied Søren's glass. "Well, you see. Twice this week, a man waited for Anna on the landing. Someone she doesn't know. Or, at any rate, she can't figure out who it might have been."

"When exactly was he waiting for her?"

"When? When?" she snapped. "A couple of days ago. I no longer keep track of insignificant events. Two long days ago." She refilled their glasses, and Søren seriously considered whether alcohol might not be good for you after all. The old lady appeared strong and fearless.

"Please try to remember," Søren asked. "Was it yesterday? Was it last week?"

"Sorry," Mrs. Snedker said. "My memory is still on summer time." She pursed her lips. "Talking about summer time . . . would you mind terribly changing the clock on my video recorder to winter time? While we wait for Anna to drag the little piglet up four flights of stairs? Look, I've found the instructions, but that's where my technical expertise ends."

Søren plodded obediently after Mrs. Snedker. She handed him a torch and a yellowing booklet. The VCR was from 1981. Søren went down on all fours and started pressing various buttons until the clock was correct.

As he got up, Mrs. Snedker said, "How funny, my memory seems to have returned. I remember it vividly. The first time the man waited was Monday afternoon and the second time was Wednesday evening." She beamed.

"Last night?"

"No, May, ten years ago," she teased him. "Of course it was last night! Yesterday, tenth of October."

"Where was Anna, since he had to wait?"

"How would I know? Up to no good, I expect."

"And Anna has no idea who he might have been?"

"No, she was convinced it was Johannes, a fellow she shares an office with at the university. Mainly because of his hair color. The man was wearing a hat, but I think some auburn hair stuck out from under it, and I told Anna that, which made her think it was Johannes. But I'm not so sure. I was busy closing my door. It could have been him, but how would I know?" Mrs. Snedker suddenly sounded hurt. "I'm not hired help here, am I?"

"What's keeping them?" Søren said, suddenly impatient. Even with a toddler in tow they should have been home by now.

"Perhaps it wasn't them after all?" Mrs. Snedker shrugged.

Søren gave her weary look. "Of course it was," he said. "They must have gone somewhere else."

"The supermarket in Falkoner Allé is probably your best bet. Another glass while you wait?"

Søren declined.

"I'll come back and talk to you later," he said.

Mrs. Snedker pretended to be terribly flattered. "Perhaps you would be kind enough to buy me a small white loaf?" she called out after him.

Søren spotted Anna and her daughter almost immediately. They were plodding along very slowly and had only just passed the spot where Søren had parked his car. He followed them at a distance and when they crossed Ågade and walked down Falkoner Allé, he crossed to the other side and followed them on the pavement. He couldn't hear what they were talking about, but he observed their body language. The child was walking at a snail's pace. She kept stopping to look at things, and several times she sat down on someone's doorstep. In one hand she held a soft toy, which she dragged along the muddy pavement. Anna seemed lethargic. Her body language told Søren she needed every ounce of her strength to stay calm. One hundred feet from the supermarket, Lily sat down in the middle of the pavement. Anna pulled her arm. The situation boiled over and Anna stomped off after yelling at Lily so loudly that Søren could almost make out the words. When Anna had almost reached the entrance, she stopped and buried her face in her hands. Lily was still sitting on the pavement, sobbing her little heart out and several passersby threw anxious looks at the toddler. Anna went back and picked Lily up. At first, the child kicked her legs in anger, but Anna whispered something in her ear and the crisis passed. For the time being, at least. Anna carried her daughter inside the supermarket, and Søren crossed the road and entered as well. He waited at the entrance where some sad-looking flowers were hoping to find a buyer and watched Anna put a coin in a shopping cart, remove Lily's snowsuit, and ease her into the child seat. Their first stop was the bakery at the front, where they bought a snail-shaped pastry for Lily. Anna took off her jacket and beanie and briefly looked up. Søren took a step backward and when he looked out again, Anna and her cart had gone down an aisle. Her face was grimy and her hair flattened and greasy from the wool beanie.

Once they were out of sight, Søren found a basket and started doing his own shopping. He trailed them around the store, keeping a suitable distance. He could hear snippets of their conversation. Lily wanted to get down from the cart. As soon as Anna lifted her down, she ran off. Anna caught her, and Lily laughed out loud. Anna wasn't laughing. Anna grabbed her firmly to put her back in the child seat. Lily went rigid. The two of them struggled. Søren watched them and felt an urge to pick up the child. The girl was the same size as Maja would have been, Søren imagined. Not that he knew anything about children. Lily looked huge in Anna's arms, like a wild animal Anna couldn't control, but Søren knew the child would be tiny in his arms. She would curl up like a mouse and fit perfectly inside his shirt pocket. Together, they could smell funny cheeses in the delicatessen or find a bicycle with training wheels and colored streamers on the handlebars while Mommy did the shopping.

"Now stop it, just stop it, Lily," Anna screamed. "Do you understand? Or there will be no ice cream for a week, no, a whole month!"

Lily howled and Anna plunked her hard into the body of the cart and stormed off. They stopped at the vegetable section and Anna patted Lily's cheek to make up. Lily sniffled. Anna hugged her.

"I'm sorry," she whispered. "All we need now are some potatoes and we'll be done."

"Me do it," Lily yelled.

"No, darling," Anna said, exhausted. Søren was very close to them now. Anna and Lily both looked dreadful. Tired, red-eyed, and run down, mother and child both. Lily got ready to throw another tantrum, so Anna lifted her out of the cart.

"Okay." She gave in. "I'll hold the bag and you put in the potatoes."

"Lily help Mommy," Lily insisted.

"Yes, darling, that's right," Anna said.

Lily picked up potatoes with both hands and dropped them into the bag.

"Gently," Anna said.

"Gently," Lily echoed.

"Gently, I said," Anna repeated. Lily carried on. There were now ten potatoes in the bag. Lily picked up a large potato with both hands and hurled it into the bag.

"Right, that's enough," Anna said, and at that very moment the bag split and the potatoes rolled off in every direction.

"Oh, no," Anna gasped. Her hands hung limply by her sides. It was all too much. "Now look what you've done."

Lily started crying again.

"Come on, allow me," Søren said. He put down his basket, which contained a strange mix of groceries. "Let me help you, please?"

Anna straightened up and gave Søren a look of disbelief. "What are you doing here?"

"Shopping," Søren said, innocently.

Anna started picking up the potatoes. "I'm not talking to you," she snarled, keeping her eyes on the floor. "I'm not interested in anything you have to say. I don't want to hear it." She looked up at Søren and her eyes glowed yellow.

"I'm going to pick up your potatoes," Søren said. "And then I'm going to carry your groceries and your kid home."

"Oh no, you're not," Anna snarled.

"You bet I am," Søren said.

"Over my dead body," Anna said, theatrically.

"Sure, if that's how you want to do it," Søren replied, unperturbed.

Anna glared at him, but Søren held his ground. She looked like shit. Scrawny and spotty, and Lily, in the cart, looked neglected, with tears down her cheeks, snot across her mouth, and a filthy teddy in her arms. Anna hadn't even noticed the other shoppers staring at her and shaking their heads. A socially disadvantaged, impoverished single parent was precisely what she looked like. All that was missing were some beers and chips in her cart. But Søren was bowled over. It was madness—he didn't even like her. Contrary and stuckup, as she was. And he had only known her four days, during which time she had grown increasingly hostile to him. But he was completely smitten.

Lily refused to walk. Anna told her she had to, but Lily had made up her mind and was sitting down on the steps of a store that was closed. "No," she declared and stuck out her lower lip in defiance. "You *have* to walk," Anna repeated. Søren was about to say something, but Anna turned to him when she sensed his lips moving.

"She *has* to walk. If she doesn't, we can't get home. I can't carry all those bags, my books, and a child. I'm not strong enough." She was on the brink of tears. Søren emptied his groceries into Anna's least full bag, tied the two remaining ones together, and hung them over his shoulders like a yoke. Without asking for permission, he lifted Lily and put her on his shoulders.

"Keep your feet still, or you'll break the eggs," he told her.

"Okay," Lily said, proudly.

Søren started walking and he soon heard Anna's footsteps behind them. A gleeful Lily called out from her vantage point, "I can see all the cars in the whole world, I can see all the houses and all the boys and girls."

Anna didn't utter a word the whole way back, but when they reached the stairwell, she said, "Thanks for your help, I'll take it from here."

"Anna," Søren said, as he let Lily down. "I'm coming upstairs with you." He was in no mood for an argument.

Lily, now rested, started to climb the stairs. Anna faced Søren, her eyes brimming with tears.

"I know what you've come to tell me, and I don't want to hear it. I don't want to hear it!"

"Anna," he said gently, "it's not going to go away just because I don't tell you, and I have to talk to you. What the hell were you doing outside Johannes's apartment? And why did you run?"

"Mooom," Lily called out from the first floor landing. "I'm having a pee-pee in my snowsuit."

"Shit," Anna exclaimed. She raced up the stairs and tried running all the way to the top with Lily. Lily laughed. Søren followed with the bags.

Mrs. Snedker was waiting for them on the fourth floor.

"Hi, Maggie," Søren heard Anna say. "Emergency. Lily needs the bathroom."

"Aha," Maggie said. "Is that nice cop with you?"

Søren arrived in time to see Anna give Mrs. Snedker a baffled look, then she unlocked her front door and disappeared into the flat with Lily.

"Did you remember my bread?" Maggie asked him sternly.

"Yes, of course," Søren replied. He untied the knots on the shopping bags and handed her a paper bag from the bakery. Anna appeared in the doorway.

"Maggie, why don't you go back to your own apartment? I'll come and see you later, okay?"

The old lady nodded, disappointed, and left.

"Why did you give her your bread?" Anna asked while she unpacked her shopping.

"I bought it for her."

Anna raised her eyebrows.

"I was waiting for you. In her apartment. We saw you from the window and when you didn't come back, Mrs. Snedker thought you must have gone shopping, so I followed you," he confessed.

"And she asked you to get her some bread?"

Søren nodded.

"And you did?"

Søren nodded again. A tenth of a second later Søren heard Anna laugh for the first time. It didn't last long, but it suited her.

"We'll have dinner first," Anna said. "Then Lily needs to have a bath, and at seven o'clock I put her to bed. You'll have to wait. I don't want Lily seeing me when. . . . You can wait in the living room."

Søren watched her briefly. Could you do that? Postpone dealing with terrible news until a more convenient time cropped up? He went into the living room and sat down in a chair. Wasn't that precisely what he had done, when he put the four baby pictures of Maja in a box in the basement? Pressed on as though nothing had happened? Lily peeked at him from the doorway, and he smiled at her. Anna came into the living room to fetch a bowl and glanced at him quickly.

"Do you have children?" she asked.

"I called you yesterday. Twice. Why didn't you answer?" Søren said, ignoring her question.

"I was . . . out," Anna replied swiftly and headed back to the kitchen with the bowl.

"Where?"

"I'm afraid I can't tell you that."

Søren sighed, then he wrinkled his nose.

It was the second time today he had been given the brushoff.

CHAPTER 11

Anna knew perfectly well she hadn't bumped into the World's Most Irritating Detective in the supermarket by accident. She had spotted him outside the entrance to Johannes's stairwell, been aware he had run after her, and had seen him throw up his hands in frustration when the bus pulled out. How he had ended up in her living room doing a jigsaw puzzle with Lily while she was cooking dinner was beyond her. When the potatoes had boiled, she mashed them with angry movements and slammed the plates down on the kitchen table. She hated him! Since he had entered her life, less than a week ago, everything had started to unravel. How dare he buy a loaf of bread for Maggie; how dare he carry her daughter? She wanted him to leave her alone, and she didn't want to hear what he had come to say. Johannes must not be dead. Tears started rolling down her cheeks. The steamy mashed potatoes were in a bowl in the sink, and suddenly she slumped forward as if she had been stabbed.

When she had composed herself, she fetched Lily from the living room.

"Dinner's ready, Lily," she said and shot the World's Most Irritating Detective a look of disapproval. If he thought she would invite him to eat with them, he could think again. Once he was off duty, he would undoubtedly go home to his trophy wife with her shiny white teeth and her golden skin, and they would cuddle up on their designer sofa and he would think how lucky he was with his Pernille or his Sanne or whatever her name was, everything so picture perfect. But now, while he was still on duty, he was playing at being a social Robin Hood, watching her, poor struggling Anna, with his dark brown eyes and his healthy freckles; he might at least have the decency to leave his freckles in his locker when he arrived for work in the morning; his farm-boy freckles were an insult to criminals everywhere and to Anna in particular. How she hated him!

Later, when Lily had fallen asleep, she went to the living room and found the World's Most Irritating Detective in a chair by the window. He was looking down at the street.

"It's very cold and dark outside," he remarked.

"Really!"

The World's Most Irritating Detective slowly turned his head and looked at Anna, who had sat down on the sofa, as far away from him as possible.

"Why are you so angry?" he asked.

Anna scowled at him. The scent of Lily still lingered on her clothes; putting her to bed had been a struggle and when she had finally nodded off, Anna had sat on the floor watching her. Eventually, she had got up and left the bedroom, suddenly pleased Søren was there, glad she wasn't alone.

"I'm so angry I could kill someone," she hissed, and looked first at her hands and then at him. Søren leaned forward and looked compassionately at her.

"Johannes is dead. But I imagine you've already figured that out. He was murdered."

Anna stared at him blankly.

"Anna, did you kill him?" Søren said gravely.

"Yes, of course I did. Heaven forbid I should have a single friend left in the world," she said, sounding forlorn.

"Is that a no?" he asked.

"Yes. That's a no." The tears started falling and she wiped them away with an irritated movement.

"What happened?" she asked. "Who did it?"

Søren shook his head as though he was deliberating what he could or couldn't tell her, but in the end he seemed to reach a decision. Even sitting here, off duty, in the living room of a potential suspect was compromising, Anna thought, so he might as well go the whole hog.

"I don't know," he said. "He was killed in his apartment. That much I do know. He's been dead about twenty-four hours, and . . ."

Anna's eyes widened.

"That can't be right," she exclaimed, triumphantly, as if it meant Johannes couldn't be dead after all. "I got a text message from him this morning." She fetched her bag. "See for yourself," she said, tossing her cell to Søren with the text message open. He studied the message for a long time and scrolled down, she noticed, probably to check the date and time the message had been received.

"What does it mean?" Anna asked.

Søren said nothing, nor did he look at her. Instead he stared into space and seemed to be pondering something. When he finally became aware of her, his eyes were somber.

"The text message is from Johannes's killer."

Anna was mystified.

"We haven't been able to locate Johannes's cell phone," Søren continued. "It's likely the killer took it and, to buy himself time, he probably replied to your message and any others, so no one would get suspicious." He looked at Anna.

"Johannes was killed by repeated blows to the back of his head. It was messy, blood everywhere," he went on, observing her closely. He noticed when she moved her foot and when she cleared her throat, his face contracted imperceptibly. It was eerie, and suddenly Anna felt scared.

"This is completely illegal, isn't it?" she demanded. "Aren't you being totally unprofessional? Waiting for me in the supermarket, pretending to be shopping when really you were following me? That's harassment."

Søren got up and sat down on the sofa next to Anna.

"Hey," she growled and tried to get up, but Søren grabbed hold of her and pulled her back down.

He held her by the shoulders and hissed, "I've had enough of you, Anna Bella." His grip was vice-like. "I've had enough of you refusing to cooperate. I've been a police officer for many years, and I've never had a case as impenetrable as this, and the last thing I need is a stubborn suspect who, for reasons utterly beyond my comprehension, acts as if the police in general and me in particular were put on this earth to annoy her. I can see it's not easy for you, Anna. I really can. A young child, a demanding dissertation, and now two sudden deaths. I can understand you're scared and angry and beside yourself. But I don't understand why you're angry with me. I'm your only friend in this whole crappy business." He let go of her.

Anna yelled, "You've bruised me. Are you out of your mind? You can't manhandle me, you unprofessional shit."

Søren got up and went to the window.

"Then make a formal complaint, Anna. Go to the station tomorrow and do it. You've been uncooperative, and you're technically still a suspect. Did you kill Professor Helland? Is that what you do when you get angry? Do you get so mad that you kill? And what about Johannes? Did you get angry with him, too? Did he tell you a few hard truths and you went berserk? Was that what happened? And what about Lily? Judging by your behavior, I ought to have her taken to child protective services. You're mentally unstable, anyone can see that, and it might be better for your daughter to grow up away from you. So, go ahead, Anna Bella. You file that complaint." Søren looked calmly at her while he spoke, and when he had finished, he turned again to the window.

Anna's heart was racing and she gasped for breath. Søren had said terrible things, he suspected her, he had found her Achilles' heel, but to hell with it. She couldn't imagine life without Lily. Søren stared into the darkness. Anna noticed his right hand was shaking.

"I'll help," she croaked. "I promise to help you."

Søren turned around slowly and looked at her for a long time, then he nodded.

"Some woman was in love with Johannes, and she . . . bothered him," she said. "A woman he had met at this club he goes to . . . the Red Mask."

"A woman?" Søren raised his eyebrows and looked at Anna.

"I'm not sure . . . I assumed it was a woman. I thought that's what he said. Someone he got along with, but he wasn't in love with her, and I think she freaked out because she was in love with him." Anna squirmed as she realized how little attention she had paid. "He told me last Monday, but I was too preoccupied with my own problems," she added, miserably. "But there was someone who wouldn't leave him alone, who kept calling and . . ."

"We've found some e-mails on Johannes's computer," Søren said, looking pensive. "They were sent from an account in the name of Donald Duck and the sender calls himself YourGuy, so we think it might be a man. Ring any bells?"

Anna shook her head and stared out of the window.

"It just seems . . . so extreme to kill Johannes," she said. "He's the nicest person in the world! He never argues with anybody. That's what makes him so irritating," she added. "Johannes sees the good in everyone." She froze, realizing she had used the present tense.

"Johannes had falling out with Professor Helland," Søren protested.

"No, definitely not. Helland and Johannes were friends. Johannes got really uptight if I ever dared criticize Helland even a little." Anna replied as though Søren's statement had been a question.

"Anna, I'm telling you Helland and Johannes had clashed. We have it in writing, a long e-mail exchange that began before the summer and was still ongoing. Helland wasn't pulling his weight regarding a paper they were meant to cowrite. Johannes appears to have been dissatisfied with Helland's contribution and upset that Helland was making so little effort. Did Johannes ever mention this?"

Anna looked wretchedly at Søren. "No," she whispered.

"And you never noticed his relationship with Professor Helland was strained?"

"No." She jerked her head and stared at Søren. "You're not insinuating Johannes killed Helland, are you? That's outrageous. Johannes is the sweetest man I know, he would never . . ." She clutched her forehead.

"Anna," Søren assured her. "I'm not insinuating anything. I'm just trying to make sense of it. That's all. Why do you think Johannes never told you anything?"

"Because I'm utterly self-centered," Anna said in a chastened voice.

"Pardon?" Søren said.

"Nothing," Anna replied.

Lily appeared in the doorway, dangling Bloppen in one hand.

"I can't sleep," she said, drowsily. "Bloppen is being noisy."

The World's Most Irritating Detective sat down and looked at Lily. Now alert, she glanced from her mother to Søren.

"Darling, you need to go back to bed," Anna said, wearily.

"Bloppen is jumping up and down in my bed," Lily complained.

"It's late, darling," Anna pleaded and got up.

"But Bloppen is reading my books," Lily persisted. "While he sings."

"No wonder you can't get to sleep," Søren said. Anna wanted to explode. Pig! How dare you talk to my daughter when you've just threatened to take her away from me? Søren looked at Lily.

"He makes so much noise," Lily said, shy, but pleased to have an audience.

"Why do you think he makes a noise when you're trying to sleep? That's not a nice thing to do."

"Bloppen teases me," Lily complained.

She toddled further into the living room, past Anna as if she didn't exist, and up to Søren where she stopped in front of his legs.

She reached almost up to his chest and her nightgown touched the floor. She dumped the naughty toy dog on Søren's lap.

"Shall we ask him why he's so noisy?" Søren suggested.

Lily nodded.

"I'm a police officer," Søren said, conspiratorially. "It's better if I ask the questions, isn't it? Then Bloppen might think you've called the police because he was noisy."

Lily thought that was an excellent idea.

Søren picked up Bloppen, narrowed one eye and looked at him sharply. "Bloppen," he said. "Why are you noisy, why do you read Lily's books, sing, and jump in her bed so she can't sleep?"

Lily stared at Bloppen, she was mesmerized. Søren barked like a dog.

"Oh, no," he said. "I'm afraid I don't understand what he's saying."

Lily looked terribly disappointed.

"However, I believe you speak dog language. I think your mom told me."

Lily turned to Anna, beamed, and looked back at Søren again.

"Oh, yes," she said. "Bloppen says he's only teasing me because he feels sad."

"What's he sad about?" Søren asked.

Lily asked Bloppen very earnestly and listened carefully when he barked his answers.

"He's sad because someone's teasing his mom. Teasing her a lot. And now she's not happy anymore."

Søren looked at Lily for a long time before he said: "Shall we agree I'll catch the people who have been teasing Bloppen's mom, so Bloppen will be happy again and you can get some sleep?"

Lily nodded.

"Shake on it," he said, offering her his shovel-size hand. Lily gave him her small pink hand. "I'll tell Bloppen and you as soon as I've caught them, promise."

Lily nodded, satisfied. Then, somewhat at a loss, she turned to Anna, who said, "Come on, darling. I'll take you back to bed."

"No, I want him to do it," Lily said, pointing at Søren.

"No, Lily."

"Yes," she said, pouting. "I want him!"

Søren rose and sent Anna a placatory glance. Then he took Lily's hand and off they went.

Then something happened that had never happened before. Lily let go of Søren's hand, went back to Anna and kissed her. A small, dry kiss on the cheek.

"You love me, Mom," she said.

Ten minutes later Søren returned. Anna sat on the sofa, still dazed. Søren took the chair from the window, placed it with its back facing Anna, and sat down astride it.

"Anna," he began. "Three and a half days have passed since Lars Helland was found dead, and all I know is how he died; apart from that I've got nothing. Today we found Johannes's body and, again, I've got nothing."

"Do you think I did it?" Anna breathed.

Søren looked at her for a long time.

"Right now I can't eliminate anyone. But if you ask me, off the record, now that I've carried your shopping home and put your daughter to bed, I'm pretty sure you have nothing to do with Helland's or Johannes's death. But I have to get to the bottom of this, and I need your help."

"How?" Anna suddenly detected a flicker of growing interest.

"Number one, stop being so hostile," he said. Anna looked down. "Do you think you can do that?"

"Suppose so," she mumbled.

"Number two, keep your eyes and ears open around the institute and report back to me. Your world is uncharted waters to me, and I'm ashamed to admit I'm having problems navigating it. Everyone's cooperating, answering the nice policeman's questions, but I get nowhere. You can help me because you speak their language, you understand their rivalries, you can see through them—I hope. Or better than I can," he added. "Help me find Dr. Tybjerg, for example. I think he's hiding, but why? Help me understand Johannes.

You were his friend. You must know what he was like. Are you sure he wasn't gay? Was he seeing someone? Can you think of anything that might help the investigation? Did he ever mention anyone who might have reason to dislike him? Everything, Anna. I need help with everything!"

Anna studied him as he spoke. "But what if I did it?" she asked.

"Then I'll arrest you, take you down to the station, have you put before a judge, and request you be remanded in custody; you risk a lengthy custodial sentence. But I don't think you killed Helland or Johannes."

"Why not?"

"Because you have too much to lose."

They sat for a while.

"Mrs. Snedker said Lily doesn't have a father," Søren remarked.

"None of your business."

Søren raised his hand as if to deflect a ball.

"Be nice," he warned her.

"Sorry," she mumbled.

"Though you're right, it's none of my business. I'm just curious."

"Lily has a father. His name's Thomas and he lives in Stockholm. He's a doctor. He opted out." Anna shrugged and looked around the room. "Out of all of it. Lily, the responsibility, and a girlfriend who turned out to be unlovable. Who wants to be stuck with a worthless shit like me?" she said harshly and glared at Søren. "He says he left me, not our child," she muttered. "That's what he *says*. But we haven't seen him for two years. Satisfied?"

Søren nodded and got ready to leave.

"I want you to come to the station tomorrow and make a statement."

Anna was surprised.

"My hunch isn't enough. I need to interview you, as I would any other witness. When can you get there?"

"Tomorrow's not good for me," Anna squirmed. "I'm going to Odense."

"No, you're not."

"Yes, I am." Anna looked defiantly at Søren.

"What are you doing in Odense?" he asked, irritably.

Anna twirled a box of matches between her fingers.

"There's something I need to find out. I'm going with Lily. It's a long story," she added and sighed when she saw the way Søren was looking at her. "Okay," she explained. "I've discovered that my parents have been lying to me. On top of everything else." She threw up her hands in despair. "They're lying, and I don't know why."

"Sorry, but you'll have to cancel," Søren insisted.

Anna rose and looked resolutely at him. "I'll take Lily to nursery school tomorrow morning, then I'll come to the station to be interviewed." She weighed her words. "Ten o'clock. I'll be at your disposal until one o'clock. Then I'll pick up Lily and go to Odense. I have to go. I'll be back tomorrow night, and if you're going to Helland's funeral on Saturday you'll see me there." She closed her eyes. Johannes was dead. "Christ, Johannes." Her face crumpled. "It makes no sense at all."

Søren watched her in silence, then he said: "Okay. I'll let you go to Odense between one and midnight tomorrow. But you promise not to hurt anyone or make a run for it."

"This isn't a joke," Anna objected weakly.

"No," Søren emphasized. "It isn't. And I want you to start taking this seriously. Do you hear? Do you know where Dr. Tybjerg is?" His question came out of the blue.

Anna's eyes flickered. If she told him where Dr. Tybjerg was, the police would pick him up immediately and her dissertation defense would be canceled.

"No," she lied.

Søren locked eyes with her. "Okay," he said and went on, "Is there anything at all you want to tell me now?"

Anna looked at him for a long time. "I know what killed Professor Helland. I know about the parasites."

Søren groaned. "How?"

"The rumor's all over the Institute of Biology," she sent him a knowing look, "and from Professor Moritzen. She called me into her office, told me you had visited her in her cottage and why. She wants me to contact her if I hear any suggestions the parasites might have come from her department. Though I can't imagine how anyone could know. It's not as if the little bastards are ringed. But if you can determine their origins, or whatever, and trace them back to her stock, then she wants to know."

"Why?" Søren asked.

"They're closing Parasitology. Hanne has three years to complete her research, then her department will be dismantled. However, she's convinced that the Faculty Council would love to get rid of her before her three years are up, given half a chance. They would need a reason to dismiss her, and if it turns out the parasites came from her department, if she has so little control of her stock that parasites ended up in her colleagues' tissue, they can fire her on the spot. Obviously, she wants to be prepared and doesn't want to go down without a fight.

"And I'm sure Mrs. Helland is lying." Anna fed the shark, hoping he would forget all about Tybjerg.

"What makes you think so?" Søren was fascinated.

"She claims Professor Helland was fit and healthy. There were no limits to his vigor and vitality, according to his wife and that's bullshit. I saw him, I know he was sick as a dog." Anna told Søren about the incident in the parking lot, suddenly embarrassed that she hadn't mentioned it earlier. "He scared the living daylights out of me, and he was clearly seriously ill," she concluded.

"When did you speak to Mrs. Helland?" Søren asked.

"I visited her today," Anna admitted. "I got this." She lifted the pendant free from her blouse and looked shyly at Søren. "Helland must have had it made for me. My graduation present. Mrs. Helland wanted to give it to me before the funeral."

Søren was deep in thought.

"She's lying," Anna repeated.

"Anything else?" Søren asked, scrutinizing Anna. She had never felt so cooperative in all her life.

"I think Professor Freeman is in Denmark."

Søren nodded slowly. He already knew that.

"How do you know?" he said.

Crap. She had this information from Dr. Tybjerg. She decided to lie.

"There's a bird symposium at the Bella Centre," she said. "I saw his name in the program."

Søren bought it.

"Any chance Dr. Tybjerg's disappearance is linked to Freeman's arrival?" Søren suggested.

"No, how could it be?" Anna said, innocently.

"Anna," Søren said earnestly. "I need to be clear about this. In your opinion, could Helland's and Johannes's deaths be linked to your dissertation? Your topic is a scientific controversy about the origin of birds, which Helland was heavily involved in, right? Helland, Tybjerg, and the Canadian scientist, Clive Freeman. But where does Johannes fit in? I can't see it. I'm just a stupid cop, and I can't see it. Murders are usually triggered by jealousy, drugs, money, or family issues, and I just don't buy that someone might kill because their scientific reputation was threatened; because of a dissertation."

Anna pondered this.

"Johannes helped me," she said. "He is . . . was a science theorist and very talented. He helped me extract aspects of scientific theory that are relevant to controversies in biology. I've used those arguments to demolish Professor Freeman." Anna suddenly looked directly at Søren. "That's what my dissertation is about. I destroy him." She gulped. "Johannes knew a vast amount about Karl Popper and his ideas about falsification, about Thomas Kuhn, who introduced the concept of paradigm in the 1960s, and especially about Lorraine J. Daston and her concept of scientific moral economies . . . I know, it took me weeks to grasp, so don't feel ashamed if you think I'm speaking gibberish. The point is that plenty of vertebrate scientists and ornithologists have attacked Freeman over the years. Attacked his anatomical conclusions and his fossil analyses, and let me tell you something: he doesn't care; he evades the issue, no matter what's thrown at him. Before 2000, before *Sinosauropteryx* was found in China, you would often hear Freeman say, 'Show me a feather that grew on a dinosaur, then I'll believe your non-sense.' And when he was finally shown a feathered dinosaur, his response was either: 'That's not a feather!' or, if he couldn't deny the structure was a feather, he would say: 'That's not from a dinosaur, just from a very old bird, which would, of course, have feathers!' The problem is Freeman's so well-versed in anatomy and physiology that it's impossible for most people to take him on. But no one has ever tried to attack his underlying scientific principles. No one has ever proved he breaks the most fundamental scientific rules."

"Which are?"

Anna was on the verge of giving up.

"It's a bit complicated," she began. "But internal contradictions, for example, are banned if you want to call your work scientific, and Freeman's work is littered with inconsistencies. Further, he rejects generally accepted analytical methods. He's entitled to do so, but only if he can argue convincingly for an alternative, and we don't know if he can because he has never tried." Anna paused and looked at Søren. One of his eyes was drooping slightly.

"I don't believe for a moment that Professor Freeman has anything to do with this. If Freeman wants to prevent my dissertation from being published, then there are several people he needs to kill before Johannes and Helland. Me, for example. And Dr. Tybjerg."

"Yes," Søren said, looking at Anna. "But the reason we can't find Tybjerg might be that he's dead. I'm starting to think you should be put under police protection."

"*If* there is a link between the two deaths," Anna objected. She had absolutely no desire to have the World's Most Irritating Detective following her round the clock. And, besides, Dr. Tybjerg wasn't dead.

"Yes, if," Søren said, suddenly looking very tired.

"I know the cysticerci were between three to four months old," Anna continued. "I think this means even though Johannes and Helland died in the same week, they were technically killed at two completely different times. Johannes yesterday"—she swallowed—"and Helland possibly as far back as June or July."

"We won't know until tomorrow whether Johannes was also infected with cysticerci," Søren said quietly. Anna stared at him.

"Who is the man who has waited for you twice, Anna?" Søren suddenly asked.

"How do you know about him?"

"Mrs. Snedker told me," Søren said.

"I don't know," she replied honestly. "But I know it's not Freeman. Maggie says he was young."

"Haven't you wondered about it?"

"At first I was convinced it must have been Johannes," she said, "and I texted him to find out. When it turned out not to be him, then I started wondering. But if . . . if his killer has his cell," Anna gulped, "maybe Johannes really was here, and the text messages are lying. . . . Perhaps Johannes came to tell me something? But then, why would he run away? That doesn't make any sense." She looked away.

Søren rose. "Tomorrow at 10 a.m.," he said, pointing at her, "and don't be late."

Anna shook her head.

When she had closed the door after him, she gave him the finger.

Thirty seconds later, someone rattled Anna's mail slot. Anna opened the door.

"So, what's the latest?" Maggie whispered. Anna could hear that Søren hadn't even reached the ground floor yet.

"Maggie, I'm exhausted," Anna whispered back. "Tomorrow."

Maggie looked disappointed and had turned around when something occurred to Anna.

"Maggie," she said, taking the old lady's hand. It was velvety. "If the man who waited for me comes back, then . . ." She looked gravely at her. "Then I want you to call the police."

Maggie looked momentarily frightened, then she said, "I'll tell you one thing, you're a much more exciting neighbor than Mrs. Lerby. When she lived here, nothing ever happened."

Anna smiled feebly and said goodnight. She sat down in her living room, barely able to keep her eyes open. For the first five minutes she just sat there. Johannes was dead. Her brain refused to accept it. She couldn't tell Jens and Cecilie. They would freak out completely and refuse to allow her ever to set foot in the university again. Jens would stomp up and down and threaten to expose the department in the press. Then she remembered neither of them was talking to her. She kicked off her shoes.

She wanted to cry, but her chest tightened and no tears came. She mourned Johannes. Then she called Karen.

Karen picked up the telephone immediately and was thrilled when she realized who it was. She wasn't the least frosty or guarded, as Anna had feared. Karen chatted away. She was a student at the Royal Danish Academy of Fine Arts and had lived in Copenhagen since August. She loved it, Copenhagen was a great city, and she had made lots of friends in no time. She knew where Anna lived but hadn't called her. She admitted, frankly, that she needed to summon the courage after all these years, but last Tuesday she had bumped into Cecilie in the street. Cecilie had told her Anna was super-busy and one of her supervisors had died. Cecilie had promised to e-mail Karen with the date of Anna's dissertation defense, and they had arranged for Karen to be there. As a graduation present.

"Imagine, you're a real biologist now!" Karen exclaimed. "I'm so proud of you!"

Karen wanted to know everything about Lily. Brown hair, red hair, Anna's color? What did she like? Could Karen buy her a present? A doll? Or a Spiderman apron so they could make models out of clay together? Anna was filled with regret. Why hadn't she kept in touch with Karen? It seemed beyond silly, and Anna had an uncomfortable feeling it was her who had chosen not to see Karen, rather than the other way around. Her throat tightened and she responded monosyllabically to Karen's joyful outbursts. Finally, Karen asked how she really was, apart from busy.

And the whole story poured out of her. Thomas, their shipwrecked relationship, Cecilie picking up the pieces, but who now stuck to her life like a barnacle, her graduate work at the department of Cell Biology and Comparative Zoology, about her supervisor and a fellow student, who both appeared to have been murdered. At this point, Anna burst into tears and Karen insisted on coming over—there's no way you can be alone right now, she said, horrified.

"I don't want to be by myself, either," Anna sobbed. "But would you be able to come over tomorrow evening instead, please?" she asked in a small voice. "Would you like to stay with us over the weekend? Help me with Lily, so I don't have to call Cecilie? I don't want to call Cecilie. I feel so ashamed." Karen agreed without a moment's hesitation. She would love to come; there was nothing she would rather do. "I've missed you so much," Anna said and hung up before Karen had time to reply.

Afterward, she was unable to fall asleep. The thoughts were churning inside her head. Finally, she sat up in her bed. Johannes was dead. He was in cold storage somewhere, on a stretcher in a mortuary. And she had never apologized to him. She had yelled at him, she had punished him for what he had said to the police, even though she wasn't even seriously angry about it. Now it was too late, and Johannes had been right. She acted as if the whole world revolved around her.

Anna got up, walked through the apartment, past the nailed-down door to Thomas's old office, and into the nursery where she picked up her sleeping daughter.

Once they were cuddled up under Anna's comforter, she felt guilty. It was one thing when the kid toddled in during the night wanting to get into her bed, another to actually pick her up. Lily was a human being, not a hot water bottle. Cecilie had a tendency to act as if she was entitled to Anna. Not in an evil or calculating way, Cecilie wasn't like that. But situations and clashes often had an undercurrent of "but you're my daughter and I'm your mom." As if that justified everything. It didn't give you the right to cut corners and cross boundaries whenever you felt like it, it didn't allow you to just take and keep on taking. And here Anna was, getting high on her own child. Inhaling the smell of Lily's hair in the darkness, unfolding her sleeping fingers, caressing a warm, round shoulder. She couldn't hold back the tears. The bedroom was dark and the street below very quiet. The bed linen absorbed her tears, but they kept on coming. She wanted her love for Lily to be pure. She wanted to be able to love her child. She desperately wanted to be the constant sun, warming her from afar, warming Lily, an eager seedling who wanted to grow up, up and away, grow lush green leaves and scarlet flowers and juicy pods. But her heart felt numb.

She stuck her arm under the pillow where Lily's head was resting and pulled her closer. Anna had never been able to delight in things the way Karen could. Karen would be delirious with joy when she saw Anna after summer vacation, or when she cut school and spent the day shopping and going to cafés in Odense with her mother, with whom she had a seemingly great and uncomplicated relationship. Karen loved movies, spaghetti Bolognese, the beach, card games, and musicals, which she would play at maximum volume and dance around to with her wild curls. Karen never hinted her approach to life was better than Anna's. Karen danced and sang at the top of her voice. Anna would hesitate, then tap her foot a couple of times. They had been friends. And Anna had messed it up.

Was Anna even capable of enjoying herself? Her parents mattered. A great deal. Just as Lily meant the world to her. But her worth came from the head, not the heart. She turned away from Lily, ashamed to entertain such thoughts while the toddler clung to her. She looked at the light from the city, which seeped in through the coarse curtain fabric.

When Troels had walked out that day ten years ago, the summer they graduated from high school, Karen had been beside herself. She had looked for him everywhere, called his parents; they had to find him, she wanted a reconciliation, she said so over and over, even though it was Anna who had done the damage. To Karen it was unbearable that they weren't friends, and Anna tried to empathize with her friend's anxiety. Where was he? What had she done? Deep down, she hadn't actually cared, but merely pretended. He had been a bad friend. He no longer mattered. They could go to hell. All of them.

But there had been one great love. The thought was banal, trite even, but it filled her with horror because she longed to love Lily the way she had once loved Thomas. Passionately, unconditionally, non-negotiably. Anna let go of Lily completely and sat upright. It couldn't be true that she had been able to love him but not her child. That had to be impossible. She didn't want to be someone like that. Thomas was the past. Lily was the present and the future, she was forever. Anna swung her legs over the edge of the bed. She checked the time; it was 3 a.m.

She left the bedroom and closed the door behind her so as not to wake Lily. She made coffee, a large mug with warm milk. She lit a fire in the living room and pushed the armchair in front of the open doors of the stove.

Why are you so angry, Søren had asked? For a moment, his eyes had been tender and curious. As if he truly didn't understand. Perhaps she didn't understand it, either. That was just the way she was. Anger was her most powerful emotion. Much stronger than love. The thought paralyzed her. She was angry with Thomas, but her anger was ultimately futile. They hadn't seen him for over two years, and all she knew was that he worked in Stockholm and she had his number somewhere, but apart from that she knew nothing and he never contacted them.

But she was also angry with Cecilie and feelings ran high every time they saw each other. And Jens annoyed her. When he picked his nose, when he was late, when he couldn't quit smoking, or generally failed to pull himself together. She was incapable of tempering her irritation with concern and tolerance, she simply blew a fuse. At the slightest thing. And then there was Lily. Anna obviously wasn't angry with her three-year-old daughter, but neither did she possess the patience she so desperately longed to have. Lily was demanding and impossible to negotiate with, she was stubborn, she acted as if she had no common sense, and she clearly hadn't because she was only three years old!

She had been angry with Helland, Tybjerg, and Johannes. Johannes, who massaged her shoulders when she had slept badly. Johannes, who listened gently and attentively and made her laugh. Her rage triumphed every time. It made no sense. Why was she so angry? She put her mug on the floor and pressed her knees into her eyes. The fire was roaring now and warmed her thighs.

She got up, feeling livid. No way did she want to be angry with her child! Children couldn't handle that! A child loves because it feels loved.

Anna studied the photo of Cecilie, Jens, and her younger self, a girl with sparkling eyes. Noted the contrast between her parents' smiling mouths and their sad eyes; stared at her own, oblivious innocence. Something had happened back then. She would visit Ulla Bodelsen tomorrow. A child loves because she feels loved.

Her interview at the police station on Friday morning lasted just under two hours. Søren was clean-shaven, and his treatment of her was equally smooth. Nothing in his behavior revealed he had tucked her daughter in bed and held her hard by the shoulders last night. Another officer was present during the interview; perhaps that explained why. She left just after twelve and had an hour and a half before her train to Odense. She was in need of fresh air and decided to walk down Frederikssundvej. It was cold and a couple of birds on the pavement couldn't even be bothered to take off when Anna walked past them.

Further down the street she noticed a man who reminded her of Troels. Karen hadn't mentioned him, and Anna had avoided the subject completely. But perhaps she had to face it at last? Maybe it was time to get in touch with him and apologize for what she had said? Even though she didn't feel genuinely sorry? Handsome Troels. Anna stared—surely she was seeing things? How could anyone look so much like him? It couldn't possibly be him. Troels wouldn't just show up out of nowhere, after ten years, on Frederikssundvej; there was no way he could know that Anna would be there or that she had got back in touch with Karen the day before. That simply couldn't happen.

But there he was. He was standing outside a grocery store, casually, as though he was waiting for a cab on the corner of Second Avenue and Fifty-eighth Street. Troels stared into the distance, across the road, across the cars, and Anna tried to follow his gaze.

She just had time to think that he was posing, that he must have seen her and was now trying too hard to pretend he hadn't, when he turned his head and looked straight at her.

"Hi, Anna!" he exclaimed, astonished. "Wow, Anna, hi!" he said again. His voice sounded delighted and genuine, and Anna couldn't help laughing when she embraced him.

"What the hell are you doing here?" she said into his oilskin jacket. It smelled of nicotine.

"I was just wondering," Troels laughed, squeezing her, "if Anna Bella Nor had learned to speak like a lady or whether she still swears like a sailor! How are you? I hear you've become a dinosaur expert, or an archaeologist or something?"

"That's about it," Anna smiled. "But who told you that?"

Troels looked fantastic. He had flawless skin and his dark eyebrows and lashes were exquisitely groomed and beautifully arched. A green stone sparkled in one eyebrow, and he wore a St. Pauli hat with the famous skull emblem pulled over his ears.

"I ran into Karen a couple of days ago. Imagine running into you both within the same week, how weird is that? She told me. It sounds really exciting! We talked about getting together."

Anna frowned. Get together? Him and Karen? Or did he mean Karen and Anna and him? He didn't seem angry, not at all. More like exulted, bordering on nervous. She certainly was. Through her clothes, her armpits felt clammy.

"A dinosaur biologist, Anna Bella, you show-off! I always thought you wanted to do something else."

Anna wrinkled her nose. "Let's walk," she suggested. "It's too cold to stand still."

He glanced at his watch, then he nodded. They started walking.

"If I were to hazard a guess, I would have said you would become a sergeant in the army or something hard-core, where you could boss a lot of people around," he laughed.

Anna gave him a wounded look.

"Ten years and you're still full of opinions about things you know shit about."

"Hey, Anna Bella," he said, amicably. "Let's not argue."

"Why not?" Anna snapped, taken aback by how quickly her old rage flared up. "You've always had completely the wrong impression of me!" They had only been walking for 150 feet, and Anna wanted to stamp her foot. Troels seemed unperturbed.

"Why didn't we keep in touch?" was all he said. "You, me, and Karen. You were my best friends, and suddenly you disappeared."

"No, *you* disappeared," Anna protested. "It was you who disappeared."

It was Troels's turn to frown. "Whatever," he then said.

"So, what have you been up to?" Anna said, changing the subject.

"This and that," Troels said, unenthusiastically. "Went to Milan first, that was all right. Then I moved to New York. Made some money modeling, but perhaps you already know that?"

"No," Anna replied.

"Seriously? And here was I thinking I was famous for my good looks." He laughed a hollow laugh. "In New York I started to paint. That's why I've moved back to Copenhagen. I applied to the Royal Danish Academy of Fine Arts. That's where I bumped into Karen, at an open evening. It was unbelievable. We had a beer afterward and talked about you. Unfortunately I was rejected, but I'll apply again. Since then we've gotten together a couple of times." Troels smiled. "In fact, I saw her last Tuesday. We had a burger at a café. Karen wanted me to come with her to your dissertation defense. As a surprise. I think she would like us to be friends again." Troels temporarily looked shy, and they walked on in silence.

"Karen said something about someone in your department dying?" Troels remarked.

"He wasn't just anybody, he was my supervisor. Heart attack. He was only fifty-seven," Anna muttered. It was none of his business. Cecilie should not have told Karen, and Karen should certainly not have told Troels.

Troels was quiet for a while, then he said: "No, one of your friends. A young guy."

Anna stopped in her tracks.

"How do you know?" she said in a low voice.

"From Karen," Troels said, casually. "She called late last night," he admitted. "After you had spoken to her. She suggested that we kiss and make up, as she put it. She said you were upset. Distraught, in fact."

Anna stared at him in disbelief. "And she called last night to tell you that?"

"Yes," Troels said, as if this were quite normal. "I'd gone to bed, but I was reading. It was way past midnight. She was worried because you were so distressed. She said you needed help immediately; you needed your old friends. She said your voice had sounded strange." Troels smiled gently. "It's uncanny because I've wanted to contact you for a long time. Forget what happened back then and start over." He laughed briefly. Anna eyed him suspiciously.

"So the next day you just happen to bump into me?" She took a step backward.

"Okay," he confessed, grinning broadly. "It's not a coincidence. I saw you on the bus this morning. I was sitting at the back. You got on at Rantzausgade and got off at Bellahøj. I got off there, too, and I waited outside the police station. I've been a chicken. I've been back from New York since February, and one of the first things I did was find out where you and Karen lived. I wanted to call you so many times, and I don't really know what stopped me." He suddenly seemed timid.

"And I suppose I feel embarrassed," he added. "Toward your parents as well. After everything they did for me. For years they sent me letters and presents. And I never wrote back. So when I saw you this morning, I thought, it's now or never. I waited for you outside the police station. I had nearly given up when you finally came out. I was freaking freezing." He laughed and patted himself to warm up.

"Well, there's not much meat on you," Anna blurted out.

"Or you," Troels said, affectionately. Spontaneously, Anna stuck her arm under Troels's. He smiled.

"It must be tough," he said. "Have you been interviewed by the police?"

"Hmm," Anna replied, evasively. "I'm helping the police a bit. They don't really get the world of academia," she said and fell silent.

Troels looked at her. "What did they ask you?" he pressed.

Anna stopped and glared at him. "Honestly, Troels. What happened back then?" she challenged him. "Why did you leave? Why did you disappear? Karen looked for you for weeks."

"Does it really matter now?" Troels asked.

"If it doesn't matter, then why did you leave? Drama queen."

Troels withdrew his arm from hers.

"Don't do that!" His eyes glowed.

Anna planted her hands on her hips. "Don't do what?" she fumed. "I'm not doing anything. You've been spying on me, following me, and behaving very strangely. And now you say that it doesn't matter. You dropped off the face of the earth for ten years. That does matter! I can't have people just disappearing like that, it's a rotten thing to do!" She was jabbing her finger at him now and her eyes turned shiny with anger. Troels's face hardened.

"You were my best friend," he almost whispered. "I trusted you. You and Karen and your parents. And that night you behaved just like my dad. And you know it. You were vicious." Troels clenched his jaw.

Anna simmered with rage and knew she was about to lose her temper again. She only restrained herself because the image of the World's Most Irritating Detective appeared on her retina.

"Listen, why don't we say good-bye now and meet up after my present my dissertation?" she forced herself to say in a controlled voice. "Karen and you are welcome to attend it, it's a public event," she added and glanced at him. "Only I'm a bit pressed for time now, Troels. I'm sorry. I want to get on. On my own. I've got some things I need to process. And I've a train to catch."

For a moment his face looked outraged and she thought he was shaking, but then he relaxed.

"Okay," he acquiesced. "It's all right. I understand you're under pressure. First your supervisor, then Johannes. That can't have been easy."

Anna thawed a little. "Hey," she said, reaching out for his hand. "I'd really like to see you, Troels. In a couple of weeks, all right?" She tried to calm things down and remembered Søren telling her to be good. She had almost managed it.

"I'm going this way," Troels said weakly, and pointed toward the intersection. "I don't live far away."

"Okay," Anna said. She hugged him and their embrace felt hard and bony. Anna gripped his arm and briefly held him at a distance.

"Friends again?" she asked.

"Of course," Troels smiled. "Bad timing," he added. "I just couldn't help myself when I saw you this morning. I had been thinking about you and then, presto, you get on my bus. I should have waited." He moved a lock of Anna's hair from her forehead with his gloved hand.

"See you, gorgeous," he said and crossed the road. Anna looked after him.

Lily was in high spirits all the way to Odense. They had found seats in a family carriage and the first thing she did was empty her rucksack of toys out on the table. Her cries of delight quickly attracted two other children and soon Lily was handing round teddies, dolls, and Lego bricks. Anna watched her daughter from her window seat. Then the train attendant arrived with her trolley, Anna bought hot dogs and two cartons of juice, and when they had eaten their lunch, they were practically at their destination.

At Odense railway station, Anna was struck by how everything had changed and yet it remained the same. There was a multitude of shops now and the place looked more like a shopping center than a station. An escalator had been installed, and there was a new parking lot at the station entrance. Nevertheless, she was overcome with nostalgia.

While Anna and Lily walked—at a painfully slow pace—along the pavement, she wondered if she knew anyone in this city. Several of her and Karen's old school friends were bound to live here, but she couldn't recall the names of any of them. Karen's mother still lived here, she believed. Anna sighed. Karen was coming over tonight.

Anna had printed out a map and had been delighted to discover that Ulla Bodelsen lived within walking distance of the train station, in a narrow street called Rytterstræde. Lily toddled along with enthusiasm in her snowsuit, and it wasn't until she slipped and fell that she insisted on being carried. Anna sweated. What the hell did she think she was doing? Ulla Bodelsen had to be around eighty years old and bound to be senile and confused. And how many children had passed through her hands since Anna? Anna decided she was an idiot for thinking this was a good idea. She made a mental note to buy flowers for the funeral tomorrow.

Her cell rang. She shifted Lily on to her hip and managed to retrieve it from her pocket. It was a man from the examination board confirming the exact time for her dissertation defense. When the conversation had ended, Lily said: "Was that my daddy?"

Anna was astonished. "No, darling," she replied.

"Don't I have a daddy?" she wanted to know. Their eyes were very close and Anna could feel Lily's warm breath on her chin.

"Yes, darling. You have a daddy. His name is Thomas, and he lives far away. In Sweden. He's a doctor and he makes people better."

"Andreas's daddy is called Mikkel," Lily said. "I want a daddy, too."

"Yes, I know," Anna said.

"Poor Daddy," Lily said and squirmed to get down. She had spotted something shiny on the pavement. "Look, Mom, gold!" she called out, ecstatically.

"Why poor Daddy?" Anna asked.

"Look, Mom. Real gold." Lily picked up a bottle top of golden foil. Someone had smoothed it out and it looked like a small sun. "Gold. Gold!"

Anna gave up.

Ulla Bodelsen lived in a ground floor apartment in a small cobblestoned street. Anna hesitated before she rang the doorbell and started sweating when she heard quick footsteps behind the door. Lily marched straight in when it was opened.

"Look, we found gold," she informed the old lady. "What's your name?"

The elderly, but well-groomed woman bent down, cupped Lily's face in her hands and studied her closely.

"Yes, it's clear to see," she said, enigmatically "My name's Ulla. What's yours?"

"Lily Marie Nor," Lily said with emphasis. "Please may I have some squash?"

Ulla Bodelsen laughed and looked at Anna.

"Hello," she said, warmly. Anna shook her hand. Ulla Bodelsen's eyes were green and bright, her hair was cut in a short, modern style, and her skin surprisingly smooth. A kayak was leaning against the wall behind her.

"You're a canoeist?" Anna exclaimed, amazed.

"Yes, well, I kayak," Ulla Bodelsen replied, patting its fiberglass hull as she led Anna into the living room. "I retired, reluctantly I admit, some . . . twelve years ago or thereabouts. When I turned sixty-two. The thought of doing nothing was rather alien to me." She laughed. "I loved my work, you see. But now I'm extremely pleased that I did. In fact, I'm busier now than I ever was." She laughed again. "I've trained as a swimming instructor. I teach beginners three times a week, and I've become hooked on kayaking."

The walls in the room were white, the furniture stylish and simple, and on the wall hung a poster from the 1996 Copenhagen Jazz Festival. Ulla Bodelsen gestured toward a black sofa and Anna sat down. The old woman had baked rolls and had made tea and there was a bowl of rock candy.

"Look what I made for you," she said to Lily, peeling plastic wrap off a plate and handing her a selection of apple slices, melon, a peeled mandarin, three Gummi bears, and some mixed nuts. While Lily inspected her treat, Ulla Bodelsen fetched a toybox, which Lily explored with glee.

"Help yourself," Ulla Bodelsen said to Anna, nodding toward the coffee table. "I've just got to get something." Anna buttered a roll and added milk to her tea. What kind of old woman would Cecilie become? Would she be like Maggie? Like Ulla Bodelsen? Bursting with life and joy even though time was running out? Anna found that very hard to imagine.

The older woman returned with a white envelope, which she placed on the table. They ate rolls and drank tea for a long time, and they discussed the communes in Brænderup, which now had either been knocked down or renovated beyond recognition. They even discovered that one of Anna's old teachers turned out to be married to Ulla's nephew.

Eventually she said, "The envelope is for you." She looked at Anna. "I don't know precisely why you're here, and . . ." she hesitated. "And you don't need to explain anything if you don't want to. That's quite all right." She hesitated again. "I can't figure out how I could have ever met you before, but after last night, after we had spoken, I went through my files." Ulla gestured to the dining table at the other end of the room. On top of it stood four cardboard boxes with metal edges. "Our conversation kept troubling me. I found the photo at the bottom of the third box. There are hundreds, if not thousands, of snapshots in those boxes. Of children and their parents during all my years as a health visitor. And there was one of a father and a child whom I remember, Jens and . . . Sara. Some corner of my mind remembered that photo, and I found it." She looked away.

"The health visitor, who had initially been assigned to the family, moved to Greenland when her husband was offered a job up there, and I took over when Sara was around seven months old. The mother had injured her back during the birth and had been in chronic pain ever since. She had had several operations and had been hospitalized repeatedly for long periods and whenever I visited, the father was always alone with the baby."

"Is there a record? Did you make notes about . . . Sara?"

"Yes, and that's what triggered my memory last night. I remembered that Sara's record was missing," Ulla said. "When I took over, everything was in a state of flux. We had just been merged with Odense Nursing School, and the result was chaos. Before my first visit to the family, I looked for her record, but I couldn't find it. When I explained this to a colleague, she convinced me that my predecessor must have left it with the family with instructions to pass it on to their new health visitor. But when I asked for the record, the father said it had never been given to him. So together we created a new one. Sara was thriving and gaining weight, and there was really very little for me to do. During what would be my first and only visit, Jens was delighted to share his good news with me. Sara's mother had had another operation, at a private clinic somewhere, in England I think it was, and it had been very successful. That was the day he gave me the photograph." She nodded toward the envelope. "I was very moved when I left. I looked forward to visiting the family three months later, to finally meeting Sara's mother, and I hoped it would all work out for them. But I never saw them again. Jens called to say there was no need for me to come."

"And you never got an explanation?"

"No," Ulla replied. "Life moved on. New children, new family histories."

"The other health visitor . . . what was her name?" Anna wanted to know.

"Grethe Nygaard. She's dead. I saw her death notice in the local paper three years ago. She died in Greenland."

Anna cast a sidelong glance at the envelope.

"Open the envelope, Anna," Ulla said, gently. Anna reached for the envelope and her hands were shaking. I'm going to die, she thought. She opened the envelope and carefully pulled out a picture. She looked at the back of the photo.

"Jens and Sara Bella Nor, August 1978" it read. Anna stared at it. Then she turned it over. It had faded slightly, but only a little. The background showed hessian wallpaper and part of a brown window frame. There were two people in the picture. A very young Jens with masses of hair and a beard. He was looking into the camera and his smile was crooked, but his expression was dark and mournful. On his lap sat a small girl in a pinafore dress and a diaper. She was the spitting image of Lily. The tears started rolling down Anna's cheeks.

"There can be no doubt," Ulla said carefully. "You're like two peas in a pod." She looked gravely at Anna. "And I swear on my Hippocratic oath: the little girl in that photo, that one," she pointed, "her name was Sara. I wrote her name on the back of the photo. I've always been meticulous."

Ulla Bodelsen got up and sat down next to Anna on the sofa. Lily was absorbed in play under the dining table where she had lined up the teddies and the dolls. Anna wanted to get up, but instead she leaned into the other woman and Ulla put her strong, old arms around her.

Anna didn't want to leave, but Lily had started rubbing her eyes so Anna decided the time had come to say good-bye. She returned the photo to the envelope and put it in her bag. Then she dressed Lily in her snowsuit and hugged Ulla Bodelsen. They didn't speak much. Anna said thank you and the old woman said take good care of yourself. Lily wanted to be carried, and just as they boarded the train to Copenhagen, she fell asleep on Anna's shoulder. Anna was soaked with sweat. She settled Lily across two seats, unzipped her snowsuit, and bought herself a large cup of tea with milk. Soon she found herself ringing Jens without having decided what to say to him.

"Jens." He sounded tired.

"Dad, it's me," Anna said.

"Hi, sweetheart," he murmured.

"Why haven't either of you called me?" she asked, as calmly as she could manage. "Have you decided to gang up on your *only* daughter?"

"Anna," her father said. "I've called you lots of times, but you won't answer. Your behavior is ridiculous. Honestly. You've no reason to scream at your mother and lecture me. We're only trying to help you. You're stressed, we're aware of that, and Cecilie and I think it's crazy that Lily can't be with us, with Cecilie, until your dissertation defense. But she's your child and, of course, we can't make the decision for you. We just don't understand. Surely it would be much better for Lily to be with people who've got time for her, wouldn't it, Anna, my love? But if you don't want to—" He would have carried on talking, but Anna interrupted him.

"I love you, Dad, do you know that?" she said hoarsely. "But you're spineless." The tears forced their way out. "Not everything Cecilie says or does is the law. And right now Cecilie isn't good for Lily or me. And I think you know that. I've been so unhappy these last two years because of Thomas, and I don't know how I would have managed without your and Cecilie's help. But you've got to stop now. Both of you. Lily and I need to be mother and daughter; there may only be two of us, Jens, but we're a complete family. And you need to leave us alone. You can be Lily's grandparents who visit on Sundays and bring sweets, and you can borrow her during summer vacation. But Lily's my daughter, and I'm a good mother. Not perfect, but I want to be her mother. Do you understand?" She was hissing now from trying to keep her voice down. There was silence down the other end.

"I've never been able to understand why you're so aggressive." He sounded hurt.

"Who is Sara Bella?" There was no stopping her now.

"Pardon?" Jens switched the telephone to his other hand, and Anna imagined he had been lying on the sofa and was now sitting up.

"Who is Sara? I'm Sara, aren't I? My name was Sara when I was a baby, wasn't it? Why? What the hell is wrong with you two?!" She regretted the latter as soon as she had said it. Jens would only hear her swearing, not the message. As had happened a thousand times before. And she was right.

"Anna," Jens said quietly. "Don't speak to me like that. You're stressed, I understand, but you've gone too far."

"I don't give a damn how I speak to you, Dad," Anna said, icily. "You've lied. You're still lying. There was a girl named Sara Bella, I saw a picture of her today. She's the spitting image of Lily. On the back of the picture it read 'Jens and Sara Bella.' I'm her, I know I am. *Why?*"

"Where are you?" Jens was sounding genuinely shocked now.

"On a train between Odense and Copenhagen," Anna sighed. Silence followed.

"Where's Lily?"

"I abandoned her in an orphanage and made a break for it. What do you take me for? She's asleep next to me."

"What were you doing in Odense?" The fear in Jens's voice was so obvious that Anna mellowed a little.

"Silly Daddy," she said. "We went to Odense to visit Ulla Bodelsen. My health visitor. Who helped you all the times Mom was in hospital. You want to know why I'm angry? I can't explain because I don't know, either. But *you* do." She exhaled.

"My birth certificate," she suddenly remembered. "The date I was named is almost eleven months after the day I was born. It's not true you named me as late as you've always maintained, is it? You changed my name. *Why?*" The latter came out as a not very quiet roar. Lily jerked, and a man wearing earphones turned and gave Anna a look.

There was total silence down the other end.

"Anna," Jens pleaded. "We need to talk. I can explain."

Anna held out her cell and scowled at it. Then she remembered that the World's Most Irritating Detective had told her to control herself. She put the phone back to her ear.

"Anna," Jens called out. "Anna?"

"I'm here," she said tonelessly.

"Cecilie can't know about this," he whispered. "Promise me you won't mention this. I can explain. It would destroy her completely."

"Dad," she said patiently, "if the truth will destroy her, she'll have to be destroyed. It's over." She hung up. Her cell phone rang immediately. Jens's name came up on the display. She switched the phone to silent and stared at it. He called eight times before he gave up. He left no messages. Anna leaned back and tried to look out into the dark night, but all she saw was her own reflection. She looked tired, but not angry. Not in the least. She closed her eyes. She began to fit together the pieces of what had happened almost thirty years ago, when she was born. But only the pieces. A girl who started off as Sara, then became Anna. A lie.

Slowly she calmed down. She went to the restroom, and when she returned she covered Lily with her jacket. Then she called Karen.

"I was just about to give up on you," Karen said happily. Anna had spent the day being cross with Karen for calling Troels the night before, but she was no longer angry. Instead she said: "It took longer than I had expected. I went to Odense. It's a long story. We're on the train. We get in at 10:08."

"I'll meet you at the station," Karen said.

"There's really no need," Anna said.

"I know. But I'll be there anyway."

CHAPTER 12

On Friday October 12, Søren rose at six o'clock and showered. Two hours later, he arrived at Bellahøj police station, in plenty of time for the morning meeting at nine. He stood in his office, staring out the window at the running track, while he reviewed the case. Two days after a murder, four days after a suspicious death, which was very likely also a murder, and what did he have? Not even the beginning of a theory. He should be rushing around, getting the investigation moving, pumping suspects for information and chasing every last piece of evidence.

He thought about Anna. He had never asked anyone for help. He had never been so unprofessional. And he had picked her—of all people. An unbalanced lioness with a threatened cub. A woman with something to hide.

He watched the sky above the city and was consumed by a deep urge to touch her; to kiss her and make love to her. He imagined it was New Year's Eve, they had gone somewhere, Anna and he, to a party with lots of people, women in beautiful gowns, men in black tie. Anna stood by the window and Søren watched her from across the room. She was wearing a black dress, her yellow eyes were made up and looked dramatic, and Søren knew every man secretly desired her. Later that night, she danced. Drunk and vulgar, throwing propriety to the wind, her hair in a mess, her thighs bared where her dress had ridden up. He would find her in the darkness and put out her fire with gasoline. It would never go out. Never ever, as long as he lived.

He froze. Where had she been last Wednesday night when he had called her, twice? What could she have been up to that was so private she refused to tell him? It was odd that Henrik had said something similar. That *he* had been with someone and he had screwed up? Søren was suddenly convinced Henrik had visited Anna. That he had used the case as a pretext for seeing her and they had. . . . He checked his watch and stormed off to the morning meeting, itching to pick a fight with someone.

He briefed his team, distributed that day's tasks, and answered a few questions. He didn't look at Henrik directly, but watched, out of the corner of his eye, how Henrik doodled on a pad, paying absolutely no attention. It wasn't until Søren announced he intended to visit Johannes Trøjborg's mother, Janna Kampe, that Henrik reacted and wanted to know why. Had Søren come across something? After all, they had already spoken to Mrs. Kampe.

"I want to know whether Johannes was gay or—" Søren began.

"Of course he was." Henrik interrupted. "If Johannes was straight, I'll watch the next season of *The Bachelor* with you."

Søren glared at Henrik. "What do you mean?"

"They like that kind of thing. They fuck each other up the ass and watch cheesy shows." A few people tittered.

"Just like you're some fascist pig who sits in his patrol car all day, stuffing his face with doughnuts?"

Søren expected his comeback to trigger howls of laughter, but it didn't. Suddenly he became aware of how angry he had sounded.

Anna showed up at ten o'clock, exactly as they had agreed. He could clearly forget all about a truce. She stared daggers at him during the entire interview but never looked at Henrik once, not even when he addressed her directly, or when she replied to his barrage of questions. She was clearly making a point.

"Jesus, she's hard work," Henrik said, as he looked down the corridor where Anna was disappearing. Søren followed his eyes.

"What's your problem?" Søren snapped, went into his office and slammed the door shut behind him. Henrik opened the door, wanting to know why the hell Søren was so uptight. At that moment the telephone rang, and Søren gestured for Henrik to come in.

It was Bøje.

"Yes?" Søren snarled.

"Someone been raining on your parade?" Bøje asked.

"Just get to the point," Søren said.

"There wasn't a single parasite in Johannes Trøjborg's tissue."

Søren didn't know whether to be relieved or disappointed. Now he was looking for two killers.

"What else?" he demanded, impatiently.

"I've found several semen traces on Johannes's body," Bøje continued and Søren heard him flick through his report. "Crime scene officers have isolated samples on the floor and at the bottom of two table legs in a radius of about 20 inches from the spot in the living room where he was killed. I don't need to tell you the semen didn't come from Johannes, do I?"

Søren held his breath.

"What's your conclusion?" He could hear the rustling of paper, then Bøje took a breath.

"Johannes Trøjborg died as a result of six injuries to the back of his head, of which four would have been severe enough to kill him on their own. Judging from the forensic report, which I have in front of me, and the injuries sustained by the victim, he was thrown up against the far right corner of the sofa, which penetrated the back of his head. Two of the injuries were inflicted prior to the victim's death and probably rendered him unconscious but didn't kill him, then he suffered another four which . . ." Bøje hesitated. "Well, it's the equivalent of someone stabbing him with an ice pick.

Johannes Trøjborg undoubtedly died from the first blow, and it begs the question, why did the killer carry on? The victim was of medium build, which suggests the killer was either very strong or very angry or both. By the way, what an extraordinary piece of furniture," he added, and Søren assumed he was looking at a photograph of Johannes Trøjborg's sofa.

"It looks like Count Dracula's sofa," he commented. "Everything indicates someone went berserk and we're *not* dealing with a calculating killer, but rather some dude who went nuts. You have to be good and angry to attack an unconscious man and continue assaulting him after he's dead, wouldn't you agree?"

"What does the semen tell us?" Søren asked.

"Well, that's something of a mystery. Semen traces were found on the body. On the body but not inside. So they didn't have sex, and it wasn't rape." Bøje paused and waited for the penny to drop.

"And?" Søren prompted him after a long, ominous pause.

"What bothers me is that we're talking about very little semen."

Søren was perplexed.

"I don't follow."

Bøje hesitated.

"Well, it's as if . . . as if the killer ejaculated while he manhandled the body. Very confusing and difficult to explain. Even for me."

Søren groaned. A parasite freak and a necrophile. What the hell was going on?

"Are we talking about necrophilia?"

"No, I don't think so," Bøje replied. "Do you recall that man from Søborg who killed an armed robber by throwing him against a stove?"

"No," Søren said.

"Well, anyway, we found traces of the man's DNA on the intruder. In the form of semen. We were speechless, to put it mildly. The man called the police straight after the attack and nothing suggested he had time to satisfy his necrophiliac urges before calling for help, and besides, it made no sense whatsoever. He was a regular guy whose wife was holding an almost newborn baby in her arms, and I didn't think for one moment he had ejaculated over the body. Besides, there simply wasn't enough semen, if that was the explanation. We found traces, but nowhere near the amount we find in rape victims, for example, not even half a load. So how on earth had his semen ended up on the intruder? We were all going crazy because we couldn't figure it out. You were on leave or something and that hopeless idiot, what was his name, Flemming Tørslev or Tønnesen?"

Søren groaned for the second time.

"Hans Tønnesen," he said.

"Right, thanks. Well, that dimwit was convinced the husband was a pervert and had masturbated over the intruder after hurling him against his stove. What an idiot!" Bøje remarked as if it was Søren's fault that Hans Tønnesen was a mediocre detective. In a way, it was. As a result of Søren's sudden absence, his colleagues had to tolerate Tønnesen's modest talent for three months in 2005. Elvira had died, and Knud was ill. And then there was the breakup with Vibe. And the business with Maja. Søren had burned out and the only way he could hide it was to take time off. Hans Tønnesen had been the only senior officer at Bellahøj police station who could replace him. When Søren returned to work, he had been made to pay for his colleague's incompetence by buying everyone pastries for an unreasonably long time.

"Eventually the husband admits, under questioning, that he had been naked on the toilet, masturbating over a porn mag. At the very same second he ejaculates, he hears the intruder climb through a window. He runs into the living room where he attacks the intruder, leaving semen traces on him. As well as in the bathroom, in the hallway, on the door to the living room, and every other surface he touches. Minuscule amounts, obviously, but enough for us to track him from the bathroom to the living room. This case started off as an enigma, but make a note of this, my boy: sometimes the utterly improbable explanation is the right one."

Søren felt a headache coming on.

"And now you've found traces," he said, "but not enough to prove direct sexual contact?"

"Bingo."

"And you still rule out necrophilia?"

"I can't rule out anything, but I've seen three cases of necrophilia in my time, approximately one every fifteen years and in every one of them, there was either a full amount of semen in or on the body, or no semen at all, because even the most deranged necrophile appears to know DNA makes great evidence. Here, the semen proves neither one thing nor another, just like in the Søborg case. Johannes didn't have sex with anyone prior to his death. He had some old tears to his rectum, which suggest he may have had anal intercourse in the past, but even that's difficult to establish. Tears can happen for all sorts of reasons, and in this case, they bear no relation to the cause of death. My opinion is we're dealing with the same type of coincidence as in the Søborg case. The killer is masturbating, and while he's doing that an argument starts, he ejaculates, gets angry, and attacks Johannes, and that's how the traces end up on him."

"Have you checked the semen?"

"Yep." There was a scrambling noise down the other end. "Negative. He's not on our database."

Søren was silent for a moment, then he asked: "Any connection to Lars Helland, in your opinion?"

"The parasite-riddled guy from the other day?"

"Yes," Søren sighed.

"Infecting someone with parasites is what I would describe as cold-blooded. You don't do that in the heat of the moment, do you? It takes planning. I don't think we're talking about the same killer. I can see why you would like it to be: the victims were close colleagues and you could kill two birds with one stone, but if you ask me, we're talking about two different ones. A ruthless bastard, who carried out a carefully planned revenge, and a hothead who gets a bit too rough with his lover during a fight, and who explodes with rage when said lover dares to spill his brains all over the floor."

Søren pricked up his ears.

"What do you mean by *lover*?"

Bøje was quiet for a while.

"You're right, I'm not sure about that," he said, surprisingly timid all of a sudden. "The victim had a pierced penis, through the urethra and out on the underside of the head, which makes him a bit out of the ordinary, don't you think? Ordinary men, real men, I mean men like us, don't sport a Prince Albert, do we? The victim must have been queer."

Søren was tempted to agree with him.

After his conversation with Bøje, Søren dealt with a few things in his office and ate his lunch behind a newspaper in the cafeteria, so no one would be tempted to join him. Just before two o'clock he drove to Charlottenlund to pay Mrs. Kampe a visit.

The Kampe family home looked like a mansion, and when Søren drove up the poplar-lined avenue he couldn't help thinking of Johannes's shabby apartment. Could this really be the place where little Johannes had grown up? It was a three-story house with a broad two-winged staircase that led to the main entrance.

It was as silent as the grave.

Søren rang the doorbell. The door was opened by a woman who looked at him with Johannes's intelligent eyes. She shook his hand and invited him in. There were ornaments and furniture, rugs and stuffed animal heads, and hides from floor to ceiling in the three rooms Søren managed to see before they reached a large drawing room where a fire was burning in the fireplace. Two royal-blue sofas faced each other and Søren noticed a woolen blanket and a hastily folded newspaper on one of them. Janna Kampe gestured toward the other sofa and sat down opposite him. Søren began by telling her that the preliminary autopsy report didn't suggest there was a link between the murder of her son and the death of Professor Helland three days earlier. Mrs. Kampe looked momentarily skeptical. Then he changed the conversation to the cause of Johannes's death. His training had taught him to say as little as possible without being downright obstructive. Mrs. Kampe looked away when her eyes welled up.

"It's very important for the investigation that we form as clear a picture of Johannes's social life as possible. His circle. People he spent time with, his friends. That's why I'm here."

Mrs. Kampe looked at him for a long time, before she said, "I wish I could help you, but I can't. I didn't know Johannes very well. This Christmas, it'll be two years since we last saw each other. I've no idea who his friends are. Or I should say . . ." She got up and returned with a scrapbook. Søren watched her face. Maintain the façade, it told him, keeping up appearances matters more than anything. She handed him the scrapbook.

"I know a little. I saved some newspaper clippings."

Søren opened the book. The pages were covered with various items featuring Johannes. Søren studied a picture of a beaming Johannes who had just received a distinction for his dissertation. He was holding several bouquets and, as far as Søren could see, the article was from the university's newsletter. In another piece, Johannes was part of a crowd and Søren read about a seminar in the caption; a third article was about the communication of science and had been published in the journal, *Dagens Medicin*. Here, Johannes had been photographed with his colleagues from the department of Cell Biology and Comparative Zoology and Søren was startled when he recognized Anna. She looked straight into the camera. Johannes was standing next to her, smiling gently, and behind them was Lars Helland, distracted and looking at something outside the photo. Søren carried on. There were roughly forty articles in the scrapbook, cut out and filed like prized stamps.

"May I ask why your relationship was so strained?" he said. Mrs. Kampe looked at him for a long time.

"I married into all of this," she said, gesturing toward the elegant drawing room. "My late husband, Jørgen, wasn't the children's real father. Their father died when they were very young. My daughter wasn't even a year old and Johannes barely four. We became financially secure for the rest of our lives," she said, not looking happy at all.

"My children have never really appreciated their good fortune," she continued. "Of course, my daughter could be excused, but

Johannes . . . Johannes has always seemed . . ." She searched for the right word. "Uninterested. As if he were trying to prove something. Jørgen was a strict stepfather, but he also offered Johannes the chance of a very privileged life. Johannes, however, simply rejected it. Johannes could have been more . . ." She frowned and decided to change tack.

"With money comes responsibility," she stated. "And the plan was that Johannes would join the firm. Jørgen had taught Johannes everything about the business. Everything. And suddenly, he wanted out." She gave Søren a dark look. "He was adamant he wanted to be an academic, just like his biological father. It was very difficult for Jørgen to accept. It caused deep rifts between my husband and Johannes. They had huge arguments, but Johannes had made up his mind.

"When their feud was at its peak, Johannes started to deliberately provoke Jørgen. He showed up in a skirt and wearing eye makeup for dinner on St. Martin's Eve—would you believe it—I don't know what he was thinking. His appearance had been becoming increasingly bizarre: the black boots in the hall, which I nudged behind the coats, and his hair, of course. He dyed it red. I noticed other details. The edge of some item of jewelry. His pierced ears, which he had the decency to keep unadorned when he visited us. I regarded this as a concession because Johannes knew his stepfather would fly into a rage. Jørgen didn't approve of people being different." Mrs. Kampe shook her head. "But that night, he showed up in a leather skirt and wearing eye makeup. At first I thought he must be drunk, but he wasn't. His hands were shaking, I remember, but his eyes were challenging, as if he had decided to declare war. I knew there would be trouble." Mrs. Kampe looked at Søren, her eyes filled with the trepidation and defiance she had previously attributed to her son.

"Jørgen always saw Johannes in his study. That evening, I waited in the kitchen for an eternity. I solved a crossword. The food grew cold." She smiled sheepishly. "Suddenly I noticed the door to my husband's study was open. Jørgen was behind his desk, flicking through a hunting magazine. I asked him where Johannes was, and he said, 'He's gone and he won't be coming back.'"

"And did he?"

"No," Mrs. Kampe replied. "He didn't. Not while Jørgen was alive. I called him many times. I missed him. Johannes wanted me to get a divorce. He said it as if visiting me depended on it. But, of course, I wasn't going to. I loved Jørgen. So he started saying all sorts of vile things." She hesitated.

"Such as?" Søren wanted to know.

"Things like I was a prisoner in my own home. That Jørgen was a tyrant, and I wore an invisible ball and chain. That if this was my idea of love, then I was blind." She looked down.

"Jørgen left Johannes nothing when he died. Or rather, he left him one of the stag heads in the corridor. It's still there. Johannes refused to collect it. He was furious, but what did he expect? My husband had heard nothing from him for the better part of a year, not even when he was admitted to hospital and had only weeks to live. When Johannes found out he would inherit nothing, he was furious."

Her exasperation flared up, then her façade cracked.

"I wish Johannes was still a little boy. He was a wonderful little boy. Gentle and industrious. He did as he was told and he was never any trouble. Neither of my children was. But as adults . . . I don't know. We must have done something wrong. And now it's too late." She straightened up.

"Why could Johannes's sister be excused?" Søren asked.

"Mental health problems," Mrs. Kampe replied. "It started when she reached puberty. She lived with us for many years, but eventually the burden grew too heavy. So she moved into a residential home."

"Was Johannes gay?" Søren asked suddenly.

"His sister said he wasn't," Mrs. Kampe replied. "I obviously suspected he might be. I mean, leather skirts and makeup? I've never met any of his boyfriends, but what do I know about gay men? I don't approve of them and yes, for a time I believed he was gay. My daughter said he was merely a member of some club where men wore skirts and corsets. That he definitely wasn't gay. She knew that because she had met his girlfriend. An older woman."

"I'll need to speak to your daughter," Søren said.

"No," Mrs. Kampe replied.

Søren regretted his strategy.

"I'll need to speak to someone who knew Johannes," he said kindly. "A friend, an ex-lover, or his sister." He gave Mrs. Kampe a pleading look. "Right now, I've got nothing to go on."

Janna Kampe looked at him for a long time. Then she took the scrapbook and flicked to the third page. Søren had noticed the picture, but paid no attention to it. The photo showed a curvaceous woman around forty, with thick curly hair held in place by a spotted bandana. Her smile sparkled. Søren skimmed the text. The article was about a vintage furniture store in Nordre Frihavnsgade. The owner's name was Susanne Winther; she was a trained psychotherapist and now a passionate furniture collector. She loved spending her weekends tracking down hidden treasures at flea markets in and around Copenhagen, with her boyfriend Johannes. His name was highlighted, and the article was published two years ago.

"My daughter gave me this. She said the woman was Johannes's girlfriend. She told me to tell Dad, to tell Jørgen. So Jørgen wouldn't think Johannes was . . . a shirt-lifter."

Søren wrote Susanne Winther's name and the date of the article in his notepad. Johannes had had a girlfriend. Calling it a breakthrough might be an exaggeration, he thought wryly. But it was a start.

"It's helpful," Søren said. "But before I speak to her, I really want to talk to Johannes's sister. I presume her surname's also Trøjborg? Where does she live?"

"In heaven," Janna Kampe said quietly. "She took her own life last summer. She suffered from schizophrenia and was frequently hospitalized. In the end, she gave up."

Søren sat, shaken, in front of a woman who had lost both her children. He had run out of questions and got up to leave. Mrs. Kampe escorted him through the fine, cold house, and he promised to call her with any news.

When he drove back to the city, he could smell his own sweat.

* * *

Under normal circumstances, he would have dropped by Bellahøj police station and picked up Henrik, but suddenly he found himself at the junction with Jagtvejen, a long way from the police station, very close to Nordre Frihavn, and still angry with Henrik. He parked on Strandboulevarden and walked up Nordre Frihavnsgade where he soon found Susanne Winther's store, which was called The Apple. When he entered, the first thing that caught his eye was a dozen apple-shaped bowls arranged on a teak table, which could easily have come from his childhood home in Snerlevej. Faint music could be heard and there was an aroma of apples and cinnamon.

"Be with you in a minute," a voice called out from the back room.

Søren sat down in a high-backed armchair, which someone had updated by decorating its worn armrests with red appliqué apples. He thought about Vibe. About her open face, eyes that had trusted him since that high-school disco. He thought about Maja. The memory of the last time he saw her hadn't faded. Her singular smell, sweet and enticing, and her foot, tiny inside her booties, even smaller in his hand. The lie weighed him down. Knud had urged him to live his life right, free from lies, free from secrets. He had said lies never expired, but Søren had been arrogant and believed his lie would dissolve and evaporate. And when that had happened, his life would once more consist of manageable fluctuations within a normal range. No more hurt. No more pain. Like all the years with Vibe. A nice, quiet life, free from drama, free from loss. Now he had ended up with the exact opposite. He was attracted to Anna. It was unprofessional and risky. Anna had upset his careful balancing act. What was it all about? Her yellow eyes, her volatility, her devil-may-care attitude. He didn't even dare to think how scared he would be, all the time, if she were his. All that drama, every day, upending every stone, stirring everything up, turning everything inside out.

There were apples everywhere in Susanne Winther's store. A mirror with a plastic apple frame hung on the wall, and on the floor lay a crocheted rug with a picture of a large red apple.

"Hi."

Søren instantly recognized Susanne Winther from the picture. She was obese and very beautiful. White flawless skin, freckles down the bridge of her nose, and an impressive head of cascading curls, kept away from her face with a headband. She was wearing an apron with a large red apple and green trimming, and she offered Søren a plate.

"I've been baking," she said cheerfully. "And made a fresh pot of tea. You looking for anything in particular?"

Søren suddenly realized how hungry he was and took a slice of cake.

"Someone's got an apple obsession," he remarked.

Susanne Winther laughed.

"I've seen you before, haven't I? You were looking for a dining table? I happen to have one in the back. Do you want to have a look? You did want a solid wood one, didn't you? That was you?"

Søren stood up abruptly.

"I'm with the police," he said, feeling guilty as he wiped a crumb from the corner of his mouth. Susanne Winther chuckled and winked at him. Then she froze.

"Please tell me you're joking?" she said. For the second time that day, he pulled out his badge. Susanne Winther buried her face in her hands.

"Is Magnus all right?"

Somewhere, at the back of Søren's mind, an alarm went off.

"I'm here because Johannes Trøjborg's dead, and I have reason to believe you knew him." Søren waited for her reaction. She seemed relieved.

"Sorry," she said and slumped down on a sofa. "But that's dreadful. What happened? Christ Almighty. I've a little boy. Magnus. He's seven months old, and he's at home with his daddy. For a moment, I thought something terrible had happened to them. That they had been killed." She gave Søren a dazed look. "So Johannes is dead? How? Did he have a crash? Why are you here?"

"Were you Johannes Trøjborg's girlfriend two or three years ago?" Søren asked.

"Yes, we were together. For a year. But we haven't seen each other for a long time." Again she buried her face in her hands. "But, Jesus Christ, I spoke to him recently," she said, "less than two weeks ago. We were really good friends, or whatever you call it when you don't see each other very often. He wanted to see Magnus. He promised to call soon and arrange a time when he was less busy. That's why I didn't worry when I hadn't heard from him. So he's dead?" She stared at Søren.

"Did he have a crash?" she asked again.

Søren shook his head.

Susanne Winther closed the store and called her husband. Søren could hear her speak in a low voice in the back room. It sounded as if she were crying. Søren helped her carry two chests on the pavement back inside the store. Together, they walked to his car and Søren opened the door for her. The sun was shining, and he put on his sunglasses. He slid his cell into its holder and inserted his earpiece. Two messages. The first one was unimportant, and the other was from Henrik, wondering where the hell he was. There was still no sign of Dr. Tybjerg, and Henrik wanted to know if they should issue a wanted by police notice or what? They needed a breakthrough, no matter how small. Søren hated it when Henrik lectured him and was about to get annoyed when he spotted a newspaper headline outside a newsagent.

PSYCHO PROF KILLS AGAIN it said in large letters, and below that *Cops clueless*. At the same time he heard Henrik's recorded voice:

"I don't know if you've seen the tabloids today, but the Police Commissioner just charged past the office with steam coming out of his ears. He's looking for you as well. I think the time is ripe for a press conference, and you need to find something we can feed the sharks with. So, see ya! Honestly, dude, what do you think you're doing?" And he hung up.

Søren and Susanne Winther drove in silence. Suddenly, Søren's cell rang. It was Henrik again.

"Where the hell are you?" he shouted.

"I'll be at the station in three minutes. Can you find an interview room for me? I'm with Susanne Winther, Johannes Trøjborg's ex-girlfriend."

"I get the impression you suspect me of something," Susanne began, when Søren had hung up. "An interview. That sounds very serious." She looked at Søren. "Johannes and I were together for just under a year, a couple of years ago. It seems a little over the top to be picked up by the police and brought in for questioning without warning."

Søren was tempted to exploit her uncertainty and let her roast in the silence. He was good at that.

"We don't suspect you of anything," he said, kindly. "Of course we don't. But I need to understand what kind of person Johannes was in order to find out who killed him. I need your help. I really need your help."

Susanne Winther sighed.

"All right," she said.

Susanne Winther met Johannes on the goth scene. They got talking at the bar in the Red Mask, a candlelit semicircle in a crowded room, somewhere in Østerbro. Relatively soon afterward, they began a sexual relationship wherein Susanne dominated Johannes. Later, Susanne introduced Johannes to the fetish scene and Inkognito.

Johannes was ten years Susanne's junior and, to begin with, when their relationship was purely sexual, this had been irrelevant. However, when they grew closer and Susanne told Johannes she would like to have a child, Johannes had cooled. Not in a hurtful way, not at all. They talked about it at length and their subsequent split came with considerable sadness. Johannes didn't want to have children, and she did. They were equally insistent. That was the bottom line. Now she was married to Ulf, whom she had met at a fetish event.

"Johannes and I really liked each other, but we had incompatible views on children. Our breakup was final and clean. Soon after, I met Ulf, I got pregnant, and we stopped being part of the scene."

"Why?" Søren wanted to know.

"Because we were in love, pregnant, and needed no one else."
Susanne smiled. Søren studied her face. Her expression was open
and trusting.

"Just now you described Johannes as 'gentle,'" Søren said, flicking
through his notes even though he hadn't made any. "Earlier today I
spoke to Johannes's mother and she paints a different picture of her
son. She describes him as both 'ungrateful' and 'provocative.'"

Susanne's eyes darkened.

"Don't listen to a word she says," she scoffed. "She destroyed her
own daughter, and she tried to destroy Johannes, too."

Søren looked up in surprise.

"When I spoke to her today, she seemed deeply affected by the
loss of her son," he objected, baiting her.

"I don't buy that for a moment," Susanne sneered. "All right, she
might worry about what to say to the ladies from the bridge club.
It's fashionable to have successful children in those circles. My son
the CEO, my son the lawyer, and so on. I can imagine how inconvenient it must be for her to have to explain why she has no children
left. Johannes's sister killed herself, but you probably know that," she
added, when Søren failed to react. He nodded slowly.

"I thought the tension came mainly from the stepfather,
Jørgen . . . ?" Søren continued flicking through his notes.

"Kampe," Susanne prompted him. "As in Kampe Furniture. Yes,
of course, a lot of it came from him, but at some level it suited Janna
just fine to have a tyrant for a husband. It meant she never had to take
responsibility for anything. And that was precisely how she wanted
it. She behaved as the defenseless little wifey who couldn't help having married a domineering brute who, in my opinion, abused his
stepchildren. Not sexually," she added quickly when Søren's eyebrows shot up. "Metaphorically. His sister escaped, to some extent,
by disappearing into her illness and by becoming just as passive and
long-suffering as her mother. Johannes took the brunt of it. He was
four years old and his sister was a baby when Jørgen entered their
lives. And Jørgen cracked the whip from morning till night. Again,
metaphorically speaking," she repeated. "It was about elitism and

winning. The kid should learn to ride thoroughbreds, play golf, sail, dive, stand at attention. He even criticized Johannes's build; a real man didn't weigh one hundred and forty pounds, a real man was over six feet tall, real men didn't have slender, piano-playing fingers. Certainly not in Jørgen's eyes." She stopped talking and studied her own hands. They were large and her fingers thick, but the backs of her hands were freckled and soft, and her nails gleamed. Søren looked at the beautiful woman in the far too heavy body.

"I spent my teenage years thinking I should be different." She glanced shyly at Søren. "My twenties were hard. In those days I truly believed visible ribs equaled happiness. If only I could lose weight, I would find a boyfriend with designer stubble, healthy interests, and a car. If only. When I turned thirty, I hit rock bottom. For nearly two years I languished in a prison of my own making . . ." She smiled at her choice of words and winked at Søren. "But then things changed. I went to therapy, I traveled, and I trained as a therapist myself. I worked as a therapist for nearly five years, then I had had my fill of navel gazing and bought The Apple. I know it might sound absurd, but suddenly I just knew I wanted to do something with apples and furniture. It was fun," she said, sounding genuinely happy. "Building up the business from scratch. I was thirty-eight, and I was finally having fun. One of my customers, Stella, asked me if I wanted to check out the Red Mask. I knew of their parties, obviously, I had been active on the fetish scene for years, and many of the fetishists belong to both scenes, but until then the goth scene had never really appealed to me. I had joined the fetish scene purely for sex and, quite honestly, I couldn't see the point of goth culture. But when Stella invited me, I gave it a try. Stella organizes goth and fetish events, and she often pops into the store," she interposed and continued, "The goth scene changed my life. Here you're accepted, respected, and valued right away and it continues like that, if you live and let live. Openness and tolerance toward anything outside the norm. I took to it like a fish to water. The third time I attended, I met Johannes. And do you know something?"

Søren shook his head.

"It was like meeting myself. Only as a ten years younger man. To begin with, I wasn't sure if he was worth the effort. His lack of self-esteem. It reminded me of everything I had worked so hard to leave behind . . ."

Søren was mesmerized by her.

"But then I realized how complex he actually was. Of course, he was affected by the humiliation he had suffered as a child and, in some respects, his self-worth was like a sieve." She looked pensively into space. "However, the interesting thing about Johannes was that he had decided to break the pattern, so in some areas he was strong and determined. He had made up his mind not to go through life like a whipped dog, even though he had been treated like one most of his childhood. That's why I fell in love with him. He offered me a challenge outside the bedroom, but at the same time, he could handle that I dominated him sexually. It was a very harmonious relationship.

"We had been together for six months and were blissfully happy," she continued. "Then I started talking about having children. I was shocked when I realized he didn't want any, but we remained friends. I have always known I wanted children. We were both very sad, but the split was inevitable." Susanne fell silent.

"Do you have any idea what was happening within the family at that point?" Henrik asked. Søren and Susanne turned to Henrik in unison, as though they had simultaneously remembered his presence.

"You mean Johannes's family?"

"Yes."

"I think we had only been together for around five weeks when Johannes had a falling out with Jørgen and, consequently, Janna. Johannes tried to reach out to his mother several times, but Jørgen always got in the way. It upset him, obviously. He never found the strength to stand up to his stepfather and, as an adult, his survival strategy had been to ignore Jørgen's shit. We talked about his options. Johannes hoped Jørgen's death might create an opening. Shortly after the funeral, he visited his mother and learned Jørgen had disinherited him. Johannes didn't care, but it killed him when Janna insisted he was only there for the money. That night, he closed the door to his childhood home forever. Johannes told me everything when he came home . . ." for a moment she looked hesitantly at Søren. "I never met them myself, but . . ."

"And yet you sound so certain when you describe them," Henrik objected. Søren shuffled his feet, annoyed at the interruption.

"I trusted Johannes. You could do that. At some level, he was damaged by his childhood," she grimaced, "but he was a very fine human being. He made a real effort with people, and he would never have invented the scene with his mother. No one could have made up that story, and certainly not Johannes. He was far too . . . introspective." She looked firmly at Henrik and turned to Søren again.

"I would like to pursue my question," Henrik insisted. Susanne looked at him as though it was highly inappropriate for him to intervene and Søren couldn't help enjoying himself.

"What if you were wrong? What if Mr. and Mrs. Kampe were well-meaning, decent people, and Johannes was the one who had gone off the rails?"

"It wasn't like that," Susanne stated. "I would know. And so would you." Again she looked at Søren as though Henrik was of no consequence. "You know when you're being played. You might choose to ignore certain signals at the time, but deep inside, you know. I believe that."

She swallowed and continued. "Johannes may have been carrying some heavy baggage, but he had changed himself into a capable and very loving human being. Someone who had dealt with his past, who faced the future with optimism."

"Was he bisexual?" Henrik asked bluntly. Susanne held Søren's gaze for a moment longer, then she slowly turned to Henrik.

"No," she declared.

"Are you sure?"

"Absolutely. We began our relationship with complete sexual openness. No code, no core, no truth. And this applied to our sex life, too. Everything was allowed, nothing was taboo, and no, Johannes wasn't bisexual."

"But he wore a freaking dress," Henrik snapped, pointing furiously to the case file lying on the table in front of him. "I've seen several photos of him in a dress."

"Yes, he did. But wearing a dress doesn't make you gay. Nor does wearing pants make you straight." Susanne looked long and hard at Henrik's '80s jeans.

"Johannes got off on being dominated, and he was a transvestite. He liked going to the Red Mask wearing a skirt and full makeup. And a slightly more adult outfit at Inkognito." Søren was aware of Henrik's growing frustration.

"But transvestites are gay," he snarled. Søren scratched the back of his head.

"And bikers are thugs and all pedophiles have mustaches," Susanne Winther remarked calmly. Her gaze lingered on Henrik's mustache, which was in dire need of a trim. "I don't think you've done your homework," she said. "Transvestites get a kick out of cross-dressing, wearing clothes traditionally associated with the opposite sex. Transsexuals are men and women who feel they have been born into the wrong body and want to switch to the right gender through a sex change operation. However, transsexuals aren't homosexual, even though they are sexually attracted to their own sex, because . . . well, it's obvious. If you're 90 percent female and love a man, but you happen to have a dick because hospital waiting lists in this country are so frigging long, then that doesn't make you male. Being a man isn't just about having a dick, is it?" Again, she looked at Henrik's jeans.

Søren was aware that the situation was about to ignite.

"We're digressing," he piped up. Susanne Winther looked straight at him.

"Johannes wasn't bisexual," she declared. "Anyway, why is it even an issue?"

"We have reason to believe Johannes was killed by a man. Certain evidence from the crime scene, which I can't discuss with you, reveals—"

"That's quite all right," Susanne said.

"Er, thanks," Søren spluttered. A pause followed.

"And to be honest," he said, driven by a sudden urge to confide. "I started off thinking he was gay. Because of his clothes and his way of life. We've seen photos on the home page of the Red Mask. It's clearly unfortunate that we . . ." Søren cleared his throat. "Well, that we . . . that I didn't know the precise meaning of the terms. And our assumption . . . er . . . our very slender assumption . . . which . . . okay, here goes: traces of semen were found at the crime scene, and they didn't come from Johannes."

Henrik's jaw dropped.

"And it looks like Johannes was subjected to a violent attack which caused his death."

"What the hell do you think you're doing?" Henrik shot up and jabbed his finger at Søren. "Are you out of your mind?" Henrik's hand was an inch away from Søren's face, and Søren grabbed his wrist.

"Sit down," Søren said, guiding Henrik back to his chair. "I know what I'm doing."

"You're leaking information to a witness, which she might abuse," Henrik hissed. "I've had it up to here with your ego trip, do you hear? You've lost your judgment, Søren. What the hell's wrong with you?"

"I trust her!" Søren roared. Henrik and Susanne Winther were both startled. "I trust her, for Christ's sake! I trust what I see." Incandescent, he pointed at his own two eyes. "Don't you get it? We've got nothing to go on in this case, because we only see what we saw yesterday, the same old shit. We've been blinded." The pitch of his voice started to drop. "I've been blinded. Everyone's lying and I can't see a bloody thing. I'm changing tack, don't you get it? I'm starting where there's some clarity. And I know when someone's lying." He fixed his gaze on Henrik's face and narrowed his eyes slightly. "I promise you, that I—of all people—I know when someone's lying. And she isn't. You're not lying." This was addressed to Susanne Winther.

"No," she said.

Henrik didn't say another word. When they took a break, he stormed out, and when they resumed the interview, he sent Lau Madsen in his place. Not a problem. Søren couldn't care less if Henrik made a complaint about him. Sometimes you just had to trust people. This also applied to the police. And Søren.

Søren escorted Susanne Winther outside.

"Good-bye," she said, holding out her hand. It was firm and cold, just like a ripe, washed apple. Her eyes were shining.

"Good-bye," Søren said. "I'll call if there's anything else."

"Please do." She turned around. Søren looked at her coat. A reflective disk, shaped like an apple, dangled at the knee-length hem. She waddled across the parking lot.

Susanne had given him a name. Stella Marie Frederiksen. Stella Marie was the woman who had invited Susanne to the Red Mask. Søren had noted her name, and now he was sitting in his office staring at it, distracted by his clash with Henrik. He couldn't work out what had prompted it. Henrik had a short fuse and had been grouchy, he thought, both yesterday and today—as though he felt guilty about something. About Anna? Or was Søren becoming paranoid? He clutched his head. Henrik was spot on. Søren preferred going it alone, or, as Henrik had put it, ego tripping. He couldn't think of a more appropriate description of his life.

He looked up Stella Marie Frederiksen's address and discovered she lived in the Nørrebro area, in Elmegade. He found a landline as well as a cell number. He called her landline.

"Stella here." The telephone rang only once before she answered it. She sounded out of breath. Søren hung up. Then he got up and walked down the corridor. The door to Henrik's office was open. Henrik sat behind his desk, hammering away at his keyboard. A red patch had spread from his cheek and all the way down his neck. Søren slipped inside and managed to observe him for a while before he suddenly looked up and glared at Søren.

"No," he snapped.

"No what?" Søren asked.

"Don't you dare come in here telling me you promise to share all your little secrets with me from now on. I've had enough." Henrik banged his fist on the desk. "You and I are supposed to interview a suspect together, but do you know what I am? Window-dressing. You just do whatever the hell you like. You tackle one of your own team and dribble the ball across the pitch like a maniac, that's what you're doing." Henrik stabbed his finger at Søren. He was livid.

"Your private life is one thing," Henrik went on. "And perhaps we're not as close as I thought we were. When push comes to shove, it doesn't seem to mean anything that we've known each other since we were twenty. Perhaps you're right only to let me in on major developments. Perhaps that's just the way you are. Hermetically sealed, though we all can see that you're up shit's creek."

"You've got secrets, too," Søren said with clenched teeth. Henrik looked surprised.

"I've no secrets from you, Søren. But you're right, it's been a long time since I told you anything, and do you want to know why? To test you, to see if you would even notice, and do you know something? You've acted like it suited you just fine that I clammed up as well. And I'm cool with that. If you want us to work together like two fucking oysters, then we will. We were on the job yesterday. There was no way I could tell you that . . ."

"What?" Søren could feel his throat tighten.

"I'm having an affair, all right?" he hissed. "It's been going on for five weeks. It's a shit thing. I don't want to leave Jeanette, but I don't want to talk about it right now, okay?" Henrik threw a glance in the direction of the open door.

"For five weeks?"

"Yes. It's a girl from my gym," he continued. "Her name's Line. It just happened." Henrik looked out of the window. Søren closed his eyes for a moment.

"Anyway, we were talking about you," Henrik continued. "Not me. You pretend everything's hunky-dory, but we all know it's just a front. Everyone knows that your sudden absence almost three years ago had fuck all to do with burning out. It wasn't the job, no way. Something happened that Christmas. I know it. But like I said, it's your life and if you don't want to tell anyone, that's your choice."

He looked up at Søren and his eyes turned frosty. "But when you're at work, it's another matter. No one keeps secrets here, and do you know why? Because we're a team."

"I'm your governor, Henrik," Søren protested.

"I don't care if you're the prime minister," Henrik roared. "You can build walls between you and the rest of the world on your own time. When you're at work, you're part of a team. I've put up with it for years. You act like Sherlock Holmes, and I'm that clown, Watson, staring gormlessly at the great detective while he sits in his bay window, playing his violin, high as a kite, incapable of sharing his ideas and thoughts with those closest to him."

Søren said nothing. He wanted to defend himself, but he couldn't think of anything to say. What was there to defend?

"And it hits me twice as hard because I also happen to be your friend," Henrik said, very subdued all of a sudden. "You've shut me out of your private life and your work. As if you don't need me but would rather do everything on your own. And I don't believe you can do everything alone, not for a second." He fell silent, just like in the car the other day, as if he had run out of steam. He started fidgeting with his key ring. Søren closed the door to Henrik's office. It was now or never.

"Henrik . . ." he began.

Henrik looked up.

"Almost three years ago . . ." Søren swallowed.

It took him ten minutes to tell Henrik the story. He told it staccato. Henrik's face changed from blotchy red to chalk white. Søren didn't know what to do with his hands when he had finished. Henrik got up and hugged him.

"Christ almighty, dude," he said in a thick voice. "Why didn't you say anything?"

And Søren had no idea why.

Just before 5 p.m. Søren and Henrik visited Stella Marie Frederiksen in Elmegade. She opened the door wearing a rust-colored sweatsuit and slippers shaped like bear paws. Her thick black hair had neon pink extensions. She looked obligingly at the two men and didn't seem particularly surprised at being visited by the police. She offered them coffee. It wasn't until she realized why they had come that she went pale. She had been under the impression they were there in connection with her ex-husband, she stuttered. She had gotten a restraining order against him, and a police car had been outside her house for the last three weeks because her husband was wanted by the police.

Yes, she knew Johannes well.

"Is he dead?" she whispered, lifting a small child from the floor and hugging her. The child had burning black eyes underneath thick eyelashes, and Søren instinctively wanted to reach for her.

But before he could answer she said, "Hold on a moment, please, I'll just put on a DVD, all right? This is too much for little ears."

When she had settled her child, they sat down in the kitchen and Søren let Henrik begin. The last time Stella Marie had seen Johannes was at the Red Mask's September event. The atmosphere at their parties was usually great, but that Friday really had been something special and it was mostly thanks to Johannes. He tended to wear quite restrained outfits and drink beers with his friends, but every now and then he went to town and would arrive dressed up to the nines and set the place on fire. Besides, there had been a goth concert in Horsens so the Red Mask had been relatively quiet that night. Around a hundred people had been present, Stella Marie estimated, and it resulted in an airy and pleasant feel.

"Johannes stood in the corner." She narrowed her eyes as she retraced the events in her mind. "To the right of the bar, where people tend to congregate. He wore leather, skirt or pants, and some sort of corset under a black string vest, hey, hang on . . ." She rocked back on her chair and woke up her computer.

"I've got lots of pictures from that night."

Before Søren could say they had access to photos from the Red Mask website, Stella Marie had opened a file and started a slide show. Black-clad goths of all shapes and sizes emerged. Some pulled faces and showed their pierced tongues, others had been captured just enjoying themselves, beers half-raised toward lips painted black or in a fit of laughter that caused heavily made-up eyes to squint. Søren instantly recognized Johannes.

"There he is," Stella Marie said.

"Do you know the person standing next to him?" Søren asked. Stella Marie and Henrik peered at the screen.

"Is anyone standing next to him?" Henrik asked.

Søren pointed to something black flanking Johannes. What he was pointing to wasn't necessarily a person, but it might be. A part of someone's back, or thigh, something dark, certainly, brushing against Johannes's leg. The fabric seemed to be ribbed, and Søren had to concede it might be part of the background.

"We have different seating areas in the bar, crates and old chairs we cover with black cloth to create an impression of total darkness. It might be a table next to him." Stella Marie shrugged. "I don't remember exactly who he spoke to," she added. "I think he spoke to everyone. Like I said, he was on a roll."

"Does the name YourGuy mean anything to you?" Søren asked.

"No," Stella Marie shook her head. "But it's standard to use alibis on our scene. It's part of the game."

"What's yours?" Henrik wanted to know.

"Surprise," Stella Marie replied.

"I would like a copy of your mailing list," he said. For a moment, Stella Marie looked doubtful.

"All right, I don't suppose that's a problem," she muttered eventually, returned to her computer, opened a file and pressed print. They sat in silence and Søren studied a shocking pink hair extension that stopped halfway down Stella Marie's back. When she turned around, she hesitated before she said: "Actually, there was one thing about that night that puzzled me." She looked tentatively at Søren. "There was a guy I had never seen before. . . . And he really stood out. It's probably not important, but I'll tell you anyway."

"Can we flip through the photos again," Henrik interrupted her, "and you can point him out to us?"

"I was just coming to that." She suddenly looked shy. "This guy was absolutely stunning, he had auburn hair, but not dyed like Johannes's or a lot of other goths, it was genuine. And he was tall. When I saw him, I got the feeling I had seen him somewhere before. I noticed him when he arrived. He was alone, and I've no idea if he knew anyone. Later, I saw him by the bar. He was by himself, but it was obvious that people were staring at him. The women circled him like sharks. I started taking pictures for the Red Mask homepage, and I thought it was a good excuse to chat with him. At that point, he was on the right-hand side of the bar where later I saw Johannes entertain the masses." She smiled. "But when I tried taking his photo, he wouldn't allow it . . ."

"Wouldn't allow you to photograph him?"

"No, he put his hand on my camera and pushed it down. He wasn't aggressive or anything, he just didn't want his picture taken, and I respected that, of course. When I had uploaded the pictures to the computer, I went through them to see if I had accidentally caught him in one of the other photos. I was curious. But he wasn't there. Like I said, I took around two hundred and fifty pictures, we were around one hundred guests, so in theory each guest should appear two and a half times, but not this guy. It was as if he hadn't even been there. But several of my friends had noticed him. He was gorgeous," Stella Marie emphasized.

"Can you describe him, please? What was he wearing?" Søren asked, his pulse quickening. A man with auburn hair had been waiting for Anna.

"He wasn't in costume. But that's normal. There's always a crowd that shows up in regular clothes, people wear what they feel like. So I can't really remember. Black clothes, I think." She shrugged. "And like I said, I had a funny feeling of having seen him before. I thought about it the next day, but since then . . . well, I've got a lot on my plate." She nodded in the direction of the little girl who was watching cartoons. "But he might come next time, who knows? Why don't you join us, you're both more than welcome." Stella Marie's eyes moved teasingly from Søren to Henrik.

"By the way, do you know when the funeral is?" she added. "I'd like to attend. I know plenty of others who would want to go too. It's tragic that Johannes has died." A vertical furrow appeared on her forehead. "We're really going to miss him."

"Check with the family," Søren said abruptly. "Johannes's mother is still alive, so you should contact her."

"Ah, Johannes's mother," Stella Marie exclaimed. "I heard Johannes came from a rich family, but he had turned his back on it. Susanne Winther told me when she was going out with him. And one day, while I was cleaning up after a Red Mask party, a delivery guy came in with two sofas, would you believe it? I was convinced it had to be a mistake, but the guy insisted. Two sofas from Kampe Furniture to be delivered to Stella Marie Frederiksen. Sponsorship. At that point I didn't know Johannes's family owned Kampe Furniture, but Susanne told me. I didn't get a chance to tell Johannes until our next party, and he nearly had a heart attack when he heard it. We never found out how his mother knew about the Red Mask, and I don't think Johannes ever asked her. But that night he kept saying, 'My mom loves me!' He was ecstatic! He made us all laugh because it was so touching."

"What happened to those sofas?" Henrik asked.

"They're in our van with the rest of our gear. The bar, the lights, and so on. They're ultra cool. Black leather, obviously. We don't really do chintz." She laughed.

Once again Søren had the feeling that a minute twist to the kaleidoscope had resulted in a completely different picture.

When they were back in the car, Henrik said: "Are you absolutely sure you can trust Susanne Winther?"

"Yes," Søren said.

"Would a repressed and downtrodden housewife send two sofas?"

"Perhaps it's not that straightforward, Henrik. There might be a positive side to Johannes's mother. Things aren't always black and white."

Henrik was driving. Søren buried his face in his hands.

"Hey, are you okay?" Henrik said. His anger seemed to have evaporated.

"Do you know what my life has been like?"

"Er, no."

"Things were just as they looked. A led to B, B led to C, D, and E."

"Right, and that's not how it is?"

"No," Søren said. "Sometimes you've got no idea how your life ended up the way it did, there's only the end product, E, and the starting point, A, and the rest is unknown. The path between the two points is lost."

"Søren," Henrik said gently. "I don't follow."

"That's how I operate," Søren carried on regardless. "I need to be able to retrace my steps and understand what happened. I want life to be like that!" He slammed his hand on the glove compartment. "But sometimes it isn't, is it? And do you know what that means?" Søren didn't wait for Henrik's reply. "It means not everything is what it seems. Many things are. But not all."

"I still don't follow," Henrik said, amicably.

"It's okay," Søren said. "I just need to change my life."

"You need to talk to someone about . . . about Maja," Henrik said out of the blue. "You really do."

Søren nodded. They drove on in silence.

"My parents died when I was five years old," Søren said suddenly.

"I know. You grew up with Knud and Elvira. I knew that."

"Yes, yes, of course," Søren clutched his forehead. "I'm all over the place right now. I really am."

"You need to talk to someone about Maja," Henrik repeated. "If it had happened to my daughters, Christ, I couldn't have sat here today, no way—"

"Do you think it was enough?" Søren interrupted him.

"What do you mean?"

"My parents dying. When I was five. Unexpectedly. Do you think that's enough to traumatize a child?"

"It depends on the circumstances." Henrik sounded confused.

"And that's precisely what I don't understand," Søren said in a hoarse voice. "Of course, losing your parents is tragic. But for God's sake, I can't even remember them. And Knud and Elvira loved me. I couldn't have had better parents or a better upbringing and I'm not just saying that." He looked out of the side window. "And yet it's as if something inside me is all crumpled up. Completely tangled. I'm scared."

"What are you scared of?"

"I'm scared of . . . Vibe is like a sister to me, for fuck's sake!" Søren threw up his hands in despair. "She has been, ever since I met her at that disco. My sister was my girlfriend for seventeen years! I was scared to have children with her. All the things it takes guts to do. . . . When I see Vibe with her big pregnant stomach, I thank God she left me. I would never have been able to forgive myself if she hadn't had children because of me. She deserves so much better." An embarrassed silence followed.

"I don't have real friends, either," Søren continued. "I've got you and Allan. And Vibe and her husband, obviously."

"What's wrong with me? I'm a decent enough guy," Henrik said, looking like he was simultaneously offended and amused.

"Nothing. I can't complain. But you said it yourself this morning. I don't trust anyone. I don't give anything back. You don't really know me, do you?" Again he threw up his hands. "Plenty of children are orphaned, and some of them go into foster care or are adopted and they turn out fine. I was playing in my grandparents' garden when the crash happened, and it was the best garden in the world. *That* I do remember. But I don't remember them dying, I don't recall shedding a single tear. Nor have I ever been angry that they died, and I haven't missed them. Not really. Knud and Elvira were my parents. They were. I can't see any reason why I'm such a fucking coward." He paused. Henrik cleared his throat.

"You've just done it," he said eventually.

"Done what?"

"Opened up. Taken a chance."

"I see my daughter's face before me all the time," Søren said. "Suddenly, she's everywhere. I thought I could get away with it. Can you imagine what it was like lying next to Vibe and not be able to tell her what was really going on? She thought I was upset because we were splitting up. She comforted me and assured me that we would always be friends. She came over with dinner for me, and I kept lying to her." Søren pressed his fist into his mouth.

"You need to talk to someone," Henrik said for the third time. Søren looked out of the window. How could he ever have doubted Henrik?

"Yes, I do," he said.

At 7:50 p.m. Søren rang the bell of an apartment in a residential block on the outskirts of Nørrebro. The name on the door read *Beck Vestergaard*. Søren hadn't looked Bo in the eye since the day before Katrine, Maja, and he had gone to Thailand.

"Make sure you take good care of them," Søren had ordered him, fixing Bo with his eyes. Bo had bristled with irritation. Since then, he had seen Bo once. In the church and only from the back.

Søren had called earlier to say he was coming, but he barely recognized the man who opened the door. Bo was unshaven, and he was wearing jeans and a vest. His stomach bulged like a ship's fender. He stared at Søren, turned around, and disappeared into the apartment. Søren followed him into a small living room that opened into a laminate kitchen. To the right of the kitchen, an open door led to a room where Søren could see an unmade bed. The curtains were drawn and the television was on in the background.

"What do you want?" Bo scowled. He had sat down on the sofa and lit a cigarette. Before Søren had time to reply, he went on: "I don't know why you're here after all this time. But if you're hoping to be forgiven, you can leave right now. You lost any chance of that when you stopped answering your phone; when I couldn't get hold of you. Not even at the station. Bastards threatened to get a restraining order against me. A fucking restraining order! If I didn't stop calling. Like I was the criminal. Ha, if only they knew!"

"I couldn't bear to hear what had happened. They were dead. I couldn't bear the details."

Bo sent him a brief, lost look.

"I wasn't trying to hassle you, but that was how I was treated. Like a stalker. I just wanted to talk to you. I had just lost my wife and my child. Our child. For fuck's sake, I just wanted to talk to you!" Bo buried his face in his hands.

"I was a coward," Søren admitted. "I was wrong."

A pause followed, then Søren said, "I want to hear it now, please. The details. I want to know why you're here and they're not."

Bo went deathly pale, and started panting.

"Are you saying it's my fault? You total shit . . ." He made to get up, but his excess weight dragged him back down on the sofa. He accepted his fate and started talking.

"Our hotel room was some distance from the beach, and I woke up that morning when water started coming in under the door. It was total chaos outside. A roof had been ripped off, people were screaming and running away from the beach. I called out for Katrine and headed for the beach. I still didn't know what had happened, but suddenly I realized I wouldn't have a chance unless I started running. So that's what I did. In the opposite direction, away from the coast and up a slope, where I ended up on a hill along with fifty other people. I didn't want to look down at the bay. I didn't want to. I lay curled up under a bush, praying they were alive. But my prayers weren't answered." He laughed a hollow laugh. "I drank too much wine the night before; we had held an improvised Christmas lunch and I had had too much to drink. My guess is Katrine went down to have breakfast with Maja on the beach when she woke up, so as not to disturb me. They were helpless when the tsunami came. So they died. They were found farther along the beach. That's what happened, Søren. Happy now? I failed to save them because I was asleep. Because I had a hangover." Bo retreated into himself.

"I went to the funeral," Søren said. "I sat in the back."

"I know, I saw you."

"Thank you for arranging such a beautiful service. The flowers on their coffins, the silk ribbons and all that."

Bo said nothing. He looked like he had given up. He eased himself out of the sofa and got another beer. He didn't offer Søren one. That was all right. Søren's daughter had died, and he had hidden, like a coward, at the back of the church, convinced that Bo hadn't seen him. He didn't deserve a beer. He didn't deserve anything. A long silence ensued. Bo was staring dully at the television, drinking from the bottle. Søren was numb. When he got up to leave, Bo said: "Guys like you, in their late thirties, going for the big confession, hoping for the grand, all-embracing forgiveness for all their sins, you're all pathetic." He hurled the empty bottle into a corner.

"I'll call you," Søren said. "I'll visit."

"No, you fucking won't."

Bo didn't look up when Søren left. Søren opened the front door. Just as he crossed the threshold, he heard Bo say: "But Maja smiled at me. At me! She never knew who that asshole was."

With a heavy heart, Søren walked past the trash cans and old bicycles that lined the concrete walkway.

Vibe's stomach greeted him first when she opened the door. Her head was bullet shaped and her swollen feet were stuffed into Birkenstock sandals. She was grinning from ear to ear.

"I'm the happiest hippo on the planet," she said, hugging Søren. "How lovely to see you! I thought you were working around the clock and would visit once the police were no longer 'clueless,' as the papers say." She scrutinized him. "Hey, what's wrong? You look completely shattered."

Søren hung up his jacket.

"Vibe, I need to talk to you. My timing's crap," he nodded toward her stomach, "but it's urgent. I can't wring a single constructive thought out of my head until I have spoken to you."

"That sounds serious," Vibe said, lightly.

Her husband, John, was sitting on the sofa and the television was on. A bottle of massage oil stood on the coffee table, and John had a towel in his hands. There were also two glasses of red wine. Hers still full, while his contained just a drop. They were watching a cop show. John got up and shook Søren's hand.

"Hiya. Sorry about today's papers, eh?"

"It doesn't matter," Søren mumbled.

"Can I get you anything? A glass of wine? Are you hungry?" Vibe asked. Søren hesitated. He was starving. Vibe read his mind.

"Darling," she said to her husband. "Please would you heat the leftovers for Søren and pour him a glass of wine? He wants to talk to me. It's important."

John's eyebrows shot up.

"Is it okay if we go into the dining room? Then we won't disturb you."

John checked his watch. "I'll heat some food for you," he said, glancing at Søren. "And then I'll take Cash for his walk, so you can talk."

"I'm really sorry," Søren apologized. "I didn't mean to ruin your night."

"That's all right," John replied, putting his hand on Søren's shoulder for a moment.

Twenty minutes later Søren was eating goulash with mashed potatoes. He tried to remember when he had last eaten. Vibe poured him a glass of wine, and they made small talk while the food disappeared. When he had cleared his plate, he carried it into the kitchen so Vibe wouldn't have to get up. In the kitchen, he drank some ice-cold water from the faucet and splashed some on his face. Then he went to the living room. Vibe was sitting in the corner of the sofa, looking expectantly and anxiously at him.

"I've been dreading this moment for twenty years," she said.

Søren stopped in his tracks. "I don't understand," he said.

"Ah," she said quickly. "I'm getting ahead of myself." She looked away. "Sit down, get it off your chest, you look so tormented."

It was Friday October 12, and it was pitch-black, cold, and nasty outside. Søren leaned back and stared at his hands. Then he told Vibe the reason for his visit.

Could she remember going on that course in Barcelona in December 2003? Yes, of course she could. Did she remember Søren going out with Henrik? Søren had told her about their night out when she came back, about the restaurant, about the girls at the neighboring table they got talking to, who had come with them to a club where they had danced. Vibe remembered it well. The night he had gone home with a woman named Katrine. Vibe's eyes hardened to begin with, but then she started to smile, wanting to know if Søren was here to confess to an old infidelity. "Bad boy," she said, wagging her finger at him, "but honestly," she went on, "we were together for seventeen years and I was perfectly aware that it might happen, that it might already *have* happened, there's no need to look so guilty," she said. Søren shook his head. No, there was more.

"I couldn't say it," Søren said eventually. "I couldn't make myself tell you. I didn't want a child with you, but I had gotten another woman pregnant. I just couldn't. It was also because of our relationship, Vibe," he said, as though she had protested. "We were like brother and sister, for God's sake! We weren't lovers. There was no spark. Not really. I mean, take John. Even John treats me as if I were his brother-in-law, not a hint of jealousy even though I've slept with his wife more times than he has." Vibe couldn't help smiling. "Apart from the fact that I truly didn't want to be a dad, then our relationship was enough of a reason for us not have a child together. And then Elvira and later Knud died . . . I just couldn't tell you Katrine was pregnant. At least, not then." Søren swallowed. "So I decided to wait a little. Until the storm had passed. Just like we decided not to tell Knud and Elvira we had broken up."

"Did they know about the baby?" Vibe whispered.

"No, Vibe, they knew nothing. I would never have done that to you. No one knew anything. Not Henrik, not anyone. I kept everything to myself. But I couldn't keep the secret for ever, that was obvious . . . but . . ."

"You have a daughter . . ." Vibe whispered. She shook her head in wonder as if her entire world had just been smashed.

"I *had* a daughter," Søren said brutally. Vibe blinked.

"On the eighteenth of December Bo, Katrine, and Maja went to Thailand for Christmas. To Phuket. They died in the tsunami. Not Bo, but Maja and Katrine."

Vibe put her hands in front of her face, her eyes darting from side to side as if she was rereading old documents and everything finally made sense.

"But you didn't have your breakdown until January," she said, baffled. "After we had split up. Quite a while after Elvira's death, and while Knud was still alive—though no one knew how long he would last. And that was after the tsunami, wasn't it? In early January."

"We were in Sweden, remember? We had no idea what had happened until we came back and saw the papers. I wanted to tell you about Maja in Sweden, but I couldn't. You were so relaxed. When we came home and heard what had happened in Asia, I looked for their names and I couldn't find them. I thought they had survived, that they hadn't called me because everything was chaos. After all, I was just a sperm donor. All I could do was wait for Katrine to get in touch. On January fifth, in the evening, Bo called. He was crying and screaming. I couldn't understand a word he was saying. I calmed him down. In a situation like that you think all sorts of crazy things. I imagined that Katrine had been hurt and was in hospital. Bo was so upset and emotional. Deep down, I couldn't believe that they were really dead. After all, they weren't on the dead or missing persons' registers. But they had died. Bo had identified them."

"Oh, no." Vibe was sobbing, the tears ran in two straight lines down her cheeks.

"That was it. I had a breakdown. I took time off. Forgive me, Vibe. I know you blamed yourself for my suffering. I couldn't talk about it. I suppressed everything about Maja. When Knud died soon afterward, I added my grief for Knud to my grief for Maja. So no one would know."

Vibe stared silently into space.

"I can understand if you hate me," he said.

"I don't hate you, Søren," she said. She leaned forward as best she could and took his hand.

"It must have been terrible for you," she said. Søren could feel his toes curl and he looked away.

"So why now?" Vibe wanted to know, as she stroked his hand. "Why tell me now? Is it because I'm pregnant? Has something happened?"

Søren closed his eyes so he wouldn't cry. Having succeeded, he turned to look at her.

"It's this case I'm investigating," he said, softly. "It's not especially tragic—all things being equal—and it shouldn't be so harrowing, either. Not for a detective. No children have been hurt, and both the victims . . . well, of course they have friends and families, but even so. No suddenly orphaned children staring at me with lost eyes. Do you know what I mean?"

Vibe nodded.

"And yet it's the worst case I've ever been involved with. It touches every raw nerve. Everybody's lying to me! Or, most of them are. They're lying to protect something that isn't worth protecting. Something they believe must remain hidden at any cost. Just like I did with Maja. The investigation only started five days ago. The papers call us clueless, but that's a load of rubbish. It took us four weeks to solve the Malene case and we were praised for our swift work. They just write that because I'm not coming across very well." He looked embarrassed. "And I always used to. I spoke to two reporters the other day. The headlines could have been worse. They should have said *Top cop gets personal* or something like it." He swallowed.

"And I've fallen for with one of the suspects," he said. Vibe didn't reply. When he looked at her, she had turned to one side and didn't appear to have heard his last confession.

"Are you okay?" Søren asked, scared. He thought about John, who had taken the dog for a walk and Vibe's massive stomach, which looked as if it might burst at any moment.

"Don't worry," she said. "I'm not about to go into labor." She smiled. "But . . ."

"But what?"

"I've got something to tell you, too."

And then Vibe told Søren something that changed his life.

Afterward Søren thought long and hard.

Henrik had been right. Things weren't always black and white.

CHAPTER 13

As promised, Karen was waiting on the platform when Anna and Lily arrived at Copenhagen central station after their visit to Odense. She was carrying a plastic bag full of chips and bottles of wine, which she nearly dropped when she hugged Anna. Anna froze, but Karen whispered, "Never let me go," and Anna cautiously put her arms around her.

Lily's turn was next. Sleepy and groggy, she received the greeting of her life from a woman she had never met. Anna had to laugh, and Lily showed how wrong all theories on how quickly an object can melt could be. She radiated, even more so when Karen conjured up a teddy. Lily wanted to hold Karen's hand, Karen wanted to hold Anna's hand, and together they walked through an almost deserted station to the taxi stand.

When Lily had been put to bed, they made themselves comfortable in the living room. Karen wanted to know everything. Anna showed her photos from Lily's birth, of Thomas in the maternity ward, sitting down with Lily in his arms, and standing, smiling, flanked by Cecilie and Jens. Karen made no attempt to hide her interest and looked at the photographs for a long time.

"Well, it's obvious," she said, at last.

Anna didn't understand. Karen pointed to Thomas.

"He's way out of his depth."

Anna took the photographs. She thought Thomas was gorgeous. Relaxed, calm, on top of things. Everything she had ever dreamed of. His chin was lifted, his gaze was confident.

"Watch his hand." Anna followed Karen's finger. "You don't clench your fist in the hospital when you've just become a dad. And look into his eyes."

Anna looked into his bright blue eyes.

"His fear is killing him. And you're probably just as terrifying." Karen's eyes flashed. "If you're a wimp, I mean."

Anna mulled it over. Then she started to laugh.

"What are you laughing at?"

"At you," Anna replied. "At your ability to wave your wand and put everything into perspective. By the way, what on earth were you thinking, calling Troels after we spoke last night, you dork. Are you trying to save the world?"

"How do you know about that?" Karen asked, not looking the least bit embarrassed.

"I saw him today." Anna was serious now. "It was really weird. It started off all right. In fact, I was pleased to see him. But then it went wrong, somehow. There was something . . . strange about him."

Karen looked at Anna for a long time. Her gaze was warm. Then she said, "I really wanted us to be friends again. All three of us. Like in the old days. It was the best time of my life. The years with you. I want that again."

Anna hugged her.

"You hopeless romantic," she said into Karen's hair. The ice was broken, it had melted and the water was warm. They drank all the wine and ate all the chips. They put the world to rights. Anna found she couldn't stop talking, and Karen laughed at everything she said. If only Søren could see me now, Anna thought triumphantly. Anna in her living room, relaxed, tipsy on red wine, in the company of a good friend. She began to cry. Karen gave her a worried look and took her hand. "What is it? What's wrong?" she wanted to know.

"Do you know who Sara is?" Anna said, looking straight at Karen. Karen's mother had been Cecilie's best friend. Always and forever. And Karen and her mother were close and shared everything. What if everyone knew who Sara was? Everyone except Anna?

"Nope," Karen replied. "I don't know anyone named Sara. Who is she?"

An idea occurred to Anna. The photograph. It was hanging to the right of the stove in its lacquered wooden frame, looking at her, like a face. She got up.

"What is it?" This unexpected shift in mood mystified Karen who straightened up in the sofa.

"Hang on." Anna wiped her eyes and took down the picture.

"How old am I here?" she asked.

"I don't know . . . two? I don't know anything about children," Karen said, apologetically.

"It's summer in this photo. I'm wearing a vest. Cecilie is in a bikini. So I must be between eighteen months and two and a half. And I don't think it's the latter. I still have those chubby breastfeeding cheeks. So my guess is eighteen months. Do you agree?"

"Er, all right." Karen scratched her head. Anna fetched her handbag and took out Ulla's photograph. She showed it to Karen.

"That's you and Jens, right?" Karen said. "Gosh, Lily looks so much like you!"

"This photo was taken in August 1978. I'm roughly eight months old in that photo. So I'm eighteen months in one picture and eight months in another, do you follow?"

Karen nodded. Anna fetched a letter opener from her desk and placed the framed photograph face down.

"What are you doing?"

"My parents are lying," she snorted. The old frame was an obstinate devil. The small brackets had practically rusted into the cardboard backing.

"About what?" Karen was completely lost.

"Turn that photo over." Anna nodded in the direction of Ulla's photograph on the table while she struggled. By now, she didn't care if she broke the stupid frame. Karen sat diagonally behind her, curled up in the sofa, and Anna sat on the edge, using the coffee table as her workspace. Finally, the stubborn brackets started flying.

"Sara Bella and Jens, August 1978," Karen read out loud. "I still don't get who Sara is?"

"Don't ask me."

Anna slipped the letter opener under the cardboard backing.

"Spooky," Karen mused. "Perhaps you had a twin sister who died?" Anna stopped in her tracks. This was an explanation she hadn't even considered. She examined it quickly.

"That baby," she pointed the letter opener at Ulla Bodelsen's photograph, "is me. And this baby," now indicating the picture she was easing out, "is me as well. The girls are identical."

"Identical twins," Karen whispered, dramatically.

"It makes no sense, Karen. Why would my parents keep it a secret that I had a twin sister who died? Anyway, that can't be it. Ulla, the health visitor I saw today, said nothing about twins." The cardboard came off, underneath it the faded backside of the photograph appeared. Anna cheered. On it someone had written *Anna Bella, Dad, and Mom. July 1979.*

Anna placed the two photographs side by side on the coffee table. They sat up and studied them.

"It's the same child," Karen stated. "But in August 1978 she was called Sara and the following July, her name was Anna. That's just weird."

They sat in silence for a long time, lost in thought. Anna felt a strange sense of purpose. She wasn't alone. Karen was there.

"Why would you change a child's name?" she asked Karen.

"Why don't you just ask Jens and Cecilie?" Karen suggested.

"True," Anna said. "And I'm going to. But let's play detectives. I want to be prepared."

"Okay," Karen said, indulging her. "A name usually marks the beginning of a life. You're named and you go through life with that name. You keep that name—unless you visit a numerologist who tells you you'll win the lottery, if you change it to Solvej, or something like that."

Anna started to smile.

"So, a name marks a beginning," she said slowly. "Cecilie was ill. She had problems with her back."

"Hmmm," Karen said. "I do remember something about that. My mom used to say that's why you were so close to Jens. Because he carried you everywhere during your first year."

"He was practically a single dad," Anna said. "Cecilie spent a lot of time in the hospital. Though I think he managed quite well," she added.

Soon afterward they went to bed.

Saturday morning Anna woke up and, for a moment, she didn't know where she was. She sat upright, feeling dazed. It was past ten and she was in her bedroom. She couldn't recall the last time she had slept past ten. She heard muted laughter and got up. She went to the kitchen. The door to Lily's room was open, and Karen and Lily were sitting on the floor drawing pictures. They had taped paper to the floorboards and were drawing houses and roads as seen from a bird's perspective. Lily had started furnishing one of the houses with small teddies and furniture from her doll's house. The radiator was on at full blast, and she could smell toast.

"Hi," Anna said.

"Mom," Lily shouted, dropped everything and threw herself into Anna's arms. Anna lifted up her daughter and sat down on a chair in the kitchen. Lily's body was warm and soft under her PJs.

"Did you sleep well?" Karen asked. Anna nodded.

"Cool afro," she said, giving Karen a nod of approval. Karen's hair was—if possible—even frizzier in the morning. They both burst out laughing.

"Why are you laughing?" Lily asked, confused.

"Auntie Karen's monster hair," Anna explained.

"Auntie Karen has a lion on her head, Mom," Lily said.

Karen and Anna laughed even louder. The kitchen was welcoming, and Anna wanted some toast. With lots of butter and cheese. It was just like the old days. Karen and Anna rolling down a hill in the sunshine, laughing and rolling. They could take on the world. The cow pies they rolled over, the spinning globe, hunger, thirst, everything. As long as they were together.

Karen joined Anna at the table while she ate her breakfast. Lily went back to play in her room. Karen had made coffee. It tasted heavenly.

"What's behind that door?" Karen asked, pointing over Anna's shoulder. Anna swallowed her toast and turned around to look at the door to Thomas's old office, as if seeing it for the very first time. Then she stole a look at Lily who was absorbed by her game.

"It was Thomas's office when we lived together. I nailed the door shut when he moved out. We didn't need all that space." She smiled bitterly.

"What's inside it now?" Karen wanted to know.

"Nothing," Anna said, taking another bite of her toast.

"Aha," Karen said. A short silence followed. Then Karen remembered that Jens had called.

"Seven times on your cell and twice on the landline. I unplugged it so it wouldn't wake you." Karen gave Anna a searching look.

"Did you speak to him?"

"No. Your cell is over there." She gestured to the kitchen counter. "I saw his name come up on the display."

Another pause. Karen turned on the radio.

"Okay," Anna said, eventually. "Would you answer it when he calls back? I'm going to Professor Helland's funeral at one o'clock." She checked her watch. "Shit, I need to buy flowers . . . how long is a funeral? Two hours? Three? Would you tell Jens I can meet him at four thirty? At his place. Without Cecilie. And I want him to respect that. I can only stay an hour because I have an important lecture at the Bella Centre at six o'clock, and if Cecilie is there, I'll leave immediately. All depending, of course, on whether you're prepared to babysit Lily? I'll be back between seven and eight," she added. Karen thought it over.

"Yes, that's fine," she said. "But I want a favor in return. I want you to promise me you'll meet with Troels, properly. I want to be there. I want all three of us to get together and see if we can be friends again. If not, well, then I'll just have to accept it. But I want you to give it a try, Anna."

Anna mulled it over, then she held out her hand.

"Deal," she said.

"Great," Karen replied.

Jens called while Anna was in the shower.

"He sounded surprised I answered your phone," Karen said. "I told him you were showering, but you would be at his house at 4:30 p.m. And no Cecilie. He protested to begin with."

"Yes, it's tough to do anything without Cecilie." Anna towel-dried her hair angrily.

"Anyway, he agreed eventually. He sounded really upset."

Anna disappeared into her bedroom to find some suitable clothes. She decided on black jeans, a thin black sweater, and Chuck Taylors.

"You can't wear that," Karen objected. "Chuck Taylors?"

"I wear what I want," Anna said. "They'll just have to take me as is."

They hung out in the living room for another hour. Lily and Karen played with Lego bricks on the floor, and Anna sprawled in an armchair she had dragged to the window. She looked across the rooftops. There was a huge lump in her throat, and every time she closed her eyes, she saw Johannes. His bad skin, his soft gaze, and his hair with the awful red dye that was growing out. Lily came over to her chair.

"Mommy's crying," she said. Anna looked at her daughter. She was about to shake her head, deny it, wipe away her tears, and lie, but suddenly the light outside changed and it was as if Lily's small head glowed.

"I feel really sad," she said. "Because I have a friend I can't visit anymore."

"Why not?" Lily asked.

"Because he's dead. He's in heaven." Anna pointed to the clouds, which had parted and for a moment the columns of light beamed down to the earth. Lily looked in the direction of Anna's finger and narrowed her eyes.

"He's kicking a ball around. I think he's happy. Heaven is a good place, but I'm here on earth, and I'm sad because we can't see each other."

"I want to go to heaven," Lily said, looking longingly out of the window. Anna lifted her daughter onto her lap.

"You will one day," she said. "But first you need to be here on earth with your mom for a long time." Lily snuggled up to Anna for a few seconds. Then she climbed down.

"I want to play with Auntie Karen," she said.

Karen had been watching them.

"It's terrible what happened to . . . your friend," she said quietly. "What was his name?"

"Johannes."

"It's terrible what happened to Johannes."

Anna nodded.

Shortly afterward Anna put on her army jacket and pulled the hood up.

"You're wearing that?" Karen stared at Anna in disbelief. Anna zipped her jacket up to her chin and flashed her yellow eyes at Karen.

"Yep," she replied. Then she left.

Anna recognized Professor Freeman immediately. He stood outside the church, next to an impeccably dressed younger man, digging his shoe into the gravel like a child. Anna approached with caution and tried to hide inside her jacket, until she remembered that Freeman didn't know what she looked like. She positioned herself fifty feet away from him, and when he entered the church she followed and took a seat in the pew opposite, two rows behind, where she could keep an eye on him.

Birgit and Nanna Helland were standing beside the coffin. Anna watched Mrs. Helland. She smiled feebly, she hugged some mourners, put her hand on her daughter's neck, smiled again, spoke to someone. Suddenly she looked straight at Anna. For two seconds. Deeply into her eyes, eyes filled with pain, before she quickly averted them. Mrs. Helland never looked at Anna again. Not once.

Søren appeared next to her.

"Good to see you," he said, putting his hand on her shoulder as though she were a prisoner who had been allowed out on leave and who had defied everyone's expectations by returning to the prison on time. Anna nodded.

"Hello," she sulked.

Søren glanced at her.

"Any news?" His eyes scanned the church restlessly. Did he think she had solved his murder-mystery overnight? Anna leaned toward him.

"The butler did it," she whispered. "In the library."

Søren glared at her. His eyes were cold. Without a word, he walked to the back of the church and sat down. He didn't look at her again. Not even when Anna tried to catch his eye a little later. Honestly. Had he no sense of humor? The organ started.

Anna was bored stiff during the sermon. She spotted her flower arrangement and was relieved flowers and cards were delivered separately. This meant Mrs. Helland would never make the connection between her card and the pathetic-looking bunch of flowers she had bought. She struggled to keep her sweaty feet still. The church floor was mired in dirty water and gravel, and the room was steaming up. They sang. Anna tried to focus on the coffin, tried to reflect. Nanna's ponytail bopped up and down in the front row, and when the music paused, the girl's heart-rending sobbing could be clearly heard. Anna looked at Professor Freeman several times. She couldn't help it. At first, she tried to be discreet, but as he started shifting in his seat and looking around; she stared at him openly.

The trouble that man had caused! A small, insignificant old-timer in an oversized parka. If the world's scientists could simply let everything he said go in one ear and out the other, Freeman's scientific position would have dried up and dropped off like an umbilical cord. Anna would have written her dissertation on another subject, she would have had a different supervisor, and might barely have noticed that Professor Helland had died. She would merely have read his obituary in the university newsletter, and Johannes might still be alive. She shuddered.

Dr. Tybjerg! Shit! Anna jerked so violently that the man sitting next to her raised his eyebrows. She clasped her hand over her mouth. Jesus Christ, she had forgotten about Dr. Tybjerg. How could she? She had seen him last on Thursday and today was Saturday. He had been on his own for two days. How could she be so thoughtless? She kicked the pew in irritation. Fortunately, the organ was playing at full force. The man next to her gave her a look. She was surprised at how contrite she felt. The image of Tybjerg's helplessness burned onto her retina, the way he had wolfed down the sandwich she had brought. She meant to bring him more food, a clean towel, a blanket, ask him if he wanted her to wash his clothes. But she had forgotten him. Then again, it was hard to remember other people's existence when you were so busy contemplating your own navel. She kicked the pew again. This time, the woman in front turned around and glared at her, and the man next to her made no attempt to disguise his disapproval. The organ played on. Then there was silence. Anna was mortified. She turned to catch Søren's eye. He ignored her deliberately. Even Freeman was looking away, first at his hands, then at the stained glass window above the altar. Nanna rose. She was sobbing and her ponytail swung youthfully while she spoke, her voice faint, but composed. Her eulogy was fumbling and a little banal, but then again how old was she? Eighteen? Suddenly, it all hit Anna, and she rested her head on her knees. *Why am I so self-centered?* she thought. I would never give my dad such a eulogy. I would never stand up and say something banal, youthful, and very loving to him if he died. I would be far too busy feeling sorry for myself in the front pew, furious he had had the audacity to leave me, how dare he? Nanna stood tall and proud, looking vulnerable. Anna sat in her army jacket with gall in her veins. She couldn't even take care of Tybjerg. The coffin was carried out. Nanna was one of the pall-bearers, Mrs. Helland another and behind them were four men around Helland's age. When the coffin had been placed in the hearse, the church bells began to toll. People stopped and bowed their heads. When the crowd dispersed at last, Anna made herself scarce. It was only a little past two o'clock. She caught a local train and got off at Nordhavn. She shopped at Netto, tossing groceries into her basket. She'd rarely been so angry with herself. She had forgotten Tybjerg. For two whole days.

The university was quiet. She swiped her keycard and entered. It was nearly 3:30 p.m. and she was meeting her father in an hour. Their meeting now seemed a picnic compared to this one. What if Dr. Tybjerg had died? She shook her head. Of course he hadn't. You couldn't starve to death in two days and, besides, he had probably left his hideout to forage. She unlocked the door to her study and hung up her coat. She didn't encounter a living soul when she walked from the institute to the museum. The building was hushed and the corridors dark, but the light was on in front of the collection. She stopped cold. Had someone just left or recently arrived?

She unlocked the door to the collection. The smell took her breath away. She switched on all the lights. The ventilation system whirred. She walked past the display cabinets and called out for Dr. Tybjerg. There was no answer. She ignored her fear. She called out again. "Erik?" She had never called him by his first name before. "I forgot about you. I'm so sorry! Where are you? If you're here, please would you come out?" Her voice was loud and she wondered whether she was talking to herself, to him or both. She peered between the rows of cupboards.

Suddenly, he stepped out into the central aisle and Anna jumped. He had long, black stubble and his eyes looked just as dark. He stared at her shopping bag.

"Did you bring food?" he croaked.

"Yes," Anna said, trying to compose an apology, but had no idea what to say without revealing Johannes had died. So she said nothing.

"He was here," Dr. Tybjerg whispered.

"Johannes?" Anna's eyes widened.

"No. Clive Freeman. He was here for hours. I hid in the back." Anna saw a drop of sweat trickle down his forehead. "Why did he come? He pretended to be looking at the moa skeleton. He fiddled with the bones. Then he left. What did he want?"

They walked back toward the light.

"Er, to have a look at the moa skeleton?" Anna ventured. She turned around so they were facing each other.

"Erik," she said. "Professor Freeman is a wizened old man. He's not going to kill you. What would he gain from that? Honestly? It wouldn't help him win the argument."

But he would shut up his most vociferous opponent, Anna thought. Helland had been permanently silenced. It was very convenient. She checked her mobile. No signal. It was 3:50 p.m. and she was meeting Jens in forty minutes. She had run out of ideas and rubbed her head in frustration.

"Erik," she pleaded.

"I'm staying here. I'll come out when he has left. Call me stupid; call me paranoid. I don't care." Tybjerg looked defiant.

"Has Helland been buried?" he asked.

"Yes," Anna replied.

"Did you send flowers from me?" Dr. Tybjerg asked.

"Yes," Anna lied. "A beautiful bouquet from both of us. Freeman attended the funeral."

Dr. Tybjerg nodded.

"There you are," he said, enigmatically.

"I need to go," Anna said. "But I'll be back tomorrow."

"All right," Tybjerg said, sitting down at one of the small desks. Anna grabbed his arm.

"Listen. I'm on your side!" she exclaimed.

Suddenly Dr. Tybjerg looked at her with great insight and said quietly, "Research is my life. It's what I live for. If I can't research, then nothing matters. I'm staying here. Please let me know when he's gone. I'll come out then. Then I'll talk to the police. But not until then." He turned back to the desk.

"When I get tenure, I'll build up a new vertebrate department from scratch. A dynamic research unit, a young team," he vowed.

Anna was close to tears. So she left.

Jens lived in Larsbjørnsstræde in central Copenhagen, on the top floor of an old printing works, through an archway and a backyard. He had lived there since leaving Odense and divorcing Cecilie when Anna was eight years old. There used to be a garage in the backyard, and some unkempt trees and scrubs. Anna would visit him often.

These days she hardly ever saw her father. On rare occasions, she picked him up from Larsbjørnsstræde and they would go for lunch at Sabines or to Magasin to buy a Christmas present for Cecilie. Now the backyard had been renovated, smartened up and shiny new cars were parked there. The old printing works looked decidedly out of place, surrounded by trendy advertising agencies, architects' offices, and bicycle messengers delivering sushi or props for photo shoots. They would never believe that anyone actually lived there. Anna walked up the wooden staircase and reached a dilapidated walkway. Jens's front door was at the far end. Socks were drying on a clothesline. She rang the bell. Jens emerged from the kitchen. She could see him through the window. His hair stood out on all sides, and he looked like he had the mother of all hangovers.

"You look awful," Anna blurted out. She gave him a quick hug and noted to herself she had been right. He reeked of stale booze.

"I had a late night, and when I finally went to bed I couldn't get to sleep."

"It's an old wives' tale that booze helps you sleep. It prevents it, in fact," Anna said.

"I would have preferred a bad night's sleep to no sleep at all," Jens mumbled. They sat down in the living room. The sofa frame was made from varnished bamboo, and the cushions were ancient. A low coffee table, piled high with newspapers, stood in front of it. The apartment had a sloping roof and consisted of a large room divided up by a wall that reached all the way to the ceiling. On the living room side, the wall was covered with books from top to bottom; an ingenious contraption consisting of an iron pole and a ladder enabled Jens to reach the top shelves. Anna caught a glimpse of the open-plan kitchen on the other side, a loaf of bread half out of its bag, a stick of butter. A lumpy patchwork rug lay on the floor.

"Why don't we go out," Jens suggested, apologetically. "I don't mind. I could buy you a hot chocolate?"

Anna stared at him in disbelief.

"Are you trying to wriggle out of this?"

Jens gave her a weary look.

"Yes, I suppose I am. Let's stay here. Do you want some tea?"

"No, thanks," Anna said. "All I want is an explanation."

Jens looked haggard. Then, all of a sudden, he began to sob. Anna was shocked. She had never seen her father cry.

"We never meant to hurt you, Anna sweetheart," he said. He stood with his arms dangling, looking lost and lonely in his jeans and shirt; his stomach had grown too big and he needed a haircut. Anna gulped. Jens sat down on a worn armchair, facing her. For a long time he stared at his hands which now rested in his lap.

"Cecilie doesn't know you're here," he began, with trepidation. "I spoke to her yesterday, but I didn't say anything. I thought the two of us should talk first . . ."

"That's all right," Anna said, calmly.

Jens looked momentarily relieved.

"But you can't shut me up." Anna's eyes flashed. "You're going to tell me who Sara is, where she is, and why I've never heard about her. I'll listen to what you have to say, and I'll try my best to understand."

Jens gave her a frightened look.

"And if you ever lie to me again," her voice was trembling, "you'll lose me. I'll count to ten, Jens. I mean it. You have ten seconds to start talking." When she reached three, Jens cleared his throat.

"Everything was fine while Cecilie was pregnant. We were in love; we were looking forward to the baby. I couldn't believe my luck. I had yet to turn twenty and this wonderful, attractive, older woman had chosen me. I had moved into her apartment, she went to work, I was studying, the summer seemed endless. We decorated the nursery. Your mom put up a Che Guevara poster above the changing table and made a giant, foam-filled snake for you. Her belly grew; the sun was shining. Then you were born. It was winter and pitch black. I was there at your birth. It was a long labor; Cecilie fought hard, and finally, out you came. It was minus ten outside and the sky was full of stars the night I came home to Brænderup. I remember standing in the conservatory, gazing at it. I was a father. You came home five days later between Christmas and New Year." Jens clutched his head. "And I knew instantly that something was wrong."

Anna realized she was tense all over.

"Mom's back?" she asked.

Jens gave her a dark look.

"She had postpartum depression. She didn't want you. We made up the story about her back."

Anna was dumbstruck. Jens's revelation hit her like a thunderbolt that went in one eye, across the roof of her mouth, down her throat, and into her stomach, where it lodged itself like an anchor on the sea bed. She wanted to throw up.

Jens looked away.

"I didn't want to admit it. But I could see it. She wouldn't look at you when she fed you. You looked at her. You could barely open your eyes and yet you were trying with all your being to get her attention. But she looked out of the window, at the birds on feeder. When she had fed you, she would put you down quickly. In your crib or on a blanket on the floor. She would sit down to read. I'm just tired, she would say whenever I summoned the courage to challenge her. After only a short time, Cecilie said her milk had dried up, and I believed her. But then I saw her in the shower one day. Her eyes were closed and the water jet was aimed at her face. I happened to be in the bathroom to fetch something. And the milk was running down her belly, dripping into the drain. When we went to bed that night, I confronted her. It was mid-January, you were about a month old, I think, and she freaked out, like I had never seen her before. She screamed and she shouted and slapped her own face. 'I'm a bad mother. Is that what you're saying?' You were in your crib, crying and crying. In the end I took you to my study. It was awful. I settled you down, but you woke up in the middle of the night, hungry. I went back to the bedroom where Cecilie was sleeping, but she didn't want you. Take her away, she said. I didn't know what to do. I ended up feeding you milk with a spoon. We had nothing else. No bottle, no formula. Cecilie had been looking forward to breastfeeding you all through her pregnancy. The next day I went shopping for everything, bottles, nipples, and formula. I left you at home while I did it; it was still freezing cold outside. Cecilie was sitting by the window, staring at the garden, when I left. You were lying on a blanket with your blanket over you. I remember asking Cecilie if she wanted to pick you up. 'Not now, she's asleep,' she snapped. I drove into town and bought what I needed. I was gone an hour, maybe. You were still asleep when I came back, but Cecilie wasn't there. I looked in all the rooms; I called her name. She returned two hours later. Covered in powder snow, her cheeks flushed. She was in a slightly better mood. I prepared a bottle for you and asked Cecilie if she wanted to feed you, but she preferred to have a bath. 'You do it,' she said. 'I already know how.'" Jens breathed in deeply. "A few days later I went back to work."

Anna could see his Adam's apple bob up and down.

"It was fine," he said, and his eyes grew dark. "No, it wasn't, not at all. But I couldn't bear it, Anna. I couldn't bear watching it. I don't know how else to explain it. When you were five weeks old, the health visitor returned. She had been there, twice, the first few weeks, while everything was still new. She had told me not to pressure Cecilie into breastfeeding. Bottles were okay. Most mothers got the baby blues. You were a healthy little girl. To call her with any worries.

"On her next visit, she raised the alarm. You hadn't gained enough weight, and she couldn't get you to respond properly. Our lives changed that afternoon. Cecilie didn't like feeding you. She told the health visitor to her face. She thought it was disgusting when your diaper needed changing, when you puked up milk. Our house was a total mess. I was at my wits' end. The health visitor asked so many questions. A doctor arrived soon afterward. Cecilie said that yes, she often wished she had never had you. Sometimes, she would leave you by yourself, she said, bluntly. That was when I realized how thin Cecilie had become. Scrawny, like a twig. The health visitor gave me a look I'll never forget. It said: Don't you realize that children can die through lack of love? They can die!

The doctor examined Cecilie and spoke to her. They left shortly afterward. I held you while the health visitor packed up your things.

"We need to look into this," she said. "We need to decide the best place for your daughter to be. It might be a while before you get her back." Her eyes were a mix of condemnation and compassion. Then she took you away. It wasn't until then I snapped out of my trance. I ran around the house, howling like an animal."

Anna wiped away a tear, and Jens looked at the floor.

"The system took over. Your mother was hospitalized. She didn't want to see you. She would barely see me. She was far away, didn't care. For a long time it looked like I wouldn't be allowed to keep you. Three, four weeks. I took time off work. Endless meetings, hearings, and examinations followed. It was 1978. There weren't many single dads in Denmark." He smiled quickly. "They had nothing to compare with. Finally, the case was decided. It set a precedent, in fact."

For a moment he looked proud. "You were allowed to stay with me at home. I felt terrible. I had let down Cecilie, and I had let you down, too. Physically, you recovered quickly. I fed you to the gills." He smiled. "We slept in the same bed at night, and when you woke up . . . I looked into your eyes the whole time." He blinked away a tear. "To begin with, you wouldn't look at me, but I won your trust. We would lie on the bed, gazing at each other for hours."

Anna was crying openly now.

"I met with Cecilie's doctor. Cecilie was suffering from severe postpartum depression, he told me. It wasn't her fault. A woman's hormones alter dramatically following childbirth, and it can trigger varying degrees of depression. Cecilie was badly affected. She had been prescribed medication and had started intensive therapy. For months she didn't want contact with me or you." Jens sent Anna a look of infinite love.

"I named you Sara. It means 'princess' in Hebrew." He was silent for a moment, then he continued.

"I was exhausted and miserable, but I coped. I bought a baby sling and carried you on my back when I started working again. I raised my desk, so I could write standing up. Of course, I couldn't work as much as I used to, but we muddled through. You hung on my back babbling, waving your arms and kicking your legs. At times, it was quite distracting for my political analysis of the effect of the Cold War on European policy." He laughed briefly. "We had a new health visitor by then, the previous one having gone to Greenland. I remember the day she came to say good-bye. She was proud of me, she said. We stood in the doorway and she hugged me.

"'You can do this, Jens,' she said. I knew she was right.

"In the late summer Cecilie improved and began visiting us. She thought you were cute. She wanted to come home. Slowly, I began to hope. The medication made Cecilie tired and irritable, but the apathetic look in her eyes had gone, and it was wonderful to see her take an interest in you. You were happy, chubby, and bore no grudge; on the contrary—you kept reaching out for Cecilie.

"There were only two flies in the ointment. Cecilie was adamant that no one must know about her depression. She felt ashamed and demanded that I help cover up her shame. To explain her hospital stay, she wanted us to tell everyone that she had developed serious back problems after the birth. When the new health visitor came, I realized I had accepted Cecilie's lie. I told her I didn't have your records, even though the last health visitor had given them to me and asked me to pass them on. It was an easy lie. I burned your old records and started spreading the story about Cecilie's bad back.

Nine months had passed and, of course, people had noticed that something was amiss. We had friends, especially in Copenhagen, people we knew from college, but no one knew the truth. The first year with a new baby is tough, everybody knows that. When we were finally ready to visit friends and relatives again, we told them the story about Cecilie's bad back and they understood. Everyone was sympathetic.

"It was easy to lie at home in Brænderup, too. We had moved into the house shortly before you were born and it wasn't until later, when things had improved, that we became a part of the local community—the main reason we had moved out there in the first place. Another year and we would never have been able to keep such an illness a secret. It was as if it had never happened. Cecilie blossomed. Decorated the house and made new curtains. Enjoyed being a stay-at-home mom. That autumn you got a new name. That was the second fly in the ointment. Sara's such a beautiful name. So is Anna, of course," he hastened to add. "But I was used to calling you Sara. For years I would call you Sara when no one was listening. Do you remember me suggesting it for Lily?" Anna nodded. Jens seemed to have run out of words. Anna's tears had dried, and she didn't know what to say. Jens gave her an anxious look as if he was aware the jury was out.

Anna said: "You're a hard-nosed political analyst, feared and admired, and you're so weak when it comes to Cecilie." Even she could hear her voice was more loving than she had intended it to be. "How on earth could you agree to something so outrageous?" she continued. "I simply don't understand. Mom was seriously ill, and for two months I was home alone with her, every day. That's bad, Jens. And it shouldn't have happened. But it did. I would have understood. Cecilie was ill, it wasn't her fault. But you chose to keep it a secret. I really don't get that."

She looked pensively into space before she continued.

"If only you knew how the pieces are finally starting to fall into place."

Jens briefly raised an eyebrow.

"I was eighteen years old when I met Cecilie," he said. "She was twenty-five. I was still living with my parents." He smiled. "Cecilie bowled me over. Seven years older than me, mature and . . . a real woman. I admired her. She was beautiful, and she had her life figured out. She had just finished teacher-training and bought her own apartment when we started seeing each other. Cecilie was always the stronger."

"Certainly the more dominant," Anna interjected.

"Call it what you will. I've always been more reticent and invisible. The guy in the corner who never said much. Cecilie had courage. She set the agenda. Allocated roles and it suited both of us very well. At political meetings, Cecilie would speak out with a clear vision. I wrote whatever needed writing, but I never said anything. I'm sure people wondered what she saw in me. But we complemented each other. Cecilie was extrovert, vociferous, radical. I was loyal, flexible, and I worshipped her. That's why we split up. Because it just wouldn't work. Cecilie wanted a challenge. I tried, but I couldn't give her what she wanted. And yet, we've never separated properly. We still loved each other, Anna. We still do. And, back then . . . back then she asked me to keep silent about what had happened. She wanted to forget it. She wanted to start over, wipe the slate clean. She couldn't see why we should stir up something it would be in everyone's best interests to forget. Not least you. Deep down I always knew there would be consequences. But she convinced me it was for the best. As a teenager you were unbelievably angry with us. We discussed at length whether you might have some lingering notion of what had happened. An imprint on your earliest memory, perhaps? Cecilie consulted several experts and received a lot of contradictory information, which only served to confuse us even more. In the middle of it all, Troels entered our lives. By the way, Troels . . . he dropped by . . ." Jens hesitated. He had interrupted himself and shook his head.

"We knew we loved you. We knew we had patched up the past as well as we could, and though you were one angry teenager, you were also utterly gorgeous. Extroverted and full of life. We met Troels and saw in him a child who so obviously needed us. Cecilie, especially, saw him as a project. At times, it was almost too much. I was terrified that you might get jealous. Luckily, you were also very fond of him. 'Here's a boy who's never had anything,' Cecilie said one evening. I don't quite know how this related to you, but somehow it did. The reasoning was . . ." He looked away. "There was always someone worse off." Anna flexed her foot in irritation.

"Dad," Anna said quietly. "Have you ever asked Cecilie about those two months? When I lost weight, when I grew nonresponsive?" She twisted the knife deliberately. Jens looked at her for a long time. He shifted in his armchair.

"No," he gulped, eventually. "I've never asked her." He slumped back in his chair like a fallen king. Anna could see he was bracing himself for the worst, but she felt calm inside.

"That's all right," she said. "I will."

Jens gave his daughter a wretched look, but he said nothing.

"You and I have looked after Mom my whole life," Anna continued. "Because Mom had been ill. Mom was frail. Please, don't shout, no, don't tell Mom, it'll only upset her. You've protected her because you thought it was for the best. I understand." Anna leaned forward across the coffee table and looked straight into Jens's eyes.

"But it was a shitty thing to do, Jens Nor," she said. "It really was. And now it's over."

Anna glanced at her watch. Professor Freeman's lecture was starting in half an hour. She had to go. They got up and walked to the door. Anna had put her hand on the handle when she turned around and pulled her father toward her.

"Silly old fool," she said. "That's what you are." Jens rested his head on her shoulder and let himself be held. He still hadn't spoken. It wasn't until she was some way down the walkway that he called out to her.

"Anna, hold on." He came up to her, shivering in the cold. "What I was about to tell you just now . . . about Troels. I nearly forgot. But he was here the other day. Wednesday night." Anna stopped on the stairs and walked back up two steps. Something inside her turned to ice.

"Here?"

"Yes, I was dozing in front of the TV when I was woken up by a knock on the door. It was Troels. I could barely recognize him! We tried to figure out how long it had been. Ten years, we concluded. I made him some tea, he was shivering with cold. He had been to the Student Union, he said, and decided to drop by on his way home. It appears he has been trying to contact you. I was excited he wanted to apply to the arts school. I never really had much faith in the modeling business. And Karen. Troels told me she is already studying there. That's brilliant, eh? Did you know? I'm so pleased you've started seeing each other again." Jens suddenly looked happy. Then he noticed the expression on Anna's face.

"What's wrong?"

"That's weird." Anna hesitated. "Because I saw Troels yesterday. In the street. And he never mentioned he had tried to get hold of me."

"He seemed a little out of it, to be honest." Jens was really freezing now. "At first I thought he might be on drugs. He was shaking and seemed a bit manic. But it stopped once he came inside and warmed up. And he was ridiculously underdressed. I lent him a sweater. Both his parents have died, did you know? First his mom, breast cancer, and then his dad, the year before last. Troels told me he hadn't seen much of his dad since his mom died, and his sister is a lawyer working here in Copenhagen. I don't think he sees much of her, either . . ." Jens tailed off.

"Karen and I have agreed to meet with him. I just need to get a few things out of the way. My dissertation defense and . . . Cecilie."

"Do the right thing, sweetheart," Jens said. Anna was on the verge of asking if that meant she should keep her mouth shut, but she suppressed her antagonism.

"I will, Dad," she said quietly. Then she walked quickly down to Nørreport station and took the metro to the Bella Centre.

Anna stuck her key in the lock just before eight o'clock. Karen and Lily were playing with Play-Doh in the living room. Lily was in her

PJs and wore a plastic apron. She could hear music in the background and on the table lay four colorful drawings, a combination of Lily's shapes and Karen's eye for color matching.

"They're lovely," Anna said, and meant it. "Did you make them?" Lily was clinging to her.

"Yes, I did them all on my own with Auntie Karen."

Anna ate the leftovers from Karen and Lily's dinner. The kaleidoscope pieces were still whirling around inside her head. Outside, the autumn weather raged; Dr. Tybjerg was hiding in the Vertebrate Collection, and somewhere the World's Most Irritating Detective was probably putting his feet up after one of his yummy wife's gourmet dinners. Screw him. Anna's tomato soup tasted delicious, and when she put her daughter to bed, she snuggled up to her in the darkness and told her a story about a bird that was hatched with skis on its feet. Anna lay next to Lily until she was asleep.

Karen was reading on the sofa when Anna came out and sat down beside her. Karen looked up. *What happened?* her eyes asked.

"Cecilie suffered from severe postpartum depression when I was born. She was at home with me for the first months until it was discovered how much weight I had lost. She didn't like feeding me. She was admitted to the hospital, and Jens became a single dad. He called me Sara. When I was nine months old, Cecilie came home. She was well again, or well enough. She didn't like the name Sara, so I was renamed. Like a computer file." Anna fell silent. Karen's jaw dropped.

"Tell me honestly, did you know? Did your mom ever say anything?" Anna looked at Karen.

The light in Karen's eyes changed, then she cupped Anna's face in her hands and gently pulled her toward her.

"Anna," she said, tenderly. "I promise you, I knew nothing about it. Absolutely nothing. I don't know if my mom knew. But I didn't. Why on earth did they keep it a secret?"

Anna withdrew from Karen's protective embrace.

"To protect Cecilie," she said blankly. "In our family it has always been very important to protect Cecilie."

They sat in silence for a long time.

"What a stupid thing to do," Karen declared.

They drank wine. Anna rested the back of her head against the sofa and closed her eyes.

"Troels," Karen suddenly exclaimed. "You haven't had second thoughts, have you?"

"We had a deal. I always keep my promises." Anna smiled, her eyes still shut. Now she opened them.

"Incidentally, you could say he has indeed decided to return to the land of the living," Anna remarked. "He visited Jens last Wednesday, and if I were to call Cecilie now, he'll probably be there, wrapped in a blanket, having milk and cookies." She let out a noise that was supposed to be laughter.

"I think he's scared, Anna."

"Scared of what?"

"Of you."

"Why?"

"Because you have dragon's teeth and a sting in your tail."

Anna looked annoyed and was about to defend herself when Karen continued.

". . . and if you happen to be a wimp, well, then someone like you might be a tad intimidating."

"That's the second time you've suggested that. Do you think I'm a monster?" Anna asked quietly.

"No, I think it's liberating to be with you. Your excesses and mine cancel each other out, and when we're together I don't need to spend all my time wondering how I come across. I can just be me. That's why I don't understand why we haven't seen each other for ten years."

"You got so angry with me that night."

"Yes, I did. And what of it? Can't you handle a taste of your own medicine?"

Anna shrugged.

"That night," Karen said. "We were high. And Troels had come out of the closet. Maybe not to the world, but to us. We knew he was gay. And yet we come up with the insane idea we should all have sex . . ."

"The two of you came up with it." Anna corrected her.

"Whatever." Karen tucked her legs up under her. "He and I started kissing while you had gone to the bathroom. I had a massive crush on him. He was divine." She looked dreamily into the distance. "And I wouldn't accept that he was gay. I was nineteen years old, and I suppose I thought I could turn him or something." She laughed. "Anyway, we started kissing and I remember thinking that him being gay was all an act because he got an erection! Gays aren't meant to be turned on by girls, and there was Troels with a massive hard-on! And everything was going really well until you gave him that Kung Fu kick and he landed on the floor. And then you went mental. You screamed and shouted, you attacked him. He just stood there with his now limp, gay dick, while you beat the hell out of him." Karen couldn't stop herself from laughing.

Anna was stonefaced.

"It's not funny," she snarled.

Karen winked.

"Given how many Molotov cocktails you've thrown in your time, you're incredibly touchy," she observed.

"That night . . . what did I say to him?" Anna wanted to know.

"You don't remember?"

"Not really. I just remember being angry. I opened my mouth and I saw red."

"You humiliated him," Karen said, calmly. "You said—"

"Actually, I don't want to know," Anna interrupted her. She held up her hand and turned away.

"And it doesn't matter now," Karen said, in a conciliatory voice.

"I was high on coke."

"I didn't understand it then, but the other day, he told me he left because he was this close to punching you. Beating you up, just like he beat up his dad." Karen gave Anna an uncertain look. "Come on, we all knew what went on in Troels's house. His dad humiliated him. But what we didn't know was that the abuse got physical when Troels became a teenager. His dad would goad him until Troels lashed out. And then his dad would hit him back. They never stopped fighting. He told me so the other day. His dad was in the oncology ward at Odense Hospital, dying from cancer, thin as a skeleton, with tubes coming out of him, but he still attacked him verbally, mocked him. Troels hit him and his dad retaliated. We ended up laughing about it because it was so grotesque! His dad managed to rip the drawer out of his bedside table and hurl it at Troels. Troels had to go straight from his dad's deathbed to the ER!" She chuckled briefly.

"And that night you humiliated him. The very thing guaranteed to push him over the edge."

"Stop it, Karen." Anna got up and went to the window. "And now what?" she whispered. "He wants to be friends with me again? Because ten years have passed? Because he has lost the urge to beat me up?"

"We've all changed, Anna."

Anna went to the bathroom. When she came back, Karen had put on a CD of eighties music and was singing along to it.

"Did someone called Birgit manage to get hold of you?" she said, halfway through a verse.

"No." Anna froze. "When did she call?"

"At five o'clock. Birgit Helland. I got her number, and I gave her your cell number."

Anna hurried to her jacket. Her mobile showed one message. Birgit had called just after five and left a message: *"I need to speak to you. It's important. Nanna and I are going to our cottage tomorrow afternoon. Please could we meet before? Tonight, preferably. I'm begging you. Please call me. I can pick you up. Thanks."*

Anna went to the bathroom and splashed cold water on her face. Then she applied a little makeup and brushed her teeth. Before she left the bathroom, she called Mrs. Helland. They spoke for less than a minute. Mrs. Helland would leave her house now and pick Anna up on the corner of Jagtvejen and Borups Allé in twenty minutes. Anna checked her watch. It was almost eleven. Then she went to the living room and asked casually: "You're sleeping over, aren't you?"

Karen turned and smiled. "I told you, you're not getting rid of me that easily. Hey, where are you off to?" She whistled softly.

"I've got to do something." Anna couldn't help smiling. "I have to go to Birgit Helland's house. She wants to talk to me. She's coming to pick me up. I'll be back in a few hours." Anna looked at her watch. "But if I don't. If I'm not here when you wake up tomorrow morning," Anna swallowed, "call Superintendent Søren Marhauge and raise the alarm, okay?" Anna gave Karen a note with Søren's cell number.

"What do you mean? What could possibly happen?" Karen stared at Anna.

"Nothing," Anna said, lightly. She went to the hall and Karen followed her. Anna put on her army jacket, checked the battery level on her cell, and opened the cupboard in the hall where she kept her toolbox. She stuffed two cable ties and a small, sharp screwdriver into her pocket.

"What do you need those for?" Karen wanted to know. Anna grabbed her shoulders and looked firmly into her eyes.

"Karen. Don't worry about me. God help anyone who tries to hurt me." She smiled. "I'm merely taking precautions because I'm a paranoid bitch who doesn't want to end up dead." She kissed Karen's cheek.

"See you soon," she said and before Karen could respond, Anna had closed the door.

It was snowing lightly outside, but the tarmac was wet and dark. She waited on the corner, in the doorway of a bicycle shop. A girl's bicycle was on display. Pink with a basket. There was a strawberry on the basket.

A horn beeped.

Mrs. Helland pulled over, leaned across and opened the passenger door. Anna got in. Mrs. Helland looked exhausted.

"Hi, Anna," she said, weakly. Anna put on her seatbelt.

"Is it all right if we drive back to my place? It's so cold. I don't really want to sit in the car or go somewhere there are other people. It's been a long day." She smiled faintly.

Anna nodded.

"Thanks for coming to Lars's funeral." Mrs. Helland focused on driving.

"Not at all."

"No, I don't take it for granted. I appreciate it. I understand why you didn't come to the wake. I was close to not showing up myself." She laughed a brittle laugh.

"I had to be somewhere else."

"It's quite all right." They drove on in silence.

"Where's your daughter tonight?" Mrs. Helland asked, looking at Anna.

"At home," Anna replied, trying to sound calm. "My friend Karen is with her."

Why the hell did Birgit Helland want to know that?

When they pulled up in front of the house, it was almost half past midnight. The road was deserted, but the cars parked on either side indicated the houses weren't empty. The light was on and Birgit must have put another log on the fire before picking Anna up, because it was roaring merrily when they entered the living room.

"No, not for me, thank you," Anna said, declining an offer of wine. Mrs. Helland poured herself a glass and downed two large mouthfuls. Anna wondered how much she had already drunk. Had she been over the limit when she drove? Mrs. Helland emptied her glass and refilled it.

"Come on, we're going upstairs. I've something to show you."

Anna had hung up her jacket in the hall but put her cell, the cable ties, and the screwdriver in the back pockets of her jeans. Warily, she followed Mrs. Helland up the stairs. There was a powerful scent of flowers, and when they passed the bathroom Mrs. Helland pushed open the door.

"I brought some of the flowers home," she said in a flat voice. On the bathroom floor stood a large cluster of white plastic buckets with multicolored bouquets. They continued down the corridor, past a half-open door leading to a teenage bedroom, tasteful and tidy compared to how Anna's room used to look when she was that age. The bed was covered with an old-fashioned crochet blanket, and next to the bed stood a low makeup table with a round mirror, bottles of perfume, and an iPod on charger. The curtains were drawn and the windows glared ominously at Anna.

"Nanna insisted on seeing a friend." Birgit raised her arms and let them drop. "Life goes on."

They had reached the end of the corridor and Birgit opened the door to a surprisingly large room. To the left, a desk was pushed against a bare wall and, to the right, there was a built-in couch with scatter cushions covered in coarse fabric. The end wall was one large window and a magnolia tree, naked in winter, grew outside. On the desk was a computer, which turned out to be on when Mrs. Helland nudged the mouse.

"I found something today . . ." she began. Anna looked at the screen and recognized the logo of an online bank she used herself. Mrs. Helland logged on using a pin code she copied from a piece of paper. A screen picture of account activities emerged.

"Look at this," Mrs. Helland said, pointing to the screen. Anna followed her finger, but found it hard to figure out what she was supposed to be looking at. The blood roared in her ears.

"What is it?" she stuttered.

"Payments. Every month during the last three years. I've checked our bank statements. Seven thousand kroner per month, money Lars transferred from his private account to an Amager Bank account. And do you know who owns that account?"

Anna shook her head.

"Erik Tybjerg."

They both fell silent.

"So what does it mean?" Anna asked, slowly.

"No idea. But we're talking about a quarter of a million kroner." Birgit let the amount linger in the air. Anna swallowed. Her brain was annoyingly sluggish.

"And you knew nothing about this until today?"

"No. The money came from Lars's private account. I found the pin code in his desk drawer, and I logged on to see how much money he had left. Nanna got worried today and asked if we could afford to stay in the house, and I wanted to know where we stood. When I had accessed the account and found the transfers to Tybjerg, I went through Lars's office systematically. Every drawer, every cupboard." Mrs. Helland had been bending over the computer, now she straightened up and looked at Anna. The tears started rolling down her cheeks.

"You were right," she whispered. "Lars was ill. Much more so than I could have imagined in my worst nightmares."

"What did you find?" Anna dreaded the answer.

"A bag filled with blood-soaked tissues."

"What?" Anna thought she must have misheard. Mrs. Helland went over to the couch, pulled out a drawer, and retrieved a plastic bag. It was stuffed full, but seemed light, precisely as if it really was full of tissues. Blood-soaked tissues. Fear started spreading through Anna's body.

"I found another bag. Behind this one." She swallowed. "Full of support aids. Support bandages, a neck brace." She gave Anna a look of despair. "And a teething ring, the kind you give to babies, with deep teeth marks. The police told me he was covered in bruises, like after a fall. Old injuries. That he must have fallen, and he had fractures to several of his fingers and toes—they even found two healed cuts to his scalp, which weren't sutured though they ought to have been. I had dismissed what they said, you know, because they suspected me. The police always leave something out, and they always say things that aren't true. They lay traps." Mrs. Helland was panting now.

"Erik Tybjerg was blackmailing him," she whispered, "and I've spent all evening thinking about what he might have had on him."

Anna waited for her to continue.

"Lars was diagnosed with a brain tumor nine years ago. He had surgery and made a full recovery. There has been nothing since. Last

August we held a barbecue for Nanna when she graduated from high school. Lars was tending to the grill when he suddenly collapsed. We were frightened, but he made light of it. He sat on the lawn for ten minutes to collect himself and was in great shape the rest of the evening. He flipped burgers, happy as a clam, and joined Nanna and her friends in a croquet tournament." Mrs. Helland looked at Anna. "Lars's greatest fear was losing his intellect. Being slowly stripped of everything and ending up a vegetable. Shortly afterward, he moved out of the bedroom and into his study. I wondered why but not for very long. He didn't want his snoring to disturb me, he said. And he was right, it had gotten worse, I must admit, so it suited me fine." Again the tears rolled down Mrs. Helland's cheeks in an asymmetrical pattern. "But this was the real reason." She gestured toward the plastic bags. "He didn't want me to know that his illness had returned. That the tumor had started growing again." She looked into the distance. "I think Tybjerg knew about the tumor. He knew Lars had been seriously ill. Perhaps he tried to use it against Lars? Tybjerg has always been envious because Lars had tenure and he didn't. I'm convinced Tybjerg was blackmailing him. What else could it be? Seven thousand kroner per month. That's a lot of money. I've been trying to contact him today, but he's not answering his phone or replying to e-mails. And do you know what really puzzles me?"

Anna shook her head.

"He didn't attend the funeral. Isn't that odd? Even Professor Freeman was there. But not Tybjerg. Anna, I think he killed Lars." Mrs. Helland looked at Anna with burning eyes.

"You need to tell all this to the police."

"I know."

"Why did you call me, Mrs. Helland?"

"When you were here last, I could tell from looking at you that you thought I had killed my husband. You looked at me with contempt written large across your face. I couldn't stand that."

"I don't think you killed Lars," Anna said, gently.

"I loved Lars," Mrs. Helland said.

*   *   *

Anna walked home from Herlev. It took her ninety minutes. The cable ties and screwdriver were back in her jacket pocket; the mission had been called off. The night was crystal clear and the wind had died down. The cold was biting. She walked briskly, swinging her arms. For a moment, she was the only person alive, the only one who millions of stars had come out to see.

There was a beeping sound from her back pocket. It was almost one thirty a.m. It was probably Karen who had woken up and was worried about her. She fished out her mobile and stopped under a bus shelter.

It was a text message from Johannes.

Can we meet? it read.

Anna stared at the display in disbelief.

CHAPTER 14

On the morning of Saturday October 13, Clive went looking for a florist, and when he found one he meditated on the vagaries of life. Here he was, buying flowers for Helland's funeral. He had skipped breakfast at the hotel, and when he had got the flowers he stopped for coffee and a bagel. He thought about Kay. About what she might be doing. They had met through mutual friends. Kay hadn't been the most striking woman present that night, but she had exuded something old-fashioned and meticulous, which appealed to Clive. They quickly became a couple and married on the anniversary of their first date. A common enough story, Clive thought, and there was nothing wrong with that. Franz and Tom had followed in quick succession and Kay stayed home with the children while Clive went to work. So far their marriage had been undramatic. In fact, it reminded Clive very much of his parents' marriage with one exception: Clive made an effort with Kay. He knew she didn't always understand his work, but he made a point of keeping her informed about major developments. They had always spoken politely to each other, both when they were alone and in front of the children. Clive knew he had behaved well.

He had no interest at all in other women; he didn't drink or gamble. Nor had he ever hit Kay. Until now. He looked out at the gray capital and cursed Jack. Jack was responsible for the vast majority of drama in Clive's life. He was a thirty-year curse that had refused to release him. Clive had never suffered as much as he did when Jack became a teenager, lost interest in him, and moved away. Not even his intellectual clash with his father had cost him so dear. He had been unable to sleep and had desperately wished for Jack to come back. The anguish faded only slowly. He thought it must be fate when he met Jack again. Clive was a scientist and didn't believe in fate, but when he spotted Jack in the university lobby, he refused to accept it was a coincidence. Their paths kept crossing and all they had to do was reach out. But Jack didn't reach out. Clive had given him hundreds of chances, but Jack hadn't followed him since childhood.

Clive massaged his eyebrows. He wouldn't think about Jack. His lecture was at six o'clock and before that there was Helland's funeral.

The church was full to the rafters when Michael and Clive entered. The tall superintendent, Marhauge, sat right inside the door, in the last row, and he nodded kindly to Clive. The usher took his flowers, and Clive looked for a vacant pew. Michael fell behind, but Clive was pushed forward and ended up sitting near the front. At least two hundred people were there. The coffin, decorated with flowers, shone brightly in front of the altar. In the first pew, to the right, were two distraught-looking women in black who spoke in hushed voices. They had to be Helland's family. Clive found it unreal that Helland had a family. Helland, that evil man. Several men sat in the front pew to the left, suggesting Helland had been one of several brothers. He had certainly had many friends and colleagues.

Diagonally behind him, Clive spotted a young woman who was looking in his direction. She had light brown bobbed hair, sneakers on her feet, and she wore jeans and an inappropriate army jacket with a hood. She seemed very angry.

What on earth was she staring at? He tried to follow her gaze, but no one stood out in the sea of people in front of him. Everyone was busy taking off their coats and opening hymnals. He realized the young woman was staring at him. At that moment the service began.

Later, at the Bella Centre, Clive noted to his delight that around one hundred and twenty people had shown up to hear him speak. He trawled the audience for familiar faces but found none. A heated debate followed the lecture. Clive knew the routine and had, by now, been on the receiving end of so many attacks that he would have been very surprised if his audience had responded with silence. Yet he noticed the results of the cartilage condensation experiment weren't considered as revolutionary as Michael and he had hoped.

"It's an interesting experiment," someone said. "But it doesn't cancel out the 286 apomorphies linking modern birds to dinosaurs."

"I agree," another said, nodding in Clive's direction. "The ontogenesis of the bird hand is one of the weakest areas of the dinosaur theory. But we have to live with that. We can't know the embryonic development of dinosaurs, for obvious reasons. But even without an insight into embryonic development, we have more than sufficient evidence to conclude that there's a relationship. We really do, Professor Freeman."

"Yes," a third person called out. "It's the equivalent of doing a thousand-piece jigsaw of the New York skyline. Only one piece is missing, and yet you claim you can't see what city it is."

"I agree," a fourth person said.

Clive inevitably reached the point where he simply stuck to his guns and dismissed all criticism. Two people walked out, fewer than usual. He wasn't facing a polite and sympathetic crowd who lapped up his every word, but they weren't bad, either. He thought their eyes showed evidence of genuine interest.

One hour later the room was deserted. Clive couldn't hide his disappointment. A few members of the audience had come down to shake his hand, but he didn't feel the cartilage condensation experiment had won over anyone. He couldn't see why. It was a good experiment.

"What do you think?" he asked Michael. "It felt like they didn't quite follow." Clive shook his head with frustration. Michael seemed distracted by something. He had been busy taking down the large, colorful posters but had stopped.

"Michael?"

Michael didn't react until Clive was right next to him.

"Earth to Michael," Clive said.

"Clive," he said. "I'm really sorry."

Clive looked baffled.

"The department is closing," Michael explained. Clive gasped. "The decision has been made. Our department will be merged with the department of Vertebrate Morphology and you . . ." Michael touched his head and said in an anguished voice, "There isn't a position for you. That's the official version. You're being made emeritus professor. On paper. Of course, we'll continue to include you. Well, I'll include you in my projects, definitely. I was supposed to tell you before we went to Europe. But I couldn't. I'll understand if you're angry."

"But why?" Clive stuttered. He was stunned.

"I'm on your side, Clive," Michael hastened to add. "It's not that. Look at the condensation results. I support you. But every day new evidence emerges suggesting we could be wrong. We have to allow for the possibility that we might be wrong. The department of Bird Evolution, Paleobiology, and Systematics has become synonymous with your scientific position and that was never the intention. It can't happen; it's hurting UBC. We're known as the Creationist Faculty. We have fewer students than ever, and you know what that means." He rubbed his thumb and index finger together. "No one takes our graduates seriously, they can't find work, and the faculty desperately needs money. We have to change course if we're to have a hope of increasing our student numbers. And you're too well known, Clive. The feeling is that we can't save the sinking ship as long as you're the captain."

Clive stared at Michael.

"I've secured funding for the department for more than thirty years. Every single time money was handed out," he whispered.

"And that's why you need to stop now. While the going is good. It can't last. You will be given fewer and fewer grants and, finally, none at all. Besides, the University Council demands it. An immediate merger and your retirement."

"I'm in my prime," Clive objected.

"I should have told you before we left. Or on the plane, at least," Michael said, "but it wasn't easy."

"Business class tickets and a Michelin star dinner? Was that the department's attempt at a golden good-bye? And what about the meeting?" Clive shouted triumphantly. "That meeting which I, very conveniently, failed to be invited to."

"I'm really very sorry," Michael said again.

Clive clenched his fist.

"I want to be alone," he hissed. Michael threw up his hands.

"I'm sorry, old boy," he said in a convivial tone. "Life goes on, eh? You made a huge contribution, we all know that . . . without you the department wouldn't have had such a high profile, and—"

"I want to be alone," Clive roared.

"Calm down. It's not my decision," Michael said, hurt, and headed for the exit. He shook his head lightly as he left. He was merely the messenger.

When Clive was alone, he stared at the huge PowerPoint screen. He felt numb and consumed with hate. When he heard footsteps, he thought Michael had come back. But it wasn't Michael, it was the young woman from Helland's funeral. She held out her hand, and he shook it out of pure reflex.

"My name's Anna," she said. "I would like to talk to you, please."

"You were at Helland's funeral," he said. "Why were you staring at me?"

"I was surprised to see you," she replied calmly. "Curious."

Her eyes were almost yellow and there was a touch of defiance about her mouth.

"And why is that?" Clive started gathering up his papers and returning them to his briefcase.

"I'm Professor Helland and Dr. Tybjerg's postgraduate student," she said. "I've written my dissertation on the controversy surrounding the origin of birds. There are some anatomical details I would very much like to discuss with you. I've come to ask if you would meet me in the Vertebrate Collection. Tomorrow . . . ? Or is Monday better? Will you still be here on Monday?"

He stared at her.

"Being Professor Helland and Dr. Tybjerg's postgraduate student is your problem," he sneered as he picked up his jacket and his briefcase. "What's there to talk about? Helland is dead, and I'm sorry about that. Tybjerg . . ." He glanced at her. "Tybjerg didn't even have the decency to attend my lecture today. I've nothing to say to their protégée. Good-bye." He climbed the broad steps between the seat rows. The young woman followed him.

"I've got something for you from Dr. Tybjerg," she said. Clive stopped and gave her a sharp look.

"What is it?"

"I can't tell you here." She glanced over her shoulder as if the walls had ears.

"Why doesn't he deliver it to me in person?" Clive persisted.

"I'll explain later. It's a bone . . . it's complicated." The young woman straightened up and said softly: "Imagine how you would feel if you finally had to accept that you had been wrong. Your entire scientific career."

"Ha!" Clive snorted. "Hell will freeze over before Tybjerg admits he's wrong."

He continued walking, reached a corridor, and increased his pace. The young woman called out after him.

"Professor Freeman! Monday, eleven o'clock. In the Vertebrate Collection. Do we have a deal?"

"I guarantee you we don't!" he said, shaking his head as he left.

Michael was waiting for him in a taxi in front of the Bella Centre. He was sitting in the back with the door open, the meter was already running. What was he thinking? That Clive would act as if nothing had happened and drop the subject? Michael was on his cell, reporting back, most likely, oh yes, everything had gone fine, he had finally managed to say it, the old fool was history. Who was he even talking to? Someone from the department? The Head of the Institute? Michael moved to make room for Clive.

"Don't you ever wait for me in a taxi again," Clive screamed into Michael's astonished face. Michael lowered his phone.

"Relax, Clive," he said quietly. "Get in the taxi."

Was he not listening to him? Not anymore. That was the message. Clive stomped across the parking lot to the subway station. He didn't look back.

He got off at Nørreport and walked down a random street. He had trusted Michael. He had taught Michael everything he knew. Without Clive, Michael was a mediocre researcher with a—to all intents and purposes—superfluous knowledge of bird evolution. It struck him he wasn't any better than Jack. One of a scientist's most important qualities was the ability to stand firm. Through stormy weather, starvation, and torture. Otherwise you were nothing but an amateur. Jack and Michael were amateurs. Cut from a different cloth to him. He would remain firm even if it was the last thing he did. To be honest, he had respected Helland and Tybjerg for that very characteristic. You could say what you liked about them, but they stood firm and defended their position, just like him. It was the only valid stance. U-turns were for politicians. He would pay no heed to that silly girl. Tybjerg would never admit to being wrong. If he could, it never would have come this far! Tybjerg would stick to his guns just as stubbornly as Clive's father had done. A bone. Ha! What a joke.

He entered a round tower that appeared on his left. The ascent was almost without steps, a smooth spiral, and he tripped and fell on his knees. Thinking he was alone, he swore out loud, but a younger man, on his way down, stopped and looked shocked. Clive exploded and screamed at the young man, who retreated, said something, but left in the end.

Clive was alone. What was happening? In the old days, when he was younger, the sun had shone and when he leaned across his desk to look out into the garden, he would see Kay sitting there, wearing a broad-brimmed hat, and the boys dipping their toes in an inflatable pool, squealing and drinking lemonade through curly straws. Once, a respectful silence had accompanied his arrival at work; Michael had been twenty-two years old, bright green like a newly hatched grasshopper, delirious with happiness because he had been promised a postgraduate place in two years' time and grateful for being allowed to type out Clive's lecture notes and laminate the covers of all Clive's reference books in the meantime. Once his sons had looked at him with admiration in their eyes, once Jack had loved him.

Clive felt the cold and he stood up. He needed Kay. It was no good without her.

He called her from a telephone booth. Around him, people fought their way through darkness and it snowed lightly. Clive's heart nearly exploded when Kay answered the telephone. Not Franz, not Franz's wife. Kay.

"Kay, I love you," he whispered. "I don't want to live without you. I can't live without you. I'll change. I'll never hit you again. I'll make it right with the children. Take me back, please. I'll try harder. I promise." Clive struggled to hold on to the handset; the wind seemed to change direction, it started blowing directly at his back and the hand that held the telephone. His telephone card counted down. There was silence down the other end.

"Kay?"

"Call me tonight, Clive," she said, suddenly sounding tender. "I can't talk now. I'm going out with Annabel. But tonight I'll be . . . in our house. You can call me then." She hung up.

A flash of jubilation exploded in his chest. It wasn't too late! Kay loved him!

He went back to the hotel. Michael had left three messages. Clive left one for him. If he didn't get the meaning of that one, he had to be an idiot. He went to his room and switched on his computer. He wanted to book a trip for Kay. She had never been across the Atlantic and had often mentioned how much she would like to see Paris. It was sixty degrees in Paris, nothing like the raw cold that dominated Copenhagen. He checked flight departures and began to plan. There was a departure from Vancouver, via Seattle, over London and onward to Copenhagen the next day at 1:20 p.m., arriving at Copenhagen Tuesday morning at 6:20 a.m. Clive could meet Kay here and together they could fly on to Paris at 12:35 p.m. He paid for the ticket with his credit card. Almost two thousand Canadian dollars for a return flight. It was a lot of money. But then he remembered he hadn't bought Kay a present for their silver wedding anniversary. He also remembered he didn't want to be alone. He tried to call her at Franz's, but no one answered. He imagined she would like some time to pack. Soon afterward he fell asleep. He slept heavily and only surfaced a couple of times, when the telephone in his room rang angrily, but he slipped back to sleep the moment it stopped. At first, he dreamt about Helland, about Kay, about the boys, about Michael and Tybjerg. They all apologized to him. The dream changed and became about Jack. Jack stood close to him, smiling, as he said something. Clive couldn't hear what it was because there was music playing. Clive asked Jack to repeat himself, but when he did, Clive could still not hear it. Suddenly, Clive realized that Jack's face was that of a child. He was as tall as a grown man and wearing a grown man's trousers and thin sweater, but his face was a boy's; the sharp upper lip, which had pointed at Clive for nearly forty years, his eyes filled with a child's admiration. Clive's groin throbbed. Jack smiled and nothing felt wrong. You're allowed, Jack said. The music had stopped. It was very quiet. Clive knelt in front of Jack and carefully pulled his trousers down over his slim hips.

Clive woke up with a start and sat bolt upright in the bed. He was dripping with sweat. He dried himself furiously with a towel and tried to rub away the stains on the sheet. His watch on the bedside table glowed fluorescent green. The alarm would soon go off to remind him to call Kay. Clive showered and when he sat, clean and refreshed, in the chair by the telephone, he called Kay. She answered after four rings.

"Hi," she said gently. "I'm glad you called."

Clive breathed a sigh of relief. He didn't want to be alone.

"Do you know what you're doing tomorrow?" he said.

"Looking after Annabel. She has tonsillitis," Kay replied.

"No, you're going to Paris!"

"Paris?"

"Yes, I've bought you a ticket. If you check your e-mail, you'll see. Your flight leaves tomorrow afternoon at 1:15 p.m. from Vancouver, via Seattle and London, and on from there to Copenhagen. I'll meet you at the airport, and we'll fly to Paris together." There was silence down the other end.

"I can't."

"What do you mean?" Clive was flabbergasted.

"I can't. I have plans tomorrow."

"But I've already bought the ticket," Clive protested.

"You should have checked with me first."

"Can't you cancel your plans? What are you doing, anyway? You can look after Annabel some other time."

Pause.

"Kay?" he said.

"I don't want to," Kay said quietly. "You should have checked with me first. I want to go to Paris, but I'm looking after Annabel tomorrow. It's important to me. She's looking forward to it. You should have checked with me first."

When their conversation had ended, everything around Clive went black.

CHAPTER 15

In 1975 Søren's parents, Peter and Kristine, had rented a vacation cottage on the North Sea coast. Søren suddenly remembered the cottage. It was wooden and painted pale blue, situated in the corner of a vast plot, surrounded by tall trees. The beach lay a little further away with the fishing village beyond it. The accident happened one week into their vacation. Søren's father was busy fixing the car and had stripped it of everything: wings, bumper, silencer. The sun came out and it was time for ice cream. The stand was only two miles down a tiny road, but they took the car because Søren's mother wanted to come, and she couldn't ride her bicycle because she was heavily pregnant with Søren's baby brother or sister. They only had one major intersection to cross. They would be fine.

The car was squashed into a cube when it hit the truck. Søren didn't die. His face was badly cut, he broke several ribs, and he suffered a concussion. It took the emergency team more than an hour to cut him free. Søren remembered nothing. Not the drop of sweat trickling down the nose of one of the ambulance men, the smell of coffee, the golden wheat swaying in the summer heat. Nothing.

Blackout. His parents had sat in the front of the car, which was squashed flat.

At the hospital, no one knew who Søren was or where he came from.

The doctors and nurses asked him over and over, but he said nothing. He was in the hospital for nearly three days and didn't utter a word. Something terrible had happened, he was alone, and he was five years old. It was important to be very quiet. Knud and Elvira hadn't come, either. No one loved him.

Knud and Elvira had no idea what had happened. They were attending a seminar in Finland. They weren't at home when they heard the news, nor did Knud go out into the garden to tell Søren about the accident, like they had told him. It was a lie. They were in Finland.

After three days, Søren said: "My grandfather's called Knud Marhauge, he lives in a red house outside Ørslev in Denmark." After that, everything happened very quickly, a telephone call was made, a friend housesitting for Knud and Elvira answered it, another call to Finland, and Knud and Elvira flew back to Denmark to pick up their grandson.

When Vibe had finished her story, she looked anxiously at Søren. His arms hung helplessly by his sides, and he stared at the candles in Vibe's white ceramic candleholders, burning infinitely slowly on a bookcase in the living room. Søren had been playing in the garden when the accident happened! At the far end. Knud had come down to tell him. He remembered it, though he was only five years old and had moved to Copenhagen soon afterward. The house outside Ørslev had been red, there were three apple trees in the garden, and Elvira had a large barrel for collecting rainwater into which Søren would tip tadpoles he found in a nearby lake. Peter and Kristine had been on their way to Ørslev to pick him up when the accident happened. His grandparents had been looking after him for the weekend, and he had been playing with a red car when Knud came down to him at the far end of the garden. Later, they had had ice cream. It wasn't like Vibe had said.

"Why did you keep it secret?" he asked. His sweater was sticking to him, something was howling inside his head.

"I've known since I was seventeen," Vibe said. "I've known it since the summer I saw the wedding photograph on the sideboard and discovered that Elvira and Knud were your grandparents. I was shocked your real parents were dead. Dead! It was the first time I realized you can lose someone you love in an accident. When I went home, I was beside myself. That night, when my mom said goodnight to me, I burst into tears. You had lost your parents, and I was terrified of losing mine. I was seventeen years old," she defended herself. "I told my mom what Elvira had said. How awful it had been for Knud to find you in the garden and tell you about the accident. She had stayed in the house, slumped against the wall in grief. My mother hugged me and promised not to die.

"The next time I was at the library, I couldn't help myself. I looked up the accident on a microfilm. I wanted to see a picture of your parents, read about the accident, mourn the terrible fate my boyfriend had suffered, wallow in it a bit, I suppose." Vibe looked down. "I had almost given up when I found a newspaper clipping. 'Tragic vacation mystery solved' was the headline. 'The five-year-old boy from Viborg, who miraculously survived the car crash that claimed the lives of his parents three days ago, has finally been identified and reunited with his grandparents.' I stared at the photo that accompanied the article; the police had released it in an attempt to find out who you were. It had been taken in the hospital and it was like a bad joke. You were black and blue, swollen, and unrecognizable. With bandages around your head. The caption read: 'Five-year-old Søren has finally been reunited with his family.' I ran out of the library, terrified and furious. That night, I called you. Knud answered the telephone, and I told him what I knew. They had lied and they must tell you the truth. Knud asked to meet me the next day, by the embankment behind our school.

"He was sitting on a bench staring at the water in the moat when I got there. It was windy and I was cold. He hugged me. Elvira didn't want Søren to know, he said. She was adamant that you had suffered enough and didn't think you needed reminding of the tragedy, if you couldn't remember anything yourself. If it ever surfaced some day, they would be there for you, explain it to you and support you. But until that happened, they would keep their mouths shut. Suppression is the body's way of protecting you against the unbearable, was her opinion.

"Knud had serious doubts that this was the right thing to do, he told me, and I got the impression that it had driven a massive wedge between them. Knud was convinced that children were survivors; they healed quickly; they adapted and compensated like plants that wither in the shade and thrive in the sun. But Elvira said no. In the end, Knud reluctantly gave in, however, he did so in exchange for Elvira's promise that if ever any scrap of your memory returned, they would put their cards on the table. That was the deal. They shook hands on it.

"'Dear Vibe,' Knud whispered to me. 'Please don't tell him. Leave it alone. We have peace at last.' He beseeched me. I said I would think about it. Elvira knew nothing, neither did you, but in the days that followed, Knud looked at me, observed me, hoping and praying. All of a sudden telling you seemed pointless. You were seventeen years old and at high school. You were head of the student council, sporty, clever, popular, and easy-going. Why would I reveal a secret that appeared to have had no ill effect on you? I asked you about Peter and Kristine. You never wondered why; after all, I had just learned that your parents were really your grandparents, so you answered me willingly. You said, of course you thought about your parents from time to time, especially when Knud and Elvira mourned them at Christmas and on Kristine's birthday in May, when Elvira and Knud would light a bonfire in the garden, even if it rained. You were supposed to look a lot like your dad, and it might have been fun to have a dad you looked like. But Knud and Elvira were the best parents you could wish for and, at this point, your eyes always grew tender and compelling. Think of all the fun we have, you said. And you did. The house was full of life.

"I met with Knud and told him my decision. He was relieved. My knowledge of your secret faded into the background. We left high school, we moved in together, life was easy. You applied to the police academy," Vibe smiled, "and, at the time, I never wondered why you were so preoccupied with mysteries. We were good together; our relationship grew stronger. It wasn't until I wanted to have children that the secret surfaced, when you simply said 'no' without any explanation. I forced you to dig deeper, but all I could deduce from your many excuses was that you were scared. Why would you be scared of having children? We were in our late twenties and we loved each other. Or, at least, I believed we did." She glanced up at him. "And you clearly had the capacity for loving a child. You had been loved yourself and you were good with children, I had seen you with them. You can't fake something like that. The only explanation that made sense was that the secret terrified you subconsciously. In your mind children were abandoned, lying alone in a room with a high ceiling and no one coming to get them . . . so no wonder you didn't want children.

"For the second time I grew convinced that telling you the truth was the right thing to do," she said. "Knud and I had lunch in town and he was clearly shocked when I brought up the accident again. At first, he didn't want to talk about it; you promised, he said. But then I asked him if he had ever considered there might be a link between it and the fact that you didn't want children. It made a deep impression on him. After all, he really wanted some great-grandchildren," she smiled, and Søren felt a spot in his heart glow red-hot.

"And suddenly it made sense to both of us. There had to be a connection. When we parted that day, I felt confident, but very nervous. We had made a decision. I had no idea how you would react, or how furious you would be with Elvira and Knud, whether I should tell you that I already knew or pretend that I didn't. . . . We had to plan it down to the last detail, I decided. Knud had promised to call once he had spoken to Elvira.

"Only he never called back. It was one of the worst weeks of my life. I grew more and more angry and desperate. I was so fed up with your stubborn, no-nonsense attitude and deeply hurt you wouldn't even consider having children with me. I slept in the living room and every morning when I woke up, I wanted to rip your head off. Knud still hadn't called, but it no longer mattered, I told myself.

"That Sunday we went to have lunch with them, as we always did, and that's when I realized why Knud never called me. . . . That bloody illness," Vibe burst out and stared blankly into space before she continued.

"The grotesque part was that I met John in the middle of it all. When Knud died, I was in love. I visited Knud two days before he died, when he was deteriorating rapidly, but he still had plenty to say. For the first time ever, he begged me directly.

"Please don't tell him, Vibe. Let it rest. Give my boy peace. He's hurting so much. Give him peace." I held Knud's hand and I was consumed with doubt. Perhaps he was right? You were only just coping; Knud was right, I had never seen you in such pain. Why would I hurt you even more? I was so confused: did silence equal peace? I still don't know. But I just couldn't do it. Defy Elvira's wish, defy Knud who was about to die, and push you into an abyss where none of us could foresee the consequences."

"Does John know?" Søren demanded.

"Yes, he does."

Søren groaned.

"Why now?" he asked.

She waited a little. Folded her hands around her stomach.

"When you called today and said you wanted to talk to me about something important, I thought you might have found out. There's not much on the Internet, but there's a bit. Besides, the old microfilms are still available, in regional archives and at the central library. You might have become suspicious and searched the archive yourself. After all, you're a detective," she laughed. "Perhaps you had decided to investigate your family history, what did I know? But I prepared for the worst. And . . ." Her face crumpled. "Never in my wildest dreams had I imagined it would be something so awful. That you had a daughter and she died. You poor man," she said suddenly.

"You poor, poor man." She uttered the words so tenderly, and when she embraced Søren he rested his head on her shoulder. She smelled warm and familiar, her huge belly was bursting with life and she stroked his hair for a long time. John came back. Søren got up and the two men had an awkward hug. Vibe felt uneasy about Søren going home.

"You can sleep on the couch," she assured him.

But he wanted to go home. "I'm okay," he said.

When Søren woke up Saturday morning, he was angry. He was angry while he ate his breakfast, angry while he showered. He was angry when he stopped off at Bellahøj police station to switch cars, and angry when he reached Herlev Church for Professor Helland's funeral. He sat in the back row watching Anna, Professor Freeman, Mrs. Helland, and the other two hundred mourners. His anger didn't abate until the service started. Helland's coffin was covered with colorful flowers. The roar of the organ opened the floodgates of his thoughts and he almost calmed down during the sermon, watching the backs of Anna's and Freeman's heads, one more stubborn than the other.

Maja's funeral had been the worst day of his life, he had thought at the time. He had arrived late on purpose and was the last to enter the church. A funeral could be pompous, or almost euphoric, or indifferent, but when the coffin was the size of a box of dates, it was a nightmare. Søren's nightmare. No one knew who he was, and he didn't think Bo had seen him. During the service, Søren had wanted to stand up and scream: "My daughter's in that coffin. *My* daughter." But he had said nothing. It had been the worst day of his life. Or so he had thought.

Søren attended the wake after Professor Helland's funeral. It was held at a funeral home not far from the church. He stood in a corner, watching everyone, speaking to no one and reeking of police. Mrs. Helland was distant. She was steadily drinking wine, speaking to people, but never for very long, and Søren noticed her gaze flutter like a butterfly. Just before five o'clock she made her excuses and left. Her daughter, Nanna, stayed behind. People began to trickle home. Søren could hear Nanna apologize. Her eyes were red, but she seemed more self-composed than her mother. She tidied up a little, and around six an older man offered her a lift home. She said good-bye to the remaining mourners, shook hands and was hugged. Søren went to his car. He had only attended the wake because he was desperate. He had even brought handcuffs, ready to slam them on the wrists of anyone who looked suspicious. How ridiculous.

Søren had reached Bellahøj police station and had just switched to his own car when his cell rang.

"It's Stella Marie," a voice said.

"Hi." Søren was surprised.

"I know where I've seen that guy before."

Søren was about to drive out of the basement garage, but pulled in and waved a colleague past.

"Go on."

"He's on the outside of Magasin. I drove past this morning. There's a huge poster on the front of the building." Yes, she was sure. Søren thanked her and drove into the city center rather than home. He parked at Saint Annæ Plads and walked a few hundred meters down Bredgade, past Charlottenborg and up to Magasin. The giant poster faced the square. It depicted a man and a woman. The woman smiled flirtatiously, baring her bright white teeth. She was wearing a soft pink sweater and tight jeans, and she held out her hand behind her to the man who was about to slip an ostentatious gold ring on her finger. The man was handsome, even Søren could see that. Auburn hair, brown eyes, scattered freckles. He smiled, mischievously, but he appeared sure of his success. Behind his back, he held a Swiss army knife with multiple functions, and the message of the poster was that once the Magasin sale started, the man would be able to afford the ring for her and the knife for himself. Søren stared at the man's face. He was around thirty, a little less perhaps, and he didn't look like someone who frequented the Red Mask. Søren quickly came up with a plan: contact Magasin's marketing department and identify the model. But that couldn't be done until Monday morning. Damn! He looked at his watch. He was off duty now, but he had no urge to go home to his silent empty house. He called Henrik.

"No problem," Henrik said. "Come over."

Henrik lived with his family on the outskirts of Østerbro, and Søren spent the rest of the evening there. They ate together, and Søren was fascinated by Henrik's teenage daughters who were simultaneously distant and omnipresent. One man had a daughter who would never grow bigger, a tiny daughter with tiny feet in tiny socks, another man had two daughters, with curves, who picked at their food, answered back, and had bright eyes. Søren liked Henrik's wife and couldn't imagine why he was having an affair. Jeanette was five years younger than her husband and worked as an administrator at a nursery school. After dinner, the men cleared the table, the girls disappeared to their bedrooms, and Henrik's wife went to the gym. For a moment, Henrik looked nervous.

He and Søren got two beers and discussed the cases. As far as Helland was concerned, Henrik, too, was of the opinion they had to check out Hanne Moritzen. Professor Moritzen was the only person who really knew how to handle parasites, and even though they could attribute no motive to her, there had to be one. They agreed Henrik would investigate her on Monday to see if he could establish a link between her and Professor Helland.

But Henrik frowned when Søren went on to suggest that Helland might have been murdered by his wife.

"Why would she kill him? She has no motive," Henrik objected. "And she knows nothing about parasites." The two men looked at each other.

"Tybjerg, however, has a motive," Henrik continued. "He's fed up with standing in Helland's shadow and decides to get rid of him. He may not know much about parasites, but he is a biologist, so he can find out."

Søren remained unconvinced.

"Birgit Helland is hiding something. I can feel it."

"So is Anna Bella Nor," Henrik said. "And she has a motive."

"Which is?"

"She's a killer bitch from hell who eliminates any man who crosses her path. Possibly even Johannes. You have to agree it's odd that two men, whom Anna Nor has been around since she started her graduate program, die within three days of each other, or is that just me?"

"I don't think Johannes Trøjborg's death is related to Helland's. I think we need to visit Count Dracula's castle if we're to have a hope of finding the man who killed him. Or woman."

Henrik nodded and they agreed to check out everyone who had been to the Red Mask on September 7.

"I still think Anna is an enigma," Henrik insisted. "Perhaps she and Dr. Tybjerg are an item and they killed Helland together? To be crowned the new king and queen of the dinosaur experts."

"I don't want to talk shop anymore," Søren said, stretching out.

"Fine by me. But I don't want to talk about you-know-what. I told her today that it's over." Henrik's eyes flickered.

They drank more beer. Henrik leaned back and said: "Ahhh."

Then Søren told him a story about a little boy who went on vacation to the North Sea coast and got trapped in the car with his dead parents.

They got drunk. Not very, but enough for Søren to relax. Just after midnight he called for two cabs. One to take him home and another to drive his car back. When the cabs beeped their horns and Søren was about to leave, he went to shake Henrik's hand, but Henrik would have none of it. He hugged him. For longer and harder than the other day.

When Søren got home, he went to bed and slept soundly for thirty minutes, exactly, before his cell rang. He was deep into a weird dream about dogs with thick, glossy coats. He was looking after them, or he owned them, and he could control them by winking. He was the only man in the universe who could do that. Dazed, he sat up in bed, clammy with sweat though there was frost on the outside of the window. The ringing stopped, but when he swung his feet over the edge of his bed, it started again. It was charging under his clothes, which he had left in a pile, and when he finally found it, it had switched to voice mail. He entered the pin code but before he had time to do anything else, it started ringing again.

"Hello," he said in a rusty voice.

It was Anna.

"Why don't you answer your phone? What's the point of having a policeman's cell number if he isn't there when you need him?" Anna shouted. Søren wondered if her teeth were clattering as well. He looked at his alarm clock. It was 1:55 a.m.

"I was asleep," he said. "What's happened?" He was awake now. He switched on the light and fumbled for his clothes.

"I've just received a text message from Johannes," she informed him.

Søren said, "Hang on." He quickly got dressed then he picked up his phone again.

"Where are you?" he wanted to know.

"Right across from Bellahøj police station, as it happens. I was in Herlev and I decided to walk home. I received the text just as I passed the Lyngby highway exit and it was quite dark, so I ran. Now I'm here. It's cold, I'm sweaty, and I'm going home."

He was puzzled.

"What were you doing in Herlev?" he asked.

There was silence down the other end.

"I'm calling to say I got a text message from a dead man," she said at last, "and perhaps you need to ratchet up your investigation a notch before his cell is switched off again. It's probably too late already, given what a heavy sleeper you are. It's been a long day. Good night."

"Stop, Anna!"

Søren was cut off.

"Damn!"

He called her. It went to voice mail.

It was 2:05 in the morning and he was wide awake.

"Damn!" he said again.

He called the station and spoke to the duty officer who had been just about to call him. Johannes Trøjborg's missing cell, which they had been keeping an eye on since last Wednesday, had just been active. The activity was traced to the corner of Schlegels Allé and Vesterbrogade, and the phone was moving down Vesterbrogade toward the city center. One minute and twenty seconds after sending the message, it was switched off. Søren hung up and very slowly ate five apples. It felt like they started fermenting in his stomach right away, something was certainly brewing. He called Anna's number ten times, but got no reply. He stared into the forest; the moon hung huge and round over the ragged line of the treetops. He touched the window and could feel the cold through the glass like a faint electric current. Was he protecting Anna because he was attracted to her? Was Henrik right? Had Anna killed Helland? Out of hate? Had she killed Johannes? But why? Had they been too quick to discount Professor Freeman? Had he sat in a church with a killer today and let him go? Was it Mrs. Helland, was it obvious to everyone except him? And Dr. Tybjerg. Where did he fit into the picture? And where was he? Dead? Or had he gone underground because he was guilty?

Søren showered. As he stood, heavy and naked, on the cold bathroom floor, he suddenly felt things were about to change. There were no more obstacles in his path. He got dressed and made coffee. He spent two hours making notes, drawing stick people on pieces of paper and moving them around on the floor. Then he lay down on the sofa and slept for a couple of hours. At eight o'clock he got up and made oatmeal. While it simmered, he splashed water on his face. He thought about Susanne Winther. The terror in her voice when she thought something might have happened to Magnus, her little son. He had loved his daughter just as much, though he had only seen her a few times while she was a baby, the size of a bean. What had Søren said the night Bo called from Thailand? Had his eyes widened and had he whispered: "Is Maja all right?" No. He had screamed: "Pull yourself together, you fucking freak!"

What was it Professor Moritzen had said?

The very first time he called her.

She had whispered: "Is Asger all right?"

It was nine o'clock, it was Sunday, and a huge weight fell from Søren's shoulders; he had finally gotten his touch back.

CHAPTER 16

When Anna got home, she climbed into bed next to Karen and slept soundly. In the morning she made pancakes and treated Lily to a bubble bath. Every time Karen passed her, Anna gave her a hug. Karen was overjoyed but confused.

"What are you up to?" she wanted to know.

Anna smiled softly.

"It's just that . . ." She shook her head.

Karen asked if she could get Lily out of the bath, so Anna went into the living room. She had received another text message from Johannes's mobile.

Can we meet at my place? it said.

Anna replied: *No. The Natural History Museum. 3 p.m. Or I call the police.* Then she returned to the bathroom. Karen was sitting on the toilet seat with a towel in her lap. Lily was squealing with delight at a plastic Bambi bath toy with a Santa-Claus-style foam beard. Anna's heart sank. She was about to make Karen very sad. Gently, she put her hand on Karen's back.

"I thought it might be a good idea to visit Cecilie," she suggested. Lily stood up among the bubbles and held up her arms.

"Granny, Granny," she shouted. Karen turned around and gave Anna a baffled look.

They walked through Assistens Cemetery. It took them nearly an hour. Lily was in her snowsuit and insisted on climbing everything. Anna and Karen wandered side by side, taking in the snow-covered landscape.

They bought cakes filled with chopped pistachios and a bag of dry, sweet rolls from an Arab bakery in Nørrebrogade. Anna and Lily stopped outside every store and admired the displays. Anna pointed and said, "Look at that" or "Isn't that cute."

"Come on," Karen implored them, shivering. "Walking slowly isn't going to get you out of it."

Anna shot her a look.

Karen and Lily raced each other up the stairs. Anna followed. She heard joyous commotion when Cecilie opened the door.

"Hunnybunny!" Cecilie exclaimed. "Hi, Karen! How lovely to see you. Come here, sweetheart, let me give you a big hug. I've missed you so much."

When Anna reached Cecilie's apartment, Cecilie had lifted Lily up and was holding her tightly. She spotted Anna over Lily's shoulder and paled.

"Hi, Anna," she said, putting Lily down. Lily slipped into the apartment with familiar ease.

"Hi, Mom," Anna said, her cheek brushing her mother's.

"Come in. It's freezing outside."

Inside the hall Lily quickly pulled her toys from a big blue box and started playing. She was still in her snowsuit and wool hat. Karen helped her out of them.

"Look, this is my bed when I'm at Granny's," Lily chatted. "And look, I've got dollies, too. A little dolly and a big dolly. And teddies and books." Karen admired everything. Anna remained in the hall. Cecilie smiled nervously.

"Aren't you going to take off your jacket?"

"No, I'm not staying. There's something I need to do. Is that okay with you, Karen?"

Karen looked puzzled, but she nodded.

"Are you still sulking?" Cecilie wanted to know. "Am I still banned from helping out with Lily?" She smiled patronizingly.

"Have you spoken to Jens?" Anna asked.

Cecilie blinked.

"I speak to Jens every day, Anna."

Cecilie's gaze was expectant and a little wounded, as if she was waiting for Anna to apologize for shouting at her the other day. Anna watched her mother in silence, aware of how uncomfortable Karen was at being monkey-in-the middle. Then Karen took charge of Lily, lifted her up, and carried her into the living room with a book. Cecilie suddenly looked ill-at-ease, as if she sensed that something was wrong.

"I know everything, Mom," Anna said in a thick voice.

Cecilie blinked again.

"Sorry, what?"

"I know you had postpartum depression when I was born. I know you couldn't take care of me, that you didn't feed me properly. I know my name used to be Sara, because Dad loved that name; I know he took care of me as best he could. I know you came home from the hospital when I was nearly a year old, and I know you didn't want anyone to ever know you had been ill. I know everything."

Cecilie's jaw dropped.

"I also know you love me," Anna continued. "That you try to make up for it every day. I know you love Lily more than anything, and I know you're afraid I will fail her, as you failed me. I think you got scared when Thomas left and I was so distraught I could barely take care of her. I hit rock bottom, and you thought history might repeat itself. You were afraid I might hurt Lily, like you hurt me."

Cecilie had said nothing. Now she gasped for air and let out a dry, agonizing howl.

"But I'm not you, Mom," Anna said, gently. "I'm Anna Bella, and I've never been ill way you were. True, I struggled . . . I felt angry and impotent because Thomas had abandoned us. But I was never ill, and I have never failed Lily." Anna fixed Cecilie with her eyes. She stepped forward, took Cecilie's hand, and pulled her toward her. Cecilie was rigid with fear and resisted, but Anna kept hugging her.

"What happened was bad, Mom," she said into Cecilie's hair. "But it happened. I can live with it. Now that I finally know," she added. "Lily loves you. You're her granny. But don't try to protect her from something that has nothing to do with us." Anna grabbed her mother's shoulders.

"Do you understand what I'm saying?" she said, firmly.

Cecilie's face dissolved. She still hadn't uttered a word. She nodded. Anna embraced her again.

When Cecilie composed herself, Anna kissed her daughter and Karen good-bye, gave Cecilie another hug, and left.

Anna opened the door to the Vertebrate Collection, stepped into the twilight and called out. "Dr. Tybjerg, where are you? I need to talk to you."

She was impatient and when she heard a noise coming from the far end of the room, she marched directly toward it. Suddenly he appeared in front of her, just like the last time. Dark-eyed and surrounded by shadows.

"Why are you shouting?" he asked.

"Why did you blackmail Professor Helland?"

Dr. Tybjerg's eyes widened. He didn't look like he intended to give her an answer.

Anna leaned toward him and, very calmly, said, "I ought to suspect you, you know."

"Of what?" he said, genuinely surprised.

"Of killing Helland. You're the only one I can think of who actually has a motive. You were Helland's crown prince, and now the king is dead."

"That's utter garbage," Dr. Tybjerg said. "Lars was my friend."

He retreated into the darkness. Anna followed him.

"But you were blackmailing him?"

"The two things aren't remotely connected," he said. "One is about science, about research; the other is about friendship. Friendship and science are two irreconcilable entities. Lars would have done the same, he said. Everyone puts pressure on you. That's just how it is. Desperate times call for desperate measures. And the times are truly desperate." Dr. Tybjerg gave her a fraught look.

"But *why*? Seven thousand kroner a month for three years. That's serious money."

Dr. Tybjerg momentarily looked stunned, then he shrugged.

"To fund my research. I've already said so." He took another step into the dark and Anna pursued him.

"How did you blackmail him? Come on, help me out here."

Dr. Tybjerg shrugged again.

"I discovered Lars had an illegitimate son. His name's Asger."

Asger. The name rang a bell.

"Asger used to be my friend, but not even Asger knew he was Helland's son. It was a scandal. Or rather, it would have been had it become known that Professor Helland had had an affair with one of his students. She was a nineteen-year-old undergraduate and Helland was her tutor. Asger's mother hasn't told her son who his father is." Dr. Tybjerg suddenly looked horrified at Anna. "Asger attended lectures given by his own father and he never knew, can you imagine? Asger and I aren't friends anymore. He changed when he lost his job. Grew strange. He used to be good. The best. He was a coleopterologist; still is, I suppose. He sailed through his studies. His PhD was approved, he wrote his doctoral thesis, the whole shebang in record time. He was the youngest staff member in a tiny department whose elderly professor was about to retire, leaving the Chair vacant for Asger. The future looked bright. And do you know what happened then? The Faculty Council closed the department. They claimed they had sent Asger a letter, but it somehow had gotten lost. We were still friends then. When he came back after the summer break, ready to start a new term, to teach and research, the department was no longer there. The end. Terribly sorry, et cetera . . ."

"How did you find out Asger was Helland's son?"

Dr. Tybjerg looked torn, then he sighed and continued.

"Asger's mother is a professor here, but she works in a different department. One day I saw her with Helland. They were having an argument, which was clearly personal. It happened in a corner right by the entrance, and I watched them from the stairs, unnoticed. It sounded like Asger's mother was threatening Helland—she was very angry. At the time, I had just finished my PhD and my dream was to research, but I wasn't entirely sure how to go about it. I don't know what prompted me, but shortly afterward I dropped a hint to Helland. We were working together—over there, as it happens—by those long desks, and it was a chance shot. Turned out to be a bull's eye. I could see it in his face. He went pale, and his reaction told me I had stumbled onto something much bigger than I had initially suspected. I brought up the subject every time we met, until he asked me outright to keep quiet. I agreed, of course. Shortly afterward I was given an office in the basement. Helland arranged it. Remember, I wasn't demanding astronomical sums of cash and all sorts of perks. However, I could see how government cuts were affecting us, we were all hanging on by the skin of our teeth and I feared redundancy. I have devoted my life to reaching this level of expertise, and there's no way I'm joining a retraining program for the unemployed." He sounded outraged now. "So I suppose you could say I twisted Helland's arm a little. But like I said, we struck a deal. I did him a favor by keeping quiet, and he did me a favor by sending work my way. I got a small office, one that no one else wanted, and an invitation to join in his research. That's why we did so many things together, papers, posters, and research proposals. But it wasn't the only reason. It was killing two birds with one stone, see? We worked within the same field, and together we made a strong team. One of the strongest in the world. Over time, my arm twisting faded into the background."

"Why didn't Helland want it known that Asger was his son?"

"Well, why do you think? Number one, he would have been fired on the spot, and number two, his wife would have been less than thrilled."

"Who is Asger's mother? Do I know her?"

"Possibly. Her name is Hanne Moritzen; she's a parasitologist. She has an office on the ground floor."

You could have knocked Anna down with a feather.

"She's his mother?"

"Yes," Tybjerg said. "Asger's mother is Professor Moritzen."

"Why do you think that?" she said in disbelief.

"You don't think Asger would know his own mother?"

"But I know her," Anna said, vehemently. "She doesn't have children. She always said she never had children!"

"Then she was lying," Dr. Tybjerg declared.

Anna was at a total loss. Hanne had a son with Professor Helland. Anna was only distracted for a second, but Tybjerg managed to retreat so far into the darkness that he vanished. Anna heard the sound of his shoes, heard him mutter something, and then the rattling of a cupboard door. She stared into space, stunned.

"I have to go," she muttered to herself.

Anna left the Vertebrate Collection and let herself into the museum. Her heart was pounding and she was starting to have second thoughts. Should she have told Søren what she had discovered? Was her plan too dangerous, after all?

Then she spotted Troels. He was waiting for her in the doorway to the Mammoth Room. He touched the artificial glacier with trepidation and withdrew his hand in wonder. He wasn't wearing a jacket and had stuffed his wool hat into his back pocket. His auburn hair fell in skillfully cut locks across his forehead.

Anna's breathing quickened as she watched him, her weapon safe in her pocket. When she had managed to calm down, she approached him and gently put her hand on his back. He turned around.

"Hello again, Anna," he said. His eyes were flickering.

"Come on, let's go," she said, softly.

Slowly, without speaking, they drifted through the exhibition. They even stopped in front of some exhibits before ending up in the Sperm Whale Room, where they found a bench. A group of noisy kids shuffled their feet, waiting impatiently for headsets to be passed around. Anna and Troels sat close together.

Anna said, "What have you done?" and turned to him.

"I didn't mean to."

Anna gasped.

"What happened?" she whispered.

"I fell in love with him," he confessed.

"With Johannes?" Anna raised her eyebrows and, for a moment, her horror gave way to confusion. "But Johannes wasn't gay . . . he . . ."

"I know," Troels replied, quietly. "But I was still in love with him."

"So what happened?" Anna probed.

"We met at the Red Mask. I went there with a couple of guys I don't actually know very well. I had never been there before, but I liked the place. I noticed Johannes almost immediately. He was standing at the bar, looking amazing. He wasn't actually very handsome, was he? But he outshone everyone and made us all laugh. He was surrounded by people. I moved closer and we started talking. I drank some more beer—I had already had too many. We talked for a long time, and I struggled to keep up." Troels looked embarrassed. "He spoke about complex subjects, gestured with his hands, touched my shoulder, stabbed his finger into my chest, ruffled my hair. For a new acquaintance he was very physical, and I lapped it up. I've been on the gay scene for years," he smiled, "where, usually, quick physical contact equals sex, and I thought . . . he wore a leather skirt, fishnet tights, and army boots. Johannes, however, spoke about everything but sex that night. He talked endlessly about the theory of science, which didn't really interest me. But *he* mesmerized me. He seemed completely indifferent to how other people perceived him, waved his arms around whenever he felt like it. Take me or leave me. That was why he was a magnet, of course. I've always admired people like that.

"At dawn, we left together and walked to Enghave Plads. He hugged me and said it had been great to meet me, that he would like to see me again."

"Johannes wasn't gay," Anna protested. Troels looked away.

"We met a few days later. I couldn't get him out of my head. He invited me to dinner at his apartment; we drank wine. I was totally confused. He sent out such contradictory signals and in the end, I asked him outright. I said I was very attracted to him; I wanted to have sex with him. He said he wasn't gay. At first, I got angry. I felt he had strung me along. With the wine, the meal, and the ridiculous clothes he was wearing. But then I realized there was more to it. He wasn't gay, but . . ." Troels hesitated.

"He wanted me to . . . humiliate him. Sexually, but without us touching. I was allowed to hit him and to verbally abuse him, but I must never touch his dick. He got off on being humiliated. He had tried it with women, but it wasn't really working for him. So that's what we did that night. I've tried something like that before, but never anything that real. I lived in the US for years and I was a part of that scene, going to S&M clubs, I've been the dominant one in all my relationships, the aggressor. But with Johannes it was . . . so hot. Because it was new for him. Because I was the first." He glanced shyly at Anna who was sitting very still, staring at the sperm whale on the wall. The noisy children had gone, and a family of four had arrived. The father lifted up the younger boy.

"I hit him, and . . . no, it doesn't matter. He masturbated until he climaxed. Obviously I wanted to touch him, but every time I tried, he turned away. He didn't want me. In the end, I was deeply frustrated. I wanted to have sex with him. I tried, but the magic disappeared. Johannes got upset, went into another room, and told me he was disappointed in me. That it wasn't what we had agreed. I apologized, but it was no good. He just wanted me to leave. Get out, get out, he whispered. Very quietly, as if I had failed him. So I left. In the days that followed I was beside myself. He was all I could think about. I e-mailed him, but he never replied. On the goth scene I'm known as YourGuy." Troels peered at Anna. "Most people on the scene have aliases. It's part of the game. It suited me just fine. Copenhagen is a very small town. And I've just come back from abroad and, to be honest, I'm scared shitless of ending up on the front page of the tabloids. 'Supermodel into S&M' or something like that. I'm actually quite famous in the US," he added, "but getting work back here, when I returned last spring, was really tough. But finally I was about to land a huge campaign, a well-paying one, so I preferred going to places where no one cared who I really was. Anyway, Johannes never replied, and I was getting desperate. Then we bumped into each other, accidentally, in a café. He seemed pleased to see me. As though he had forgotten what had gone wrong during our last meeting. He had been busy, that was all. We agreed to meet again, the next day.

"That night I realized the two of you knew each other. He had mentioned you several times that first evening. Anna, my colleague; Anna, the woman I share a study with, without me making the connection. But when we met again, he referred to you as 'Anna Bella,' and it clicked that it had to be you. I knew where you lived, and I had meant to get in touch ever since I moved to Copenhagen. Only I was too ashamed. Ashamed I had run away back then. Your parents . . ." Troels shook his head. "I heard from them for years. They had my address in New York, and they wrote faithfully to me every Christmas and on my birthday. Your mom even sent me an advent calendar one year. They urged me to get in touch if ever I came back to Denmark." He laughed bitterly. "And I never replied. When I moved to Copenhagen, I thought it would be easier to get ahold of Karen first. I missed you the most, but . . . Christ, how you freaked out at me that night." For a moment, he looked at her with tenderness.

"So much that you were afraid you might beat me up?" Anna asked. She felt her anger rise through her shock. It wiped the smile off Troels's face.

"I don't know why you had to humiliate me," he said. "You were just as bad as my dad that night. You kicked me, Anna. You hit me and you screamed. And group sex was a seriously shitty idea. Whose was it?"

"Yours and Karen," Anna snapped. "You and Karen got the idea, and . . ." and the words spilled out of her. "You were always trying to shut me out. You became Karen's best friend just to hurt me. And it was the same that night. I might as well not have been there. And my parents favored you. Poor Troels, he's such a nice kid, we'll take good care of lovely, little Troels," she mimicked. Troels stared at Anna in amazement.

"Anna," he said softly. "I've always loved you more. Karen is my friend, she's straightforward and uncomplicated. She always was. You had everything I wanted. I worshipped you and I loved your parents. I wanted to live with you, always, be with you always. But there were times I thought you hated me. That night, I thought you hated me. And I couldn't cope with anymore hatred. I wanted to shut you up, and that's why I ran. The week before I had knocked out all my dad's teeth, for fuck's sake. With a wood plank. He told everyone he had forgotten to wear his seatbelt and had had to brake hard. But it was me. He shut me in the basement and said the most awful things to me, provoked me, baited me, called me queer. Finally, I ripped a shelf off the wall and bashed him across the face with it. I couldn't take being hated anymore, do you understand? And I was scared of how I might react that night. Really terrified. I've thought about it hundreds of times since. How jealous you must have been. You were an only child and always landed on your feet, always, born with a fucking silver spoon in your mouth, and then I come along like the serpent in paradise. By the way, I never understood what your parents saw in me. Since they already had you," he added. "But . . ." He fell silent.

"You know nothing about me," Anna said, quietly. Troels stared ahead with a blank expression, as if he hadn't heard her.

"During that evening I realized Johannes was in love with you. He talked about you all the time. Not directly . . . but he would mention your name, no matter what the conversation was about. I would ask questions, from time to time, as though you interested me and he answered them willingly. Very quickly I knew most of it: you had been dumped by your boyfriend, Thomas, who never visited your young daughter, never sent Christmas presents, and only paid basic child support—even though he was a doctor and you were a student—you struggled with your rage; you felt completely powerless; you were about to get your masters; Cecilie had moved to Copenhagen, and your relationship with her was strained. Johannes never found my questions odd—he was quite keen to talk about you. His eyes lit up. It was bizarre. I was madly in love with him, and he was madly in love with you." Troels smiled. "Seems to be my curse. You get everything I want.

"That night," he continued, "I crossed the line. Johannes wanted a repeat of last time. Wanted me to abuse him verbally, humiliate him, and slap him. Mostly on his body, but also across his head. He masturbated while I did it, but flinched whenever I tried to touch him. I could do the same, he said. Get my dick out and have a tug. I didn't want to. I was delirious, a bit drunk and in love. And I was the stronger; I was in charge. I managed to enter him. I held him down. For fuck's sake, I only lasted five seconds. I came inside him, and he went berserk. He cried; he screamed and threw me out. On the fetish scene this is a total no-no," Troels muttered, ashamed. "You go right up to the line, but you never cross it without the other person's consent. Johannes asked me to stop many times that night, but I didn't listen.

"The days that followed were terrible. I called him. I e-mailed. He didn't reply. It took a week before I got ahold of him. He sounded really pissed off with me. I had crossed the line, he said. It was unacceptable. The rules had been crystal clear. We were experimenting with the balance of power, but there was to be no direct sexual contact. I had agreed to that. I had broken our deal. He never wanted to see me again.

"Some weeks passed. I met with Karen, twice. I told her I was in love, but that it wasn't reciprocated. She consoled me." Troels smiled. "And we talked about you. I asked her if she thought we might be friends again. You and I. The three of us. Asked her how you were. She became a little subdued. Then she told me the two of you hadn't kept in touch, either. That really surprised me. But she had met Cecilie, and Cecilie had told her you were alone with your daughter. You had had a rough time, Cecilie said, but she made no effort to conceal she and Jens were enormously relieved Thomas was out of your lives. They never liked him. He was highly intelligent, but shallow. That's how Cecilie had put it. They worried about you, Karen said, and they helped take care of your daughter, Lily. I would like to meet her someday," he smiled.

"Karen suggested we get in touch with you, but Cecilie asked us to wait until you had defended your dissertation, so we agreed to meet afterward. Karen was wildly excited about our plan. She was missing us so much, she said. Her joy inspired me. One day, I visited Cecilie and had tea with her. It was a lovely afternoon. I apologized for my years of silence, but Cecilie said it didn't matter. I told her I had had a hard time and asked her not to mention to you that I had been there. I said I wanted it to be a surprise, but really . . . I was scared you would get angry again. Jealous and angry. That we would end up back where we started. I wanted to establish some ground rules with you. You must never humiliate me again. I can't take it. In return, I would keep a low profile, as far as your parents were concerned—if that was what you wanted.

"I also went to see Jens. I waited for him outside his office, saw him come out. He had aged, I thought, he looked withered and gray. I followed him home, but I chickened out. So I got in touch with my sister instead. Karen's joy, Cecilie's open arms . . . I got carried away and called my sister. She was as cold as ice. "Don't you ever call me again," she said. "Don't ever come near me or my children, or I'll call the police." He smiled, embarrassed. "My dad and I fought when he was in the hospital, terminally ill with cancer; I smashed a vase across his head, and he threw a drawer at me. My sister always got so upset when we fought." His smile started to fade. "At his funeral, six days later, I still had seven stitches in my forehead from the drawer he'd hurled. I don't know how he got the strength. He was weak and dying. I still have a scar." Troels turned to Anna and ran his finger along a thin white line.

"It never occurred to my sister to ask if I was all right. She refused to sit next to me at the funeral. She and her family sat on the opposite pew. Afterward, she came up to me and said if I ever contacted her again, she would have me charged with assault. Our dad was eaten up by cancer, but according to her logic, I had killed him with a vase." For a moment Troels looked exasperated.

"When I called my sister that evening to attempt a reconciliation, it soon became clear she had no intention of forgiving me. When I hung up, I had a small breakdown. I was thinking about Johannes all the time; I was scared of what I had done, scared he might file charges against me, and all the while I just wanted to be with him. Karen suspected nothing. We met a couple of times; we had coffee and Karen chatted away about the great reunion that was to come. Suddenly, I had to see you. It seemed to be the only right thing to do. Perhaps you could speak to Johannes . . . I don't know what I had imagined. I waited for you—twice. Found your address online and got into your building, hoping you would be there. I deliberately didn't call you first, because I didn't want you to turn me away. I was convinced that if only I could speak to you, everything would be all right again. I chickened out both times. One time I panicked. The woman below you came up to check on your daughter. I found out you had gone for a run. She left the door open, and I followed her in. I sat down and pretended to be an old friend. She threw me out. Told me I had to wait outside. She gave me such a hostile and suspicious look, her eyes flashed as if she had seen through me, caught me in the act. That's when I panicked. I ran down the stairs and suddenly I heard you come back. The door downstairs opened, you were out of breath, I could hear that it was you. You coughed. I hid in the meter box. You and your neighbor looked for me, as if I were a criminal, as if I were a danger to others." His voice sounded tired. "Just like when we were back at school, right? My dad had to be strict or he wouldn't be able to control me, he told my teachers. No, of course he didn't hit me. But he made himself clear, he assured them, he set boundaries. They understood that. They, too, had a job controlling me. Your parents were the only people who didn't buy the story.

"I curled up inside the meter box, and you walked right past me. When I heard your footsteps above, I got out and ran. I found myself in Vesterbro. In front of Johannes's building. I looked up at his windows. The light was on, and after a while Johannes appeared—he was on the phone. I stood outside for a while, then I knocked on his door. And when he answered it, I forced my way in. I had called him every day for two weeks, I had sent flowers, I had begged for his forgiveness, and sent him several e-mails. I had heard nothing from him.

"He was very scared when I got inside his apartment. I'm much bigger than he is, that's what made it so perfect between us. I got aroused. There was something in his eyes; I caught a glimpse of something in his eyes. He wants me to, I thought. He wants to be dominated, controlled, humiliated; at that moment everything became clear. He had tricked me, tricked me good." Troels's eyes shone now.

Anna carefully slipped her hand inside her pocket and shivered, as though she was cold.

"I closed the door behind me and unzipped my jeans. It was what he wanted. I felt so sure. He walked backward, just as he was supposed to. I held my dick, I rubbed it, while I ordered him to take off his clothes and told him to suck me off. He was good at acting scared, he got it just right. He resisted. I called him lots of names . . . and suddenly I came. All over my hand and the floor. I buckled, consumed by a deep urge to hug him, to snuggle up. I closed my eyes for a second and when I looked at him again, he was armed. I don't know where he got it from, but he was holding a knife. His eyes grew black. I said something. I raised my hands. 'You mustn't threaten me,' I said. I wanted him to calm down, but he attacked me. Waved the knife in the air, stabbing at me. I tried to warn him, told him to put down the knife, to stop. His tenderness was gone, as was the fragility, which I loved about him. His voice had changed, too. It was dark and strange. He wouldn't stop. He came closer to me wielding the knife and ordered me to leave. He screamed in a high-pitched voice, I felt drops of spit on my cheek." Troels glanced at Anna.

"This time I didn't run. I wanted him to shut up. He had to shut up." Troels fell silent.

Anna got hold of one of the cable ties in her pocket and curled it up so it lay like a coiled snake in her hand. She pretended she wanted to change position and leaned forward. Her heart was pounding.

"Afterward I visited Jens," Troels said, casually. "I don't know how I got there, but suddenly I found myself in front of his building, without my jacket, my trousers soaked. All I could think was that I was about to be arrested. I wanted to talk to Jens first. Just talk to him. So we talked. For hours. I calmed down a little; I thought it possible that Johannes mightn't have been seriously hurt. Did I even hit him? I started to have doubts. Jens poured me a whiskey, he lent me some clothes. You've got great parents, Anna."

Anna nodded.

"They're very fond of you, too," she said, kindly.

"I'm leaving soon and I won't be coming back. I don't want to go to jail." He laughed a brittle laugh. "I've been in prison all my life."

"Why did you text me?" Anna wanted to know.

"Do you know what a big thing it was to me that we had a falling out? Massive. I didn't want to leave without seeing you first. I wanted to unburden myself, tell you I didn't mean to do it. Not then, not now. I don't think you'll betray me again," he said. "I don't think you'll get up now and betray me again." He smiled a crooked smile. "I think you've changed. Your little girl. I must meet her sometime."

"I knew you did it."

"Yes, I'm impressed." He smiled again. "I thought it would take you longer. What did I write?"

"That you were trying to tell me something," Anna replied. "It was the way you phrased it. But that's not why. It was when you mentioned Johannes by name. When we met last Friday. You knew his name. You pretended that Karen had told you." Anna turned to Troels and her eyes glowed yellow. "But Karen didn't know his name. So how could you? Suddenly, it all made sense. You waiting for me; you showing up everywhere. Karen met you, Jens met you, and so did Cecilie, apparently. And Johannes's stalker. . . . At first I thought it was a girl, but when the police told me they were looking for a man . . . YourGuy. That was one coincidence too many."

Troels gave Anna a rather drowsy look.

"Did he really say that?" he said, dully. "That I was stalking him?" Anna leaned toward her friend.

"And you're right. I won't betray you again," she said, softly into his ear. Troels turned to face her. His eyes were shiny.

"I'm sorry about Johannes," he whispered. "I love him. I hope he gets better. I hope he's not too upset."

"He's dead, Troels," Anna said, gently. "Johannes is dead."

Troels stared vacantly at her, then he turned away and Anna knew he was about to leave. This was the moment when she mustn't betray him.

It only took ten seconds. She rested her full weight on his arm, blocking his view with her body, then she slipped the cable tie over his arm, looped it around a slat, and clicked it shut. He grunted, not realizing why she was lying across him. She pulled hard, he yanked back his arm, "What the hell are you doing?" Shit, she was too late, someone screamed. It wasn't until she found herself on the floor three feet away, dazed and brandishing the screwdriver, that she discovered she was the one who was screaming. Troels thrashed about and tried to stand up. The bench groaned ominously. Anna gasped for air. The loop was tight, but Troels pulled at it. He shouted. Called her names. Threatened her. "I'll kill you," he screamed. "I'll kill your kid." People came running. The loop started to give. The plastic stretched white. She returned to him. He lashed out at her with his free arm, kicked her. Punched her on the side on her head. She saw stars. She forced herself to focus and slithered under the bench, where she looped the second cable tie around his arm, pulled it through the back of the bench, and tightened it. He lashed out again, stabbing a bent index finger against her temple, a direct hit. His arm started to go red. Anna rolled out of reach. His whole arm was tethered to the bench now. A crowd had gathered. "What's going on?" someone shouted. Anna got out her cell, her hands were shaking. He answered it immediately.

"Søren," Anna said. "Help me."

*   *   *

Anna left the museum before the police arrived and ran down Jag-tvejen, where she jumped on a bus. She was incandescent with rage when she rang Hanne Moritzen's doorbell.

"Why is everyone lying to me?" she yelled when Hanne had let her in. Anna stamped her feet. Then she saw the look on Hanne's face.

"Why did you lie about having a son?" she continued, somewhat appeased. "With Professor Helland! It makes no sense. Why didn't you tell me?"

They were in the large white hall, the door to the living room was ajar, and Anna could see a white, comfortable sofa and a brass dish with polished seashells. Suddenly, Hanne slumped to her knees. She grabbed Anna's hands, pressed them against her face, and the noise that erupted from her throat cut Anna to the quick. Shocked, Anna helped her into the living room. They sat down on the sofa and Anna let Hanne cling to her, realizing how close she was to solving the mystery. When Hanne had calmed down, she told Anna about her son.

"It's my fault," she said. "I thought if I buried it, it would go away. It's all my fault."

Anna didn't contradict her.

They spoke for almost two hours. At the end, Hanne asked Anna to go to the police.

"I can't report my own son," she whispered. When Anna had agreed, Hanne asked, "Would you like to see a picture of him?"

Anna nodded and Hanne fetched a box full of photographs. Anna had expected a recent photograph of the Asger Moritzen who apparently worked three floors above his mother, whom Anna must surely have passed in the corridors at the institute or might even have had as her dissection tutor on an Introductory Morphology course. But the box Hanne brought out contained pictures of Asger as a child. Photos of a smiling dark-eyed toddler with his mouth open, shiny saliva dribbling down his chin and a stripy rattle in his chubby hand; winter pictures of a child in a snowsuit with open and inquisitive eyes, like blotting paper, completely unspoiled.

"I have to get back to Lily," she whispered.

Hanne and Anna said good-bye in the doorway. Hanne refused to let go of her.

"I'll be there for you, I promise," Anna said.

Hanne smiled feebly and released Anna's hands.

"I'll call the police when I get back," she went on, "and you'll take it from there, okay?"

Hanne Moritzen nodded.

Anna walked down Falkoner Allé, crossed Jagtvejen, and went around the National Archives. She felt relieved and calm.

She unlocked the entrance door and for a moment she stared into the darkness, her hand on the door handle, then she opened the door and walked up the stairs. She could hear singing from a children's television program and something that sounded like an exuberant child bouncing up and down.

It was nearly over. All she had left to do was to meet with Professor Freeman tomorrow.

CHAPTER 17

When Søren arrived at the Natural History Museum, Anna had vanished. He had been driving to Copenhagen when she called and his blood had turned to ice.

"*Help me,*" she had said. He could hear her breathing heavily. "*My friend Troels killed Johannes. He's here. In the Whale Room at the museum. I've tied him to a bench. But I have to go now.*" Then she had hung up. Søren called Bellahøj police station for backup and accelerated. A patrol car with two officers reached the museum at the same time as him. He told them what little he knew as they raced up the stairs. "The Whale Room?" he shouted to the young woman behind the counter. She pointed dutifully to the elevator. When they reached the fourth floor, they ran through the foyer and into a large room. A whale was mounted on the wall, several people had gathered and it was mayhem.

Søren pushed through the crowd. The man he had seen on the poster outside Magasin was sitting on a bench. He must be Troels. Søren was astonished. Troels was pulling and yanking his left arm, which was tied to the back of the bench. His wrist was bleeding, and he snorted like a wild animal.

"Sit still," Søren ordered him. Troels refused.

"Sit! Still!" Søren thundered.

Troels turned his head and sent Søren a furious stare. His eyes were bloodshot. Then, with all the strength he could muster, he kicked Søren's shin with his boot. Søren hobbled out of the way and let his colleagues take over.

"Now calm down," one of them said. The other cut the cable ties and handcuffed Troels.

"What's your name, apart from Troels?" Søren said, amicably, limping closer.

"Not fucking telling you, pig." Troels scowled.

"Where is Anna?" Søren asked him instead. Troels's eyes flashed.

"I'll kill her when I see her."

"Of course you will," Søren said, humoring him. "It's 3:22 p.m. and I'm arresting you and charging you with . . . assaulting a police officer." Søren was aware that his colleagues were looking at him, but he ignored them. In a few hours, when he had more information, he would charge Troels with Johannes's murder.

"You do not have to say anything, but it may harm your defense if you do not mention when questioned something that you may later rely on in court. Anything you do say may be given in evidence," he added. The light in Troels's eyes changed; he opened and closed his mouth, then he accepted the situation. "Take him to the station," Søren ordered his colleagues. "I'll follow shortly."

Søren went through the museum, but Anna was nowhere to be found. He called her several times with only a minute's interval, but she didn't reply. Finally, he left a message telling her he wasn't prepared to run around the museum looking for her and expected her to call him as soon as possible. He thanked her for making a citizen's arrest and requested a proper explanation. As soon as possible, he emphasized.

At five thirty Søren still hadn't heard from Anna. He sat in his office debating his options. He had spent two hours trying to get Troels to tell him his surname. Troels refused. In the end, Søren had telephoned Stella Marie Frederiksen. She was visiting friends, but agreed to take a taxi to the police station. She spent fifteen minutes there, looked at Troels through a one-way mirror and confirmed that it was him. No doubt about it. She also provided Søren with a guest list for the Red Mask on September 7. Troels's full name would be on it. Søren scanned it but was none the wiser. There were two guests by the name of Troels. One called Vedsegaard, the other Nielsen. He scratched his head and looked at the clock.

Tick tock.

He ate a sandwich.

He wrote a report.

He stared out into the darkness, but couldn't see past his own reflection.

When Anna finally returned his call, his nerves were twitching.

"Where are you?" he practically shouted when she said her name.

"At home now," she said, calmly. Søren relaxed.

"It's Vedsegaard," Anna confirmed, glumly, in response to Søren's question. "He was my best friend . . . when I was little. I promise to explain it all another time. I'm sorry for running off."

Søren underlined the name *Troels Vedsegaard*.

"He confessed," Anna said.

"I assumed so, since you arrested him." Søren couldn't help smiling. "You need to be at the station tomorrow morning at ten." A pause followed.

"I have something else for you," she said.

"Aha?"

"I know who infected Professor Helland with *Taenia solium*."

Total silence now.

"Are you there?" Anna said.

"What did you say?"

"I know who infected Lars Helland."

"Who?"

"His name is Asger Moritzen. He is Lars Helland and Hanne Moritzen's son. His address is 12 Glasvej, northwest Copenhagen. Dr. Tybjerg revealed the link. He has been friends with Asger since they were undergraduates. Asger used to work at the university, but was laid off when his department was closed. Dr. Tybjerg told me Asger had no idea that Professor Helland was his father. Tybjerg discovered it by chance and was blackmailing Helland with the knowledge. When Asger finally found out, he became very odd and distant. Tybjerg said they're not friends anymore."

Søren tried to break all this information into bite-size pieces.

"Go on," he said, brusquely.

"I spent almost two hours with Professor Moritzen today. That's why I couldn't wait for you and I didn't answer my cell. I had to see her. Hanne is my friend, and she lied. She has a son! I was really angry when I got there, but she . . . she told me everything. She has known all weekend that Asger killed Helland. She wanted to go to the police, but . . . mothers and their children," Anna suddenly burst out. "Mothers will do anything to protect their children."

Søren was about to say something when she continued.

"I promised Hanne you'll take good care of him when you pick him up. Asger's mentally frail, but not dangerous, she assured me. I think he's mostly scared."

Søren swallowed.

"So you know where Dr. Tybjerg is?" he said.

"Yes," Anna said. "I've known all the time. Sorry."

"Why didn't you tell me?" Søren said, angrily.

"Dr. Tybjerg is on the verge of a breakdown, so I couldn't run the risk. I want to have my dissertation defense next Monday. I have to get it over and done with. I have a three-year-old daughter. I have to become her mother again."

"So where is he?" Søren said, appeased.

"I'll tell you later." Anna's voice was calm. "Tomorrow. But I can't be with you at ten. There's something I have to do first. I'll be there at one. And now I've got to go."

"Anna, I demand to know where Dr. Tybjerg is!"

"Trust me."

And she was gone.

Søren sat at his desk, staring at the telephone.

*   *   *

Søren went to visit Professor Moritzen.

"Come in," she said, hoarsely, buzzing him in. She was wearing a soft gray outfit and was waiting for him in the doorway when he came up the stairs. Her hair was wet as though she had just had a shower.

They sat down in the living room. Like her vacation cottage, her apartment was carefully furnished, limited to bamboo and white, broken only by splashes of bright red and orange. Professor Moritzen perched on the edge of the sofa and waited for Søren to begin.

"I'm here because Anna Bella Nor called me an hour ago and told me—"

"I asked her to call you," Professor Moritzen interrupted him.

"So you suspect your son, Asger Moritzen, infected Professor Helland with parasites?" he said.

She nodded.

"And the late Lars Helland was your son's biological father?"

She nodded again.

"Why do you think your son infected his father with parasites?" Søren wondered if Professor Moritzen was mentally ill. Did she even have a son or was she making it all up?

"Asger told me last Thursday," she said. "He was very scared, but he felt better after telling me. When will you be picking him up?" She looked beseechingly at Søren. "Asger is very delicate. You can't just barge in on him. You need to go there, alone, and talk to him. You won't just barge in, will you?" she repeated. "He has dangerous bugs and reptiles in there," she added.

"In his apartment?" Søren frowned.

"Yes, he has tanks full of them," she replied. "So, are you going to get him?"

"When did you last speak with him?"

"Perhaps you could just let me tell you the whole story," she said.

CHAPTER 18

"Asger's a good boy," she said and didn't seem to have heard his question. "Please don't hurt him. He didn't mean to kill Lars. . . . The silly boy thought he had given his father a tapeworm. A tapeworm! He just wanted to annoy him a little, but he didn't mean to kill him, of course he didn't. But you don't get a tapeworm from eating a piece of one! And you don't get a tapeworm infection from eating its eggs, either! Stupid boy." Her voice became shrill. "I'm a parasitologist, and my own son commits such a howler. And he's a biologist, too." Professor Moritzen looked mortified.

"At least you know where the 2,600 cysticerci came from," she added, dryly. "From my silly boy. Of course, I wondered how Asger got ahold of the material, and I've discovered that. . . . There was one weekend in May when my keys went missing and I had to use my spare set. My keys reappeared and I thought nothing of it. Asger had let himself into my lab and took the tapeworm from the in-vitro supply. I honestly believed I knew precisely how many specimens I have. After all, I count them. But he had only taken one and when I checked, it seemed to add up to me." She gestured apologetically. "I have samples in cold storage, for dissection, and I have living specimens, which are kept in artificial conditions, like the ones found in the small intestines. At least he had been smart enough to take a living specimen, but his knowledge stopped there," she said bitterly. "That Monday he went to the department of Cell Biology and Comparative Zoology to have lunch with Professor Ewald in her office across from the senior common room. They know each other from a project when Asger was still an undergraduate. At some point, Asger went to fetch some salt, and while he was in the senior common room he opened the fridge and placed the tapeworm segment in Lars's lunch."

"How did he know the food belonged to Lars Helland?" Søren interjected.

Professor Moritzen sighed.

"The stupid idiot had planned it all down to the last detail. He had gone to the senior common room twice the previous week. On both occasions, he had found an empty cool bag with the initials L.H. and once when Asger passed the senior common room, he had seen Lars eat leftovers from it. He was very careful. He certainly didn't want to infect Professor Jørgensen or Professor Ewald. Asger was angry. I told him Lars Helland was his father shortly after I was told I would be laid off. I had always told Asger he was the result of a one-night stand and that I knew nothing about his father. But I was in love with Lars and got pregnant by him during my second year as an undergraduate. Lars was already married to Birgit, and he was shocked when I confronted him. He told me he didn't believe the child was his. But I knew it was. We reached an impasse and people started talking. Someone had seen us together, and now I was pregnant. Lars got completely paranoid and offered me money. He would have been fired on the spot had it become known that he had got an undergraduate pregnant. I accepted his offer. I moved to Århus and had Asger. Lars bought us an apartment on the condition that I signed a document stating he wasn't Asger's father. I listed my son's father as 'unknown,' and, to be honest, I forgot all about him. I was twenty years old, I lived in Århus, and was busy with my studies and my little boy. I met other men. Do you want some tea?"

Søren nodded and Professor Moritzen disappeared into the kitchen. Shortly afterward, she returned with a small bowl with steaming contents, which she handed to Søren. She sat down on the sofa and blew carefully into her own bowl.

"After all those years why did you decide to tell Asger that Professor Helland was his father?"

Professor Moritzen heaved another sigh.

"Asger grew up without a father, but it was never a problem. When he turned nineteen, he decided he wanted to study biology. To begin with, I was dead set against it. An academic career isn't for the faint of heart. It's one long uphill struggle. For money, for recognition, for elbow room. I genuinely doubted if Asger was cut out for it. He's a loner, wary and ultra-sensitive. But he was adamant. He had followed my work his whole life, and when he wanted a butterfly net for Christmas and an aquarium for his birthday that's what he got. I don't know why I expected anything else." She shook her head. "In 1998 I applied for the post of professor of parasitology at the University of Copenhagen, never thinking for one minute I would get it. But halfway through the summer break, I got a phone call. The job was mine. Less than a week later Asger got a letter. He was offered a place to read biology at the University of Copenhagen. That summer we moved. I sold the apartment in Århus and bought two apartments with the money; this one and the one Asger lives in, on Glasvej.

"Asger began his studies and the same week, I spotted Lars. Of course, it had crossed my mind he might still be working there, and yet I was genuinely shocked. It was nineteen years since we had last met, and there had been no contact in between. It was almost four months before we met. Odd, really, given his office was only two floors above mine. It happened just before Christmas. The strange thing was that he appeared pleased to see me. He ran up to me from behind, twirled me around, and kept saying how marvelous it was. He had no idea what had become of me, if I had even graduated. Oh yes, I replied. From the University of Århus. He never mentioned our son, as though he had truly wiped from his memory that he had gotten me pregnant. At that moment, Asger appeared and Lars shook his hand.

"'This is Asger, my son,' I said. 'He's in his first year.' I stared at Lars, but his face gave nothing away. He simply pressed Asger's hand and welcomed him.

"Professionally, I got very busy. The field of parasitology was growing rapidly due to a government increase in foreign aid. The focus of public attention turned to bilharziasis, and I was made responsible for three huge research projects, two of which took place in Central Africa. Asger was happy. He cruised through his studies. I was pleased for him, but also rather concerned. He had no friends, and he never went out. It was all about studying and preparing for the next exam, and when he finally had time off he would tinker with his growing number of tanks, attend conferences, read, or collect insects. I tried encouraging him, but every time he smiled his silly smile. "People don't interest me, Mom," he said. "I'm a scientist like you." What troubled me the most was that he always said it with an element of complicity, as though he and I were the same. I didn't want to be someone with no friends because my work took up all my time. But the truth was this was precisely who I was.

"One day, Asger finally made a friend. Erik Tybjerg, Anna's external supervisor, would you believe it? Yes, you're thinking we're all as thick as thieves, and I suppose you're right." She laughed briefly. "Asger was writing his dissertation, and the two boys spent a lot of time together. Their friendship revolved around science, but all the same, it looked like a genuine friendship. Asger remained strangely content in the way he always was. Nothing upset him. If it hadn't been for all those As he got, I would have started thinking there was something wrong with him." She smiled. "But he's bright and knows everything about natural history. He knows practically nothing about anything else. I consoled myself that at least he seemed happy." She sighed, deeply, once more.

"One day I dropped by unannounced. I knew he was recovering from flu, I had bought some cakes and I wanted to surprise him. As I walked down the street, I tried to recall when I last visited him. One thing was for sure: it was too long ago, and in that moment, I felt so bad for not visiting him more often. Asger used to tease me and say 'My biologist mom is scared of bugs'—he thought it was hilarious. Of course I wasn't. But I didn't like them or what they represented."

"Which was?" Søren probed.

"Only nerds have tanks," Hanne said, bluntly. "You don't live with snakes and scorpions!" she scoffed. "I don't share my home with the parasites I work with, do I?"

Søren glanced around the austere apartment and suddenly he couldn't decide which was worse: bugs or loneliness?

"And every time I was confronted with that side of my son, I felt guilty. I desperately wanted him to have friends. Other young men he could go out with, run a half-marathon with, whatever, what do I know? And I wanted him to have a girlfriend. Live with her, so I could visit them on Sundays, and he could start a family one day. But if he managed to persuade a girl to come home with him, she would surely leave the moment she saw all his bugs and reptiles. At the time, I knew he kept a small nonpoisonous snake, four bird spiders, and some mysterious-looking, over-dimensioned stick insects. I made no attempt to disguise my disgust, but Asger merely laughed and said that was why children left home. I stopped bringing it up; we met mostly in my apartment and that's why so much time had passed.

"He was delighted to see me. He was wearing his dressing gown over his pajamas, his hair was tousled, and he was grinning from ear to ear. Everything was fine. I entered the hall and took off my coat. The air was stuffy, but that was understandable. He had been ill for three or four days. It was also a little dark, but I presumed he had just been asleep.

"Asger took my coat, put it on a hanger, and opened a built-in closet to put it away, when something fell out and hit his head. It was a bundle held together with string, and it appeared to contain clothing and shoes. Asger asked me to hold the hanger while he struggled to push the bundle back in the cupboard. When he managed to close it, he hung my jacket on a door handle instead and went to the kitchen to put the kettle on. I stayed in the hall and called out to ask him why it was so dark, but the water was running and if he replied, I didn't hear him. I switched on the hall light, and as the door to his bedroom was wide open, I entered and turned on the light.

"It took five seconds before I realized what I was looking at. He had three tanks. I was almost relieved, three isn't excessive and, at first glance, they appeared to be empty. Then the shock came: there were bundles of clothes everywhere. The first bundle had merely seemed strange, but this obsession with bundles worried me." Professor Moritzen looked hesitantly at Søren. He forgot to drink his tea. "His comforter, his pillow, and sheets were rolled into a bundle on his bed, and the bundle was held together with," she gulped, "the cord from my dressing gown I had been looking for for ages. Along the wall facing the street were another three bundles, one with books, two apparently stuffed with Asger's clothes—one was slightly open and over the buckle of a belt I could see the pair of expensive Fjällräven trousers I had given him for Christmas. Shoved under the bed was a bundle with what looked like a bathroom scale I had given him, and on a small desk in the corner, to the right of the window, was a bundle that appeared to contain an open laptop and next to it, smaller bundles. I was staring at them when I suddenly became convinced there was someone behind me. I could hear Asger whistle in the kitchen, hear cups clattering, so I knew it wasn't him. I spun around and, on the wall in front of me, Asger had mounted three shelves, as wide as floorboards, and they were filled with jars of insects in ethanol, small tanks with live bugs, Styrofoam sheets with skewered insects and butterflies, and numerous reference books on the anatomy and physiology of insects.

"I left the bedroom and went into the living room, which was pitch black. I sensed the window must be covered with a heavy curtain, and I hoped desperately it was because he had been napping. I yanked the curtain open, but the room stayed dark. That was when it dawned on me that the room was alive: Asger had transformed his living room into a terrarium.

"'I painted the window black recently,' he casually told me when he returned with the tea. 'The plumber came and he opened the curtains though I had expressly told him not to. My South Chilean tarantula was about to lay her eggs, and she can't tolerate daylight when she does that. Not at all. In their natural habitat, the female buries herself in the ground so the eggs are exposed only to moisture, cold, and darkness. That plumber ruined it.' He was angry. 'I haven't been able to make her lay eggs since.' He put the teapot and the cakes on a coffee table that I could only just detect the outlines of.

"'But I can switch on the light, if you want me to,' he said, and before I had time to reply he flicked the switch. He explained it was a special light that filtered out all the red beams. You can't read in it, but you can find your way around. He asked me if it was all right or whether I would rather sit in the kitchen.

"The living room now looked as if it was lit by twilight. The walls were covered with tanks from floor to ceiling.

"'Spiders?' I whispered.

"It turned out that he had seventy-two spiders, of which thirty-four were lethal, thirty-nine scorpions, all lethal, four venomous snakes, as well as cockroaches, mice, and crickets for food. He explained it all very cheerfully. Along the wall to the left were more bundles. Books, binders, science journals, and CDs would be my guess.

"I asked him why he kept his possessions like this, and he replied it was nature's way of storing her possessions. Eggs and food, always packed in clusters, piles, and heaps. He was merely emulating nature.

"He told me it was just an experiment and it was just for fun, but he hesitated." Professor Moritzen stopped and stared at Søren.

"I don't really know why I'm telling you all this."

Søren cleared his throat.

"Please go on. It's important." Søren gazed straight at Professor Moritzen who briefly looked as if she had lost the thread.

"I don't know . . . I left . . ." she shuddered. "And I was sad . . . but also angry with myself. It's not like I had found child porn or caught him forging checks . . ." She sighed. "So what was going on?

I gave it a great deal of thought in the weeks that followed. I bumped into Helland often. Every time I looked out the window, he would be chatting to a colleague or putting on his bicycle helmet, always busy, always charismatic. I had seen him with his daughter a couple of times. She looks nothing like Asger. Lars's treatment of them was completely different, too. Asger was invisible to him the day they shook hands, but his daughter was the apple of his eye. You could tell from the way he rested his hand on the back of her neck, the way he listened to her, tilting his head. She would have been twelve, thirteen years old then. Something inside me contracted. Why couldn't he love Asger as well? I was in turmoil. Since my visit to Asger's apartment, I had started wondering if I should reveal his father's identity. I spent hours examining my motives. Did I want Asger to have a father or was it about my own need to discuss Asger with someone who also loved him? There was no denying I was driven by the latter. I imagined sitting with Lars on this sofa, talking about our son. But he clearly had no wish to do so. He knew perfectly well Asger was his, but he never expressed a desire for Asger to be a part of his life. He never even glanced through my windows when he walked by. It was only when we met at seminars or at lectures that he would greet me, warm and effusive, as before. Then Lars and I had a meeting about research funding. His department and mine had jointly applied for a grant, and now it was time to share the spoils. The financial situation of the departments was really tight, but none of us could have foreseen how bad it was about get." She gave Søren a dark look. "Anyway, we agreed two representatives from each department would allocate the money to a range of projects. I showed up with a younger colleague and Helland arrived with one of his. I knew instantly that something had happened. Helland looked tired and out of sorts. His hearty personality, which sometimes annoyed me, was nowhere to be seen. During the meeting he was irritable and brusque, and he appeared to think not a single one of our projects was worthy of funding. I wondered what was troubling him, but I didn't know him very well anymore. I concluded his usual invincibility had vanished or was weakened, and

I spotted an opportunity to stick the knife in." Professor Moritzen looked straight at Søren. "After the meeting I caught up with him. I told him I had decided it was time to tell Asger the truth. He replied he had no idea what I was talking about.

"Two days later I was officially informed that more than three quarters of the grant had been awarded to my department, specifically to two of my projects. I arrived at my office to find champagne corks popping. My younger colleague, who had attended the meeting with me, beamed and said that whatever I had said to Helland, it had worked. And he congratulated me. He hugged me. I was speechless, and for five naive minutes exactly I thought we had been given the money on merit. Then I understood. Helland had bought my silence.

"In the weeks that followed, I was torn. Morale in the department was sky-high, and we held one ambitious strategy meeting after another. We could afford a new electron microscope, we could invite three postgraduates on a planned trip to our overseas projects, and we could afford to participate in two upcoming symposia in Asia and America. The atmosphere was euphoric. I saw Helland several times, but still he never once looked through my window, even though I'm certain he knew I was in my office. I also saw Asger several times. He was radiant, having been offered a fellowship at the department. I had never seen him so happy. It was more food for thought. Should I let Helland get away with buying my silence?

"I made up my mind one afternoon when I saw Asger with Erik Tybjerg. They walked right past my window, laughing out loud at something, so Asger completely forgot to wave. The next day, I informed Helland that his blatant bribe had been accepted on one condition. He would put himself forward for the next election to the Faculty Council, and when he was voted in he was to make sure my department would never be short of funds again. I tried to gauge how badly he wanted Asger to remain a secret. It was clearly of the utmost importance, because he consented. Asger remained fatherless, I became a blackmailer, and Professor Helland kept his job. I lost no sleep over this. Our parasite research saved lives in the Third

World, and my son was spared a father who didn't want him. It went on for years." Professor Moritzen blinked. "Lars was good at securing grants, exceptional, even. Once the grants were awarded, he got creative. The money was allocated across the system and when it reached individual budgets, it was disguised and moved along so that when it finally came to us, no one was keeping an eye on it anymore; no one asked questions."

"So what happened?" Søren wanted to know.

"There was an election, and the new government had other plans," Professor Moritzen said bitterly. "It slammed the money box shut and threw away the key. From now on, every unit within the institute had to submit a half-yearly report explaining how grants had been spent, along with research results. Every kroner had to be accounted for. The new government was highly mistrustful, and it soon became clear it cared nothing for our work unless it was profitable. There was a major management shuffle, and Professor Ravn was appointed as the new head of the institute. In consultation with the Faculty Council, he decided to close Coleoptera Taxonomy—"

"What's that?"

"A small unit, specializing in beetle systematics. It had a staff of two: one was an older professor of taxonomy on the verge of retirement and the other was a young, upcoming invertebrate morphologist . . ." Professor Moritzen looked at Søren with tears in her eyes.

"Asger."

She looked away.

"Asger had spent the summer in Borneo collecting samples and returned the day before the start of the new academic year. He was tanned, and I had never seen him looking so relaxed and contented. The institute claimed they had sent a letter and an e-mail, that they had tried hard to contact him, but whether it was Asger's fault or they were lying, he showed up, unsuspecting, and found his department closed. There was a photocopier, still in its bubble wrap, waiting outside the door for Asger to clear out his things, so his office could be turned into a photocopying room. Not long after I said hello to him I saw him storm out. He had arrived with his buckets and specimen jars, wearing a too-warm jacket, smiling from ear to ear, his backpack tucked under his arm, and now I saw him head for the parking lot without his things and in a T-shirt. I worried and waited for him to come back. After half an hour, I knew something was wrong. I called Asger's former colleague, but calls to that line were forwarded to his secretary. She gave me his home number. When I called him, my hands were shaking. Afterward I called Lars. It was a very unpleasant conversation. 'There was nothing I could do,' he said, over and over. 'It was the smallest unit at the institute. There was nothing I could do.' I wanted to kill him, even if he was telling me the truth. Lars assured me he had done everything he could, but he had been the only one to vote against it. 'Did I know what a majority vote meant, had I heard about democracy?' The department was closed immediately. The older professor retired, and Asger was . . . let go." Professor Moritzen looked out of the window, at the building across the road. It had grown dark.

"Obviously I went straight to Asger's. He didn't open the door. I called out through the mail slot. I should have known it all along. His joy, his optimism, Borneo, his glowing skin, which almost made him look normal. It was an illusion. Underneath it Asger was what he always had been: a misfit. Someone who couldn't cope with the world, and it was all my fault. I had worked too much, and he didn't have a father. In the end, I called a locksmith and broke in. Asger lay on his bed, staring at the ceiling. I sat beside him, stroking his arm." Professor Moritzen looked at Søren.

"I promised him it would be all right. I said I would make sure he didn't become unemployed. Thanks to Helland, my department had enough money, and I hired Asger as an assistant in the Department of Parasitology. I twisted Lars's arm further—I told him to get a grant for Asger for two annual trips to southeast Asia to collect samples, and offer him three lectures a year in Lecture Hall A. To a full house. Or I would start talking.

"Needless to say, Asger was far from content. He languished. His life had changed for the worse. He traveled regularly to southeast Asia, he classified animals, wrote papers, and helped out in my department. But it wasn't what he really wanted to do. He didn't want to be a gofer at the University of Copenhagen. He wanted tenure, his own office, to teach, to contribute to growth and debate in the world of research. He didn't want to be an ultimately insignificant freelancer. I asked him if he still saw Erik Tybjerg, though I knew he didn't.

"In the end I hated Lars Helland." Professor Moritzen suddenly looked straight at Søren. "Hated him because . . ."

"He refused to be Asger's father," Søren said.

"He was Asger's father," Professor Moritzen said, defiantly. "And I hated him for not acknowledging it. But the person I truly despised was myself. Research grants are to us what steroids are to athletes. Whoever gets the most, gets the furthest. And I made sure I got plenty for myself." She gave Søren a remorseful look.

"Last April I was made redundant and given three years to conclude my research. The Department of Parasitology at the University of Copenhagen will be shut, and the Serum Institute will take over our work. It happened during the Easter break. In contrast to Asger, I received a letter and a telephone call from the head of the institute. He apologized profusely. They had to make cuts. The government had the knife to the institute's throat. When I returned after the break, I went looking for Lars. He seemed to have vanished, and his door was locked. I called, I e-mailed, but he didn't reply. Finally, I called him at home and his daughter answered the telephone. Her voice was bright and happy. She was Asger's sister, they shared genes, how could she sound so happy? My dad's abroad, she said. At a dig. He wouldn't be back for another ten days. That weekend I told Asger. After years of deliberation, when I had sworn to myself I would never tell him in anger, I told Asger that Lars was his father. Because I was hurting. Because I had been laid off. Because the money had run out. Because it would no longer trickle down to Asger. Because I was bitter that Lars's daughter sounded so happy. For all the wrong reasons," she said, wearily. She fell silent and stared at her hands.

"Why didn't Anna know you had a son?"

Professor Moritzen looked up.

"She asked me the same question a few hours ago." She smiled weakly and fidgeted with her clothes. "She was angry with me because I had kept it a secret. She shouted at me, in fact." Another feeble smile. "But we didn't see each other outside work. We met at a summer course where I taught terrestrial ecology. We started talking, and I was fascinated by her. She was so different from Asger, from my own child, and she reminded me of me, when I was a young biologist and a single parent. We had lunch together, maybe five times. It was lovely sitting in the cafeteria with her. It made sense. Anna's life isn't easy, is it? Living on a student grant with a young child. She never told me her story outright, but today she admitted she felt ashamed because her boyfriend had left them. And do you know something?" She looked up at Søren. "I, too, felt ashamed. I was ashamed of Asger."

Søren tried to get his thoughts in order. "And then, last Thursday, Asger told you he had infected Professor Helland with parasites?"

"Yes." She looked wretched. "But it's my fault. I should never have told him Helland was his father. But I did. The night I told him, he reacted with surprising equanimity. He seemed puzzled more than anything. He kept saying: I thought you didn't know who my dad was? As if it wouldn't sink in that I had lied. Afterward, we shared takeout and watched a movie. When he went home, he seemed pensive rather than angry. Three days later, he called to say he didn't want to see me for awhile. Then he hung up. Asger had never rebelled, not even as a teenager. He has always been my sweet little boy. I was shocked when he hung up on me. I called him back, but he didn't answer. I went to bed. I wanted to sleep on it, not compound the damage by acting in haste. After three weeks, I called him. Yes, he was fine. What day was it? Really? He sounded surprised. He responded to everything I said as though he had had a lobotomy. I invited him to dinner; I asked if we should go away for Easter break but he said no, we wouldn't be seeing each other. Good-bye. I told myself everything was all right. He was twenty-seven years old and he had the right to create some space between himself and his mother. Only I desperately wanted to talk to him, to explain to him once more why I had kept Lars a secret. I wrote him a long letter, begging for his forgiveness. I wrote I had been nineteen years old when I had slept with my tutor; I knew nothing, and today I would never have made the choices I had made then. I heard nothing, not even on my birthday in July, which Asger always used to make a big deal of. Not so much as a postcard." The tears rolled down Professor Moritzen's cheeks.

"He didn't respond to anything. To my letters or my calls. He had quite simply dropped me. Last August I started therapy. It was mainly about my relationship with Asger, about my role in his life. My therapist told me to write another letter to Asger, that he definitely read them and they made a difference even if he didn't respond. In the letter I was to assure him I would be there when he was ready, and I was to tell him I loved him and I looked forward to seeing him again. But not until he was ready. That was important, the therapist stressed. He had begun an emancipation process, she said, and I was to leave him alone. Respect him. The therapist insisted it was about time, too." She looked embarrassed. "So that's what I did. Wrote a letter, which the therapist read and approved before I sent it to Asger. Then I waited. I heard nothing, but the therapist comforted me. It was quite normal. The longer the period after puberty when emancipation ought to have taken place, the harder it was. She said it might take years. So I was so happy when he suddenly called last Thursday." Professor Moritzen looked earnestly at Søren. "I swear it never occurred to me that Asger might be implicated in Lars's death. I had speculated like crazy whether the parasite might have come from our stock, but in consultation with my colleagues, I concluded it couldn't possibly be one of ours. We hadn't been broken into, nothing had been touched, nothing had been taken. Last Thursday, Asger told me he had watched me through my office window. His plan was to make it look like I had infected Helland with tapeworm. We should both be punished, he said. He even found the prospect amusing. He knew tapeworms weren't dangerous, but they frequently aren't discovered until they're several feet long and fill most of the intestines. He thought his plan was brilliantly disgusting. He imagined how the tapeworm would grow and take up more and more space, just like Helland and I had gradually taken over his life.

"He also told me he had threatened Helland. Sent him some e-mails in English from an untraceable address. Helland was completely indifferent; he didn't even take them seriously. He had replied to a couple of them, Asger told me, though he obviously didn't know to whom he was replying, and he seemed to find the threats amusing. Asger was crushed," she said softly.

"Asger heard about Helland's death on the radio and got very scared. Last Wednesday he visited the institute. It took less than fifteen minutes to catch up on all the gossip. Helland had been riddled with cysticerci. Asger panicked and went home where he spent the next twenty-four hours thinking it over. He couldn't make sense of it. He called me Thursday night. His voice was small and timid. At first, I couldn't understand why, after months of silence, he'd called me to talk about the life cycle of parasites. Surely he could look it up in his own reference books? But he insisted. Slowly, the pieces began to fall into place and, in the end, I asked him outright: Are you involved in Helland's death? He thought so, he whispered. Then he told me everything, though he still didn't fully understand what had happened, all he had wanted to do was give his loser dad tapeworm. I connected the dots myself."

CHAPTER 19

"Will it help him that he confessed? It will, won't it?"

"He could have called the police himself," Søren said gently.

"But that's what he has done by calling me," Professor Moritzen protested. "It has been this way all his life." Again she looked ashamed. "I always made his calls. To the tax office, the housing benefit office, the student grant office. He can't call people he doesn't know. He just clams up." She looked out of the window.

"Perhaps there really is something wrong with him," she said. "But then I don't understand why he's always been a straight-A student." They sat for a while. Søren gave Professor Moritzen a break. Then he got up.

"I'm going to pick him up now," he said. "And we'll help him, okay? As much as we can."

She looked inscrutable. "Yes," was all she said.

When Søren left Professor Moritzen's block, it had started to drizzle.

It was close to midnight when Søren, accompanied by four colleagues, arrived at 12 Glasvej. Søren looked up at the apartment, which, according to Professor Moritzen's instructions, was on the third floor to the right. It was dark. He had briefed the others before they left the station and he reiterated the main points. Asger Moritzen was highly likely to be unstable. He shunned people and he was anxious, so their approach must be soft and gentle. Four heads nodded. Then they entered. When they reached the third floor, the four uniformed officers lined up on the stairs and Søren, who was in plain clothes, put his ear to the door before he knocked. There was no sound from the apartment. He knocked harder. No reaction. He called a locksmith, who promised to be there in ten minutes. Søren was tempted to kick down the door, but was reminded of what Professor Moritzen had told him about Asger.

"Proceed with caution," he had told the others in the street, and he stuck with that even though he had his doubts. He knocked lightly on the neighbor's door. A moment later, they heard footsteps. The door was opened by a puzzled-looking woman in a nightgown. They spoke for three minutes. The woman had never met her neighbor. She had lived in her apartment for ten months and she had wondered about it, of course, but decided the apartment was probably empty while its owner was traveling. She had never heard any noises coming from it. No running water. No music or guests. She shrugged. Sorry, she couldn't help them. Søren thanked her and asked her to return to her apartment. When her door had been closed, a breathless locksmith came up the stairs. Two minutes later, Søren could open the door to Asger's apartment.

"Asger Moritzen," he called out. "This is the police. We would like to talk to you." Not a sound. Inside, it was dark—only the light from the stairwell made it possible to see. Søren switched on the light. The hall was spacious and tidy. The built-in closet was closed, as were the three doors. The kitchen must be the door to the left. He signaled to the others to stay put. He called out again. Still no reply. He carefully nudged open the kitchen door with his elbow— the light from the hall enabled him to find the switch. The kitchen was tidy and impersonal. The walls were bare, and Søren could see silvery trails from a dishcloth on the work surface. The sink shone. He returned to the hall and stopped in front of the two closed doors. One had to lead to the living room with the blacked-out windows, the other to the bedroom. He opened the one to the left, again calling out.

"Dr. Moritzen. This is the police. We want to talk to you." The smell hit his nose. Nail polish remover was his first thought, some sort of solvent, definitely. The room was black and quiet.

"Flashlight, please," he demanded over his shoulder and one of the officers shone a bright beam of light into the room. There were tanks everywhere, just like Professor Moritzen had said. From floor to ceiling. In the middle of the room were a loveseat and a coffee table. Nothing stirred. Søren switched on the light and the cold, dim gleam helped him get his bearings. The smell of solvent was overpowering. Then he spotted something glowing white. In every terrarium lay a cotton ball, each the size of a child's fist.

Behind him, his colleague coughed. Søren turned around and asked him to open the window. He walked up close to one of the tanks. Then he spotted it. A bird spider, the size of a cake plate, diagonally behind the cotton ball. It didn't stir.

"The window has been painted over," the officer gasped.

"Smash it," Søren said, now desperate. Suddenly he felt faint and the smell irritated his nostrils. Two loud bangs followed, then the autumn air filled the room. Søren tapped the glass of the tank, but the spider stayed put. He checked the animals, searching for one he knew something about. What else had Professor Moritzen said? Crickets and mice. He had to find them to be certain. What did he know about the behavior of bird spiders? He found both in two tanks on the floor. One contained cricket-like beings, stacked like a pile of dried twigs. He tapped the glass. Not a single nervous twitch. The tank beside it was filled with sawdust and dead mice. Søren straightened up.

"He's killed his animals," he concluded, sadly.

He walked past his colleague and back to the hall where the other three officers were waiting, exhibiting varying degrees of tension.

"Call for an ambulance. I'm sure he's in the bedroom," he said, looking at the officer at the back. Then he put on a pair of rubber gloves and entered Asger's bedroom. The darkness practically spilled out of it. Søren called out. Same words, no response. He listened. Someone passed him the flashlight, and he shone it inside the room. Blacked-out windows, a desk, bundles neatly arranged along the wall, a bed, a human foot.

He found the switch and turned on the light.

Asger lay on the bed. His hips and stomach covered by a blanket, his torso bare and white. His eyes were closed, his hair, which needed cutting, lay like a matted halo around his face. His skin was pale and waxy, and he didn't stir when the three officers came in. Søren carefully checked if Asger had a pulse.

"He's dead," he said, softly. Spots indicating early decomposition were forming on the surface of Asger's skin. Søren thought hard. Every impression must be memorized. Soon the medical examiner and the crime scene officers would take over and ask Søren to leave. Now was the time.

"Check the expression on his face," Søren said. "Why so tortured?" He sniffed the air. Had Asger taken solvent to kill himself? Had he wanted to die like his animals? The room was tidy like the others. The bundles, the small desk with the laptop, wrapped up exactly like Professor Moritzen had described. He turned around and looked at the shelves. Small tanks, jars of preserved animals, books. How had he died? Søren carefully sniffed the body, but he couldn't smell anything, then he lifted the duvet and peered under it. Nothing.

"Søren," one of the officers behind him called out. "Watch out."

Søren had sent the officers out of the bedroom, but one had stayed in the doorway, watching him. His voice was ominous. Søren had pulled the blanket over Asger's hips and had just let go of it. Suddenly, a scorpion emerged from Asger's hair, just behind his ear. It was yellow and had retracted its venomous sting. It scampered across Asger's chest. Søren quickly withdrew his hand.

"Fucking hell," he exclaimed. "He was bitten by a scorpion." The scorpion darted across the body and disappeared under the blanket.

"There's another one," said the officer. He was right. It sat in a fold to the right of Asger's pillow. Søren looked up at the wall. There was another one.

"Okay, boys," he said, keeping very calm. "I'm coming out." He retreated with as much dignity as he could muster and closed the door to Asger's bedroom. A shiver went down his spine.

"Fucking hell," he said again.

"What do we do now?" one of the officers asked.

"No one is going in there," Søren ordered. Not that anyone wanted to.

The ambulance arrived, then Bøje, another two sergeants, two crime scene officers, and a wizened man from Animal Control who had come to remove the scorpions. He went into Asger's bedroom with two of the crime scene officers who were there to make sure he didn't destroy any evidence. Wearing special gloves, he removed eight Buthidae scorpions, he explained over his shoulder to Søren, very likely to belong to the *Leiurus Questriatus* family. Their venom was poisonous, but a sting by only one scorpion, he continued, was unlikely to have killed Asger. A child or an older person might have died, but not a young man. However, no one could survive eight scorpions, the man said and shook his head gravely.

"My guess is that he—or someone—placed the animals under his blanket," he added.

"Why?" Søren asked him.

"As a rule scorpions don't attack," he replied. "They'll only sting if they're trapped or provoked. By a blanket, for example." And off he went with the scorpions.

Asger's body was removed, and the crime scene officers got to work. Everything reeked of suicide. There were eight empty transport tanks in a hidden angle behind the bed and below Asger's half-open hand, which hung over the bed lay a book entitled *The World's Most Dangerous Scorpions*. Søren watched the stripped bed. All that loneliness, he thought. He had found a note in the kitchen. The handwriting was microscopic and the space between the lines so small that Søren could barely read it. The letter was placed in a bag, which was then sealed. Søren sighed. He knew what it would say. Forgive me. My life is dreadful. I don't want to live any longer. PS. I killed my dad. Aside from the latter, all suicide notes were written from a template. All that loneliness, he thought again. With a heavy heart, he went back to Professor Moritzen.

Chapter 20

It was Monday October 15, the first weekday morning of the autumn intersession, and Anna was woken up by Lily balancing a plate of fruit. Anna tried to appear awake. The previous night she had told Karen about Troels, Karen had cried and cried, and it had been past four in the morning by the time they went to bed.

"Rabbit food," Lily said. "Auntie Karen says it's called rabbit food." Anna could hear Karen light a fire in the stove in the living room, and she lifted her daughter up into the bed and made her comfortable.

"Yum," she said, stroking Lily's hair. "I love rabbit food."

"Do you know what it is?"

"All rabbits know about rabbit food," Anna declared.

"But you're not a rabbit!" Lily squealed with delight. Karen appeared in the door. She looked tired, smiled and said good morning.

"My mom says she's a rabbit," Lily informed her.

Karen smiled.

"Your mom is a biologist, so if she says she's a rabbit, then she must be."

Lily started eating Anna's carrot sticks, dropping only a few pieces on the bed sheets.

"Er," Karen said, looking at Anna, "are you free today?"

"Not entirely," Anna replied, checking her watch. "I've got two things to do. One is at the Natural History Museum. You want to come along? There's an exhibition about feathers and a real glacier you can touch and lots of animals and short films. Lily loves that kind of thing."

"What are you doing there?"

"I'm meeting someone. In the Vertebrate Collection at eleven o'clock. I would like you to come. I'll be an hour, max. You can have a hot dog in the meantime. Then I need to stop off at Bellahøj police station and . . . well, we'll see." She smiled and Karen sat down on her bed.

Anna felt a pang of guilty conscience.

"Are you okay?" She scrutinized Karen.

"I still don't understand it," she said and the tears welled up in her eyes.

"Come on, lie down here," Anna said gently. Karen snuggled up and Anna held her close.

"I hope they sentence him to treatment of some kind," Karen said. "That they help him."

Anna nodded.

"Where do you think he is now?"

"Bellahøj police station," Anna said. "I'm being interviewed at 1 p.m., then he goes before a judge and he'll probably be remanded in custody."

"I would like to visit him, if I'm allowed to. Would you come with me?"

"No," Anna said, stroking Karen's hair.

"Okay," Karen said into Anna's arm.

At 10:30 a.m. they arrived at the Natural History Museum. They looked at all the colorful plastic animals, pencils, and posters in the museum shop by the entrance. Karen bought Lily a dinosaur eraser while Anna hung up their coats.

"I thought you were meeting someone?"

"I am, in half an hour."

They strolled through the exhibition and lingered for a long time in front of the different displays.

"I didn't know birds were dinosaurs!" Karen exclaimed as she studied a poster depicting the 200-million-year evolution of the feather. Anna smiled.

"So a sparrow is a dinosaur?" Karen wanted to know. Anna nodded.

"And when we eat chicken, we're really eating dinosaurs?"

"Yep! And I like mine with roasted potatoes," Anna said.

"Roasted potatoes! They must be extinct by now, surely?" Karen teased her. Anna elbowed her.

"Ahhhh, Mom, that's so cute," Lily burst out. She was standing in front of a low display case containing a model of a baby Tyrannosaurus. It was the size of a small dog, had giant feet and was covered by a soft, insulating layer of down. Anna leaned forward, gazing at the small body.

"What is it?" Karen asked her.

"A feathered baby Tyrannosaurus."

"Right," Karen said.

"Fascinating, isn't it?" Anna remarked.

"What is?"

"That it has feathers."

"I think it's more fascinating that its arms are so short. Must have been a real nuisance."

At that moment, Lily spotted a sign with an ice-cream cone on it at the far end of the lobby where the café was located.

"Ice cream," she shrieked, taking off.

Karen chased after her.

"So sorry, I've ruined your daughter," she called back over her shoulder.

"That's quite all right," Anna called back. "I'll be off now. Back in an hour, all right? I'll come and find you when I've finished."

Karen waved without turning around.

*   *   *

Anna let herself into the university through a concealed door in the Whale Room, which had been painted two shades of blue to blend in. She caught a glimpse of the bench where she had sat with Troels, before the door slammed shut behind her and she was in the strange, but now familiar, system of corridors. She started walking and when she turned into the corridor leading to the Vertebrate Collection, Professor Freeman was already there. She knew he wouldn't have been able to resist! Even so, a wave of triumph rippled through her. Freeman had taken off his jacket and was holding it under his arms, which were folded across his chest. Everything about him exuded rejection. Anna's heart started pounding, and she concentrated on holding out a hand, which didn't shake.

"Hello," he said.

"Thank you for coming," Anna said, feigning composure.

She unlocked the door to the collection and switched on the light, which scrambled and rattled into action. Anna heard a chair scrape across the floor far away and knew she had to get Professor Freeman to say something, so Dr. Tybjerg would know that she wasn't alone.

"Do you have a vertebrate collection at UBC?" she asked. She said UBC so loudly that it was a miracle Freeman didn't comment on it.

"Yes, obviously," he said. "Our collection is far bigger than yours. The biggest in North America . . . but the atmosphere in here," he added, sounding almost amiable, "is really quite special. The cabinets, the systematics, it's all very old-worldly."

There was silence at the far end of the collection where Tybjerg must have heard Anna arrive with a guest and presumably figured out who it was. Anna had planned the scenario the night before, and she deliberately led Professor Freeman to the place where she had found Dr. Tybjerg last Wednesday. She lit a desk lamp, pulled out a chair, and asked Freeman to sit down. Then she opened her bag and took out her dissertation and the draft of the lecture she would give in a week.

"You said you had something for me," Freeman said.

"I lied," Anna said, looking straight at Freeman. "I want you to listen to what I have to say."

Freeman reached for his jacket, which had slipped to the floor. He looked as if he was about to leave.

"You're a coward if you leave," Anna declared. Professor Freeman blinked and let his jacket fall.

"You have fifteen minutes. Not a second more," he said through clenched teeth.

Anna gulped. Her lecture lasted an hour, and the subsequent defense, forty-five minutes. Now she had fifteen.

"I wrote my dissertation on the controversy surrounding the origin of birds," she began, "and you play a key part in this controversy."

Professor Freeman looked at her as if he couldn't be less interested in what she had to say.

"I've read everything you have written, papers and books. Gone through them with a fine-tooth comb." She studied him. "And I've read everything your opponents have written and examined that just as closely."

Professor Freeman still looked utterly bored.

"Your most prominent opponents are," Anna continued, "Walter Darren from New York University, Chang and Laam from the University of China, T. K. Gordon from the University of Sydney, Belinda Clark from the University of South Africa, and, of course, Lars Helland and Erik Tybjerg from the University of Copenhagen." She flicked through her papers.

"What your opponents have in common is that they all criticize your fossil analyses and, on that basis, reject your conclusions regarding the origin of birds; criticism that you don't accept, am I right?" She didn't wait for his consent, but carried on.

"For more than fifteen years you have engaged in fossil trench warfare, even though experts agree there's no longer anything to debate. Let me give an example of your critics' view on the origin of birds: Belinda Clark is quoted in the September 2006 issue of *Nature* as saying . . ." Anna picked up a sheet and read out loud:

"We basically try to ignore him. For dinosaur specialists it's a done deal. Birds are living dinosaurs." She lowered the sheet.

"Your opponents say they're ignoring you, but that's not entirely true, is it? The debate is still ongoing. Why?"

"Well, why do you think?" Freeman said, giving Anna a neutral look. "Because we can't agree, and why is that? Because they're wrong. Clark and Laam and Chang; Helland and Tybjerg. They're wrong."

Anna ignored him.

"No one can catch you out in terms of anatomical and fossil arguments. I've been through all the material, and the order of battle is the same: you interpret the bones differently, so you draw different conclusions. It's a vicious circle. You'll never agree."

"I was about to give up." She gave Professor Freeman a dark look. "I was desperate. You have maintained your position for so many years, so how could I—"

Freeman glanced at his watch. Anna took a step forward and looked straight at him.

"So instead, I reviewed your premise. And it stinks!"

"Allegations," Professor Freeman yawned. "Unscientific allegations. From a postgraduate." Again he reached for his jacket. Anna handed him a piece of paper, which he automatically accepted.

"Please would you read it and tell me if you agree?"

He looked baffled for a moment, then he scanned the page.

"Basic rules that should be adhered to if work is to be deemed scientific," he read out loud. "What's this?"

"Just read it and tell me if you agree."

Professor Freeman read it. He shrugged.

"It's elementary," he said. "It's the requirements for internal consistency and convincing argumentation for selection and refutation of scientific positions. Is this what they teach postgraduates here at the University of Copenhagen?"

Anna was aware she was starting to sweat.

He was walking right into her trap.

"Do you agree with them?"

"Completely." Professor Freeman let the paper rest against his thigh and looked at Anna.

"Then please could you tell me why you, in your argumentation on feathers, to name one example, are guilty of a severe case of inconsistency, which you've just agreed mustn't happen if a position is to be deemed scientific?"

Silence.

Then Freeman said, "What sort of nonsense is this?"

"Your nonsense, Professor Freeman." Anna flicked through her papers. "In 2000, Chang and Laam described *Sinosauropteryx* as having well-preserved, feather-like skin structures. Since then dinosaurs with more or less distinct, feather-like structure have literally poured out of the ground, such as *Tyrannosaurus Rex* found in 2005. Your opponents argue convincingly for the structure being homologous with feathers, and that consequently a feather isn't a diagnostic feature reserved for birds but characteristic of a wider group of predatory dinosaurs, *including* birds. One of the most important conclusions drawn from this is that feathers evolved *before* flight." Anna looked briefly at Freeman.

"You obviously disagree profoundly with this statement and in 1985, in 1992, in 1995, three times in 1997, again in 1999, and six times between 2001 and 2004, you write, in a range of scientific journals, that the evolution of feathers is inextricably linked with the evolution of flight and it wasn't until later that it served to insulate the animal. Is that correct?"

Freeman nodded in an off-hand manner.

"You also write several times that, in terms of evolution, it would be wasteful to develop complex contour feathers, which would only be used for insulation. Ergo, the structures might *look* like feathers, but they aren't *real* feathers. Rather than *Archaeopteryx*, you and your supporters point to the archosaur, *Longisquama*, as the likely candidate for the ancestor of birds, is that correct?"

"That's right." Professor Freeman had regained his footing, but Anna could tell that he wasn't enjoying it.

"So now we turn to theoretical science issues, still on the premise that you agree with the rules for scientific integrity, as stated on the sheet of paper. Do we still agree with those rules?"

"Yes," Freeman croaked.

"Then how do you explain that you, in two papers, one from 1995 and the other from 2002, are critical of the feather-like structures found on *Longisquama*, and argue these structures bear a striking resemblance to plant material, when you, in a paper from 2000 claim, in great detail, these very structures seal a homologous relationship between modern birds and *Longisquama*? *Plant material*, Professor Freeman?"

Freeman made to say something, but Anna continued regardless.

"It's unbelievable that you dare to assume *Longisquama* is an archosaur which, according to many experts is by no means certain, and simultaneously you reveal a naive understanding of falsification. It's not enough to claim *Longisquama* is bird-like, that's quite simply not a convincing reason to let *Longisquama* push *Archaeopteryx* off the throne." Anna glanced at Freeman before she went on, knowing full well Freeman was on the verge of exploding.

"I have two further theoretical science disparities associated with your argumentation concerning feathers, then I'll let you go. In an article in *Nature* in 2001, you state it's impossible to establish whether predatory dinosaur feathers are homologous with those of modern birds, because the claim cannot be tested biochemically. But elsewhere . . ." Anna leafed through her notes. "More specifically in your 2001 book *The Birds*, on page 114, you claim that it '*is not scientifically correct to use biochemical analyses to determine if* Longisquama's *appendage was animal or vegetable*,' which, for me, is a striking example of the inconsistency which characterizes most of your general argumentation. You let the validity of an argument depend on the actual situation, and that isn't in accordance with prevailing rules for good science."

Professor Freeman was white as a sheet.

"Last, but not least, you write in 2000 and in 2002, in *Science* and *Scientific Today* respectively, it's impossible to imagine that a structure as complex as a feather might have evolved independently in different situations, which is likely to be correct. However, the inconsistency arises the moment you, on several occasions in 1996, 1999, and 2000, argue brazenly that other, equally complex structures found in both birds and dinosaurs, such as the half-moon-shaped carpal, might well be the result of convergent evolution. Isn't it absurd that the feather, according to you, could *not* have evolved independently, while the half-moon-shaped carpal *could*?" Anna raised her eyebrows and looked at Professor Freeman.

"Have you finished?" he groaned.

"Yes," Anna said. "I've proven the same kind of sweeping inconsistency and absence of methodology with respect to your arguments about stratigraphic disjunction, the carpus, the furcula, the ascending process of the talus bone, the fingers of the bird hand, and the orientation of the pubic bone. However, I think my time's up."

Nothing happened for several seconds. The air stood still and Anna's heart raced. Then Professor Freeman pushed back his chair and walked out.

Anna let herself fall into Freeman's empty chair. She heard his footsteps fade away; she heard the doors close, and she sensed how his defeat was absorbed by the stillness of the room. Her heartbeat slowly returned to normal.

"You can come out now, Dr. Tybjerg," she said.

She didn't say it very loud; she knew he was close by.

Anna and Dr. Tybjerg put Karen and Lily on the number 18 bus. Tybjerg was less than thrilled, but Anna had insisted and helped him into his jacket as though he was a child.

"I'll be there in an hour," Anna promised. Karen looked dubious.

"Karen, I'll be there in an hour," she repeated, gravely. "If you make the batter, I'll make pancakes when I get home."

Lily shouted with glee and Karen relented.

When the bus had departed, Tybjerg said, "I've never met your daughter before."

And Anna replied, "No."

Then they caught a bus to Bellahøj police station. Tybjerg seemed drained and kept squinting in the light.

They introduced themselves at the reception but didn't even have time to sit down before Søren Marhauge came racing out and looked from Anna to Dr. Tybjerg, dumbfounded.

"Er, hi," he said. "Glad you're here."

They were put in separate interview rooms. Dr. Tybjerg gave her an anxious look before his interview began, but Anna shook her head gently. You'll be fine, she signaled.

The interview lasted thirty minutes. Søren's questions were precise and thorough, and she tried to reply likewise. When Søren told her that Asger Moritzen was dead, the tears started falling down her cheeks. Søren got up. He's about to hand me a tissue, she thought, to wipe away my tears, tell me to pull myself together, be strong. But he didn't. He squeezed her shoulders gently and told her she was free to go once she signed her statement.

Back at Anna's they ate pancakes and, later, lasagna, salad, and ice cream.

"We're having a party," Lily said, again and again, and Karen and Anna laughed every time.

When Lily had been put to bed, they sat in separate chairs in front of the fire and shared a bottle of wine, while Anna told Karen the story from beginning to end, even though some of it was probably confidential. She didn't care. When she had finished, Karen looked at her for a long time.

"You need to open the door to Thomas's office."

Anna closed her eyes and didn't respond.

"Anna—"

"I'll open it," she cut in. "I'm not scared of opening it. There's nothing behind it. The room's empty." She straightened up.

"But first I have to do something I really am scared of." She glanced at Karen.

"Stay where you are," she went on. "Don't say anything, don't do anything, please. Just be here, all right?"

Karen nodded.

Anna stood by the dark window, her hand on the telephone, looking down into the street, now slushy with melted snow. She could see Karen's reflection in the glass; she was sitting in the chair to the left of the stove with her legs curled up, her chin resting on her knee. Anna breathed right down into her diaphragm, then she picked up the telephone and pressed Thomas's number. It was past eleven, and it rang six times before he answered, drowsy with sleep.

"It's Anna," she said.

Thomas sighed.

"What do you want?" he said, as though she rang him constantly. "I was asleep. I'm working shifts."

"I'm calling to tell you I forgive you."

"What?"

"I'm saying," Anna cut the letters out of a large, heavy sheet of metal, "that I f-o-r-g-i-v-e you. I forgive you for messing up my and Lily's life." Her voice gained strength. "I forgive you for being a fraud. I forgive you for never really loving me, and I forgive you for being cold. I forgive you for being a coward, I forgive you for all the stuff you haven't got the guts to face, I forgive you for all your lies and your habit of blaming everyone but yourself. I forgive you for only seeing what you want to see, I forgive you for—"

"Do you know something, I don't need to listen to your crap," he said and slammed the telephone down.

Anna looked out across the street.

"No, I don't suppose you have to. But I forgive you anyway, damn you," she said and added into the telephone: "Except one thing. I'll never forgive you for depriving Lily of her father." Then she hung up.

She turned around and faced Karen, who was still sitting in front of the stove and said, "Why don't we take a look at your new room?"

Karen smiled.

Johannes was cremated on Thursday October 18. The day before Anna called Mrs. Kampe to ask when and where, and she replied it was a small and private service but Anna was welcome. When

Anna arrived at the chapel of Charlottenlund Church at 12:50 p.m.
she encountered ninety-five goths in full costume. It was a glorious
sight. Mrs. Kampe stood away from the crowd, looking lost.

Inside the church, she sat alone in the front pew, but just before
the service was about to begin, she rose and asked in a meek voice,
"Why don't you all move closer to the coffin?"

People got up and filled the front pews, and when Mrs. Kampe
began to sob, a woman with heavy black makeup and green hair
gently took her hand. Anna sat in the fourth row letting her tears
fall freely. The coffin was pure white. It should have been wearing a
Hawaiian shirt.

Chapter 21

Anna looked out across the almost fifty people gathered in Lecture Hall A at the Institute of Biology. She didn't know most of them, postgraduates from other departments and institute staff who must have seen her disseration defense listed on the internal notice board. Hanne Moritzen sat in the back row. In her grief, she glowed faintly, like a distant moon. Asger had been buried last Saturday, and Anna had attended the service. At first, they had been the only two mourners, but Dr. Tybjerg arrived at the last minute, dressed in a nice but crumpled suit and with a fresh haircut. The organ started playing and none of them heard the door open and shut again, but when the service was over and they rose to leave, Mrs. Helland was sitting at the back of the church. She said nothing, and she didn't look up.

Anna's eyes swept across the seat rows. There was Jens and Cecilie, and Karen next to them. They all watched her with excitement, and Jens's eyes were moist. Anna had asked him not to take photographs, that it would distract her and make her nervous, but she couldn't stop herself from grinning when, for the fourth time in less than ten minutes, he sneaked out his camera and snapped a picture of her.

They all had dinner together the other day, Anna, Karen, Lily, Jens, and Cecilie, and it had gone very amicably. They had talked about Troels, and Karen and Cecilie had cried. That was all right. Anna understood they were shocked. After the meal, Karen had gone to the corner store and Jens, Anna, and Cecilie had cleared up while Lily put her dolls in a drawer in the living room. Cecilie started to speak, "Er, Anna," she said, in a certain way. Anna stopped her.

"But we have to talk about it," Cecilie protested, her voice thick and Jens standing behind her, nodding.

"We do, Anna, my love," he said.

"And I want to," Anna replied. "I promise you. But not now. I'm exhausted."

Cecilie and Jens had accepted that.

At that moment, Karen returned with marshmallows, and they all played a game of Monopoly.

Her lecture would begin in five minutes. Anna was sweating. They had agreed that Karen would pick Lily up from nursery school between Anna's lecture and examination. Afterward there would be cake and champagne for everyone in the department, and Lily was, of course, invited.

Dr. Tybjerg sat in the front row, tilting his pencil. He was dressed in the crumpled suit he had worn at Asger's funeral, and he looked gravely at her. He pointed to his watch with his pencil and Anna nodded.

She lowered the lights and took a deep breath.

She opened with a short historical review and proceeded to the in-depth presentation of scientific ideals where she succinctly accounted for Popper, then Kuhn and Daston after which she extracted the basic rules for scientific integrity, the same that had been listed on the paper she had given to Professor Freeman. It took her about fifteen minutes. The next thirty minutes she spent reviewing the morphological evidence linked to the controversy. At fairly high speed, she went through the stratigraphic disjunction, the half-moon-shaped carpus, the furcula, the ascending process of the talus bone, the fingers of the bird hand, and the base of the pubic bone, whereupon she considered in detail first the disputes and then the theoretical science problems linked to the evolution of the feather. She held a small remote control in her hand, and while she explained, illustrations and keywords flashed up on the screen behind via a computer.

Anna briefly looked out into the darkness.

"After this review it should be clear that Clive Freeman, professor of paleoornithology at the Department of Bird Evolution, Paleobiology, and Systematics at the University of British Columbia, didn't adhere to the most basic rules for sober science, and his archosaur theory is riddled with major internal contradictions and a striking absence of consistent methodology. The central question is . . ." Anna paused and tried to find Dr. Tybjerg's eyes in the half-light, "why? Why is the opposition reluctant to accept that birds are descended from dinosaurs? I propose three possible reasons."

Anna took a step toward her audience.

"Firstly, it's human to see what you want to see." Anna dearly wished she could look into her mother's eyes, but Cecilie was lost in the darkness. "And in people's minds, dinosaurs don't have feathers as per previous definitions. The same conservatism applies to birds. Birds are unique and advanced, and every child can tell you they look nothing like dinosaurs. After all, they're not big scary creatures with teeth!"

A short burst of laughter from the hall.

"The truth often lies elsewhere," she went on, "in the ground, from where it must be excavated, dusted down, and interpreted as objectively as possible." She let the conclusion linger for a moment, and then she went on:

"Secondly, there's human obstinacy, here camouflaged as scientific prestige. The opposition and Professor Freeman, in particular, have obviously invested considerable resources in supporting a position, which at some stage has turned out to be scientifically untenable. Acknowledging you were mistaken is no defeat. Acknowledging you were wrong is to accept that you participate in a discipline called science, where the overall dynamic depends on scientists constantly proposing possible hypotheses and trying to support them with evidence and, more important, reject them when they can't. Not to acknowledge this is, however, unscientific. Clive Freeman can maintain his position as much as he wants to, also for reasons we cannot fathom, but he doesn't have the right to call it science.

"Thirdly, it's about the communication of science, and this is closely related to status in science, as mentioned earlier. It's one thing to understand Clive Freeman's agenda, but if you really want to appreciate why a controversy like this one endures, you need to turn your eyes to the world in which research and science exist. It's a world characterized by tough competition for scarce research grants, a world wherein the media play a shockingly big role for scientists and consequently the quality of science.

"Since the latter half of the twentieth century it has become customary to publicize scientific controversies, in order to make science accessible to the wider public. However, it's my opinion we are currently experiencing a shift in communication, where the interest in the content of a controversy has given way to a rise in interest in the feud itself. Everyone knows that Bjørn Lomborg argued with leading experts about the state of the earth, but how many lay people can explain the scientific arguments at the heart of that controversy, and how many understand its scientific implications, even though the media covered it extensively?"

Anna looked at Dr. Tybjerg and saw the pencil in his hand, which now rested in his lap.

"And *why* has controversy suddenly become so attractive?" she asked and turned up the light. It went very quiet, and Anna could now see Dr. Tybjerg's face clearly. He was smiling.

"It sells tickets," Anna said. "It sells newspapers, it sells journals, and the pressure for profit also affects highly respected journals such as *Science* and *Scientific Today*, which increasingly regard the degree of controversy as their basis for selecting which papers to print, while ignoring the quality of those papers. Dinosaurs are 'sexy,' and the question of what became of them is glamorous. In the controversy surrounding the origin of birds, it seems to have created a co-dependent relationship between the opposition and the media, where each party needs the conflict because it sells, even though it means that an expert, such as Professor Freeman, is forced to defend a scientific position that is ultimately indefensible." Anna found Karen's admiring gaze in the hall.

"Research grants are awarded by people who also read newspapers and journals and watch television. Big headlines and extensive media coverage can easily give the impression the feud is important. Bitter arguments between highly qualified scientists sell and, in my view, the opposition has exploited that. Publicity leads to media coverage, and media coverage leads to grants. You can think what you like, but you can't call it science."

The hall was very quiet.

"Thank you," Anna said and closed her laptop.

Everyone clapped.

Dr. Tybjerg rose and started examining her. A young professor from the University of Århus assisted him, and an external examiner, also from Århus, took careful notes. Anna wore Helland's necklace. The questions rained down over her and, at some point, Dr. Tybjerg handed her a box of bones and asked her to account for the evolution of the bird hand compared to the evolution of other pentadactyle hands. Anna answered and looked Dr. Tybjerg straight in the eye. Karen had left the hall to pick up Lily. For God's sake, it had to be over soon! Suddenly, the door opened and the World's Most Irritating Detective entered. He looked frazzled and tried not to draw attention to himself. He failed. When he missed a step and stumbled, everyone turned to glare at him. Christ, he was irritating. Anna flushed hot all over and smiled at him.

Dr. Tybjerg said, "Congratulations."

And, at last, Anna was a biologist.

The author would like to thank the following:

Anders Lund, Jens T. Høeg, Åse Jespersen, Jørn Andreassen, Christian Baron, Peter Makovicky, and Paul McNeice for reading the script and for their professional comments. Thank you also to Jørgen Lützen, Per Christiansen, Peter Holter, Henrik Glenner, Kristine Johanne Kurstein Sørensen, and Margrethe Noýe-Sneding for inspiration. Special thanks to Detective Sergeant Uffe Jensen of the East Jylland Police's Criminal Investigation Department for patiently explaining his profession and his work to me (I take full responsibility for any errors and artistic license). Thank you to Janne Hejgaard, Paul Gazan, Trine Rosenkjær, and Sophie Sanwald for being there for Lola while I wrote—I love you! Thank you to Trine Pallesen, Katrine Kjær, Mette Holbæk, Tina Felton, Eva Myers, Ditte Rode, Eva Kruse, Hanne Palmquist, Malou von Simson, Lisbeth Sandberg, Julie Michelsen, Lotte Garbers, Stine Hesager Lema, and Christine Elverdal for your courage under fire. Thank you to my editor, Lene Wissing, for an exceptionally fine collaboration. Last, but not least, thank you to Ea-Viola Gazan. You are the love of my life, and this book is for you.